HONORBOUND

HONORBOUND

LAURA TAYLOR

FRANKLIN WATTS
1988
New York · Toronto

PRINTED IN THE UNITED STATES OF AMERICA
6 5 4 3 2 1
Designed by Tere LoPrete

Library of Congress Cataloging-in-Publication Data

Taylor, Laura.
Honorbound.

1. Vietnamese Conflict, 1961–1975—Fiction.
I. Title.
PS3570.A9434H6 1988 813'.54 88-17256
ISBN 0-531-15092-5

Honorbound is dedicated to the following:

. . . to those who waited, and to those who still wait, often alone;

. . . to the League of Families of POWs/MIAs;

. . . to my father, Alfred J. Mattei, Lt. Col. (Ret.) USAF, and to my husband, Gordon Taylor, USMC;

. . . to the memory of AJB;

. . . and to the Black Knights of VMFA-314, El Toro Marine Corps Air Station, Santa Ana, California, 1975–78. The Muffin Lady thanks you.

Honorbound is a work of fiction. Other than those already historically documented, all of the characters and events portrayed in this novel are purely the result of my imagination.

ACKNOWLEDGMENTS

Several people have been particularly supportive of me during the years I have spent writing *Honorbound.* I thank each of them, even those who unknowingly encouraged and nurtured me during moments of creative difficulty.

The following individuals, however, deserve special thanks for their validation of my efforts . . . Pat Teal, my literary agent and a woman of uncommon character and compassion . . . Kent Oswald, my editor at Franklin Watts, my friend and a trusted ally on the journey to publication . . . Captain Ray Alcorn, USN, seven years a POW in North Vietnam . . . Captain James Hickerson, USN (Ret.), five years and four months a POW in North Vietnam, and his wife, Carole . . . Lt. Col. James Walsh, Jr., USMC (Ret.), six months a POW in Cambodia . . . Vergie A. Townley, an active member of the League of Families of POWs/MIAs and the wife of Captain Roy Townley, who has been listed as Missing In Action since December of 1971.

Laura Taylor
April 1988

PART ONE

PROLOGUE

Hawaii—September 1967

No matter how much she wanted to banish the memory of their conversation, it wandered through her mind, painfully and repetitively.

"I don't want you at the airport, Eden."

"But I'd planned to see you off."

She struggled to keep pace with him even though she knew it was impossible. He needed this now, far more than she did. It was his way, she realized, of saying good-bye. And she knew him well enough to know that he would never actually say the words to her. He hadn't the first time he'd left her. She was certain he wouldn't this time, either.

"There's no point in making the trip twice in one day. You can catch a cab when you're ready to leave. It'll be easier for you."

"Easier?" she had whispered. For you or for me? she wondered as she stared up at him. "Matthew, there isn't anything even remotely easy about this situation."

She wanted desperately to cry, but she couldn't. She ached with the need. Still, she couldn't. Her tears were locked deep inside her, hidden and throbbing in some dark corner of herself even she couldn't reach. She tried to make herself relax, tried to release her thoughts and untether her emotions, if only for a few minutes, but that, too, had become an impossibility.

Panic suddenly infused her. What if he died in that godforsaken place?

Silently, feverishly, she prayed for a miracle, all the while knowing that her one big miracle had already happened. One to a person, one per lifetime. That's all, folks! She shuddered with dread and clutched at his shoulders.

Stop thinking, she told herself. Just let yourself feel. Feel his heat and his hardness, his strength and his tenderness. But she couldn't stop thinking about how the day would end.

"It's not like we need an audience."

"Say what you really mean, Matthew."

His body quickened, and he tightened his hold on her hips. Air raged in and out of his lungs as he clasped her to him.

She heard him groan, felt the thundering urgency of his heart, and knew, in that instant, the fiercest kind of love for this man. Her man. Her lover. Her husband.

She thought again about how little time they'd had together. Grow up, she silently ordered. This is life, the real world. It won't go away, and you can't change it no matter what you do or say or promise.

He moaned her name, and she welcomed the pounding pressure of his body. He was close, she realized, very near the edge. Slowing the answering surge of her hips, she deliberately allowed her body to erect a low wall of resistance. She needed him inside her just a little longer. A few extra moments this way and then, maybe, she'd survive the long months ahead.

"I want to remember you like this . . . not standing in a crowd of strangers at an airport. I want to remember what we've shared . . . just the two of us . . . the way it's been here for us all week."

She had moved forward into his arms, trembling with love. "Come home to me, Matthew. Please come home to me."

He lifted his face from the curve of her shoulder and studied her. She saw the question in his dark eyes, and sudden guilt prodded her back to the path of his need. He didn't deserve her restraint. They both knew he hadn't earned it.

Her tears finally surfaced, and she wept, soundlessly, helplessly, heartbreakingly. She didn't even try to hold back. She knew he would never expect that of her, especially not now. With everyone else she was aloof, reserved. She'd had to learn how to protect herself from the world, but with him it had never been necessary. She hoped it never would be.

"I love you, paleface. I always will."

She had seen the pain in his eyes and knew it reflected her own. "And I love you."

She felt the force of his release the second it exploded within her body, felt its power tremor through her soul as he erupted inside her, and she prayed. She prayed that these precious moments would be the start of a baby.

Too quickly their body temperatures cooled and their respiration returned to normal. They continued to hold one another, unwilling or unable, perhaps both, to let go even after he rolled them to one side to relieve her of his weight.

She closed her eyes and savored the feel of his hands soothing and stroking her body, absorbed the steady cadence of his heartbeat beneath her ear as she rested her head against his chest. Sighing softly, she tried to ignore the relentless ticking of the clock on the nightstand.

He moved suddenly, dragging her up his body so that they were face-to-face once again. She started to speak, but an indescribable sound of remorse escaped him, effectively eclipsing her expression of concern. He took her mouth in an almost violent display of rage, hunger, and frustration, his lips and tongue and teeth hurtful and arousing all at the same time.

He released her as abruptly as he had seized her, grief etched into his features as he sat up, left the bed, and crossed their hotel room. Stunned, she didn't take her eyes off him, didn't relinquish the sight of him until he closed the bathroom door.

She forced herself not to follow him, forced herself to wait while he showered and shaved, despite the trembling inside her that threatened to shatter her heart. She focused on the week they'd just shared, thinking of the time they'd spent joyfully, and sometimes desperately, plundering one another's bodies, and of the ceaseless hours devoted to discussions of how they would spend the future. She also remembered the depth of the love that linked them beyond all earthly considerations.

Soon, though, she knew she would have to resume her vigil.

He returned to find her sitting naked in the center of their bed, the covers gathered about her hips, her thick auburn hair gloriously tangled and wild across her shoulders and down her back. He inhaled sharply and looked away, his jaw tight and his back rigid as he assembled his uniform.

She spoke; he answered. He spoke; she answered. But not once did their eyes meet. Determined not to be merciful, she watched his every move, silently willing him to look at her and see her agony despite her empathy for what he was feeling. Her own pain was simply too great to be discounted now.

She'd watched him dress before, of course, and had never been bored by the ritualistic quality of his routine. He did it quietly, his movements practiced, precise, all the while concentrating on the task as he stood in front of the closet.

She marveled at the way he carefully tucked and smoothed his shirt into his pants, heard the sound of his zipper as metal teeth gnashed, and smiled slightly as he soundlessly slid his keys into his pocket. He turned, his eyes on the nightstand. She breathed in the smell of soap, deodorant, and after-shave, distinctly masculine, distinctly him, as he walked past the bed and collected his watch and wallet.

Finally, he paused, took a fortifying breath, and met her gaze. Her heart lurched, and tears slipped down her cheeks when she saw the despair shimmering in his dark eyes. This is it, she realized. He's leaving now. She knew she couldn't stop him, knew she had no right to even try. Vietnam. She winced. The name alone had the power to wound.

He moved nearer, reached out, caught a single tear with his fingertip before it could slide into the corner of her mouth, lingeringly smoothed her lower lip with his knuckles, and then leaned down to kiss her.

She briefly touched his cheek before he straightened and turned away. Whispering, "Be safe, my love," she watched him cross the room.

He hesitated at the door, his fists clenched at his sides as he quietly said, "Don't stop loving me, Eden."

CHAPTER

I

January 30, 1968—Chu Lai, South Vietnam

Matt Benedict stood in front of the only window in the briefing room, his thoughts on the mission ahead. From the air-conditioned trailer he could see the sun-drenched Chu Lai flight line, aircraft lined up like used cars in a vast parking lot.

The trailer door slammed, and he turned to greet Jack "Eagle" Morrison, the marine lieutenant who would occupy the backseat of the F-4 Phantom now positioned at the edge of the runway and being loaded with ordnance.

Jack waved a sheaf of papers. "Weather reports." Scrubbing at the sweat dripping down the sides of his face with his free hand, he dropped the papers on a table situated in the center of the room, sank into a chair, and steepled his fingers across the bridge of his freckled nose. "Jenson's on his way over with the intelligence data we'll need for the Khe Sanh run. Those poor bastards are really getting the hell kicked out of them up there. I got a look at the casualty reports, and the numbers are grim."

Matt nodded. He already knew about the grunts trapped in the mountains near the DMZ. He also knew that there wasn't a marine on either side of the Pacific who didn't feel a sense of personal distress about the situation. "Who's the FAC on this mission?"

"Thunder."

The two men grinned at one another. An F-4 pilot by

training, Tom "Thunder" Delaney now endured his second Nam tour of duty as a forward air controller in an OV-10. The small aircraft bore little resemblance to a jet fighter, a fact his friends were quick to point out whenever possible.

Following a briefing that outlined aircraft headings, desired altitude, time on target, and the type and quantity of ordnance they would carry, Matt and Jack adjourned to a small building at the end of the flight line. There they donned flight suits and forty pounds of additional gear after placing their personal possessions in their lockers. The only remaining means of identification worn by the two men were dog tags and removable, Velcro-backed, name-and-rank-embossed leather strips affixed to their flight suits. They tied chamois headbands across their foreheads to keep the sweat out of their eyes before putting on their helmets.

Matt felt the intense South Vietnamese humidity slam into his body and add extra weight to his steps as he and Jack left the building, crossed the tarmac, and approached their fueled, bomb-loaded aircraft. Settling into the F-4, both men adjusted the Koch fittings to the regulation harnesses they wore and secured the leg restraints and lap belts that aligned their bodies to the contoured cockpit seats.

Matt initiated a checklist over the inner cockpit radio. "Okay, Eagle. Coming up on the right one."

"Roger, Warrior." Jack focused his attention on the roaring jet engine located on the right side of the plane.

"Fuel flow good, 100 percent, we've got 635 degrees, nozzles look good, oil pressure five-zero . . . hydraulics look good." Matt paused and acknowledged a transmission from a returning pilot who was taxiing his F-4 off the runway. "Now for the left side. Fuel flow good, 99 1/2 percent, we've got 630 degrees, nozzles look good, oil pressure is four-five, hydraulics look good."

"Roger."

"Eagle, controls are free. Wings down and locked, trim two units nose down, wings level, rudders look good, flaps one-half. Hook up, harness locked, pins out, guard down, panels black. All set to roll."

Jack responded to the checklist with a final confirmation, "Flaps down, circuit breakers in, harness locked, pins out, guard down. Ready when you are, Warrior."

"We'll be making a left turn after takeoff."

"Roger."

Matt experienced what had become a familiar surge of satisfaction as the powerful fighter rolled down the runway. Even an advisory transmission from the tower regarding wind velocity didn't distract him from the roaring strength of the F-4. At 160 knots, the Phantom lifted off despite the heavy racks of ordnance fixed to its undercarriage.

"Gear coming up," Matt announced.

"Roger."

"Three in the well, flaps on the way up."

"Roger."

"Landing light out."

Two trails of black smoke streamed behind the F-4 as it veered to the left and gained altitude. The Vietnamese coastline melded with the azure South China Sea and the lush tropicality of the Southeast Asian land mass.

Matt enjoyed the sight of the ever-changing terrain as the plane streaked through the sky. He knew that in the security of the F-4 cockpit he could note the unique topography of the land rather than attempt to survive in it as the ground troops were forced to do.

He half listened as Jack notified their ground radio monitor of their position and then switched their radio to the frequency monitored by the designated FAC on this mission.

"Thunder, this is zero-one-niner."

"Go ahead, zero-one-niner."

"Zero-one-niner is airborne," Jack confirmed. "Heading for rendezvous at this time."

"Roger that, Jack. Gotten any lately?"

Matt heard Jack's muffled laughter. As usual, Thunder Delaney wrote his own dialogue, often in violation of the strict parameters established by Marine Corps aviation for use of call signs during a transmission unless an emergency had been declared.

Jack clarified the ordnance they carried with Thunder while Matt rechecked the gun-sight settings of the aircraft. He also flipped several switches that prepared the bombs for release.

"How far are you from rendezvous, Jack?"

"Thunder, this is Warrior," Matt interrupted. "We're fifteen miles out and ready for a brief."

"Roger, Warrior." A fierce Indian battle cry exploded in the microphone, Thunder's historic response to any transmission from the half-Cherokee pilot he'd known since OCS. "This is one-four with a brief. Target elevation three-three-zero feet."

They listened as Thunder outlined bailout coordinates, the emergency-base frequency, and altimeter readings.

". . . ground fire in the area, Warrior. From small arms to fifty caliber. When you get in there, you can adjust according to weather. Target is known enemy location with troops in the open."

Following a brief pause, he completed his comments. "Be advised . . . quite a bit of low clouds right on the deck, but the ceiling is basically six thousand feet."

Jack confirmed the information, restating coordinates, the presence of friendly troops as well as enemy soldiers, and the existence of patchy cloud cover.

"Roger, Eagle. That's a good copy." Static briefly interrupted the transmission. "I'm directly below you at this time, Warrior. Do you copy?"

"Roger. We have you in sight."

"Target is up off my nose. Don't believe these clouds should give us any trouble. Target is clear."

"Roger, one-four."

"Target is now in the area up off my left wing. . . . It looks somewhat cultivated. I'll put in a mark."

Thunder fired two rockets. The white phosphorous smoke, known as Willie Pete, would identify their target.

Smoke began to drift up from the ground. Matt and Jack proceeded with another checklist necessary prior to dropping their bombs.

"If you have my smoke, it's right on the side of the small hill down there, Warrior."

"Roger. Target in sight, one-four."

Matt initiated his dive from ninety-five hundred feet. "In hot," he advised as he pushed the stick forward and rolled the F-4 into a thirty-degree dive angle.

Jack counted aloud their descent in thousand-foot increments. Matt, mind and body attuned to the shuddering force of the machine he controlled, eased back on the throttle. At 450 knots he released the ordnance as the F-4 reached the 4,000-foot level. The dive continued until he pulled the fighter's nose up for a steep climb that would return the aircraft to an altitude beyond the range of enemy ground fire.

"Warrior, you're taking fire from your three o'clock," cautioned Thunder.

Matt scanned the instrument panel, a feeling of unease settling in his gut. "Utility hydraulic pressure dropping." He gasped, and the sound invaded the cockpit intercom. "I'm hit."

"How bad is it?"

Taking a deep breath, he fought wave after wave of dizziness. He also tried to ignore the blood now soaking the sleeve of his flight suit.

"How bad is it, Warrior?" Jack demanded again.

"My right arm."

"Can you fly the plane?"

"Trying to," he muttered. "Trying to."

"Okay, Warrior, you're doing great. Just concentrate on my voice. Air speed starting to fall off. . . . Give me some power." To Thunder, Jack advised, "Warrior is hit. Will try to get to bailout heading zero-niner-zero."

"Roger, Eagle. Will advise Search and Rescue."

"Air speed building. You're looking good," Jack calmly encouraged.

"Can't feel my right hand." Matt gripped the throttle with his left hand while blood continued to drip from his damaged right arm onto the stick. "Hydraulic pressure down to zero."

"Roger, Warrior. We've got four-five-zero knots. Pull back on power. Can you get wings level?"

"Negative. Can't use my hand. Will try to use my knees to come wings level. . . . Controls frozen, Eagle. Controls are frozen. I can't move the stick."

Jack exhaled loudly. Matt gritted his teeth against his own frustration and the pain throbbing in his arm.

"Pull power back to idle, Warrior."

"Roger."

The dizziness returned. *"Come home to me, Matthew."* Eden's words echoed in his mind until he blinked several times to clear his blurring vision.

"We're going to have to get out, Warrior. Get into the best position you can. Is your right arm secure?"

Matt fumbled with his limp arm. He tucked his blood-covered hand securely under the weight of his right thigh. Pressing his spine against the contoured shape of his seat, he resecured his leg restraints and lap belt. He then curled his fingers around the ejection handle located between his knees, all the while feeling that every action he took was accomplished in slow motion.

"Is your right arm secure?" Jack repeated, urgency underscoring his query.

"Roger, Eagle."

"Thunder, this is Eagle. We're going to have to get out. Passing one-one-zero degrees at six thousand feet. Do you have us in sight?"

"That's a—" Static garbled the remainder of his reply.

During the moments that followed, Matt thought about the size of his body. Nearly six and a half feet tall, he'd barely satisfied the proportional requirements of the F-4 cockpit. He tightened his grip on the secondary ejection handle located between his knees. His size made it impossible for him to use the primary ejection device, known as a face curtain, positioned at the top of his seat. He knew now, as he had known during flight school, that the ejection handle he clung to was his sole option for survival.

"Warrior, are you in position?" Jack clarified one last time.

"Let's do it," he grated.

Jack took a deep breath before saying loudly, "Eject! Eject! Eject!"

The words reminded Matt of bullets being fired in rapid succession. Grasping the ejection handle, he yanked with his left hand. The forward canopy tore loose. He was jettisoned like detonating dynamite from the cockpit.

Struggling to remain conscious, Matt experienced a momentary urge to give in to the pain of his injured arm. He resisted the impulse by biting down on his inner lip. The rusty taste of blood penetrated his mind as the small drogue chute, the stabilizer of the main chute, jolted his falling body. The main personnel chute opened almost immediately.

Matt searched the sky for a second parachute, concern etching his features. Finally, he saw Jack floating earthward several meters below him.

Rice paddies stretched along a wide valley in a checkerboard pattern below the two men. The diked terrain surged up at them like the rushing tumult of an inverted waterfall.

The perimeter of the valley was thick with trees. Matt saw that the leafy vegetation reached the two- and three-hundred-foot level courtesy of the rich red Asian soil. The stench of excrement assaulted his nostrils just before his steel-toed boots splashed into a water-soaked paddy.

Matt felt the jolting impact of damp soil. Shock waves pounded up his legs and torso like repetitive blows. He leaned to his left, hoping to cushion his fall with his good arm before his parachute could drag him through the dingy water and mud. The chute tugged at his large body prior to collapsing in the surrounding rancidness.

He rolled to his knees after awkwardly releasing the harness latches at his shoulders. Despite the four-foot-high dike separating him from the adjoining paddy, he spotted Jack's deflating chute.

Matt waded through the brackish knee-high water in a low crouch. Making his way to the dike, he fumbled through his survival vest for a radio. He heard Jack's sloshing footsteps on the opposite side of the earthen wall as he sank against the muddy dike.

"One-four? This is Warrior on guard. Over."

Jack rolled over the dike, his booted feet sending up a spray of brown water as he landed on Matt's right side. Breathing heavily, he jerked off his helmet, helped Matt with his, and dragged a .45 from a holster at his hip.

"We've got company," Jack whispered as he pulled a first-aid kit and a lethal-looking K-bar knife from his survival gear.

"How many?"

"At least two dozen. Less than two hundred and fifty meters to the west. All armed." Ripping the sleeve from Matt's flight suit, Jack discarded the blood-saturated material, then sprayed a stinging antiseptic over the ragged gash above Matt's wrist and wrapped it with a waterproof bandage.

"This is Warrior on guard," Matt repeated into the radio. "Over."

Jack rummaged through his gear again. His reddish-blond crew cut was covered with beads of sweat. He swiped angrily at the rivers of perspiration draining into his eyes through the soaked chamois band wrapped around his head. Finding what he had been searching for, he leaned back against the dike, his .45 in one hand and the flare gun in his left, and listened as Matt repeated their distress call.

"One-four? This is Warrior. On guard. Over."

Matt closed his eyes as intense heat and loss of blood combined to blur his vision. He blinked rapidly and shook his head against the disorientation he was starting to feel again.

"Warrior, this is one-four. Go ahead, buddy."

"Do you have us in sight? Over."

"Negative. Lost you in a bank of clouds. Am currently descending. Will try to locate."

"Shit!" Jack muttered.

"Roger, one-four," Matt answered. "Advise . . . armed gooks advancing from valley perimeter. Two hundred meters and closing from the west. Over." His knuckles went white as he gripped the radio. We're alive, he reminded himself in an effort to counter the sense of hopelessness he was starting to feel.

Matt couldn't ignore the mental image he had of a crippled

F-4 plowing helplessly into the side of a mountain. He could almost see the destructive force of the explosion, debris flying through the air, impaling anything in its path. He also realized that fate could have been less kind, and he sobered at the thought.

He turned his attention to the man slouched in the mud beside him. Jack's brashness often concealed his professionalism. Teamed in the F-4 for more than six months, the two men had developed a profound understanding of one another as well as a strong friendship. They worked in concert in the air and on the ground, their commitment to their respective careers equally intense. A half smile playing at the edges of his mouth, Matt lifted the radio. He delayed his next distress call when he saw the look of disbelief on Jack's face.

"What the hell are you grinning at?"

Matt chuckled. "You look like goddamned John Wayne right now."

Jack grinned, the flare gun and his .45 still gripped in his mud-covered hands. "I sure as hell am glad you can laugh at this mess." He shook his head, but the smile didn't leave his face. "We're up to our asses in alligators, and the boys on the white horses don't seem to be coming in here to rescue our butts. I guess it is kind of funny, in a sick sorta way."

"I can't think of anyone I'd rather be hung out to dry with, Jack." Matt's smile reached into his eyes, although the thought of being taken prisoner shook him to the soles of his feet. He'd heard too many horror stories during survival training to ignore the gravity of their situation.

Splashing water interrupted their conversation. Quickly scanning the area, they both identified the NVA regulars approaching them in a wide semicircle.

"So much for Search and Rescue." Jack kept his gaze on the troops closing in on them. "How's your hand?"

Matt tried to flex his fingers and failed. "The bullet must've nicked a nerve. The feeling comes and goes. Right now it's gone."

"Can you handle your .45 with your left hand?"

Matt nodded. "If it comes down to it."

The radio crackled to life again, startling both men. "Warrior, this is one-four. Still do not have you in sight," Thunder announced in a voice rich with frustration.

Meanwhile, NVA troops positioned themselves on the far side of the dike, their weapons aimed at the two Americans.

Glancing at the sky, Matt released the air stored in his lungs and advised Thunder, "One-four, cloud cover increasing. Over."

"Warrior, can you give me a long count?"

"Negative, Tom." Resignation weighed heavily in his voice as he verbalized the reality of their situation. "You can't help us now, buddy. Over and out."

"It's trophy time, boss."

Matt glanced at Jack. Both men knew that downed American aviators were a special favorite of the propaganda machine controlled by the North Vietnamese government.

"I hope you like rice."

He chuckled and let the radio slide from his left hand before he stood. "Try not to get your ass shot off, Lieutenant," Matt growled.

Jack grimaced and got to his feet. He left his .45 and the flare gun in the mud of the dike.

They quietly watched the enemy soldiers form a circle around them. Matt and Jack remained at the edge of the rice paddy, their arms hanging unthreateningly at their sides and their feet widely spaced. Matt noticed their captors' surprise and wondered if their passive attitude would cost them in the hours ahead.

"Jack, go see Eden for me if we get separated and you make it out before I do."

"You got it."

"Silence!"

They glanced at one another and then at the man who'd spoken in heavily accented English. Another order was issued, this time in Vietnamese.

Matt stiffened as three soldiers approached him. Three others circled Jack, pulling him several feet down the pathway atop the dike.

"Remove all equipment except flight suits!"

They complied with the order but froze when they heard "Boots, too!"

Matt and Jack flashed startled looks at one another. Matt knew they were thinking the identical thought. Snakes. Especially those of the small green variety. Indigenous to the area and very deadly. He swallowed against the dryness in his throat and struggled with his left hand to remove his heavy steel-toed boots, as well as the remainder of his flight gear.

Feeling the press of several pairs of eyes, Matt raised his head and straightened his spine. His unflinching gaze provoked a staccatoed burst of Vietnamese from the soldiers standing nearest him. A few shook their Russian-made AK-47s at him, but none seemed inclined to approach him.

"You!"

Matt turned and stared at the ranking NVA officer. He glanced at the man's uniform, his eyes flitting to the insignia on his shoulder. He was struck by the absurdity that they both held the same rank.

"Kneel!" The order was guttural, meant to demean.

Matt hesitated. Anger flared inside him. He heard the sound of rounds filling an empty chamber. Two soldiers moved toward him. Out of the corner of his eye he saw Jack lurch protectively in his direction. He snapped, "Stay put, Lieutenant."

He slowly slid to his knees in the mud. Focusing on the face of the NVA captain, Matt expressed his contempt and loathing for the man with a hard stare.

A youth in an ill-fitting uniform stepped forward. Slipping a nooselike length of rope around Matt's neck, he held it like a leash as another trooper yanked the prisoner's arms behind him to bind his wrists and elbows together.

Forcing himself to remain expressionless, Matt suppressed the pain ricocheting into his shoulder and down his arm. He realized, in that instant, that his size had flustered his captors. Being forced to his knees was the only way for them to fasten his bonds. He watched through narrowed eyes as Jack was bound in a similar manner.

The NVA patrol soon gathered its booty and split its forces in half. Matt and Jack were led in opposite directions.

It was well after midnight when they stopped for the night. Matt fell forward and landed on his face on the floor of a deserted cave. The trail had torn through his heavy wool flight socks, and all that remained were bloodied strips of fabric hanging at his ankles. His wrists still bound, he grimaced when a soldier threaded the rope through a length of coarse hemp and looped it around his bleeding ankles, tightening it and further robbing his limbs of feeling.

He watched his captors eat cold balls of rice and drink water from their canteens. Fighting the need to relieve himself and resigned to the hunger gnawing at his belly, he drifted into a restless doze.

They set out again well before dawn, traveling north. For four days it was the same. On the fifth day Matt collapsed on the trail. Water was used to revive him. Abandoning his pride, he pantomimed his hunger and was finally fed.

By the seventh day, and even though he'd been given a meager amount of food the day before, Matt staggered at the end of his makeshift leash, barely able to put one lacerated foot in front of the other. Dizzy and numb, he slid to his knees in the center of a vine-littered trail and slumped forward.

He felt booted feet kick at him, but he no longer cared about injury or death. He closed his eyes against the saliva spattering his face as his captors rolled him over and screamed and spat their disapproval. And when he thought he could endure no more, he felt the butt end of a rifle slam into the back of his skull.

CHAPTER

2

February 3, 1968—Beverly, Massachusetts

Eden glanced at the clock above the stove as she poured hot water over the tea bag in her cup. Six-thirty A.M. She sighed and placed the steaming kettle on the stove, her nerves frayed and her thoughts focused on Matthew.

Something had happened to him. She was sure of it. Something painful and frightening. Something she had no way of verifying until she could match the dates on his letters to the entries she'd made in her journal.

He's alive, but he's in pain. I know he's in pain, and no one's helping him.

Absently rubbing her right arm, she tried to sort through the sensations she'd experienced in her sleep. But the snippets of memory from her dreams were like a partially constructed patchwork quilt, and she couldn't put an image or a name to the uncertainty that had haunted her for the last three days and nights.

She looked at the phone and wanted to scream. She couldn't simply pick up the receiver, dial the operator, and say, "Long distance to Vietnam, please." Life wasn't that simple. She couldn't call Vietnam. Only the military and the Red Cross had that option.

After fishing the tea bag from her cup, Eden walked to the window and watched a snowplow slowly make its way past her house. A station wagon, filled with neighbors who worked in downtown Boston, inched along behind the snow-removal equipment. Most of the cars for as far as she could see up and down the street were still buried under deep drifts, courtesy of a fierce storm that had blown in off the Atlantic the previous night.

She shivered as a gust of wind rattled the panes, longingly recalled the humid warmth and gentle hibiscus-scented breezes of Hawaii during Matthew's R and R, and exhaled softly. Turning away from the window, Eden fastened the button at the throat of her robe and sat down at the kitchen table.

Running her fingertips along the top edge of the box of stationery on the table, she considered the way in which she usually began each day. A letter to Matthew. Letters filled with love, personal thoughts, and plans for the future as well as frequent references to the baby conceived during those sensual tropical nights the previous September.

She stared at the blank page, her pen poised above the paper. Still, she hesitated. She knew that telling Matthew that she feared for his safety and that she hadn't known a peaceful moment for several days had the potential of distracting him from his work if he was really all right. But how many men were *all right* in a war zone? she wondered, especially when they were in a place where individuals didn't really exist except as battlefield equations or as the contents of a body bag.

Paling at the thought, Eden lowered her pen and wrote:

My Darling . . .

She paused, not certain of what to say next. Matthew always knew when she wasn't herself in a letter. The phone rang, startling her, momentarily stilling the air in her lungs. As she reached for the receiver, she reminded herself that the Marine Corps never delivered bad news by telephone. Matthew had explained the process before he'd gone overseas the previous March.

"Hello?"

"How's blizzard country treating you?"

Eden smiled at the person connected to the voice. "Hi, Tracey. And yes, I'm just fine. How are you today?"

"Warm," Tracey answered. "Very warm. But then most Californians who live in the southern half of the state don't get fifteen inches of snow in one night."

"Sixteen."

Tracey laughed. "So let's quibble about an inch. The situation is simple. . . . You're freezing your fanny off out there. When are you going to come to your senses and move back to the real world?"

"You know the answer to that as well as I do."

"Matt wouldn't mind if you put everything in storage and spent some time with me in L.A.," she argued.

"You're right, he wouldn't." Eden shrugged and ran her fingers through the thick auburn hair that fell to below the center of her back. "Being pregnant's made me lazy. The thought of facing packers and a moving van falls into the too-hard-to-do category at the moment."

"I could fly out and help," Tracey offered.

Eden frowned. "What's the matter? You invariably get the urge for me to change *my* life when *you're* between men. Where's your friend Ted?"

"Good old Ted accepted a transfer. He left for Florida a few days ago."

"So catch a flight to Florida."

"Can't do that. We had words before he left."

"Oh, wonderful! And were you your usual tactful self?"

"Something like that, but let's not waste my dime on Ted. He's ancient history. Tell me about you."

She shifted uneasily in her chair, wondering whether or not to voice her concern for Matthew. Of all the people she knew, Tracey was one of the few who would understand. Or would she? "Not much to tell," Eden hedged.

"You're lying to your best friend," Tracey told her bluntly.

She sighed. "I've got this feeling."

"And?"

"I've had it for three days now."

"I don't like the sound of this."

"And I don't like the way I feel," she countered.

"Does your *feeling* have something to do with Matt?"

Eden heard the sudden caution in Tracey's voice. She finally whispered, "Yes."

"I can be there tonight."

"No, Trace. It may be nothing."

"Don't tell me your feelings are nothing. I've known you since kindergarten, and you've only been wrong once in the last twenty years."

She groaned. "Don't remind me."

"I am reminding you," Tracey said. "I'm reminding you because I'm your friend and I want to be with you if something has happened to Matt. Even if it's something as stupid as falling off a bar stool and breaking his leg, which is highly unlikely because he doesn't drink that much, anyway."

"Arm," Eden corrected automatically.

"What do you mean 'arm'?"

"My arm hurts."

"If anybody else had just said that to me, I'd think they were nuts."

"Trace, it's not logical to build a case on an aching arm and nightmares I can't even remember."

"Forget logic. Now tell me what your doctor says about the baby."

"I had my five-month checkup yesterday. He says I'm fine. Healthy as a horse, in fact."

"You're sure?"

"Yes, Mother Hubbard. And I haven't upchucked in at least two and a half months. Feel better now? Don't you have to go to work or something?"

"Trying to get rid of me?"

"In a word, yes. I need a shower."

"You need your head examined for living in a freezer."

"Hey!"

"All right, I'll hang up, but I'll call you later in the day. Maybe a clean body will make you more civil."

"I love you, too, Trace. And I'll make the next call."

Eden replaced the receiver and sipped her lukewarm tea. She idly fingered the piece of stationery in front of her and decided, for the time being, against writing to Matthew. She wasn't ready to try and hide her apprehension, and he certainly shouldn't have to cope with her insecurities.

Placing her cup in the sink, she left the kitchen, stopped in the hallway to raise the setting on the thermostat, and walked into the bathroom. As she drew back the shower curtain, Eden heard the sound of the door chime. She assumed that one of the teenage boys from next door wanted to shovel the front walk and the driveway for a small fee.

Eden released the security chain and opened the heavy oak door, a smile of greeting on her face. Two men in wool coats and mufflers stood on the front porch. One held a Bible, the other gripped a briefcase. Short hair and painfully sober expressions confirmed that they were representatives of the Marine Corps.

She numbly looked past them and spotted a dark-colored, official-looking sedan parked on the street. Shoving shaking hands into the deep pockets of her robe, she kneaded her belly with concealed fingertips. The baby kicked, anyway, and she inhaled sharply.

"Mrs. Benedict? I'm Major Serening." He glanced at the man next to him. "This is Navy Chaplain Hughes."

She nodded and stepped aside. "Please come in. I know why you're here."

The men exchanged glances, but Eden didn't take the time to interpret the significance of their eye contact. Instead, she focused every ounce of energy she possessed on the fortress she was erecting around her emotions.

"You can leave your coats on the bench," she finally said, pointing at the low length of padded furniture in the front hall of the small house. "I'll put the kettle on for tea, or would you prefer coffee? I'm afraid all I have is instant."

"Whatever's easiest, ma'am," answered the chaplain.

They followed her into the kitchen and stood near the table until she said, "Please sit down." Silent minutes ticked by as she prepared two mugs of steaming black coffee.

She wasn't certain how she managed the task or how long it took, but a part of her realized that her dignity refused to allow her to cave in just yet. Instead, it seemed to sustain her. Placing the mugs on the table, she pulled out a chair and sat down between the two uniformed men.

The man with the briefcase cleared his throat before clarifying, "You *are* Eden Barclay Benedict, the wife of Marine Corps Captain Matthew Alexander Benedict, who is presently stationed at Chu Lai in the Republic of South Vietnam?"

Nodding, Eden raised her chin a notch and whispered, "He's not dead."

"Ma'am . . ."

"Please listen to me. Matthew isn't dead. I'd know if he . . . if he . . . I know he's in pain, but he's not dead." She placed shaking hands on the table in front of her, willing herself to breathe deeply. "I apologize, gentlemen. We're expecting a baby the first part of June, and my emotions tend to—"

"Mrs. Benedict," Major Serening interrupted, "your husband's aircraft was damaged by enemy ground fire during a mission near the DMZ. Captain Benedict and his radar intercept officer, Lieutenant Jack Morrison, were forced to bail out before their plane crashed. Radio contact was maintained until they were taken prisoner by a North Vietnamese patrol. Unfortunately, Search and Rescue didn't get to them in time." He glanced at the chaplain before continuing. "There is a confirmed report that your husband sustained some kind of an injury—"

"His arm." The ache she'd had for three days continued to throb, holding the numbness she would have welcomed at bay. "Was Matthew shot?" Eden asked.

"We think so," answered the major, his surprise carefully concealed behind a neutral expression.

"It's been at least three days. Why didn't you come any sooner?"

"A rescue team went in after them. We wanted to be able to notify you that we'd brought your husband and his RIO out."

"But you can't, can you?"

"No, ma'am."

"Did—were there any . . ." She couldn't make herself say the word.

"Bodies?"

She nodded, her eyes wide and filled with unshed tears.

"No evidence of either man was found beyond the bailout site."

"But you will continue to search?" she pressed.

"We can't risk additional personnel at this time. Your husband was taken prisoner by a North Vietnamese patrol *in* North Vietnam. Several other men—air force, navy, army, and a few marines—are being held in secret locations throughout North Vietnam. Some of the camps are as far north as the Chinese border."

"You can't do anything for him?" she whispered in disbelief.

The major clenched his fist. Eden watched his knuckles go white. A sudden cramp spasmed in her middle, and she flinched. Leaning back in her chair, she ran her fingers across her belly in soothing circular motions, breathing deeply as the pain receded.

"There isn't anything the Marine Corps can do for Captain Benedict at this time. Officially, he's listed as missing in action."

Fear flirted with her control. "That sounds as though you think he's dead."

He shook his head, his frustration once again evident. "The terminology may be somewhat confusing, but the Marine Corps *does* believe your husband's alive. As soon as we get either a live sighting or intelligence data that confirms his location, he'll be listed as a prisoner of war. In the meantime, his benefits will continue, you'll receive an allotment check each month, instructions on how to write to him via the State Department and the International Red Cross—"

Eden raised a hand and pressed her fingertips to the pulse pounding out of control in her temple. "I don't need money. Money's the last thing I need." She exhaled and squared her slender shoulders. "Matthew's a strong man. If anyone can survive being a prisoner of war, he can." She had a sudden thought and reached for the major's hand. "You hate this job, don't you?"

"Yes, ma'am, I do. It's the worst duty I've ever had," he admitted, his voice gruff but his touch oddly comforting as he patted her hand.

"In my case, you've only confirmed what I've suspected for the last few days." She smiled bleakly. "The worst part is knowing there's nothing I can really do to help him."

"And the waiting, ma'am. You have to be strong while you wait." Major Serening released her fingers and reached for his briefcase.

Chaplain Hughes finally spoke. "Is there someone we can call for you, Mrs. Benedict?"

"*I love you, paleface. I always will.*"

Eden bit back a sob as Matthew's words echoed in her mind. Standing, she walked to the kitchen window and pressed her forehead against an ice-glazed pane, eyes the color of emeralds welling with tears that soon bled down her cheeks.

CHAPTER

3

April 1968—Long Moc Prison Camp, North Vietnam

Darkness slowly gave way to slivered filaments of light as the morning sun struggled to penetrate the canopy of trees overhead. Matt heard buzzing insects, and felt their numbers as they clustered at the weeping sores that covered his flesh.

Bent forward at the waist, he rested his forehead on his knees. He felt the rocking motion of his four-foot-square suspended cell and realized that the feverish shudders of his huddled body had caused the midair movement. Taking several deep breaths, he tried to still the swaying bamboo coffin he'd been wedged into for the past two and a half months.

The sounds of morning filtered into the prison camp, and he opened his eyes. Through swollen eyelids, he studied the bamboo poles that comprised the floor of his cage. As was his ritual each morning, he dug his thumbnail into a particular cylindrical pole and added another groove to his makeshift calendar.

North Vietnamese soldiers stumbled from their barracks, a bitter reminder to Matt of his own inability to walk unaided. He knew his leg muscles had atrophied, but the knowledge provided little comfort during his daily trip to the latrine on his hands and knees at the end of a rope.

He swallowed against the acidic spasming of his stomach, a sign of deprivation, hunger, and the hatred churning inside him. Closing his eyes, he forced himself to recall tales told to him as a child of the legendary courage of his Cherokee ancestors.

The image of a small black-haired boy seated on the knee of an aging warrior flitted through his mind. He sighed, the sound ragged as another memory asserted itself. Thoughts of Eden drifted into his consciousness. He smiled sadly and lost himself in his memories of his wife.

CHAPTER
4

May 1968—Beverly, Massachusetts

Eden whimpered even as she slept. The sound shattered the stillness of the dark room. Distorted images darted through her mind like a thousand fireflies on a hot summer night. The sensation of suffocation in an airless coffin strangled her, and she gasped for air. Matthew's face, a thick maze of green, and the drone of buzzing insects finally wrenched her from her nightly trek into terror and jerked her upright on her bed.

Choking down her panic, she lowered her head to her knees and struggled to breathe deeply and evenly. Several minutes passed before her heartbeat returned to normal. The life nestled in her body soon fought her awkward position and forced her to straighten her spine. Tears filled her eyes, falling to stream like hot rivers down her face.

"I'm so tired," she moaned. "So tired."

Placing a protective hand on her belly, she used her other hand to balance herself as she got up from the bed. She padded barefoot into the bathroom, flipped on the light, and studied her reflection in the mirror above the sink. Raising still-shaking fingers, she smoothed her loosened tumble of hair from her face. Haunted eyes stared back at her, and she shook her head in frustration, a wave of anger washing over her when she realized that her appearance reflected the condition of her life.

"Damn you, Matthew! Why did this have to happen to us? Why?" Her voice cracked, and she sobbed, "I need you. Please come home. Please!"

"I love you, paleface. Don't forget me."

"Oh, Matthew. How could I forget you?" she whispered.

Eden felt a hand on her shoulder and stiffened. Scrubbing at her face with the backs of her hands, she turned and shot a rueful glance at Tracey. "I didn't mean to wake you."

"You didn't. My body clock's out of whack from my flight. I was just reading."

"It's chilly. Why don't you go back to bed?"

She yawned and tightened the sash on her robe. "I'm up. Might as well stay that way." She gave Eden a curious look. "Another nightmare?"

"Same one."

"You aren't getting more than two or three hours of sleep at night, are you? What does your obstetrician say?"

She shrugged. "Not much."

"Have you told him about your nightmares?"

She shook her head. "It won't make them stop."

Tracey took her hand and led her down the hallway and into the kitchen. Gently shoving Eden toward the breakfast table, she asked, "Hot cocoa or tea?"

"Whatever you're having is fine."

Tracey filled a saucepan with milk, adjusted the gas flame, and took two mugs from the rack above the stove. Satisfied that the milk would heat slowly, she left the kitchen, returning a few moments later with Eden's slippers and robe.

Eden smiled as the petite blonde tugged her from her chair and helped her into her robe. "You'd make a great lady's maid."

Tracey straightened and arched a slender brow. "Tell that to my mother's majordomo. He was convinced I was put on this earth for the express purpose of terrorizing the entire household staff."

"Sorry, Trace. I didn't mean to bring up the past."

"No problem. I think we've both finally adjusted to the fact that we didn't have the greatest childhoods, nor did we have parents who gave a damn about us. They had their lives, and we had ours. They're gone now, so it doesn't really matter anymore, does it?"

"At least our trust funds were generous," Eden commented

thoughtfully. "I think my money bothered Matthew at first. He wasn't too thrilled when I first told him about it."

"At least you had the good sense not to mention the money until after you were married."

Eden smiled. "A three-week courtship isn't conducive to heavy financial discussions. We were having too much fun. I honestly forgot to tell him. And then, once we were married, it seemed to matter a whole lot. I was a basket case by the time I finally brought the subject up."

"Worried about male pride?" Tracey questioned as she stirred powdered cocoa into the simmering milk.

"A little. Mostly, I think Matthew was just stunned. I'd already told him about the private schools and some of the people you and I had known while we were growing up, but I don't think it really made sense to him until I explained how Grandmother Barclay set up her estate."

"And then?" Tracey handed Eden a mug before slipping into a chair on the opposite side of the table.

"Then he was just so blasted quiet I almost exploded. But about three days before he left for Vietnam, we talked about the money. He told me he was glad that I had the financial security to depend on if anything happened to him." Eden shivered. "My blood ran cold when he said that."

"He was just being practical."

"I know that. At the time, though, it bothered me."

"Matt knows you well enough to realize that you'd never use your money as leverage in your relationship. It's there if you need it, that's all."

"That's what he said." She lifted her cocoa and sipped the hot liquid. After lowering the mug to the table, she wrapped her hands around its warmth.

"He's going to come home to you."

"I know he will."

"But maybe not . . ."

". . . for a long time," Eden finished for her. "I sometimes think I'm going crazy. I feel so empty, so disconnected from everything and everyone. What if Matthew doesn't come back? What then?"

"Then you'll do exactly what you have to do," Tracey

answered. "You'll raise your son or daughter the best way you know how. Your future is a given, my friend, whether or not Matt survives."

Eden let out a gust of air and leaned back in her chair, her eyes suddenly glittering with rage. "I loathe feeling helpless! And I loathe writing letters that get handled and read by the State Department, the International Red Cross, and the North Vietnamese. Nothing's sacred anymore."

"Finished?"

"With what?" Eden shot her a confused look. "My cocoa?"

"The self-pity routine."

"Ouch!"

"You deserved it." She leaned forward, her expression intent. "You aren't alone, no matter how you feel. Between the two of us we can get through the end of your pregnancy and do whatever else we have to do until Matt's released. No matter how long it takes. Think about it, why don't you?" Tracey suggested in a gentler tone. "U.S. troops have been in Southeast Asia since 1963 or 1964. The war can't go on much longer, especially with most of the country opposed to it."

"I sincerely hope you're right. I know I'm feeling sorry for myself and I shouldn't, but when I have that nightmare—" Eden stood and paced back and forth. "When I have the nightmare, it's as though I'm in some kind of a box. I can't even begin to describe the feeling that comes over me."

"It never changes?"

She shook her head and continued to wear down the kitchen tile. "It's the same every night. It started three or four days after I was notified about Matthew."

"But that was the first week of February!" Tracey exclaimed.

Eden pressed her fingertips to her temple as she came to a stop in the middle of the room. "I think it's just a sample of the confinement he's been subjected to since he was first taken prisoner."

"I really think you should tell your doctor, Eden."

"Why? He can't change my situation. Besides, I've only got a few more weeks before junior here is born." She patted her belly and laughed when it rippled with movement. "I think he's ready now."

Tracey stared at her middle. "Are you certain he's not playing football or basketball in there? I'm all for team sports, but doesn't it hurt when he turns cartwheels?"

Eden chuckled and walked back to her chair. "He's just getting comfortable. Don't worry so much."

"If you say so," she said doubtfully. She brought her eyes up to Eden's face, taking in the smudges of fatigue beneath her eyes. "You look beat. How about going back to bed for a while?"

"I don't think so. But a shower does sound good."

Tracey stood and carried their two mugs to the kitchen sink. "Why don't we take a walk down to the shore once you're dressed?"

Halfway out of her chair, Eden grinned. "You're starting to talk like a native."

"You know how flexible I am. Shore, beach, the words mean the same."

"You, Tracey Sinclair, are about as flexible as a slab of granite." She wagged an accusatory finger at her friend. "And taking a pregnant whale to the beach is a wonderful way of making yourself look even thinner than you already are. Your bikini stock ought to go up at least fifty points by just being seen with me on a stretch of sand."

"Take a shower before I forget about your delicate condition." She smirked and moved to the window. "I think I see a dump truck out on the street that can handle your mammoth proportions."

"Real nice, Trace!"

Eden was still grinning when she stepped into the shower. Talking about Matthew helped. In fact, talking had become a luxury to be fully explored now that Tracey was visiting. Very few people knew her situation. Those who did behaved as though she'd become invisible. Vietnam seemed to have a growing stigma attached to it, one that precluded conversation, however impersonal. People were either for the war or against it. She'd known for a long time that there was little middle ground.

She rubbed her lower back as the water hammered at her skin and thought again about her own private suspicion—that no one in Washington had a clue about what was really going on in Vietnam. She also realized Lyndon Johnson's political future had already been demolished by the undeclared *police action.* The editorials she'd read in the *Boston Globe* and *The New York Times* repeatedly insisted that it would take a new administration to heal the wounds of a divided America as well as end the involvement of the United States in Vietnam.

No one ever voiced any concern for the prisoners of war or the men still listed as missing in action. Eden wondered if Matthew and men like him would simply be lost in a bureaucratic shuffle aimed at retrieving waning political careers. That thought, the same one that haunted her every hour of every day, made her shiver despite the needle-sharp hot water sluicing down her body.

CHAPTER

5

May 1968—Long Moc Prison Camp, North Vietnam

"I'm not alone any longer," Matt whispered to himself in disbelief.

Still crammed into his bamboo cage, he wept when he first saw the American POWs being driven like cattle along the rutted jungle path that led into the prison camp. Round-eyed men clad in filth-encrusted, pajamalike garments, each carried a frayed woven mat and a single spoon. They were a dilapidated-looking trio, but they were Americans, and for that phenomenal blessing Matt thanked whichever god had seen fit to respond to his isolation.

He waited impatiently for several days before discovering their identities—days filled with agony when he was released from his suspended cage and prodded at gunpoint around the center of the compound on his hands and knees by his captors.

He felt the muscles of his body tighten and thrum in protest as he tried to walk. He tasted the rancidness of his own sweat as it poured from his body like sheets of monsoon rain. And he endured nights without sleep as his stomach heaved and shuddered, reaccustoming itself to nourishment, however unappetizing the daily bowl of gruel.

He felt his strength return, inch by painful inch.

The others nurtured him with their silent signals of encouragement. He resurrected his pride and transformed it into determination. Determination grew as he drew sustenance from the rich heritage of the Cherokee, his mother's people.

. . .

Matt studied the activity in the compound through a narrow seam in the wall of his new cell. Constructed like an outhouse, the enclosure had no windows.

Fifteen days had passed since his release from the bamboo cage. Still isolated from the other American prisoners while he regained his strength, he anxiously waited for the moment when he would be able to speak to them.

He saw large trucks pull into the center of the camp, thick clouds of red dust billowing in their wake and enveloping them when they came to a screeching stop. An overweight NVA enlisted man issued orders in what Matt now thought of as the "scream and spit" method of communication. He shook his head in disgust and knew he would never understand the Asian mind, whether at war or at peace.

He watched a group of soldiers empty the contents of the small convoy, his curiosity growing as they transported lengths of timber and what appeared to be bags of cement to a shed at the far end of the compound.

Matt straightened when he heard the bolt slide in the door of his cell. A guard motioned him forward, punctuating the request with sharp jabs of his rifle against Matt's ribs.

Matt squinted into the brilliance of the morning sun. Half smiling, he peered down at the guard standing in front of him. "What's on the recreation schedule for today, asshole?"

The guard nearest him sensed the derisiveness of his charge's query and administered several more sharp jabs to his ribs. Matt winced. The little man grinned and waved his rifle toward the far side of the camp.

"*Di! Di!*" he screamed.

Gritting his teeth, Matt stepped forward. He tried to ignore the leg irons digging into his ankles and the chain dragging in his wake. His capacity for fury had grown with each passing day of captivity, but he didn't regret the emotion. Anger and resentment, he had long ago decided, could be harnessed and used to his advantage. Emotions he would normally have considered negative now meant the difference between survival and death.

A narrow river flowed southward on the far side of the camp. Matt eagerly approached the smell of water. One of his guards stepped in front of him and motioned him to his knees. Matt narrowed his eyes and tightened his fists while slowly easing himself to the red earth. He felt cruel hands unlock and yank the leg irons from his already bleeding ankles.

"Son of a bitch!"

"Silence!"

Matt looked up. He kept his expression even.

"*Di!*" shouted the guard, pointing at the muddy riverbank.

Matt pulled himself to his feet, the prospect of his first bath since being taken prisoner dimming the pain throbbing in his ankles. He hurriedly stripped the remnants of his flight suit from his body. His fingers lingered on the filthy chamois band tied across his forehead. His token. A shabby symbol of survival. He didn't remove it.

He left a pile of rags at the river's edge and slowly waded into the welcoming flow of tepid water. For a few moments Matt forgot the threat of water moccasins, cat-sized water rats, and the cocked rifles pointed at his head.

He stood naked in the sun, ignored the guards, and allowed the heated rays to dry his emaciated body. A third guard arrived. He carried a bundle of clothing and a straight razor.

The pajama-style outfit, soiled from use, was still far cleaner than the remains of his own clothing. A guard kicked a pair of sandals made from discarded auto tires toward him once he'd dressed. Matt hurriedly stepped into them, flicking away clusters of bloated leeches still sucking at his bleeding flesh.

Forced again to his knees, he crossed his arms over his chest and closed his eyes when another guard stepped forward and dry shaved his face and head. He already knew that only those considered deserving of respect in the Vietnamese culture were permitted to grow a beard. Matt smiled grimly, convinced that the lack of hair would simply lessen his lice problem.

Two guards refastened Matt's leg irons and attached new wrist manacles. The weight of the iron dragged painfully against his injured right arm but also warned him that a new phase of imprisonment at Long Moc had begun.

The prisoners formed a ragtag work crew. Instructed to remain silent at all times, they began rebuilding a bridge that had fallen victim to heavy monsoon rains the previous year.

At first, conversation was impossible under close supervision by the guards, who outnumbered their prisoners three to one. The Americans took pains not to rouse the ire of their overseers. Late in the afternoon of the fourth day, boredom took its toll among the North Vietnamese. Communication began, and Matt formally met his fellow prisoners.

Hal Caulfield, lieutenant (jg.), USN. A tall, sandy-haired man whose innate dignity had yet to be diminished by captivity.

Chet Holt, lieutenant, USMC. A medium-sized, balding man in his mid-twenties. Serving a tour of duty at Da Nang, he'd been shot down on a bombing run near the DMZ.

Finally, there was Bill Jackson, sergeant, U.S. Army. A barrel-chested career NCO, he spent every waking moment planning his escape and shouting epithets at the guards.

The men began reconstruction of the damaged bridge by clearing away debris and broken timbers that had formed the original superstructure. Using the muddy banks of the river as a natural blackboard, each man covertly spelled out his name, rank, and military affiliation while appearing to be engrossed in his assigned task. Every time Matt climbed the slippery bank, he collected more information. His identity was the final entry of the day.

The Americans didn't complain about the long, hot days laboring for the enemy. It meant food each morning and physical activity that strengthened body and spirit.

Matt was particularly grateful for the strenuous work. His right hand showed signs of improved mobility, and his legs no longer collapsed under him like soft clay. And at night, in the dark confines of his solitary cell, he reassured himself with his fingertips that the suppurating sores on his neck and chest had begun to heal.

CHAPTER 6

June 1968—Beverly, Massachusetts

Tracey flinched every time she heard a muffled groan or a cry of pain. Concern and fatigue lined her face. Separated from the labor room by a set of double doors that periodically swung open to admit a patient on a briskly rolling gurney, she paced the worn tile of the waiting room and tried to ignore the stink of disinfectant permeating the air.

Her gaze periodically fell on the two men who sat chain-smoking on a nearby couch as she walked back and forth. Another man, older and obviously more experienced, snored noisily in a slouched position in a chair, his extended legs and unlaced sneakers the only minor deviation in her route. The television blared but held no one's attention.

She glanced at her watch, paled, and continued to pace. Eighteen hours and still no baby. A bulky figure suddenly burst through the labor-room doors, and Tracey stopped in her tracks.

"Who's this 'Matthew' person Benedict keeps calling for?"

"Her husband, but he's—"

"He's late."

Tracey stared at the woman. "Late?"

The nurse turned and lumbered back to the double doors.

"Wait! You don't understand. He isn't—he can't get here. That's why I'm here. I explained everything to the receptionist when Eden checked in."

"Husband, mother, or mother-in-law. Hospital policy is very specific."

"I realize that, Miss . . ." Tracey searched for a name tag and encountered a wide chest in baggy surgical greens.

"Mrs. Dobbs."

"Eden's husband is a POW."

The nurse frowned.

"In North Vietnam," Tracey clarified. "He's a pilot. He was shot down in late January."

"Where's her mother?"

"Dead. Look, Eden's doctor said—"

"Her mother-in-law?"

"I haven't any idea. Dr. Howard said I could be with her during labor and delivery. I won't get in your way, I promise."

Mrs. Dobbs looked doubtful. "It's no picnic in there."

Tracey drew herself up to her full five feet two inches. "I'm not expecting a party!"

The harsh-featured woman studied her, weighing the tiny blonde's fragile appearance against the determined set of her chin. "There's an exception to every rule, so follow me. But remember . . . no fainting and no hysterics."

Mrs. Dobbs led her to the changing room. Tracey silently prayed that she wouldn't keel over at the first sight of blood. Inexperience and shock widened her eyes as she approached the labor table. She studied Eden's pale face and noted the perspiration trailing into her lank hair. Touching her shoulder, she asked, "Eden, can you hear me?"

"I can't feel my toes."

Tracey laughed and then clapped a hand over her mouth. Mrs. Dobbs might think she was starting to get hysterical. "The nurse gave me a cup of ice chips. Do you want to try sucking on one?"

Eden blinked and focused on the worried face staring down at her. "Thirsty."

"Ice chips are the best I can do."

She nodded and accepted the sliver of ice Tracey slipped into her mouth. Beads of perspiration dotted her upper lip and forehead, a marked contrast to lips that were dry and cracked.

"Better?"

She nodded. "Thanks. How'd you get in here?"

Tracey grinned. "My persuasive personality, what else?"

"Your rotten temper's more like it. You'd have to use dynamite to get through Nurse Dobbs if she didn't want you in here." She stiffened and gasped.

Tracey grabbed Eden's hand as her body heaved. When the pain didn't lessen, Eden reminded herself to pant and began to draw in several quick breaths. The contraction slowly retreated.

"Are they all like that?"

She smiled and looked up. "Some are worse; some are better."

"Tell me what I can do to help."

Eden squeezed her fingers. "Just let me hang on to you for a while." She let her eyes drift shut for a moment. "I keep thinking Matthew's here."

"Mrs. Dobbs said you were asking for him."

Tears began to seep from the corners of her eyes. "I want him with me. I miss him."

Tracey shifted uneasily. "Why don't we talk about him?"

"Next best thing?"

She nodded. "Kind of."

"We used to play that game when we were kids. Do you remember the Fairmont elevator?"

Tracey groaned. "You would remind me of that fiasco."

"Best day of my life," she recalled in a hoarse voice. "Even if Matthew did think we were trying to kill him with all those boxes we accidentally dumped on him."

This time Tracey didn't try to control her laughter. "He said a mine field would be safer than being closed up in an elevator with us."

"He"—she grimaced and tightened her hold on Tracey—"was probably right. We'd just bought out most of the stores in San Francisco."

"And you went swimming in the blackest eyes I've ever seen after you dove into his arms," Tracey recalled.

"He caught me when I fell."

"He looked so fierce."

"No, never fierce. He was very gentle with me. Always gentle," she murmured.

"I was too busy getting a crick in my neck looking up at him to notice."

"You get a crick in your neck looking at everyone."

"Just because I'm not an Amazon like you—" she began.

Eden grinned. "Mutt and Jeff."

"That's us." Tracey returned her smile, forgetting for a moment where they were and what would soon happen. "It always surprised me that Matt was able to afford the Fairmont, military pay being what it is."

Eden laughed softly at the look of honest curiosity on her friend's face. Growing up with money had given them both a distorted view of middle-class life, she realized. It was still an issue they were both working on. "Officers aren't exactly peasants, you know, although Matthew did admit that the Fairmont's military discount was too good a deal to pass up while he was on leave. I think the hotel began the tradition sometime during World War II."

"Interesting."

"How about patriotic on the part of certain hotels during wartime?" she suggested tiredly.

"How about a sponge bath?" Tracey asked back, distracted from her train of thought when she noticed Eden wiping at the perspiration that was trailing across her temples.

"Please." She watched a nurse hand Tracey a shallow water-filled basin and washcloth, but her thoughts were still on those first hours with Matthew. "We made love that first night. I'd never been with anyone before."

Tracey hid her surprise. As close as they were, it still wasn't like Eden to talk about the intimate aspects of her life. "I didn't think you had."

"There wasn't any doubt in my mind about him from the start. He wanted me and I wanted him. It was the most natural thing that's ever happened to me. He seemed surprised, though, that I was a virgin."

"Glad, too, I bet."

Eden smiled and closed her eyes as Tracey bathed her face

and neck. Matthew had been surprised. Surprised and pleased. She remembered his remark: "I want to make love to you, Eden, but I know it's too soon for that, so will you stay with me tonight and let me hold you?"

"It's not too soon," she'd assured him. "I belong with you."

"We belong together." He took her hand as they sat facing one another in the sitting room of his suite at the hotel. "I won't rush you, but please stay with me."

She'd studied him then and realized that he understood the instincts that were guiding her in those early intimate moments of their relationship. Rather than try to influence her, he remained silent, trusting her to chart this new course herself.

Matthew wasn't handsome, she knew, at least not in a conventional sense. He was rawboned, big, and stunningly male. His dark complexion and ruggedly etched features suggested much more than the strength of his Indian heritage and the uniqueness of his character. When she looked into his eyes, she felt as though she were peering into the soul of a nation.

"You've never been with anyone before, have you?" he had quietly asked.

She shook her head. "I've been waiting for the right man."

"I don't want to hurt you."

She brought his fingers to her breast. "You couldn't hurt me."

He closed his hand over the fullness of her flesh, felt her nipple harden despite the fabric covering her body, and trembled. "I've got orders for Vietnam. I leave in eight weeks, and I'll be gone for thirteen months."

"I'll wait for you," she promised, momentarily surprised at herself but certain of her ability to keep her pledge.

"That's too much to expect."

She moved closer. "Nothing's too much between us." She extended her hand and made a sweeping gesture that encompassed the room. "This is right. We're right."

He had carried her into the bedroom of the suite. She experienced his tenderness as he undressed her, knew his arousal when she hesitantly explored his body after he shed his own clothing.

Lowering her to the bed, he dropped down beside her, his hands dark against the cream of her skin. "We have so little time."

"We have the future. Teach me how to love you, Matthew."

He lowered his lips to hers, whispering, "You're what's been missing from my life," before taking her mouth in a forceful display of the depth of his feelings.

They had fallen asleep in the early dawn hours, Eden content in the sanctuary provided by Matthew's embrace. Despite her fatigue, she had carried his image into her dreams. The copper of his skin, the coal blackness of his short-cropped hair, the slashing brows that complemented his large dark eyes, and the hard lines of his jaw.

While Eden drifted with her memories, Tracey tried to make her more comfortable. She continued to sponge her upper body, patting her skin dry with a small towel. She paused when she noticed the punctured strips of sheet beneath Eden's hands. Staring at the finger-sized holes, she couldn't even begin to fathom the agony that had produced such rents in the fabric.

A fresh explosion of pain brought Eden upright on the labor table. Tracey rushed to the head of the table, easing Eden back down and gently massaging her shoulders as she panted. Nurse Dobbs and a doctor Tracey didn't recognize examined her.

"Where's Dr. Howard?" she demanded, her fingers nearly embedded in Eden's quaking shoulders.

Nurse Dobbs glowered and ignored her.

Tracey abandoned all caution. "Call Dr. Howard. He's Eden's doctor."

"It's okay," Eden gasped. "Dr. Michaels is his . . . partner. Don't . . . worry." Clenching her fists, she focused her dwindling strength on the narrowing spiral of movement in her lower abdomen.

"She's just about ready. Clean her up and get her into delivery."

"Yes, Doctor."

Tracey moved while a second woman helped Nurse Dobbs transfer Eden to a gurney that would take her to the delivery room. Holding her hand, Tracey stayed at her side until she was in position on the delivery table. She stepped out of the way when one of the nurses helped Eden from her soaked gown and into a fresh one.

"Matthew!"

Eden's scream jolted Tracey forward. "You're all right. Take a deep breath and start to pant. Don't fight the contractions," she soothed. "Do it for Matt, and for the beautiful baby you're going to have. You're so close now."

Perspiration and tears wet both their faces. The minutes ticked by. Tracey continued to encourage. Eden kept chanting Matthew's name. Dr. Michaels returned, his hands encased in plastic gloves and his face covered by a sterile mask.

"You'll have to move aside, miss."

Tracey complied, too exhausted to fight Nurse Dobbs any longer.

"Blood pressure 110 over 80. Fetal heartbeat faint."

"Get the natal cart over here," the doctor ordered.

A sudden flurry of activity made Tracey straighten. She stared, fascinated and appalled, at the urgency unfolding in front of her.

"It's nearly time, Eden. I'm going to need all the help you can give me. Do you understand what I'm saying?"

She nodded. Beads of perspiration dotted her face and dripped from her chin. She grimaced as another contraction seized her.

Nurse Dobbs took her hands and inserted them into the fist-sized width of two leather straps. "Hold on to these, Benedict, and don't let go."

"Medieval-torture time," she gasped with a weak laugh. "Trace, you still here?"

"Right behind you."

"It's time now, Eden. Almost time to push. Are you listening to me?"

"Yes!"

"Start panting again. I'll tell you when to push."

Eden dragged herself up for better leverage against the harshness invading her body.

"Pant, Benedict," ordered Nurse Dobbs above the growing confusion in the delivery room.

"Can't!" she screamed, the agony tearing her body apart almost too much to bear. "Want to push. Oh, God! Where's Matthew? Need him. Can't do this without him. Damn you to hell, Matthew! I need you." She collapsed, her breathing shallow.

"Eden, pay attention to me," the doctor insisted. "You're seconds away from a healthy baby. Don't flake out on me now."

She whimpered, the sound reminiscent of a wounded animal. Without thinking, Tracey approached the delivery table. She placed her hands under Eden's shoulders for additional support and ignored the two nurses who glared at her.

"Please! I have to push."

Several seconds crept by. Tracey tightened her hold on Eden. All she could hear was the sound of her friend's gasping restraint.

"All right, Eden. Now give me one hard push."

She pushed, her body rigid with the effort.

"Again!"

Once more she stiffened, pushing with what remained of her strength. She felt her body stretch and tear. Black dots danced across the interior of her closed eyes, and she fought the urge to give in to her exhaustion. A mass of confusing sounds invaded the delivery room.

Eden heard a statement of satisfaction erupt from the obstetrician, but she couldn't make out the words. Instruments clattered on an aluminum tray, a nurse laughed, and finally, beautifully, she heard what she had been praying for—the furious cry of an infant robbed of darkness and warmth. Her baby. The baby she and Matthew had made.

"You did it, Eden. You did it."

She smiled at Tracey, amazement in her voice and fatigue-shadowed eyes. "I did, didn't I?"

Nurse Dobbs stepped forward, moisture welling in her eyes as she settled a squalling naked bundle in Eden's arms. "You did a fine job, Benedict. Here's your little man."

She cradled her son in her arms and whispered, "Hello,

Baby Drew. Your mama loves you. So will your daddy when he comes home to us."

Tracey hugged her before excusing herself from the delivery room while the doctor stitched Eden back together. Standing in the hospital corridor, she slumped against the wall and released the tears of fear and relief she'd been holding back for the last twenty-one hours.

"You've heard the news, then."

She looked up into a face filled with shock, the face of one of the men who'd been chain-smoking in the labor-room waiting area. "What news?"

"Bobby Kennedy's been shot. He died a few minutes ago."

Tracey stared at the man. Her first thought was for the Kennedy family, her second a genuine sense of personal loss, and finally, most peculiarly, the realization that Eden and Matt's son had uttered his first cry of rage at being thrust from his mother's womb within minutes of what could easily be considered a national tragedy.

She shivered, hugged herself for warmth, forced herself to smile, and reentered the delivery room, unable to dispel the uneasiness she felt for her new godchild and his mother.

CHAPTER 7

July 1968—Long Moc Prison Camp, North Vietnam

Matt listened to the jungle prepare itself for sleep. Monkeys chittered, and other small animals rustled the underbrush in their unceasing quest for survival. Drawing his gaze from the thick foliage on the back side of his bamboo cell, he focused on the North Vietnamese soldiers who shuffled drunkenly to their barracks. Poorly trained, their off-duty pursuits displayed their lack of motivation.

The camp's night guards increased the frequency of their patrols around the circumference of the compound as darkness pressed down like a heavy black cloak. They checked the cages containing the four American POWs at ten-minute intervals, instead of the usual thirty-minute passes common during daylight hours if the prisoners weren't on a work detail.

Matt whistled softly, his signal to Chet Holt that the guards were again out of listening range. Gone were the long nights of tapping out messages against the walls of their individual outhouse-shaped cells. Gone was the frustration of not being able to communicate in English.

"We're going to have to do something about Jackson soon," Chet insisted in hushed tones. "He's going to get us all shot if he keeps challenging the guards."

Matt nodded. He clenched and unclenched his right fist, unaware of the reflexive gesture as he pondered the army sergeant's behavior.

He had already noted Jackson's increasing aggressiveness in the weeks they'd spent rebuilding the enemy bridge, and his belligerent attitude had often cost them all in reduced rations and beatings. All the POWs, with the exception of Jackson, it seemed, understood that flouting the orders of several soldiers eager to reduce your brain to tiny chunks of red-and-gray ooze was just short of lunacy. But despite warnings from his fellow prisoners, he still persisted in baiting the guards. Matt wondered if he was coping with captivity the only way he knew how or if he had a genuine death wish.

He glanced at Chet. "His training as a Green Beret should've taught him a hell of a lot more about dealing with the natives, and we both know giving him a direct order to lighten up isn't going to cut it. The asshole seems to thrive on confrontation."

Chet snorted in disgust. "I sometimes think he enjoys those damned beatings he gets. There's a major problem with the way that guy operates. It still hasn't occurred to him that we're all in this mess together. When one of us fucks up, we all pay."

Matt cocked his head, heard booted footsteps, and cleared his throat. Two guards approached their cell and paused to inspect the interior. Matt squinted against the circle of light roving through the square enclosure. It glanced off his face, found Chet's, and then settled on the cylindrical pole running the length of the center of the cage. Once assured that the prisoners' ankle chains were still securely fastened to the steel rod, the guards continued their patrol of the compound.

A signaling whistle from Matt prompted Chet's final observation about Sergeant Jackson. "Confrontation makes a hell of a lot more sense when both parties are evenly matched. Maybe our favorite green beanie'll consider that the next time the camp commander tosses his ass in the hotbox."

Matt smiled grimly. Already scored into his brain was the memory of the animallike conditions he'd endured while suspended in a cage in the center of the Long Moc compound.

As he'd rotted in his own waste, he had vowed that he would survive. Matt knew that if Jackson's hostility continued, the survival of his three fellow prisoners would be threatened. His jaw tightened, and he promised himself that he wouldn't die because of another man's stupidity. He *would* find a way to control Jackson.

Accustomed to his cellmate's lapses into silence, Chet didn't question the pause in their conversation. He leaned back against the bars of their cell, silently grateful for the presence of a man he liked and respected. The periodic stoicism of the half-Cherokee pilot offset his own more verbal nature. The thought prompted a weary smile and a silent prayer of thanks for a friend in the midst of a nightmare.

Matt cleared his throat again, alerting Chet to the presence of a cluster of guards. Both men held their breath. They both realized that less than five minutes had passed since the last security round of the camp.

The sounds of a scuffle exploded in the silence of the compound.

"Get fucked, you slant-eyed son of a whore!"

"Fool!" Matt muttered. "Stupid, stupid fool!"

He listened to the sound of rounds filling several rifle chambers and then heard Jackson being dragged, cursing and kicking, from the space he shared with Hal Caulfield.

"I wonder if any of us will—"

"Don't say it, Chet. Think it if you have to, but don't ever say it aloud."

Chet nodded, his expression bleak. Matt slowly exhaled and tried to block out Jackson's cries of pain. Both men privately wondered if he would live to see the dawn. They also wondered whether or not he would want to.

Four days passed before Matt, Chet, and Hal saw Bill Jackson again. For four long days they remained in their cells and listened to the soul-stopping terror of his agonized screams and the angry voices of his interrogators. They almost didn't recognize the limp mass of bloodied humanity finally dragged into the middle of the compound, because what remained bore little or no resemblance to the cocky, barrel-chested army NCO they had all known.

Knife slashes covered his face and chest. Rope burns from being suspended from the interrogation-room ceiling marked his wrists and ankles. Matt saw that Jackson's lips had been slit, as had the bridged length of his nose. The resulting wounds flooded his face and chest with blood.

Matthew and the other POWs were doubly stunned when they saw what remained of the lower half of Jackson's body. Each tendon and ligament accessible to a knife had been severed in his legs. They hung like cherry-stained strips of limp twine from his once-meaty limbs.

Chet and Hal gagged and looked away when they saw the gouged-out stump that had once been the unconscious man's genitals. Matt froze at the sight, his mouth thinning to a narrow line of revulsion. He felt the more civilized elements of his nature withering under the yoke of captivity.

The guards hoisted Jackson by a rope coiled at his throat. They left him to rot in the sun-baked center of the Long Moc compound.

Seventy-six hours passed before he finally died—hours filled with the sight of wild birds pecking apart his already disfigured flesh, guards reproachfully spitting on him when he moaned, and maggots burrowing into his seeping wounds.

"These goddamned rats are driving me insane!" Caulfield exploded.

Opening his eyes, Matt studied the young naval officer. Even in the murky predawn light, Hal's skin had the translucent quality of a corpse.

Chet stirred and sleepily looked at his cellmates. "Give me a break, guys. I'm trying to get some shut-eye."

"The guards are awake," Matt cautioned, his eyes covering the camp in a sweeping glance.

"Don't you ever sleep?" Chet asked. He chuckled at Matt's sardonic look, while Hal shook his head in disgust. "You two insomniacs get the job of baby-sitting my kid when we get home. My wife'll never worry about a weekend trip with you two around."

"How can you joke when we . . . this . . ." Hal gestured helplessly. "We're slowly starving to death, not to mention being eaten alive by these fucking rodents, and you make jokes? I'll never understand you, Holt, not in a million years."

Chet shrugged off the criticism, as was his habit. Sweat dotted his forehead despite the early hour. "It's gonna be another killer today."

"When isn't it? Christ! There's another one." Hal swung ineffectually at a large rat scurrying into the corner of their cramped cell.

Matt noticed the bloody bites on Hal's lower legs. He didn't bother to ask how the man had slept through the experience. "Tear a strip of cloth from your shirt and wrap it around those bites. I'll try and talk the camp CO into giving you some antibiotics."

Both men looked at Matt in alarm.

Chet spoke first. "Last time we got quinine for our malaria, they cut us to half rations."

Matt glanced at his own scarred arms and legs. "Then we have a choice. We all eat a little less and Hal has a fighting chance against the infection he probably already has, or we watch him die. Slowly and painfully."

"We ask for medication," Chet insisted.

"Whatever you guys decide is fine with me." Hal turned away and curled his body into a circle of misery.

"We're going to have to be more careful about the sleeping schedule," Chet said, trying to lessen the tension he felt building in the cramped cell. "Hal's right about the rats. They're everywhere."

"In theory, a rotating sleeping schedule's a good idea. But in practice?" Matt shook his head. "Sixteen hours of work in the hot sun every day and half rations requires sleep at night. It's impossible."

"We've got to try. You can't go forever without rest, and

we both know you're the one who stands the duty while Hal and I sleep." Admiration filled his tired face.

Matt shrugged indifferently. "Just trying to stay alive. Besides, I've got enough teeth marks from those fucking rats to last me a lifetime." He shifted against the bamboo rods digging into his spine, flexed his fingers, and rubbed at the ache penetrating his manacled wrists.

"I don't care anymore," Hal moaned. "I just don't care."

"You'd better fucking care, Caulfield," Matt grated. "I'm not going to die because some candy-assed navy puke can't cut it."

"But I can't make it on only two or three hours of sleep."

"Hal, we'll help you. You can't give up. You'll die. Matt's right. If we don't fight back any way we can—together—we'll never make it out of here."

"Quit kidding yourself, Holt. We're going to die in this pisshole. The only thing we don't know is the date."

Two days following his request for a meeting with the camp commander, Matt was granted an audience. Chet's whispered "Semper Fi" did little to ease his apprehension as he was led at gunpoint from their cell.

Shuffling across the dusty compound, his leg irons punctuating his halting steps, Matt realized that he'd grown increasingly withdrawn during his months of captivity. He now traveled deep within himself in search of courage and solace.

He also realized that by seeking contact with Major Han, he had violated his own personal avenue to survival. He loathed calling attention to himself, because he had learned early on that staying alive meant becoming virtually invisible.

An hour passed before Matt heard the sound of footsteps approaching the interrogation room. Strapped to a chair in the middle of the windowless room, the stench of urine and feces invading his nostrils, he watched the camp commander enter the room.

Major Han stomped to a desk positioned under the glare of an exposed light bulb. Flinging a pair of expensive leather gloves onto the scarred surface of the desk, he studied the American officer.

"So you've finally decided to cooperate?" he demanded in French, a language both he and his prisoner spoke.

Matt stared straight ahead. He thought about death and how it seemed to emanate from the walls of the room, a suffocating presence unto itself. Shaking himself from his morose thoughts, he responded in rusty high school French, "Lieutenant Caulfield requires medical attention."

"That's not what I asked!"

Matt exhaled softly. "We have no intention of signing confessions. You already know our position on that issue, Major. We're not war criminals."

"It grows clearer to me each day that none of you took to heart the . . . shall we say, disposition . . . of Sergeant Jackson."

"Jackson's dead." He fixed his gaze on a speck of blood on the spattered wall in front of him.

"I'm pleased you took note of his demise!"

It was tough to miss. Matt took a steadying breath. "Lieutenant Caulfield isn't dead . . . *yet.* Once again, Major, I respectfully request medical attention on his behalf. His body is filled with poison from rat bites."

"You're a fool, Benedict!"

"Perhaps, sir." He felt loathing and disgust for the man and the culture he represented coil like a tight spring in his gut, but he kept his voice emotionless. "That doesn't change the fact that I'm senior officer of the remaining prisoners. And, as such, I'm responsible for Lieutenant Caulfield's well-being. Antibiotics are needed to counter the effects of rat poisoning."

"Only soldiers loyal to the Democratic Republic receive medical attention."

"So much for the Geneva Convention."

"The Geneva Convention!" Contempt filled the moon-shaped face of the North Vietnamese officer. "An Occidental innovation for weaklings," Han spat out derisively. "The Democratic Republic has fought valiantly to free our homeland from foreign invaders who rape our country of its heritage and riches. We will continue to fight until all of Vietnam is free! We do not waste precious medicines on war criminals."

Matt made a conscious decision not to become embroiled in yet another of Major Han's convoluted political lectures and remained silent.

"Look at me when I speak to you, Benedict!"

Matt ignored the direct order. "I have no desire to find myself in front of a firing squad, Major. You've executed your own men for following that particular order." *You perverse little bastard!*

"Your cleverness will one day cause your death, Benedict," he sneered. "But not until you have served the needs of the Democratic Republic. Until then, I am content to enjoy the humiliation you and your pathetic comrades must endure while in my custody."

Matt tightened his fingers on the armrests of the chair. Seething inside him was the desire to wrap his hands around the major's throat and squeeze until his palms met in the middle.

"What? No response? Come now, Benedict," taunted the camp commander. "Prisoners should never disappoint their betters. Not if they desire to remain alive."

Matt felt common sense and anger collide inside his brain. They exploded on impact. Caution abandoned, he cocked his head and stabbed the man with a steely look.

"We both know Caulfield won't last another forty-eight hours. That does not speak well of your skill as a prison-camp commander, *Major.* And we both also know that your superiors in Hanoi want us alive."

The two men stared at one another, east and west a frozen tableau of disbelief and daring.

Retribution would follow swiftly, Matt knew. He also realized that he was ready for any punishment ordered by Major Han.

The blank expression on his face provided little clue of the adrenal rush surging through him. Redirecting his gaze to the blood-spattered wall in front of him, he reminded himself that he had already journeyed once to the place of the living dead. He expected to be tested, again and again.

He focused on a heritage that had taught him to accept his own mortality. With that knowledge came the certainty that this was not his time to accept the death of his spirit.

CHAPTER 8

July 30, 1968—Beverly, Massachusetts

Sealing the letter she had just written, Eden left her desk in the alcove adjacent to her bedroom. She walked quietly down the hallway to the living room, her thoughts on Serena Benedict. She'd made every effort to communicate with her mother-in-law, a woman she had yet to meet, since Matthew's captivity earlier in the year. And despite the fact that she never received a reply to her letters or a return of her phone calls, she continued to write weekly and send snapshots of Drew.

Matthew had once remarked on his mother's reserve with non-Indian women, but Eden still wondered at her silence. Why didn't Serena want any contact with her only son's wife and child? She shook her head, puzzled by the woman's obvious indifference. Her attitude simply didn't make sense.

She turned on the late news, a nightly ritual now. Lowering herself into the Bentwood rocker Tracey had given her before Drew's birth, she waited for the reports that had become a regular part of broadcasting all over the country.

Drew's cry of hunger coincided with the start of the program, and Eden hurried into the nursery. After changing his wet diaper, she carried him to the rocker. She opened the buttons of her robe and guided his searching mouth to her milk-heavy breasts. Cradling him in her arms, she relaxed when she felt the determined tug of his hunger. Drew was the image of his father. His head was covered with hair like black silk, and his eyes, blue at birth like most infants', were now as black as charcoal.

She smoothed her fingertips across the golden skin of his cheek and whispered, "How I wish your daddy could share you with me, my sweet Drew." He waved a tiny fist at the sound of her voice, and she smiled. "Someday," she promised, "he'll be home, and then he'll always be a part of our lives."

". . . seventeen army personnel and twelve marines died when the transport plane they were in was hit by enemy ground fire near Chu Lai, South Vietnam," said the newscaster.

Eden inhaled sharply and focused on the screen.

"And in Washington today the Pentagon has confirmed General Abrams's request for additional combat troops. As yet, the White House has no comment. Coming up on the late news, a casualty report for the month of July as well as scenes of civilian losses following a guerrilla attack on a South Vietnamese village. Also, sports and weather, with the final score from an extra-inning game by the Boston Red Sox."

Eden forced herself to sit through the sports and weather segments on the off chance that some mention would be made of the American POWs held in North Vietnam. Hope suppressed her natural aversion to the casualty counts and the reports on the growing antiwar movement. She was bewildered that her country could supply a seemingly endless stream of money, manpower, and weapons to a failing regime on the other side of the world, while at the same time a growing number of voters publicly vomited their disgust via whatever forum made available to them.

Eden would have been the first to admit her political naïveté. She instinctively honored the Marine Corps' request that she not draw media attention to herself as the wife of a POW, despite the isolation caused by her cooperation, for one very simple reason. She knew it was what Matthew would have expected of her. Whatever her personal apprehensions, she kept them to herself.

News footage of sniper fire directed at Vietnamese civilians fleeing a burning village flashed across the television screen.

She cringed at the sight of the panicked people. Drew wailed, outraged by her tight grip. She loosened her hold, and he resumed his meal, his fists pressed against her skin.

As a rule, there was little mention made of the POWs. Tonight was no exception. Eden chafed at the lack of information and then reminded herself that her moods affected her son. She patted his back as she left the rocker and made her way into the nursery. He continued to sleep as she placed him on his stomach and covered him with a light flannel receiving blanket.

Wandering through the house, she closed several windows and locked the back door for the night. She hesitated when she reached the front screen door, her eyes on the porch swing as it swayed in the gentle breeze drifting in from the Atlantic.

Why not? she asked herself. It may be midnight, but I'm hours from falling asleep.

She padded barefoot out the door and across the porch, settling in the corner of the swing with her chin resting on upraised knees. She watched the front light go out across the street at the Watsons', saw Tommy Shane, one of the teenage boys from next door, pull into the driveway in his prize possession, a rebuilt 1957 Chevy, and then raised her eyes to the diamond-studded black of the sky. She sighed, the sound audible in the silence of the night and an echo of the restlessness that had plagued her for several days now.

Her thoughts wandered. Snatches of conversations with Matthew during the short months of their married life before he'd gone overseas seventeen months ago replayed in her mind. Moments they'd shared that she'd once taken for granted and that now seemed so incredibly special. Early-morning bathroom patter. The subtle dance of a man and woman sharing one mirror and one sink. The teasing words, the eye contact in the reflection of a mirror that produced broad smiles, the awareness of stepping aside when he needed to rinse his razor, and his willingness to dig through her cosmetic drawer when she needed a certain tube of lipstick.

And desperation. She shivered, recalling that it was later,

after their R and R, that she had understood and accepted the undercurrent of desperation that had haunted them both during those seven days spent in a small hotel near Diamond Head. She hadn't questioned Matthew's decision not to use the accommodations available at Fort DeRussey, the hotel used by most military personnel on R and R in Hawaii, because she sensed his need to forget everything and everyone connected with the Marine Corps and Vietnam.

He had removed his uniform and placed it in the rear of the hotel-room closet. But each time she'd opened the louvered doors to dress, she was reminded of the reality hovering at the edge of their happiness.

She shifted on the wooden seat of the old porch swing and closed her eyes. Every memory she had of her time with Matthew was rich with emotional satisfaction. She could almost feel the strength of his embrace. Her senses welcomed the remembered tenderness of his hands and mouth when they'd made love. And in her mind's eye she saw the wonder reflected in the hard planes of his face each time their bodies had come together in passion.

She also felt her body awaken to the hunger that always accompanied thoughts of her husband, and she experienced the painful swelling ache of her own flesh, knowing full well that she might never again know the intimacy she craved. Shuddering violently, Eden opened her eyes to the darkness. Tears filled her eyes, and she tightly hugged herself, trying to quiet the tremors still racking her body.

"Hang on," she whispered to herself. "Hang on and he'll come home someday."

When she finally stopped shaking, she felt damp wisps of salt-laden ocean air trail across her face. The need to be loved, she knew, would never go away. Matthew would always be the one person who had the power to satisfy her physical and emotional needs. She understood the forces at play, but she still despaired at his absence from her life.

Wiping her cheeks with the backs of her hands, Eden sped up the home movie idling in her mind. She smiled, recalling one particular morning during their R and R.

The sun hadn't even made an appearance yet, but Matthew

was busy charting the curves and hollows of her body. Prying her eyes open, she'd glanced at the bedside clock. "It's the middle of the night!"

He chuckled at her exasperated attitude. "No more sleep for now, paleface. You can do plenty of that when you get back to the mainland."

"You're impossible."

"Not me." He nibbled on her fingertips and slowly inched the sheet from her naked body. "Need I remind you that we didn't get any dinner last night?"

"Need I remind you that you have only yourself to blame for that little oversight?" she countered. "I was all ready for an evening of wining and dining, and you undressed me." She'd tried to look outraged and failed.

"Your fault. You tempted me. Admit it."

"Only if you'll admit that you had the hots for my body."

"Tell me you hated it," he challenged as his lips moved up the length of one slim arm.

"Couldn't stand it." She rolled from his loose hold without warning.

"Looks as though my number-one squaw's going to have to pay for her disrespectful nature."

Eden noticed the speculative look in his eyes. She shrugged and folded her arms across her breasts.

"I wonder if there are any anthills around the hotel."

"Anthills!"

"My ancestors always staked an errant wife to an anthill when she deprived a brave of proper nourishment." He paused and grinned before vaulting across the bed.

Eden sidestepped him quite easily. She smiled down at him, delighted with his disorderly sprawl. "This is the twentieth century. We wives tend to frown on that sort of thing."

"Good point." He grinned up at her and sighed weakly. "I'm dying of starvation, woman. Feed me!"

She smiled at his absurd behavior. "Those are my choices, huh? Breakfast or an anthill?"

"You got it, paleface."

Her stomach growled, as if to punctuate his last comment, and they both burst out laughing.

"I could always nibble on you," he offered as he seized her by the ankle.

"Later. I'm starved, too." She had leaned down and kissed him before fleeing his exploring hands for the shower.

Eden laughed softly as she stood and walked into the house. After locking the front door and turning off the living-room lights, she checked Drew to make certain he was sleeping peacefully, walked down the hall to her bedroom, and got into bed. She drifted off to sleep with the memory that more than two hours had actually passed before she and Matthew had managed to leave their hotel room. Like the intensity of their love for one another, they had come together with explosive force under a hot shower, hunger for intimacy taking precedence over empty stomachs.

Eden awakened to the warmth of the summer sun streaming across her face, not the sound of Drew's normal early-morning grunts and giggles. She smiled at his uncharacteristic behavior as she flipped back the covers and got out of bed. This was the first time her son had allowed her to sleep late since she'd brought him home from the hospital.

As she stood beside his crib, she frowned when she realized that he was still asleep. She leaned down, the movement adding to the ache in her full breasts, and stroked his blanket-covered body.

"Drew?" she whispered. "It's time to wake up, little love. Mommy needs to feed you."

Eden gently turned him onto his back. His arms remained stiff at his sides, his head cocked oddly to the left. An emotion she couldn't identify lanced through her, bringing acute, smothering pain and a sense of panic that she consciously tried to resist.

"Drew? Are you sick, Drew?" Even as she spoke, Eden mentally registered the blue-gray of his skin and the coldness of his cheek where her fingertips lingered.

"Wake up, Drew," she pleaded, unwilling to accept what she saw and felt. "Drew, please. Mommy wants to feed you."

The last word she spoke cracked and splintered into a thousand slivers of glass, each one embedding itself in her soul.

Touching his fingers, she felt their rigidity. She lifted him out of his crib and tried to separate his lips, determined now to breathe life back into him. But she couldn't open his mouth. Like the rest of his body, it was stiff with resistance.

Eden grimaced suddenly, an odd, ghostly expression that told of stepping beyond the boundaries of sanity.

"Oh, my poor little love, you're so cold," she crooned. "Mommy will make you warm, and then you can have your breakfast." She cradled him to her nightgown-covered breasts, whispering to him as she carried him down the hallway and into the living room.

"See, Drew? Mommy's sitting in your favorite rocking chair, and she promises to make you warm again. And when you're warm, you'll wake up for Mommy, won't you, little love? Won't you?" she sobbed.

The phone rang an hour later, but she didn't hear it. Still rocking, still talking to her son, Eden lost track of the passage of time. She periodically sang the lullaby her childhood nurse had sung to her, and she talked about what a wonderful father Matthew would be when he finally came home.

Morning eased into late afternoon. The phone continued to ring at thirty-minute intervals, jarring Eden with its strident sound until she finally grabbed the receiver, screamed, "Leave us alone!" and slammed it back into its cradle.

Less than a minute passed before the persistent ringing began again. Unable to bear the sound any longer, she lifted the receiver and begged, "Please let me get my baby warm."

"Eden?"

She didn't recognize the voice of the caller. "What do you want?"

"Eden, this is Tracey. What's going on?"

"Drew's cold, and I can't make him warm."

"You aren't making any sense, Eden."

"He's so cold and stiff." Tears pooled in her eyes before forging matching streams down her cheeks. "I keep rocking him and rocking him, but he won't get warm. He won't even open his eyes and look at me. Find Matthew, Trace. Find him for me. I need him to help me get Drew warm again. Please, Trace, I need Matthew," she whimpered.

Despite her own panic, Tracey forced herself to remain calm. "Eden, I want you to listen to me. Take the baby and go next door to the Shanes'."

"I can't. You come here."

"Eden, for God's sake, I'm in California. Take Drew to Mrs. Watson across the street if you don't think Mary Shane can help you. I'll call the police for you."

"No, I shouldn't leave the house."

"Why not?"

"Drew'll get even colder. He was blue when I found him."

"Oh, Jesus. All right, Eden. Listen to me. Are you listening?"

"I'm listening, but why doesn't Matthew come?"

Tracey inhaled, the sound ragged. "I'm going to put you on hold for a minute."

"You're at your office."

"Yes, I'm at my office, Eden. Will you hold on for me?"

"Hold." Eden rolled the word around in her head. "I'm holding Drew, Trace."

"Good. Hold Drew and the telephone receiver. Don't put the phone down and don't move. Stay right where you are. Okay?"

"Don't move," she repeated hollowly.

Eden waited what seemed like forever. Muzak hummed in her ear, giving life to another lullaby for Drew as she rocked back and forth. She eventually grew restless and let the receiver slip from her hand. It landed on the floor just before she stood, gathered Drew against her body, and let herself out of the house.

She stood in the front yard clutching her son, still clad in her nightgown, while her breasts leaked his milk, her hair streaming wildly around her chalk-white face and her eyes wide as she wept helpless, soundless tears.

Mrs. Watson pulled into her driveway across the street, parked her car, and walked to the mailbox at the curb. In the distance a siren shrieked, and she glanced up. What Sarah

Watson saw then momentarily rooted her to where she stood before she dropped her mail and hurried toward Eden.

Eden looked blankly into the concerned woman's face. "Drew's cold. I can't make him warm. Will you help me?"

A police car screeched to a stop at the curb, the siren dying like an aborted scream. Neighbors, drawn by the sudden commotion on their normally quiet residential street, wandered out of their homes. Two uniformed patrolmen approached Eden. One held her by the shoulders while the other man eased Drew from her rigid arms.

The officer holding Drew lifted his gaze from the baby and shook his head at the questioning look in his partner's eyes. "He's been gone for several hours. Probably happened sometime last night."

Eden shivered and wrapped her arms around herself. "Did you make him warm yet?"

"Ma'am, why don't we go inside?"

She searched their faces. "Where's Matthew?"

"Her husband," Sarah Watson confirmed to the two policemen. "I believe he's a prisoner of war in Vietnam."

Eden started to laugh, startling the three people clustered protectively around her. The sound soon rose to a keening wail that became a scream of agony rooted in the depths of her soul. In a far corner of her mind, she wondered who was making the awful sound.

One of the men led Eden to the house. She pitched forward without warning at the bottom of the front-porch steps. The officer escorting her caught her and carried her unconscious body up the stairs and into the house while his partner met the ambulance that would transport her baby son to the morgue.

". . . Almighty Father, we commend to you the soul of your faithful servant, Andrew Barclay Benedict. And for his mother, Dear Lord, we ask that you strengthen her faith in You and Your Wisdom and provide her solace in this her hour of need."

The priest paused and sprinkled blessed water over the tiny

casket, which was covered with a spray of white rosebuds. He then glanced at the two young women who stood at the edge of the grave.

"Please join me in the Lord's Prayer."

Eden nodded and tightened her hold on Tracey's hand. Their voices were hushed as the three prayed together.

". . . now and at the hour of our death. Amen," Eden finished as she swayed unsteadily.

Oh, God, forgive me. I let my son die.

She watched dry-eyed and numb as first the priest, then Tracey, showered a handful of earth over Drew's casket.

What did I do wrong? I tried so hard to be a good mother.

"Do you want some time alone?" Tracey asked after the priest expressed his personal condolences to Eden and left the gravesite.

"Please." She didn't look up from the white roses atop Drew's coffin.

"I'll wait for you in the car." Tracey squeezed her fingers before she walked down the flagstone path that wound its way through the small cemetery.

Finally alone, Eden sank to her knees, pressed her forehead to the edge of the oak coffin, and closed her eyes. "Oh, Drew, my little love," she whispered. "I didn't mean for you to die."

Why, Matthew?

Why is our baby dead?

And why weren't you here to help me with Drew? Why aren't you here now?

Oh, Matthew, how will you ever forgive me for letting our son die?

CHAPTER

9

August 1968—Long Moc Prison Camp, North Vietnam

Matt struggled to remain alert, although he longed to release his thoughts and simply drift off. The nagging desire hovered like a vulture at the edge of his consciousness, but he knew better. He'd already experienced the disorientation caused by several days in the compound hotbox.

How many times? he wondered. How often have my brains been fried and my flesh scorched on the orders of Major Han? Think, God damn it! Think!

A voice in his mind urged, "Call upon the past. It will serve you, as will the spirits of your ancestors. Trust in the lessons of the past, my son."

The voice faded, to be replaced by a primitive drumbeat hammering in his ears. He remembered the sound from another time, another life.

Matt smelled the fragrance of pine and sage, felt the comfort of darkness as night settled over the land. Cooking fires filled the air with aromatic scents. Dogs barked and horses whinnied. Mothers whispered to their children while the elders of the tribe sat in counsel.

Braves poised on the precipice of manhood waited anxiously. The harsh cry of seasoned warriors suddenly replaced the hum of village life. Matt noted the war paint symbolically slashed across proud dark faces, and he saw men's bodies, glistening with sweat, writhing and twisting in the flickering firelight. He recognized the faces of men prepared for battle and the death of their enemies, as well as the distinctive cadence of ceremonial war chants as the words echoed in his head.

The sound grew louder, almost deafening.

Matt shuddered, stricken by instinct, captured by the past. He craved oneness with his heritage, a union that would transcend the boundaries of time and space. A fierce cry emerged from deep within him, forcing its way past a tongue swollen from thirst and teeth bared in an angry growl. The sound pummeled his senses.

He welcomed the image of his great-grandfather, hearing finally his words of comfort and courage. Feeling the press of an aged hand, Matt knew of its power despite its gnarled appearance.

Matthew Benedict became a child again.

"Great-grandfather?"

"The Great Spirit is with you, my son. He has sent me as his emissary."

"They hope to crush me by degrading my body, Great-grandfather. Please help me withstand this assault by my enemies."

"You will prevail, Warrior of the Blue Sky. You are a true son of the Nation. You will not fail and disgrace your ancestors."

"I need your counsel in order to remain strong. I fear I am weakening. My body craves the long sleep."

The gnarled hand tightened on his shoulder. "You will search for and find strength within yourself, my son. And although I am only one old man, I will share your burdens. Call upon me whenever your fear threatens you."

Matt sighed. "I still fear death, Great-grandfather."

"There is no shame in such feelings. Only a fool welcomes death when it is not his time."

"Thank you, Great-grandfather."

"Be at peace, my son. Never forget that you are one with the Cherokee Nation. You have already proven your faithfulness to your people, and you will triumph in the face of your enemies."

. . .

Matt's cry of rage had invaded the compound, riveting idle NVA guards to the red Asian soil and prompting an unnatural stillness, whereas only seconds before there had been the sounds of human activity.

Chet flinched when he heard the wealth of violation contained in the primal scream. He took a shallow breath, looked at the man beside him, and closed Hal Caulfield's empty eyes.

Covering Hal's face with the filthy edge of a woven sleeping mat, Chet sank back against the opposite wall of the bamboo cell. He wondered how long it would be before the guards would discover that Hal Caulfield was dead and stop the rations for two.

He exhaled slowly and then closed his eyes. He knew only two things could end this macabre charade if the stench of Hal's rotting flesh didn't: a return to work in the fields adjacent to the prison camp or Matt's release from the coffin-shaped hell on the other side of the compound. Whatever happened, Chet realized his friend would need the food he'd concealed from the guards.

Glancing at Matt several hours later, Chet grimaced when he saw the sweat dripping from his scratched face, blood and salt water blending to form pink ribbons that flowed down the front of the large man's chest. He knew that Matt Benedict was still on his feet only by the sheer force of his will.

"It's okay if you need to ease gun," Chet whispered. "I can dig for us both."

"No."

The single word was a labored croak. Although he trembled with every shovelload of dirt he managed to extract from the earth, Matt forced himself to remain standing. He refused to show weakness to the NVA soldiers guarding the burial detail.

When first released from the suffocating hotbox, he hadn't possessed the strength to stand. He recalled the indignity of being dragged, facedown in the dirt, across the compound before he was dumped like so much refuse in the bamboo cell he shared with Chet and Hal. It hadn't taken him long to notice that Hal Caulfield was dead.

Matt steadied himself with the shovel handle. "When did he die?"

Chet kept his eyes on his work. "About two days ago."

"You've been hoarding his rations while he rotted in this heat?"

Chet nodded. "We already smell like death. The guards didn't notice the difference."

"I'd hoped that Major Han—"

Chet snorted. "That bastard wouldn't help his own mother out of a burning building, if he's even got a mother. You gave it your best shot and paid one hell of a price. I don't think I could've done what you did." He shrugged and dumped a load of dirt beside the grave they were digging. "Hal gave up weeks ago. We both know it was just a matter of time. There wasn't anything we could've done for him. He wished himself dead, and it finally happened."

Matt nodded, unable to speak. He felt bewildered by the emotions he was experiencing for a man he hadn't allowed himself to really know. Tears traced his face. They merged with sweat and blood, falling in hot splats on his hands as he leaned into his shovel. He looked over at Hal's body. Emaciated, stripped of his faded Oriental pajamas, what remained of Hal Caulfield rested a few feet from what would soon be his grave.

Emptiness gnawed at him, but Matt forced himself to dig. Tasting blood, he realized that he'd bitten into his lower lip in search of pain. Pain, he'd long ago learned, translated to alertness, but relentless waves of fatigue still assaulted him despite his efforts not to yield to his exhaustion.

"We haven't got much more to do," Chet whispered as the guards wandered away from the stink of ripe flesh. "Can you hold out a little longer?"

Matt nodded. He concentrated on the task of digging. An American aviator, he reminded himself, deserved at least a final farewell from his fellow officers, especially since the man had already been deprived of his dignity while still alive.

He smelled the smoke of freshly lit tobacco. It made him dizzy with longing for one deep drag, a single moment of pleasure. Hal's decomposing body vied with the pungent aroma, and Matt choked down the bile hovering in his throat. He forced his thoughts from his surroundings as he mechanically shoveled soil to the growing mound at his feet.

Memories of a happier time crowded into his mind. He saw Eden's smiling face and tried to imagine her round with his child. Their son or daughter would be at least two months old by now. Regret burned inside him at the thought of missing the infancy of his firstborn. Tears again welled in his red-rimmed eyes, and still he dug. The saltiness seeped down his face, and he winced as his tears stung the scrapes and cuts covering his cheeks.

Matt and Chet finally eased Hal's blanket-encased remains into the shallow grave. Both men froze when one of the guards carelessly flicked his cigarette butt into the hole. Rage blinding him, Matt started to lunge at the man. His entire body reflected menace and death as the sound of rounds filling rifle chambers echoed in the silence. Chet leaped forward and restrained him.

"Don't! It'll be all the excuse they need to make this a double burial detail."

Matt sagged against his cellmate, his fists clenched and his body vibrating with fury.

After shoveling dirt over Hal and piling rocks atop the grave, they were marched back to their cell. Chet revealed the food he'd managed to hide after nightfall. Matt ate between checks by the guards. Both men knew that the secret cache of boiled dog meat and rice balls would mean a return trip to the hotbox if discovered.

Much later, Matt studied Chet's sleeping body through narrowed eyes. Unable to sleep himself despite his fatigue, he wondered how Major Han would deal with the dwindling number of Americans still in his charge.

Shifting his gaze, he stared up at the pocket of sky visible between the towering trees that surrounded Long Moc. He watched the moon slowly drift behind a bank of clouds. A keen sense of loss, one so overwhelming that it brought chills to his weary body, made him grimace. He longed for the loving embrace of his wife, but more than anything, he craved an end to the hell that his life had become.

CHAPTER

10

August–October 1968—Beverly, Massachusetts

Eden lived the days and weeks following the funeral in a state of profound and paralyzing fear that one day soon she would begin to scream and wouldn't be able to stop.

She felt depleted, drained of her strength, unable to summon the energy necessary for even the simplest of tasks. Eating meant coping with eventual nausea. Bathing meant empty moments when her thoughts wandered and her subconscious filled in the blank spaces in her mind with the agonizing image of Drew, still and lifeless, in his casket. Leaving her bedroom meant walking past her son's nursery. Talking to Tracey meant lying to her best friend, reassuring her that, given time, she would be all right, that she would adjust to losing her son.

But, deep in her heart, she knew she would never adjust to what had happened to Drew. She simply couldn't absolve herself of the guilt she felt, and she was convinced that God never would, either.

Tracey temporarily acted as a buffer between a silent Eden and the few neighbors who, out of concern or curiosity, perhaps both, arrived carrying covered dishes and voicing their sympathy. Her departure was inevitable, though, and she returned to Los Angeles a week after Drew's funeral.

Feeling frightened and alone, Eden longed for the numbness that had enshrouded her during those first days after finding her son in his crib. She grew to loathe within herself the emotional extremes that had her alternating between sudden bouts of sobbing and untold hours spent silently staring at the walls in her bedroom.

She struggled to resume her life, but the effort soon left her feeling defeated and weary to the core of her soul. Everywhere she went—the grocery store, the post office, the park, places that had always been a part of her normal routine—she was reminded of what she no longer had.

Drew was gone, never to be a part of her life again. Armed with that knowledge, she realized that dreams were for fools and that innocence perished in the path of reality.

Even Matthew ceased to exist for Eden. She consigned to memory his love and their plans for a life together. Certain that he would never forgive her for the loss of their son, she mourned her husband as she mourned Drew. Still, she forced herself to go through the motions of living, slowly, carefully, often feeling as vulnerable as someone who had barely survived a lengthy and crippling injury.

She tried to make her way through each day individually, but her thoughts were often disjointed and her focus distorted. Most of the time she was simply relieved to reach the end of the day, and although her nights were often sleepless, the darkness and solitude of her bedroom represented a haven of sorts.

Two weeks and seven hours following her son's funeral, Eden discovered a bottle of scotch in the cupboard above the stove. As she poured her first drink, she told herself that it would simply ease the despair that shadowed her days and lessen the anguish that haunted her nights. She also told herself that it would help her deal with the insanity of her life. And she promised herself that she would never be like her alcoholic parents. They'd had no control and died because of it. She, however, was convinced that she knew what she was doing.

Six weeks later, weeks spent submerging her desolation and grief in the somewhat numbing embrace of a liquid painkiller, Eden sat in front of the living-room window, her expression blank and a half-empty fifth of scotch resting in her lap. She didn't notice the car parked at the curb in front of her house, nor did she see the uniformed Marine Corps officer making his way up the walk to the porch of her home.

David Markham hesitated before knocking on Eden Benedict's front door, his thoughts on the disjointed telephone conversation he'd had with her earlier in the day. She was either on drugs or booze. He'd seen both and suspected that she'd opted for the anesthetic of alcohol. Hell, who wouldn't? First her husband is shot down, and then her baby dies.

He exhaled slowly and squared his shoulders, reassuring himself that his appearance was Marine Corps perfect, his posture equally precise. Nerves, he realized in frustration. A combat veteran as a result of Vietnam, a career officer in the corps, Maj. David Markham was at a loss in his week-old assignment as POW/MIA Casualty Assistance Officer.

Crossing the porch, he peered through the picture window and into what he assumed was a living room. He watched Eden lift a bottle, take a long pull, grimace, and then wipe her mouth with the back of her hand.

She bore little resemblance to the photograph of the women in the file he'd studied during his flight from Washington to Boston. The lamplight cast hard shadows across her features, emphasizing the dark half-moons under her eyes and the gauntness of her face. He couldn't ignore the toll that eight weeks of grieving had taken on her. Instead of looking her twenty-five years, she resembled a woman ten or fifteen years her senior, a woman very nearly crushed by the weight of her pain.

Don't feel sorry for her, he cautioned himself. Pity won't help her now.

David moved back to the front door and knocked, momentarily wishing for the familiar, the definitive, the identifiable. Vietcong, heavy mortar fire, wounded troops, corpsmen screaming for medevac choppers. His world. A world he understood and had learned to survive. He wondered now how he was supposed to help a woman who'd just buried her infant son and who didn't know if she'd ever see her husband again.

He knocked a second time. "Mrs. Benedict?"

He tried the door after waiting several moments and discovered that it was unlocked. He let himself in, placed his briefcase and cover on a bench near the front door, and walked into the living room. Eden didn't take her eyes from the window. David got the distinct impression that she expected the darkness to reveal an answer of some kind, perhaps even an end to the madness that seemed to mark her life.

"Eden, I'm David Markham from Casualty Assistance."

She briefly glanced up at him and then back at the window.

He slowly approached her, his gaze on the emptiness in her eyes. Sudden anger, primarily with those people from Casualty Assistance who had ignored her situation, sharpened his voice. "Your house smells like a dump. When was the last time you cleaned this place? You aren't in much better shape, are you? When did you eat last?" Circling around her, he peered at her from a variety of angles before he drew up a chair, positioned it in front of her, and sat down.

Eden frowned and lifted the bottle. She felt a masculine hand halt its progress to her lips, and she stiffened, tightening her hold until her fingers ached.

"No more of this crap until we've had a chance to talk."

She tugged at the bottle. "Nothing to say."

David yanked it out of her hand and placed it on the floor beside him. "How long you plannin' on runnin' from your problems, lady? And how long do you suppose it'll be before you've managed to pickle your own carcass? You won't be worth shit if you keep this up."

If only you knew, she thought. I can't even get drunk enough to forget. But I keep trying. Damn if I don't keep trying. She shrugged. "Doesn't matter."

"Why not?"

She shot him an anguished look. "Drew's dead. And Matthew—I don't even know what's happened to Matthew."

"You aren't dead yet, but you're well on your way, aren't you? That's your plan, isn't it? Kill yourself so you won't have to deal with reality. Hell, buy a gun, Eden. It's easier and faster. That," he said harshly, pointing to the bottle of scotch, "is a coward's way out. You must think God has been playing bad jokes on you. First your husband's a damn MIA statistic, and now your kid's dead. How about I loan you my service revolver? We'll put you out of your misery in short order."

She flinched at the pictures his words painted. Tears throbbed in her throat, but she managed, "Go 'way."

"Sorry, I can't do that. I'm here for the duration."

Eyeing him warily, she asked, "Who are you?"

He smiled, the action softening the harshness of piercing hazel eyes and a stubborn chin. "Major David Markham from Marine Corps Casualty Assistance."

"Don't need you or anybody."

"Why not?"

She released a gust of air. "You can't help me. Nobody can."

"You're probably right."

Eden studied him, surprise momentarily surpassing the alcohol dulling her wits.

"I can't help you if you fight me," he clarified. "But if you cooperate, who knows?"

"People like you sent Matthew overseas," she accused.

"Correction, Eden. Your husband made a career decision when he joined the corps. Part of that decision involved following orders. Orders that in time of war can place a man in serious jeopardy. It's all part of the package."

"But he's gone. So is Drew. Everyone I love is gone." Her voice cracked, and she inhaled sharply.

"You aren't."

"So?"

"You don't give a damn about what happens to you? You don't care how your husband will feel if he escapes or is released and comes home to find you like this?"

Closing her eyes, Eden wrapped her arms around herself. She absently realized that she'd been cold to the marrow of her bones since finding Drew. "Guilt's not an effective motivator, Major David Markham from Marine Corps Casualty Assistance. I've already beaten myself bloody with that stick, so go find somebody else to bully."

David stood and extended his hands. "Come on, Eden. Self-pity's a lousy companion."

"Scotch isn't, so leave me alone."

"Sorry, no can do. It's time for a shower. Then maybe some food. After that, we'll talk."

She shook her head and remained hunched in her chair, determined to wait him out, as she had all the others.

He tugged her upright despite her resistance. "Lady, I can't be in the same room with you much longer if you don't get cleaned up. You stink to high heaven."

"So leave," she muttered.

He shook his head and steadied her swaying body. "Can't do that, either. I'm afraid you're stuck with me." Slinging her over his shoulder like a sack of potatoes, David marched out of the living room and down the hall.

Eden saw double as he hauled her into the bathroom. Nausea had uncoiled in her stomach by the time he lowered her into the tub. With one hand covering her mouth and the other braced against the tile wall for balance, she glared at him.

"Clothes off," he barked, turning on the water and pulling the shower curtain closed. "I'll be back in five minutes to check on you. I expect to find you scrubbed clean, head to toes." When she didn't answer, he peeled the curtain back far enough to study her face. "Is that clear?"

She swallowed carefully and nodded, still somewhat stunned by his behavior. The other Marine Corps people who'd come to see her since Drew's death had tiptoed around her and then escaped as fast as they could. This man didn't seem inclined to do either.

As promised, David returned five minutes later. He found Eden sitting in the tub, her nightgown plastered to her body by the force of the shower spray and her head resting on her knees. She looked up at him, squinting through the water as he removed his uniform jacket, rolled up his shirt-sleeves, and adjusted the shower head.

"It hasn't even been three minutes," she protested.

"Wrong. It's been six." He motioned her forward. "Get over here, Eden."

"Why?"

"Because if you're going to act like a baby, then you're going to get treated like one." He poured shampoo into the palm of his hand, worked up a lather, and demanded, "Do I have to get in there with you?"

She paled, scooted over to his side of the tub, and presented him with access to her dripping head. After several minutes of vigorous scrubbing, she asked, "Why do you even care?"

His hands stilled and then slipped to her shoulders. "If I had a wife in your situation, I'd expect someone to look after her."

Turning, she peered up at him. "Nobody else has stayed more than a few minutes." She giggled. The sound reminded them both that she wasn't altogether sober. "Must've been the smell."

"You mean the people from Casualty Assistance?"

She nodded.

He cleared his throat. "OCS doesn't include a crash course in caring for screwed-up wives. They probably didn't know what to do."

"How come you do?"

"I had three younger sisters."

She smiled whimsically. "Did you wash their hair, too?"

He chuckled. "Nope."

"But you were there for them if they needed you, weren't you?"

"I tried to be."

Even half-drunk she could read between the lines. "Did something happen to one of them, something you couldn't help with?"

"Yeah." David got up from the tile floor and closed the shower curtain. "Hand me your clothes and then rinse the soap out of your hair. I'll try and find you something to wear while you finish washing."

Eden peeled off her nightgown and handed the sodden mess through a narrow space between the curtain and the wall. She didn't take her eyes from the man who had just treated her with more compassion than she'd ever known from a stranger. Without understanding why, she asked, "Will you tell me what happened?"

He cocked his head questioningly.

"Your sister. The one you couldn't help. Will you tell me about her?"

David exhaled softly and then nodded. "If you'll tell me about your son."

"You don't want much, do you?" she whispered, pain vivid in her eyes.

He studied her through narrowed eyes, piercing hazel challenging faded emerald. "I want you sober, lady, and not just for a day or two."

Eden let the curtain fall back into place without answering. She'd already begun to think, to remember, and her insides felt as though an invisible claw were shredding what remained of her heart. Closing her eyes against stinging tears, she forced herself to rinse the shampoo from her hair.

Damn the Marine Corps for sending Matthew away. And damn David Markham for interfering in her life—what was left of it. He'd managed to remind her of Drew, and he'd also managed to undo the anesthetic effects of several weeks of scotch.

After her shower, Eden dressed in the clean nightgown and robe David had left on the bathroom counter. She followed the sound of clanging pots and pans and the smell of cooking food, a smell that made her empty stomach churn. Growing anger increased her pace.

"How dare you come into my home and take over like this?"

David turned from the stove and saw her standing in the doorway, her clenched fists perched on her hips. "You look a hell of a lot better. Why don't you sit down? Supper's almost ready."

"Answer me, damn it! Who gave you the right to show up here unannounced?" She noticed several grocery bags lined up near the kitchen door. "What is all that stuff?"

"Your stash." He grinned, but there was little humor in his

expression. "I've been exploring your house. The local liquor store must love you."

Her eyes traveled involuntarily to the cabinet below the sink and then back to David's face. His knowing expression made her cringe. "You've dumped it all out, haven't you?" she demanded, further enraged by his high-handed behavior.

"Every last drop."

"I'll buy more."

"No, you won't, Eden. Not even if it means I have to camp out on your living-room couch for the next six months."

"You can't do that. I won't allow it. I'll—"

"Call the police?" he prompted.

"Yes!"

He pointed at the wall phone. "Do it now. I don't have a problem with that at all, but I think you will."

"This is my home!" she shouted. "You have no right to be here."

"The Marine Corps and your husband's status give me the right, lady. You aren't going to get away with drowning yourself in a vat of scotch, not if I have anything to do with it. You can save that little exercise for when Matt Benedict comes home and can deal with you himself. But for the time being, you're my responsibility, like it or not. It's either me or a hospital. The choice is yours."

"You're unbelievable. Of all the gall—" she began.

"Shut your mouth, sit down at the table, pick up a napkin and put it in your lap, and then, if I haven't burned dinner while you've raved like the drunk you're about to become, we'll eat." He pointed at the kitchen table with the fork he held. "Now, Eden."

Tracey burst unannounced into the kitchen. "What in God's name is going on in here?" she demanded as she dropped her luggage on the floor and drew the strap of her purse from her shoulder. "I could hear the two of you shouting outside. My cabdriver even offered to call the police." Tracey stared at Eden, visibly shaken by the physical deterioration that had taken place in her since Drew's funeral. "What's happened to you? You look awful. Have you been sick? Why didn't you call me? I would've come back from London sooner if I'd known you needed me."

Eden groaned and stumbled to the kitchen table. She'd forgotten Tracey's plan to spend a few days with her while she was in transit from England to Los Angeles. Meanwhile, David removed the towel wrapped around his waist and rolled down his shirt-sleeves as he crossed the kitchen, approaching Tracey in the same cautious manner he'd used on Eden.

"Are you Miss Sinclair?"

"Yes." Her eyes traveled between Eden's stricken features and the burly man in a half-drenched uniform. "Why are you soaking wet? And if it's not too much trouble, *who* are you?"

"Eden needed some help in the shower."

She stared at him. "The shower?"

"He washed my hair for me."

"He washed your hair?"

"He has sisters," Eden supplied, still unwilling to meet Tracey's eyes.

"You people are making me crazy. Would one of you mind explaining what's going on here?"

"There's enough food for three if you haven't eaten," David offered as he moved Tracey's luggage and lined it up along the hallway wall. He then took her by the arm and led her to a chair at the table. "Eden's having a little trouble staying sober these days. I'm here to help her work on her problem."

Tracey gave him a blank look, said, "But she doesn't—" and then glanced at Eden. "You don't even like booze. How can you have a problem with it?"

David placed a platter of eggs, bacon, and toast on the table. After lowering a pot of coffee to the hot pad next to his plate, he sat down between the two women. "The trash cans outside are overflowing with scotch bottles. I've already been through all the closets, cupboards, and bureau drawers in the house. The end result is next to the back door."

"Eden, what happened?"

"My baby . . . Drew is . . ." She raised her eyes and quietly suggested, "Trace, please go home. You have a life and a job to worry about. You don't need me messing things up for you."

"I should've stayed with you after the funeral."

Eden paled, stood abruptly, and raced from the room. David continued to eat.

Tracey started to stand. "I'll go after her."

"Don't. She's going to do a lot of throwing up in the next few days. I doubt she feels the need for an audience."

"She really drank all that?" she asked, her eyes on the grouping of bags at the back door.

David lowered his fork, wiped his mouth, and poured himself a cup of coffee before answering. "That and more, I suspect. It's very likely she's already disposed of a lot of the empty bottles herself. This isn't a lark she's on, Miss Sinclair. She's going about it the hard way, but that doesn't change the fact that she's trying to kill herself, whether or not she's willing to admit it to anyone."

"This is insane."

"No, ma'am, it's life."

"It's obvious you're in the military, but who are you?"

"David Markham, ma'am. Major, United States Marine Corps, presently assigned to the D.C. office of Casualty Assistance."

"And you're responsible for Eden now?"

He nodded.

"Just Eden? The Marine Corps actually expects you to take care of her?"

"For the time being." He noticed her puzzled expression. "Why does that surprise you?

"I didn't really think anyone cared."

He bristled at her remark. "The corps cares, Miss Sinclair. We take care of our own."

"If you say so," she answered mildly.

David relaxed and asked, "You planning on staying a while?"

"As long as Eden needs me. I'll call my boss in the morning and arrange for some time off."

Tracey carefully studied him as she sipped her coffee. Surprised by his determination to see Eden through this crisis, she knew it would have been a lot simpler for him if he checked her into a military hospital and let someone else deal with her problems. "Why do you care so much about her? Unless I'm mistaken, you'd never even met her before today."

He shrugged and picked up his fork. "Let's just say I have a job to do and I intend to do it."

Tracey smiled. "That will do for now, I suppose."

He grinned, his eyes easing from her face to her ringless left hand. "What do you do in L.A.?"

"Advertising. I'm with Whitcomb, Dean, and Leighton." Tracey twisted in her chair and peered down the hallway. "I don't hear any noise coming from the bathroom. Should I check on her now?"

He shook his head. "I know drunks, Miss Sinclair. She's only enjoying a temporary break in the proceedings. Just about now, Eden's on her knees, probably hanging on to the commode for dear life. The racket'll start up again in about ten minutes. I suggest you eat while you can. We're going to have to handle her in shifts for the time being."

Eden stared at the ceiling in her bedroom. Daylight filtered through the slats of the metal window blinds. As she watched dust motes float in the still air, she heard the animated voices of children waiting for the school bus to arrive across the street. She blinked back the tears welling in her eyes and realized that her son would never sound that happy.

Thoughts of the preceding three days filled her mind, the parts she could remember, anyway. She knew she'd raved at what she considered the duplicity of her best friend, cursed the interference of a stranger in her life, cajoled, pleaded, begged, sobbed, and then screamed her outrage at being denied the one thing she craved most: scotch. The single relief she'd found against the agony of reliving Drew's death over and over again and Matthew's absence when she needed him most.

When she heard a knock on her bedroom door, she turned on her side and closed her eyes. Conversation was the last thing she wanted or needed, especially since all Tracey and

David seemed to want to talk about was her staying sober. God, what I'd do for just one drink, she thought.

"She's still asleep," Tracey said quietly.

David shook his head and approached the foot of the bed. "She's faking it again, hoping we'll leave her alone. Right, Eden?"

"Go 'way."

"What did I tell you?" He smacked her on the fanny. "Come on, Benedict. It's time for a run on the beach. You need fresh air in the worst way."

"I need the two of you to leave me the hell alone." She flipped onto her back and covered her eyes with her hand. "Please just get out of my home and out of my life."

"We had this conversation three days ago, Eden. I'm not leaving. Neither is Tracey. Get that into your head and keep it there." He whipped off the covers. "Up and dressed in five minutes. And wear sneakers, not those idiotic wedgies I saw in your closet."

Half an hour later Eden was gasping for air and holding her left side. Her legs felt like limp rubber bands, and her stomach threatened momentary eruption. David bounced up and down on the hard-packed sand like a prizefighter ready to go ten rounds.

"You're really . . . disgusting."

David grinned. "Yeah."

She glared at him. "I hate you for what you've done."

"Someday you'll thank me."

"I trust you're holding your breath in anticipation."

"No way, lady. You're a hard case." He grasped her chin in his hand, held her head still, and peered down at her. "Hate me all you want, Eden, but remember one thing. It helps if you're sober when you hate. That way you keep the object of your hate in focus."

"I am sober," she reminded him. "For the time being."

"Meaning I won't be here forever?"

She smirked at him and jerked herself out of reach. "Clever man."

"Cass was a lot like you. Proud, stubborn as a Missouri mule, and beautiful in a coltish kind of way."

"One of your girlfriends? Tracy's on her way, isn't she? Another trophy to add to your collection, Major?"

"Your friend's a lady," he answered stiffly.

"Meaning I'm not? Pardon me all to hell if that doesn't bother me at the moment."

"Cass was my sister."

Eden leaned down, took a handful of sand, and began transferring it from one palm to the other. "Was?"

"She's dead. Booze and drugs. Heroin and whiskey, to be precise. She was always kind of wild as a kid. College didn't slow her down any, either. Probably sped up the process, now that I think about it."

"I don't want to hear about your sister."

"Why? Hit too close to home?"

"I'm not a drug addict."

He shrugged and tucked his hands in the waistband of his sweatpants. "Only because it didn't occur to you."

"You have a really high opinion of me, don't you? Well, let me tell you something, Major David Markham. You don't know shit about me or my life."

"I know the important things, Eden. I know you felt like someone had torn your heart out of your body when you found your kid dead in his crib."

She flinched, turned away, and dusted the sand from her hands. "Stop it! I don't want to talk about Drew."

"Why? Because then you'll have to remember? That's the one thing you've gotta do, Eden." He grabbed her by the shoulders and shook her. "If you don't remember every detail and face it full on, then you can't let go and forget."

She stared up at him, eyes wild, her heart slamming around inside her chest like a bumper car and her breath coming in labored gasps.

"You feel betrayed, don't you? Your husband got his ass in a sling on the other side of the world, and he wasn't here to help you. You're pissed as hell, and you won't even admit it, will you?"

"Please stop," she begged, covering her ears with her hands and falling to her knees.

David dropped down beside her, grabbed her wrists, and

yanked her hands from her head. She fought him then, fought him with every ounce of strength in her body, fought him because she didn't want him to know how driven by her own pain she'd become or how much shame she felt about what she had done to her son.

"You're furious with him. Admit it. It isn't disloyal to be angry because the one person in this world you trusted blew it."

"I killed his son!" she screamed. "I killed his son! I let Drew die. I must've done something wrong. I don't hate Matthew. I hate myself." She collapsed into a heap on the sand, groaning over and over again, "I hate myself, I hate myself."

David gathered her against him and absorbed the shattering quality of her sobs. Several minutes passed before she quieted, minutes that allowed him to consider his next move. He finally asked, "Have you read the death certificate, Eden? Do you even know what it says?"

She stiffened before struggling against his hold.

"Have you read it?" he asked again, forcing her chin up so that he could see her face.

"What's the point?"

"The point is that you didn't kill Drew. His lungs collapsed. You didn't cause his death."

"But I must have. He was healthy. The doctor who delivered him said so. So did his pediatrician. Healthy babies don't just die." She scrubbed at her wet cheeks. "I need a drink. Please, David, just one drink. I can't stand this anymore. I *cannot* stand it," she whispered. "I need a drink."

"Listen to me, Eden. No booze. Not now, not ever. I won't let you do that to yourself."

"Why do you care? Why do you even give a damn about me?"

His fingers tightened on her chin. "Because I'm an idiot. I like wasting my time on a woman who has a king-size death wish."

"I don't—" she began.

"Don't you?"

"No. Yes. Maybe. Oh, God, I don't know anymore."

David released her chin and tugged her into his arms, embracing her with gentleness and compassion. "Listen to me, Eden, because I'm only going to say this once. I will not watch another human being willfully drink herself into an early grave, not if I have the power to stop it. I wasn't around for Cass when she needed me. I don't know if I'll ever be able to forgive myself for that, but I've learned to live with it. A part of me died when I found out what my baby sister had done to herself. Hell, I didn't even know she had a problem until she overdosed on heroin.

"I don't know why your son died, Eden. It happened, that's all. I can't change it, and neither can you. I'd give anything if I could, but I can't. No more than I could stop the agony my folks went through when my sister died." He paused and looked down at her. "The only thing I know much about is war. I know how a man's gut aches when he's gone without a decent meal for weeks at a time. I know what it's like to see the men you're responsible for die. I know what it means to write a letter to a mother who won't ever see her son again except as the contents of a body bag, and that's only if there's enough left of him to ship back to his family. And I know what it'll do to your husband if he makes it home and doesn't find you waiting for him. He's living in hell, just like the one you're in right now.

"If you can't be strong for yourself yet, be strong for Matt. Captivity is a nightmare. You understand better than most people what emotional devastation is like, and you'll be able to help him if he makes it out of North Vietnam alive. But you can't do that unless you're sober, can you?"

Eden stared up at him, stunned by his candor but still worried. "But will Matthew be able to forgive me?"

He shook his head in obvious frustration. "God damn it to hell, Eden, there is nothing to forgive. Nothing at all. Your husband, if he's half the man Tracey says he is, will understand that when he knows the truth."

"I always thought I was strong, but now I'm not sure of anything. I feel like such a failure," she admitted quietly. "I don't know if I can make it."

"Do you want to?"

She hesitated before answering. "Sometimes."

"I'll stay as long as it takes," David promised. "So will Tracey."

She nodded. "I know, but I'm still afraid."

David smiled, sadly, gently. "We're all afraid, Eden, but we can't let our fear conquer us. Making the decision to fight back, even against what seems like impossible odds, is the difference between existing and living."

"Maybe." She ended her study of her hands and looked up at him. "I miss them both so much. I used to keep a journal, you know. I wrote something in it every day. Little things only Matthew would understand, things about how I felt as I got closer to having Drew, my thoughts after he was born. I was going to give it to Matthew when he came home, but I haven't written in it since I . . . since Drew . . ." She hesitated, then admitted, "I feel so tired, David, so damned tired all the time. I hate the way I feel."

Compassion in his eyes, David got to his feet, brushed the sand from his pants, and extended his hand to Eden. "It's time to start over again. One step at a time. Bigger ones when you're up to it. Just don't set yourself up to fail. That's the key. Do what you know in your gut you're capable of doing. Leave the heroics to the heroes."

She got to her feet with his help. After drying her face with the hem of her T-shirt, she asked, "Will I ever really know why my son—why Drew—died?"

"I don't know," he admitted honestly, "but I'll try and find the answers for you."

David glanced up from the book he was reading as Tracey walked into the living room. "All packed?"

She nodded and sat down beside him on the couch. "Once I get the Slayton account taken care of, I'm going to ask for a leave of absence. One of the senior partners at the agency has a son in Vietnam. I think he'll understand Eden's situation, but if he doesn't, I'll resign. With a little luck, I should be back here in ten days."

David closed his book and slid it onto the coffee table. "Don't resign unless you absolutely have to. From what Eden said today, I suspect she's ready for a change of scenery. California's a good spot for her to live since it's home for both of you."

"I don't want to pressure her into a decision. Especially not now, not after all the progress she's made this past month."

David took her hand and loosely laced their fingers together. "Don't underestimate her. She's not a piece of crystal."

"I know. It's just that—"

"You want to protect her?"

Tracey nodded. "I shouldn't, should I?"

He smiled and tugged her into the circle of his arms. "Be her friend. She can handle everything else. And if she trips, help her up, but don't baby her."

"Yes, sir." She grinned before peering up at David. "Will you be here when I get back?"

He nodded. "Probably. Eden'll tell me when she wants me out of here."

"You're leaving that up to her now?"

"I think she's ready for the responsibility of running her own life again, if that's what you're asking."

"I still can't believe she blamed herself for Drew's death. I don't know anyone better suited for motherhood than Eden."

"I think she began to absolve herself of the guilt she felt once she accepted what the doctors told her about crib death."

"What a mess! I just wish Matt had been here."

David's expression grew somber. "It'll be a long time before they see one another, Tracey. A very long time."

Startled, she asked, "Who've you been talking to?"

"Nobody."

"Where'd that come from then?"

"My gut. Instinct. Maybe a combination of both." He shrugged. "I don't know."

"Sounds ominous."

"War, especially one that's undeclared, is ominous. Vietnam will probably drag on a lot longer than anyone expects."

"Even with all the antiwar protests? After what happened at the Democratic Convention in August, I'd think we'd be out of Southeast Asia in a few months."

"You may be right," he conceded.

She heard the doubt in his voice. "But you don't think so."

He shook his head and sighed, his breath ruffling the short blond curls atop her head. "No, I don't think so."

"What happens next?"

"Exactly what's been happening for the last four weeks. We take it one day at a time. Eden's system is clean for now, and AA's providing her with an outlet for the things she can't or won't discuss with us. She's preparing herself to get on with her life."

"I hope so." She moved out of his embrace and stood. "How about some cocoa? That fireplace isn't giving off much heat."

"Only if I get to help you stir," David answered, his voice intimate as he spoke to Tracey.

Eden abandoned her silent stance in the hallway as their shared laughter signaled an end to their conversation in the living room. She returned to her bedroom, more aware now than in the last month of just how far she'd come from the alcoholic maze that had contained her grief.

Quietly closing the door, she crossed the room and sat on the edge of her bed. She began to braid her hair, her thoughts on the letter she'd just completed as her fingers deftly formed the wide plait that would soon trail down the center of her back.

The words she'd written to Matthew now seemed stilted, almost terse, not the words of a loving wife to her husband. Rather, words she knew strangers would read. It was her first letter to him since Drew's death, communication that could not contain the truth because, according to David, it might be used as an emotional weapon against Matthew. And if he received this letter and the ones that would naturally follow, he would continue to assume that their child lived. Then she would have to tell him the one thing she dreaded most in this world. That the baby they'd made together had died. Her fingers stilled, dropping to her lap as she accepted the unnerving devastation wreaked by the reality that was now her life.

David had been right, even wise in his guidance. Leave the

heroics to the heroes, he'd advised. She was doing just that by taking small steps back to a world that seemed jarring and unfeeling. Steps she hoped would eventually lead her to the sobriety that all three of them had fought so hard for these last weeks.

Her thoughts drifted through the time that had passed since Drew's funeral. Nearly three months. Most of the days and weeks were a blur of muted images, overshadowed by an aching sense of isolation and emptiness. She sighed, the sound like a miniature agony, betraying only a small portion of the heartache she felt.

Eden realized that her life, her emotions, her instincts, even the manner in which she defined herself, had been permanently altered. Each hour of each day ahead now constituted a test—a test of her inner strength, her courage, and her ability to overcome the nagging temptation of taking a drink.

She also knew that she had used the scotch like a sedative to dull the edges of her grief and separate herself from the rawness of her pain—the same pain that David and Tracey had forced her to confront during the previous four weeks. She still felt the emotional and physical fatigue that had come with her acceptance of Drew's death. It was almost as if she'd been tired forever, and she wondered if she would ever truly feel rested or whole again.

She would sleep now, she decided as she set her alarm for a predawn hour. Then, before Tracey and David left the bed in the guest room they now shared, she would face the memories in the room across the hall. Drew's nursery, the one room in her home she hadn't entered since the day of his funeral.

She slept restlessly and awakened in the stillness of the night, more than an hour before her alarm would have sounded. Sliding from beneath the covers, Eden pulled on her robe, stepped into her slippers, and made her way to the nursery.

She'd discovered the key to the room in a kitchen drawer a week earlier, aware that either David or Tracey had placed it there to protect her. But she no longer felt the need for their protection. She did, however, feel the need to take one last private look at her son's clothes and toys before packing them for charity. She'd already promised herself that she alone would handle the process of sorting through his things. No one else had that right. One final journey through the past before she consigned it and her dreams to memory, she realized as she inserted the key in the lock.

Slipping quietly into the room, Eden took a steadying breath and pressed the light switch. She staggered slightly, struggling against a rush of memories and unconsciously reaching for the support offered by the bureau located just inside the closed nursery door. Snatches of lullabies she'd once hummed and the remembered sound of Drew gurgling happily assaulted her ears.

She recalled the softness of his skin, the wonderful smell of his freshly bathed and powdered body, and the hours they'd whiled away on a blanket in the backyard under a warm summer sun. A part of her, she knew, would always mourn the shortness of their time together, but, curiously, in another part of herself she had recently discovered the knowledge that *she* had the power to treasure her memories. No one could take them from her. And she knew she would never forget.

Moving forward, Eden smoothed her fingers across the top of a stack of diapers on the changing table. Like a blind woman, she felt her way through the room, fingering the enameled fairy-tale characters that covered the walls, touching the mobile of plastic ducks and birds suspended above the crib, and wiping dust from a chest that still held receiving blankets and baby-sized comforters.

She began slowly, on her knees on the hard wooden floor of the nursery, frequently reassuring herself that she could and would resolve this final aspect of her son's life and periodically wiping away the tears that filled her eyes and crept down her cheeks.

Several hours later, as dawn arrived, Eden finally stood and stretched the kinks from her back. She inspected the room carefully, her gaze lingering on empty bureau drawers, as well as the neatly stacked piles of clothing, blankets, and toys in the center of the floor. In her arms she held a teddy bear, an incomplete photo album, and Drew's baptismal gown, mementos for Matthew of the son he would never know. The rest, all things but also tangible reminders of both joy and loss, would be delivered to the sisters at Saint Mary's, who took in foundlings.

As she left the nursery, she knew in her heart that the simple yet complex act of packing up the past had been the most important step she'd taken toward the future since Drew's death. She would not live the life she had envisioned, certainly not the life she had planned, but hers would be a life of value, she promised herself. She had no other choice. Not any longer. With sobriety came responsibility; with the acceptance of death came life and the task of living, as well as the understanding that Matthew might be gone from her for many years, perhaps forever.

Where there had once been three, there was now one. She couldn't help wondering if Matthew would even want a place in the future she was about to create for herself.

Eden sipped her morning tea and studied the partial list of arrangements she would need to make. Moving across the country took planning, especially when one needed the cooperation of the Marine Corps and the spare bedroom of an old friend. She looked up when she heard the distinctive sound of high heels clicking along the hallway and then the telling silence of a brief pause in front of Drew's nursery. She wasn't surprised by the look of concern on Tracey's face when the petite blonde walked into the kitchen.

"Morning. Tea water's hot, and I just took a coffee cake out of the oven."

Tracey gave her an odd look as she prepared herself a cup of tea. "Up late last night?"

She smiled. "Up early, actually."

Tracey joined her at the table. "Coffee cake smells good."

"Tastes good, too." Eden felt the probing quality of her gaze and suggested, "Go home with a clear conscience, okay? You and David have helped me through the worst crisis of my life. I know now that I'm going to be all right."

"I noticed that the door to Drew's nursery is open."

"It was time, Trace."

"You're all right?"

She lifted her mug. "Plain tea. Really, I'm fine."

Tracey looked skeptical as she helped herself to a slice of breakfast pastry.

"Well, maybe not fine, but I will be. Drew was my son, and I needed to go through his things. I couldn't leave the job to anyone else."

"But if you'd waited . . ."

Eden shook her head. "I waited three months. That was long enough. Probably too long."

"I wanted to help you when you were ready."

"I had to do it alone. My way of saying good-bye to my little love." Her voice wavered. Glancing out the window, she cleared her throat and got herself under control. "I've already called Saint Mary's. They're sending a man over this afternoon with a supply of boxes. He'll pack up everything and take it over to the orphanage."

"Everything?"

"I've saved a few things for Matthew."

"It must have been hard for you."

"Yes, but I couldn't put it off any longer."

"Eden, you should have—"

She raised a hand in self-defense. "I've been saying, 'I should have,' and, 'What if I'd done this or that?' for weeks now. It doesn't do any good, and it won't change what's happened."

"I'm sorry."

"Don't be sorry, Trace. Please. You aren't being yourself when you have to continuously creep around me as though I'm standing in the center of ten tons of eggshells. You've got to stop it. I don't want to be handled with kid gloves any longer, especially not by my best friend. Drew is dead. He's not coming back."

Tracey reached across the table and grasped Eden's hand. "I'd give anything if I could've prevented this from happening to you."

She sighed. "I know, but it did, and we can't change it.

David was right. I had to face Drew's death and then find a way to live with it. I'm still in the 'learning how to live with it' stage. One day at a time where Drew's concerned and one hour at a time where the booze is concerned."

"Welcome back to the world," she whispered.

Eden nodded and squeezed Tracey's fingers before freeing her hand. "I'm going to give my landlord a month's notice when I mail the rent check tomorrow. I'll probably need David's help with the move, though."

"What move?" David asked as he entered the kitchen and paused to make himself a cup of instant coffee.

"I've decided to go back to California. Will I need special paperwork or permission from the Marine Corps before they'll authorize the moving company to pick up my things, or should I make my own arrangements?"

"I'll check on that after I drop Tracey at Logan this morning, but it's likely Headquarters Marine Corps will take care of all the details for you. It will probably just be a matter of requesting a packing date for your household goods and then deciding on how long you'll want everything in storage."

Eden watched him take a chair next to Tracey, his affection for her obvious as he laced the fingers of his free hand through her smaller ones and smiled down at her. Envy momentarily spasmed inside her, but she quickly dismissed the negative emotion when she saw the looks passing between the two.

"Will the fact that nearly all the furniture in the house is rented help my case? Most of Matthew's things are in storage already. I just have books from college, clothes, linens, kitchen things, and my car to worry about."

"There shouldn't be any problem. SOP for POW and MIA wives is to make certain they have whatever they need. Within reason, of course," he amended with a grin. "Your home of record is California, according to your file. Did you have a moving date in mind?"

Eden nodded. "The last week of November, if it's possible. And if the movers won't handle the car, I'll need to know right away so I can arrange to sell it. I don't want to drive three thousand miles by myself, especially not this time of year. The weather's too unpredictable."

"Sounds like you've thought almost everything through already," David mused aloud.

She nodded. "I've had a lot of time to think lately."

Tracey stood and walked to the sink with her plate and cup. After rinsing both and placing them in the dishwasher, she turned to Eden. "Do you want me to contact a realtor for you when I get back to L.A.?"

"Is that your way of telling me you don't want a roommate?" she teased.

"Of course not! You know I've got three spare bedrooms."

David chuckled. "Where do you live, woman? In a mansion?"

She returned to stand at his side and playfully tried to get a good grip on his short hair. "In a beach house in Malibu, silly."

David looped his arm around her hip and pulled her closer. "Looks like I may have to get myself some orders and head west."

Tracey dropped a kiss on his forehead. "See that you do, Major." Glancing at Eden, she asked, "What about going back to work? Do you want me to start sending you the Sunday paper?"

"Nope. For the time being, staying sober is a full-time job. Somebody very wise," she said with a smile, "told me not to set myself up for failure. I think I'll follow his advice."

"Do you want help getting ready for the movers?"

Eden saw the hopeful look on Tracey's face. Any excuse to see David and her friend would take it. "As long as it doesn't get you fired from your job."

"Never happen," she assured as she glanced at her watch. "I need to finish packing."

"Trace?"

"Yeah?"

"There's something I've been wanting to say to you both, aside from the obvious thank you for what you've been through with me this past month." She placed the pencil she'd been holding on the table before she continued. "Maybe I'm butting in where I don't belong, but I'm going to use our friendship as an excuse. It's obvious you and David care a lot about each other. For your own sakes, please don't waste a moment of your time together or the feelings you have for one another. Time goes by so quickly, and there aren't any guarantees that you can get it back if you lose it. I found that out the hard way."

Tracey silently nodded. David spoke for them both. "We understand what you're saying, Eden. And I think we know where we're headed."

"I hope so," she whispered. "I really hope so."

Tracey, her eyes filling with tears, walked around the table and hugged her. "I love you, friend, very much."

Eden swatted her on the fanny. "Go finish packing. I need a few more minutes with David."

"Are you going to ask me if my intentions are honorable?" he teased as Tracey left the room.

Eden saw the laughter in his eyes and smiled. "I don't think that's required. Besides, didn't the Congress declare you an officer and a gentleman when you were commissioned?"

David sobered. "I love her and I won't hurt her."

"She deserves to be loved. She went a lot of years without a sense of family or emotional security. We both did."

"She told me." He shifted in his chair and asked, "Didn't you have something else on your mind?"

"Will you continue as my assistance officer once I've relocated?"

"It's very likely. Given what you've been through the last few months, and because I've been here with you through a major portion of it, I suspect that Headquarters Marine Corps will want me to continue, unless, of course, you have some objection."

"No, I was hoping you could."

"As of right now, you're my only case."

"And it won't be a problem with me living in California and you stationed in Washington?"

"Let me worry about the transportation problems between D.C. and Los Angeles. It may take a while, but we'll get something worked out."

"I don't expect a baby-sitter, David. In fact, that's the last thing I want or need. What I do want and need is the assurance that there's someone I can call if I need help or advice."

He leaned forward, his expression serious. "First and foremost, I'm your friend. Even if your case is assigned to another officer, I'll always be your friend. All you have to do is pick up the phone. Understood?"

She nodded. "Understood."

PART TWO

On January 25, 1969, representatives of the United States, North and South Vietnam, as well as the Vietcong, met in Paris for the first day of four-party peace talks. The meeting signaled the beginning of a tedious trek through a diplomatic mine field that would test the ingenuity and patience of all the participants.

CHAPTER

II

February 1969—Long Moc Prison Camp,
North Vietnam

Dearest Eden:

I write to you in my mind each day. Letters I know you'll never receive, letters filled with thoughts and feelings I may never have an opportunity to express face-to-face. A voice in my head tells me that you know you've become the primary link to my sanity, my desire to survive.

My mental image of you is as sharp and as clear as a color photograph. I can't imagine a life without you, and yet I am now forced to live such a life. This isn't the world we expected to share, the world we planned for ourselves, Eden.

I keep asking myself why? Why me? Why us? My intellect provides me with the facts of how and why, of course, but my insides ache from the emptiness I feel. I remind myself that you and our baby are safe, that you still love me, but the inevitable questions arise. Do you even realize that I'm alive? How long will it be before we're together again? Months? Years? I have no answers, only the hope that you'll be waiting for me when I'm released.

I spend many hours each day wondering if we have a son or a daughter. I've told myself that I can live without knowing the sex of our child, but I can't help my curiosity. Will I someday teach my son to play baseball, or will I stand in awe of a daughter who will grow up to have her mother's compassion and beauty? Is *his* name Andrew, or is *her* name Andrea? You thought I'd forgotten, didn't you?

I've told you about Chet Holt, I think. We're still the only

Americans at Long Moc, although the number of South Vietnamese prisoners is growing. Chet's down with malaria again. Poor bastard. The nights are the worst for him. He has the sweats and then wakes up freezing. We seem to take turns with this particular malady, and that is to our benefit so far. As long as one of us can work the fields adjacent to the camp, we are given our daily rice ration. God help us if we both ever get sick at the same time.

Major Han has left us pretty much to ourselves for the past couple of months. Chet figures he just got bored having us dragged through the local village on our hands and knees at the end of a leash like dogs by the guards. I suspect some local official threatened to report him to Hanoi. Whatever his reasoning, I can't say that I mind his lack of attention. The asshole makes my skin crawl whenever I'm around him. Humiliation and degradation are his favorite pastimes, and he doesn't confine himself to the prisoners. His own troops frequently find themselves the targets of his perverse moods.

Chet and I tried to plan another escape. Needless to say, it didn't come off. Hell, it died in the planning stages. There are too many factors working against us. For the time being, we're praying for a *real* opportunity of escape, not some half-baked scheme that could get us both killed. I know you must wonder why I haven't been able to make a break for freedom in the year I've been a prisoner. Hopefully, someone from Headquarters Marine Corps has figured out our situation and has explained it to you. One fact I'm sure you're already aware of is that my height is a problem, not to mention the color of my skin. I tower above the locals. Getting rid of our leg and wrist irons, finding clothing, and stockpiling enough food for the journey south are minor difficulties when you realize that we have only a vague idea of our location.

The language barrier aside, it's unlikely anyone would risk helping us if we were able to escape. The North Vietnamese people, not just their army, are committed to uniting all of Vietnam. The hatred they feel for us is a cultural thing, not just an ideology that filters down from the leaders in Hanoi. We're political criminals to this country, not just an opposing military force. If we live long enough, Chet and I expect to go on trial for our supposed crimes. We often wonder if we will ever have a chance to say anything in our own defense. I sometimes wonder, in my darkest moments, if we'll even live long enough to stand trial.

I've probably told you things you already know about, but perhaps they bear repeating, if only to emphasize the bewildering circumstances I find myself in. I've only wanted two things in this life: to be a first-class pilot in the corps and to be the kind of husband you could always love. The first is questionable at this point in time, but I hope that I never fail in the second.

I love you more than my life, paleface. You are my hope in the bleakness that surrounds me, and you are the light that shines in my heart and mind, the same light that allows me to survive.

I am yours,

Matthew

CHAPTER

12

March 1969—Malibu, California

Eden compared Tracey's packing list against the contents of the suitcase on the bed. Satisfied that she hadn't forgotten any of the essentials Tracey would need on her trip, she zipped the large piece of luggage closed.

"I can't believe I let my boss talk me into covering Carol Walker's clients for her," Tracey complained as she walked into her bedroom. "I should've had more sense, especially considering what the weather's like in New York this time of year."

"Quit moaning. You'll only be gone for six weeks, and you *will* survive."

"Sure, as long as I carry a portable heater around on my back. Who else but Carol would take a six-week honeymoon and give just two days' notice?"

Eden laughed. "Don't knock it. You might decide to do the same thing someday."

"Okay, so I'm jealous," Tracey admitted as she stepped into a pair of knee-high leather boots and then buttoned the jacket of her wool suit. "I'd give my left arm to spend the beginning of spring in a villa in the south of France."

"But we did."

She snorted. "Your memory is failing you again. Being sent to the south of France at the age of thirteen was like being forced into exile, and you know it. Our parents pulled that trick out of their hats when we got tossed out of Weatherlake Academy for keeping a copy of *Lady Chatterley's Lover* in our dorm room. Aunt Florene's rickety old house didn't even vaguely resemble a villa."

Eden smiled indulgently and tugged the heavy suitcase off the bed. Her memories of their month at Aunt Florene's were soothing and reassuring, due in large part to the motherly nature of the woman who had cared for them. "You've very conveniently forgotten to mention how easy it will be for you to catch the Washington shuttle every Friday evening."

Tracey grinned, and anticipation made her eyes sparkle. "I did, didn't I?"

"You did."

"Maybe this trip won't be so bad, after all."

Together they hauled the piece of luggage down a flight of stairs, across the Tecate-tiled foyer, and out the front door to the cab waiting at the curb.

"Does David know about your plans yet?" Eden asked.

"I called, but I couldn't reach him, so I left a message for him with his secretary. He'll probably phone you tonight for the details." Tracey frowned before quietly admitting, "I hate leaving you in the lurch like this."

"You're not leaving me in the lurch. I've spent the last four months putting myself back together, Trace. I've also learned a lot about myself and about the choices I have ahead of me. We both know I can't afford to sit still and watch the world go by as though I'm in some kind of permanent emotional traction. Matthew wouldn't expect it of me, and I know now that I can't live that way. Besides, I'm bored, and I want a life that has some value. Until Drew died, I was a doer, not a watcher." She shrugged. "What more can I say except that I guess I'm ready to be a doer again. Escrow should close on my house in a few weeks. With all the remodeling that place needs, I've got weeks, maybe even months, of work ahead of me."

"What about your AA meetings? It's a long drive from Del Mar to Malibu."

Eden heard her concern but wasn't bothered by it. Tracey had earned the right to ask such a question. "I've already contacted my San Diego sponsor. She's mailing me a list of AA meeting locations near the new house."

The cabdriver stowed Tracey's luggage in the trunk and then loudly cleared his throat as he opened the car door for her.

Eden gave her a quick hug. "Relax and enjoy your trip. You know you love New York, in spite of the lousy weather."

"What I really love is the idea of being so close to David. It seems like forever since he was here for Christmas with us. Any messages for him?"

"Just tell him I'm sober and that I'm still taking one day at a time."

"He'll be glad."

"Get in the cab before this guy leaves you in his dust for another fare. If you've forgotten anything, call me and I'll send it to you."

Tracey did as she was told. Eden waved as the cabbie put the car in gear and sped off down Pacific Coast Highway. She walked back to the front door, still buoyed by her thoughts of the house she'd just bought, but paused when she heard a car door slam. Frowning, she turned and saw a uniformed man get out of the sedan parked at the curb.

He's been sick, she realized when she noticed the beads of perspiration on his upper lip and the way he favored his left leg as he awkwardly made his way up the walk to where she stood. The cane he gripped further confirmed his fragile physical condition, despite his broad shoulders and intensely determined facial expression. He had the look of a man who had intimate knowledge of the inside of a hospital.

"I'm looking for Eden Benedict, please. Major Markham gave me this address. I'm sorry I didn't call first."

Matthew!

Eden nodded mutely and looked past him, her expression detached, almost curious, as she waited for the arrival of a second vehicle and a second officer. That's how they do it, she reminded herself. One delivers the death notice. The other man, usually a chaplain, tries to console the disbelieving wife.

"Ma'am?"

Eden suddenly ached for a moment or two or even three with Matthew before someone told her that he was dead. Just a few private minutes in the safety of his arms. Shivering involuntarily, she took a deep breath and reminded herself of how hard she'd fought for her sanity and her sobriety.

Be safe, Matthew. Please be safe. I put our son in the ground eight months ago, Matthew. I'm not ready for another funeral. I'll never be ready for someone to tell me you're dead.

She refocused and looked into a face filled with compassion. "You're alone?" she questioned softly.

He nodded and shifted his stance, his fingers tightening on the curved handle of his cane.

Why, she wondered, had the Marine Corps given someone so vulnerable such a miserable job?

"You *are* Eden Benedict, aren't you?"

"Yes." He doesn't even know how to do this, she realized. "Would you like to come in?"

"Please."

Eden opened the front door, silently welcoming the numbness that seemed to encase her heart. Moving woodenly, she led the way through the foyer and into the living room. An open and airy portion of Tracey's home, it boasted one entire wall composed of glass that revealed a panoramic view of the Pacific.

He waited for her to sit down before sinking with obvious relief into an easy chair near the fireplace. "I've seen pictures of you."

She frowned. "Pictures? I don't understand."

"Matt carried your picture in his wallet. He even covered one of the walls in our hooch with photos he'd had blown up from your R and R. I think my favorite was the one of the two of you—"

Eden drew in a lungful of air before slowly releasing it. "You knew my husband?"

He nodded. "I thought you might recognize me, but then I guess I don't look much like my pictures anymore." Fingering the livid scar that ran the length of his right cheek, he shrugged. "I keep forgetting how different I look." He suddenly sounded self-conscious.

All the color left her face. "Who are you?" she whispered.

He stiffened when he heard the fear in her voice. "Christ! I'm sorry. I'm Jack . . . Jack Morrison. Matt's RIO."

"Eagle? You're Eagle? Why . . . how can you be here when you and Matthew . . . You're both MIAs."

"I've been in the hospital since I escaped over a year ago."

"But . . . did Matthew . . . you were with my husband." She started to leave her chair but sank back down again when she realized how disjointed her words sounded. "You said a year, more than a year, didn't you?"

"I escaped a few days after we were captured."

"You left Matthew?" she whispered, her tone one of disbelief and horror. "You left him there alone? He was hurt. How could you have done such a thing? He told me you were his friend."

"I didn't leave him, Eden. We were separated right after we bailed out."

"Then why hasn't someone told me about you?"

"I wasn't expected to live," he answered soberly.

"My God!" she exclaimed, suddenly overwhelmed by her own selfishness and insensitivity. "I'm so sorry."

"Hey! It's okay. Really. You don't have anything to be sorry for."

"But if the Marine Corps had told me, I would've come to visit you."

He shook his head. "I was out of my head for months. I wouldn't have even known you. Besides, I promised the Warrior I'd come and see you if I made it out first. I just wish it hadn't taken me so long to keep my promise."

Eden stood and paced the length of the room. She finally stopped, faced Jack, and asked, "Was his right hand or arm injured?"

He looked startled and then profoundly uncomfortable. "What did Headquarters Marine Corps tell you about his injury?"

"Very little . . . practically nothing."

"Then how did you know?"

"I just did." She saw his confusion and hastened to explain. "Three days passed between your shootdown and when I was actually notified. At the time, I couldn't shake the feeling that something extremely painful had happened to Matthew. My wrist and arm ached. They still do."

"A bullet hit him, probably nicked a nerve." Jack lifted his arm and pointed to a spot above his wrist. "Just about here. He bled a lot at first, and his fingers were numb. We managed to clean up the wound and bandage it before we were captured."

Eden wandered back to the couch, her fingertips at her temples as she massaged the pain pounding there.

"I want to tell you about the day we went down. Matt would have wanted you to know all the facts."

"Please, Jack. I need to know."

She waited several minutes for him to begin, minutes during which Jack left his chair and made his way to the windows that overlooked the ocean. Eden had already discovered for herself that it was the one spot in Tracey's home that offered a true sense of solace.

". . . and before we knew it, the NVA troops who'd captured us confiscated our gear and separated us. There wasn't time to say good-bye or even wish one another luck."

"How did you manage to escape?"

Jack heard the unasked question, as well, the same question he'd asked himself at least once a day since his escape, the one question Eden Benedict was too well mannered to ask now no matter how much she wanted to. Why hadn't Matt been able to do the same?

"I was damned lucky, in spite of how I look. The NVA captain in charge of the troops who captured us after we punched out split his force. He took Matt. One of his sergeants was responsible for me. The guy wasn't any good at his job. One night, after everyone fell asleep, there was a rocket attack. The guard assigned to watch me panicked. Things got pretty confused for a while. . . . I managed to get away and hide in the brush. Dumb luck saved my hide after that. Some friendlies found me and took me to a Green Beret unit. They radioed Search and Rescue. The rest is history."

"Your leg," she prompted softly. "When did that happen?"

"During the rocket attack. The men firing those rockets had no way of knowing I was in the area." Jack gave her a hard look when he saw the shock in her eyes. "It's the price I had to pay to get out . . . one I don't regret."

She nodded and tried to understand the rationale behind Jack's defense of the Americans who'd unwittingly caused his injuries. "Will you be able to fly again?"

He flashed a thumbs-up sign and grinned, looking relaxed for the first time since he'd arrived. "The medical types say my leg'll be back to rights in another six months or so. Until then, I'm on light duty, with physical therapy every day."

"I'm glad for you, Jack. Matthew always said you were as addicted to flying as he was."

"Is!" he insisted sharply.

She couldn't ignore the vehemence in his voice. "You believe he's still alive, don't you?"

"Don't you?" he countered, his eyes narrowing as he studied her.

"Not always," she admitted honestly. "I haven't seen him in twenty months. My last letter from him was dated the day you were shot down. It's been fourteen months now, Jack, and my emotions run the gamut on a daily basis—hope, fear, resignation, and then back to hope again. I desperately want Matthew to be alive, but I'm not always sure he is."

"Warrior is one tough son of a bitch! Don't count him out until the last bullet's been fired."

Eden leaned forward in her chair. "Try and understand that not always believing that Matthew's alive isn't a sign of disloyalty on my part. I'm just trying to be as realistic as possible in a very difficult and painful situation. Do you realize that you're the first person I've spoken to other than Tracey who even knew Matthew? When he was shot down, I felt as though my life had stopped. It took me a long time to start living again, and I'm still not doing that great a job of it yet. I also live with the very real fear that I may never see my husband again," she finished softly.

"Is there anything I can do to help?"

She read sincerity and compassion but not a speck of judgment in his face and felt the same warmth she was certain her husband must have enjoyed in his friendship with Jack. "Just be my friend, too. There are times when I need to talk about Matthew. All I'll ever ask is that you listen once in a while."

"Anytime," he promised. "I'll give you my duty-station address and phone number at El Toro and the number at the BOQ before I leave today. Until I find an apartment, I'll be at either one of those locations when I'm not down at the naval hospital in San Diego for therapy."

"I won't be here much longer," Eden confided.

"Going back to the East Coast?"

She shook her head. "San Diego."

"A lot of military families settle there while their men are overseas. It's also a great place to live."

"With all the antimilitary sentiment sweeping the country, San Diego County seemed like a good choice. I've just bought a small cottage on the beach in Del Mar." Eden didn't bother to admit that she'd been studying the newspapers for several months now. The growing tenseness in the country over Vietnam worried her, more because of Matthew's status as an MIA than any fear for herself.

"You've had a rough time this past year, especially with your little boy dying. You've got a long haul ahead of you, Eden," he cautioned. "There are hundreds of thousands of troops committed to this war. And, right or wrong, the politicians are running the show. In Nam, here at home, and in Paris at the peace talks."

"David said pretty much the same thing to me when I left Massachusetts. No one seems very optimistic about a quick victory. I personally doubt that anyone will actually win in Vietnam, but there certainly will be a lot of innocent victims," she observed, a trace of bitterness in her voice.

"You're probably right," he grudgingly agreed, "but don't quote me."

"Did David tell you about Drew?"

He nodded. "The entire squadron knew you were pregnant. Matt announced the news at happy hour the day he got your letter. Major Markham filled me in on the rest."

"Then you know about my drinking?"

Jack shifted awkwardly before answering. "Yeah, but I also

know that you're sober now and you plan on staying that way for good."

Eden smiled as she stood. "Well, since I have my wits about me, why don't you stay for dinner? Tracey left for New York just before you arrived, and I defrosted two steaks before I knew her travel plans."

Jack grinned and got to his feet with the aid of his cane. "Don't you know bachelors never turn down a home-cooked meal?"

Warmed by a memory not totally misplaced, she commented laughingly, "I seem to recall Matthew making a similar statement once."

They shared a quiet meal in the dining room. Darkness fell as they finished their coffee and dessert. The more she listened to Jack, the more Eden realized the depth of his affection for her husband. Despite how different the two men were, she understood why they had been so compatible in the F-4 they'd flown together in Vietnam. Both men lived, breathed, and talked the corps. Their commitment to that particular branch of the service was based not only on loyalty and dedication to duty but also on their deep-seated respect for the unique history of the corps and their pride in being a part of it.

Later, as she and Jack walked to the front door, Eden sensed that he'd left something unsaid during their time together. "I get the feeling there's more you'd like to say but you aren't certain if you should."

He rubbed the top of his reddish-blond crew cut with his knuckles and shrugged. "Just a suggestion, really. The naval hospital in San Diego is shorthanded with all the wounded coming out of Southeast Asia. The medical staff's really hustling down there, and the Red Cross is always looking for volunteers to help the guys in the wards."

Eden gave him a doubtful look. "I've never worked in a hospital. I majored in English in college, and the only job I've ever had was as a proofreader for a publishing house that specialized in cookbooks and gardening manuals."

He shrugged, but the gesture was less than casual. "No

sweat, Eden. It was just a thought. Hospitals aren't for everyone."

She pulled open the front door. "It's not a bad idea, Jack. I just don't know what I'd be like around sick people."

"You never know. It might make the time pass more quickly for you. Maybe even give you a sense of purpose. The guys in the wards would keep you busy. I can speak from personal experience." He grinned and tapped his leg. "I spent thirteen and a half months of my life in a place that everyone calls 'the pink palace.' "

"That conjures up images of dancing girls and men in flowing robes."

"Sorry to disappoint you, but everything at the naval hospital is blue, white, and stiffly starched." He arched an eyebrow and produced a pained expression.

Eden couldn't keep herself from laughing. "I'll give it some thought once I finish with the house."

Eden, armed with her personal belongings and a sleeping bag, left the luxury of Tracey's Malibu beach house fifteen days following her conversation with Jack Morrison. A neighbor promised to collect the mail and water the plants until Tracey returned from New York. Jack promised to visit her in her new home after she pronounced it habitable.

Meanwhile, in Washington, newly inaugurated president Richard Nixon labored over his decision of whether or not to initiate secret bombing of communist bases in Cambodia.

CHAPTER

13

March 1969—Hanoi, North Vietnam

I am dedicated to the principles that made my country free.

Matt closed his eyes each time a tenet passed through his mind. The military Code of Conduct had been ingrained in him since childhood, a gift of words from a father he only vaguely remembered. He now called upon this legacy for courage.

I am prepared to give my life for my country.

He no longer smelled the noxious fumes powering the battered vehicle in which he and Chet were being transported. Blind to the cratered earth on either side of old Highway 1 as they journeyed north, he listened to the drone of heavy bombers in the sky overhead. It was a soothing reminder that others still labored daily, their missions exacting a toll of death and destruction among the North Vietnamese.

I will keep faith with my fellow prisoners.

Ignoring the weapons pointed at his head, Matt maintained his balance on spread knees in the back of the open flatbed truck. Heavy iron encased his wrists and ankles. Chet, like a matching bookend, knelt behind him, equally silent and equally preoccupied by private thought.

Dusk crept into the sky, and shadows reached out to consume the surrounding terrain. The engine of the lurching truck strained toward its destination. While the guards kept their silent vigil, Matt prayed for an end to the day's muscle-taxing position.

Clusters of pajama-clad peasants wearing conical-shaped

hats that reminded him of inverted mushrooms looked on from the sides of the rutted road. They raised fists clenched in anger and screeched their outrage at the captured foreigners. Had it not been for their guards, Matt knew the machetes they carried would have been aimed with deadly accuracy.

Darkness finally fell as the truck pulled off the main road. They arrived at a small village a short time later. More knife-wielding locals crowded forward to greet them with barely controlled hostility, held at bay by a small contingent of what Matt assumed were North Vietnamese militia. Prodded from the truck by the guards, Matt and Chet were shoved toward a small windowless building. They heard a heavy iron bar slide across the only exit once they were pushed inside. Neither spoke for several minutes. It was the first time they'd been alone together in four days.

There had been no explanation when they were ordered from their cell at Long Moc and loaded into the truck. In the months since Caulfield's death, Matt and Chet had continued to labor in the fields adjacent to the prison camp. Their daily routine rarely changed, and they saw little of Major Han. When they did, it was an event worth forgetting.

Chet glanced over at Matt. "Do you think they'll feed us tonight?"

Matt shrugged. The movement aggravated his right wrist and arm. Chet heard the hiss of his indrawn breath, a certain sign of unbearable pain.

"How's your arm?"

"Feels like it's on fire."

"Why do you suppose they moved us?"

Matt leaned back against the wall and closed his eyes. "Who knows why these bastards do anything."

"I still don't understand why," Chet persisted, "especially after all these months. Han had you for more than a year and me for ten months. I thought the bastard was starting to like us."

Matt grinned, the facial movement emphasizing his gaunt cheeks and the deep circles of fatigue ringing his eyes. "Maybe he got tired of all the shit we used to grow his vegetables."

"Did you see the look on his face when we left? I thought that son of a bitch was gonna have a stroke."

"Let's hope he drops dead from the strain of losing his two pet monkeys."

"No way! Assholes like Han always survive. One of life's little injustices."

Chet allowed his body to fall to one side. Using the wall of the shed for leverage, he eased downward until he rested on his left shoulder. "I figure they're taking us to Hanoi."

"Probably."

"Do you remember what Jackson told us about the prison camps up north?"

Matt answered by asking, "Could it be any rougher than Long Moc?"

"Jesus, I hope not. Hell, maybe he was just bullshitting us. You know how those green beanies get when they're in the soup."

Matt shared Chet's trepidation about the treatment they would receive once they reached their destination. He suspected that Jackson, in one of his more lucid moments, had spoken the truth. "Whatever we think might happen is pure conjecture at the moment. For all we know, the gooks might stand us in front of a firing squad the same day we get wherever we're going."

"That's a comforting thought," Chet muttered. "You know, up till now I've just been pissed off at our situation and hungry all the time, but the farther north we travel, the more uneasy I get."

"Just take it as it comes. You aren't alone, and if there are other Americans where we're headed, then maybe we'll have a real shot at escaping. There's no other way to get through whatever's planned for us."

"After all your trips to the hotbox and the beatings you survived, I guess you know what you're talking about." Chet paused and squinted at Matt through the semidarkness. "Han really hated your ass, buddy. If he could've pulled it off, he'd have killed you. What do you think stopped him?"

Matt sighed and leaned forward to rest his forehead on his

knees. The manacles fastened at his wrists and ankles made comfort impossible. "I suspect there's a hell of a bounty on our heads. After Jackson died, I reminded the major of what his superiors in Hanoi might do if we all bought it. Some kind of a buzzer went off in his head that day, even though he retaliated by throwing me in the box for a good brain bake. Apparently Jackson was expendable. Caulfield flat gave up. Han couldn't have prevented Hal's death even with the medication I requested."

"Killing us outright would be too easy, wouldn't it?" Chet asked, his voice hushed.

"Yeah. I suspect we're about to get a lesson in how to live in hell. Survival school will probably seem like a romp in a park after these bastards are done with us. Look at the way they fight, Chet. The war down south had turned into a body count even before we were captured. The North Vietnamese and the VC are in this game for keeps. They intend to win. We've become pawns on a chessboard. My gut tells me they won't let us die, but they'll make sure we wish we had."

"What if we're tortured?"

Matt instinctively knew the odds were excellent. "Try not to think about it. Just take it one day at a time."

"How much farther do you think it is to Hanoi?"

"If that's where we're headed, a couple of days."

"Doesn't look like we get fed again tonight. Guess I'll get some shut-eye if you'll take the first watch."

"Fine." Matt straightened and leaned back against the wall of the shed. He stared into the darkness and tried to flex his numb fingers. Thinking back over the preceding months, he mentally acknowledged the wisdom of taking the first sleep watch. He'd always preferred it. The thought of rats, snakes, lizards, and other bold night creatures kept him awake, anyway. And Chet was dependable once he'd had a few hours of rest. Their arrangement had been successful since Hal Caulfield's death, except when Chet's malaria acted up or when Major Han ordered one of them into the hotbox.

The night passed uneventfully. Loaded into the truck at dawn, they were not fed. For three more days their routine was the same. On the last night, in a tiny hamlet near the Red River, they were given cold rice balls, chunks of raw fish, and water.

Bullet-riddled French road signs and increased mule-cart, military-vehicle, and foot traffic signaled their entrance into the North Vietnamese capital city of Hanoi. Bombed-out buildings and trash-can-shaped shelters carved into the sidewalks and streets suggested the frequency and effectiveness of the destructive force of American B-52s.

Uniformed soldiers mingled with civilians on the rubble-littered streets. The crush of humanity contrasted sharply with the jungle isolation of Long Moc. Less inhibited than their peasant counterparts, the citizens of Hanoi expressed their hatred for the American prisoners openly, hurling rocks, broken bottles, and chunks of brick at the two men. The guards laughingly dodged the flying debris. Matt was relieved when he heard a sudden shouted order from the truck driver. The circling crowd fell back, and the vehicle surged beyond their range.

Hoa Lo sobered Matt even more than the unmanageable populace of Hanoi. He stared at the old French fortress as it came into view, taking in the dry moat that surrounded it with a tense body and the reemergence of a long-discarded memory of the stories he'd read about Devil's Island as a child. The walls of Hoa Lo looked to be twenty feet high. Matt didn't miss the strands of electrified wire strung between the guard towers or the broken glass jutting skyward from the top of the thick walls. He wondered if the parallels of Devil's Island would continue once he and Chet were delivered to the interior of the French-built prison.

They had little time to observe the courtyard of the former colonial fortress. Quickly hustled into a dungeonlike section of the prison near the main gate, Matt and Chet were separated, but not before they glimpsed two men in prison garb. Both were Caucasian.

Two guards escorted Matt to an interrogation room that

was twelve feet wide and thirty feet long. He didn't know yet that his fellow prisoners had already christened it "the violent room" in a part of Hoa Lo they referred to as Heartbreak. Left standing at attention, his manacled wrists still bound behind him and anchored to a hook protruding from the concrete wall, he smelled decaying flesh and human waste.

Matt slowly surveyed the room. A desk, a chair, and a stool sat in the middle of the oblong room, a single naked electrical socket centered in the ceiling above. For two hours he stood in the darkening shadows of the room. Exhausted to a state of emotional numbness and oblivious to the raindrops pinging against the glass-paneled door that led out to the courtyard, Matt listened in stunned silence to the PA system echoing throughout Hoa Lo Prison.

He listened to the voices of other Americans calling him a baby killer. He listened to the voices of congressmen and senators, some of whom he recognized, advocating the termination of the war in Southeast Asia. And finally, most dishearteningly, he listened to the voices of men who identified themselves as his fellow prisoners; men who advised him to tell the North Vietnamese what they wanted to know because they were his friends now that the U.S. government had abandoned him.

Still reeling from the content of the recorded messages, Matt jerked his head up when the door to the room burst open without warning. He watched three uniformed North Vietnamese stride into the room. He stiffened defensively and studied the men through narrowed eyes, the pain in his body and the hunger gnawing at his insides displaced by instincts of awareness and survival.

"Captain Benedict," began the interpreter, "you are now in the custody of the commandant of Hoa Lo Prison. Until such time as the Democratic Republic sees fit to absolve you of your crimes against the people of our sovereign nation, you are judged a war criminal and will be treated as such. Have you anything to say for yourself?"

Matt released the air stored in his lungs. Struck by the absurd formality of the announcement he'd just heard, he responded calmly, "Benedict, Matthew Alexander. Captain, United States Marine Corps. Service number two-two-nine—eight."

A sound exploded from the senior member of the trio. Matt peered curiously at the three men. He noted amusement on one man's face, contempt from the other two. Their eyes, however, remained empty, totally devoid of emotion.

"The Geneva Convention is irrelevant here, Captain Benedict. Because your country has not formally declared itself at war with the Democratic Republic, that document is meaningless to us. Now," he continued briskly, "how do you respond to the charge? Will you cooperate and confess, or would you like to make this difficult for yourself?"

Matt drew his gaze from the three men and stared at the wall behind them. He repeated, "Benedict, Matthew Alexander. Captain, United States Marine Corps. Service number two-two-nine-eight-one-zero-one. Date of birth: 10 November 1936."

The interpreter shook his head in apparent disgust before he spoke to the two officers who had accompanied him into the interrogation room. They departed, and two men who reminded Matt of Japanese Sumo wrestlers replaced them. Here we go, he realized. Pain wins again. His bemused expression angered them, and they jerked him from the metal wall hook. Matt felt the jarring crunch of bone in his hips and back as he was slammed down onto the stool in the center of the room.

As he sat there, he suddenly realized that he'd forgotten his thirty-third birthday the previous fall while he and Chet rotted at Long Moc.

Matt didn't sense the blow aimed at his head in time to duck. He toppled over, unable to smother his gasp of pain as he hit the cement floor. The color red filled his field of vision when he was hauled upright by his right arm.

"Your manacles will be removed and you will receive medical attention after you sign a confession."

Matt inhaled sharply and stiffened his spine. "What am I confessing?"

"You are a war criminal," the interpreter insisted again. He shoved a sheaf of papers across the scarred wood table. "Are you ready to sign?"

"We both know I can't sign a confession."

"You will sign now, or you will sign later. It is of little consequence to me either way. But make no mistake, Captain Benedict, you *will* sign the confession." He glanced at the guards positioned on either side of Matt. "My comrades are another matter. They are amused by your stubborn attitude, and they will enjoy participating in your reeducation."

The North Vietnamese officer continued to request Matt's signature on the confession. Matt continued to repeat his name, rank, service number, and date of birth. With each reply he received two sharp blows to his head. After several hours his face felt like raw meat, and blood oozed from his ringing ears. He was convinced that it was only a matter of time before his head would explode from the pain he felt.

The interrogation room echoed with the same question, Matt's reply, and subsequent blows from the guards far into the night. Matt clung to an image firmly fixed in his mind—Eden standing on a windswept beach, her long hair teased by ocean breezes and her eyes filled with laughter and love. Even when her image blurred and he felt himself succumbing to unconsciousness, he heard her whisper, "I love you, Matthew. I will always love you. Be safe and come home to me."

Consciousness clawed at him, bringing with it waves of agony. Eyes swollen shut, Matt experienced the disorientation of free-fall. He belatedly realized that he was hanging upside down when his forehead brushed the damp cement of the floor below him. He groaned, panicked by the loss of feeling in his arms and legs. The horror of amputation slashed through his mind, and he couldn't stop the sobs that shook his body or the tears that stung the raw flesh of his forehead as they fell to mingle with blood, bits of his own flesh, and the urine puddled beneath him.

Unable to see, he forced himself to overcome his panic and go limp. Slowly, gingerly, he provoked movement in isolated portions of his body, consciously willing his limbs to respond.

He saved his arms for last. Concentrating, he commanded his elbows to bend. When they finally did, he focused his thoughts on his fingers, willing them to flex, one at a time. Several moments passed before he felt sensation traverse the swollen digits. He wept with relief, welcoming the fresh onslaught of tears that slipped from his swollen eyes. He couldn't help wondering if the fragile hold of a functioning mind in a damaged body was enough to guarantee his survival.

Morning dawned. Matt drifted into consciousness again. He heard the sound of human activity in the courtyard beyond the window. The incessant patter of rain continued, and cold, damp air invaded the room in chilling drafts.

Still suspended from the ceiling chain, he discerned the distinctive footsteps of three individuals when, late in the morning, they entered the interrogation room. He felt several hands fumble with the nylon straps binding his arms and legs. Gritting his teeth against renewed pain as he was lowered from his inverted position, Matt couldn't control the shudders that racked his body. He collapsed to his knees as he heard what sounded like an angry shout before more hands grabbed him and dragged him to the stool he had occupied the previous night. He felt the press of four hands holding him in place atop the stool.

The smell of alcohol preceded the sting when a plastic-gloved hand grasped his jaw and swabbed his face. He prayed that the person draining his ears of blood and bandaging them was at least a trained medic. Once his nose was taped and an injection administered into his upper left arm, he waited in silence. He grew more and more apprehensive as he grappled with his fear of another beating.

Despite his best efforts, Matt was unable to see the guards who took him by the arms, forced him upright, and half dragged, half walked, him out of the interrogation room. He counted twenty-seven steps before he felt the brush of another doorframe against his shoulder. He sensed that he had been moved to a smaller enclosure, probably a cell.

He flinched when a bundle of coarse fabric was thrust against his chest. He clutched the material and closed his hands tightly around it, simultaneously pressing all ten fingers into the cloth to reassure himself that his hands were still functioning. Someone turned him around and pushed him into a seated position on a slab of cement. He finally heard a door slam and then the fading jangle of keys.

Nearly overwhelmed by the sense of relief he felt the moment the cell door banged shut, he struggled to his feet despite still-trembling legs. He worked his way along the damp walls of his new quarters. His ankle irons dragged between his feet, but he ignored the scraping sound. Pacing off the distance between the walls, Matt discovered that the space he now occupied was seven feet long and four feet wide.

A raised cement platform ran five feet the length of one wall. A bucket stinking of feces sat in the far corner of the rectangular cell. Using his fingertips, he discovered that there were no windows.

Easing himself onto the cement bunk, Matt pawed through the bundle given to him by the guards. He handled each item with care: a thin bedroll, a shirt he probably wouldn't be able to button, baggy trousers he suspected would reach only as far as his knees, a spoon, and a threadbare towel.

"Things are looking up. At Long Moc I had a spoon and a sleeping mat." He laughed sardonically, the sound dwindling to a groan before he whispered, "All my worldly possessions."

"Be safe, my love."

He hugged the sour-smelling jumble of fabric to his chest and rocked back and forth.

"I'm still alive, paleface. I'm still alive."

Matt ate the watered-down soup with tasteless chunks of squash and the small piece of bread that were delivered to his cell each morning for the next eight days. Considering his experiences with Major Han at Long Moc, he decided that he could expect many more sessions with the interrogators of Hoa Lo Prison. On the ninth day, as he had anticipated, Matt was escorted to the interrogation room. This session began as the first one had—a demand for his signature on a confession, his refusal, and blows to his body. Booted feet and hard-knuckled fists punished his kidneys and groin. The pain eventually became numbness, and he slipped from consciousness. In the week that followed, his urine was blood red.

Matt endured the cyclic process for nearly two months. The North Vietnamese demand that he confess, his negative response, the beatings, each time focused on a specific portion of his anatomy, subsequent if inadequate medical attention, and time to recuperate.

Without warning, his interrogation and torture ceased. Matt, having already decided that the North Vietnamese would eventually beat him to death, made peace with himself. He forced himself to take each hour of each day individually, certain that this reprieve was a momentary thing.

So began 208 days of isolation. He received a daily bowl of soup and a chunk of dry bread. He showered once a month under heavy guard. And he periodically heard the shattered cries of other prisoners being tortured. Otherwise, he was ignored.

CHAPTER 14

Spring 1969—San Diego, California

"Home is a state of mind, not a place," Matthew had cautioned in the first weeks of their marriage.

Although Eden remembered the exact moment when Matthew had counseled her against any emotional attachments to a particular piece of property, she enthusiastically threw herself into the remodeling of her new home. She found that the Del Mar beach location of the white frame cottage she had just bought suited her need for privacy and permitted easy access to the sprawling city of San Diego.

Thoroughly convinced of the potential charm and livability of the twenty-year-old dwelling, she spent her first weeks as a homeowner pulling up old carpeting and stripping the walls of multiple layers of age-stained wallpaper. Eden didn't even try to stop herself from thinking of the cottage as a permanent part of her life, a place where she could put down roots, experiment with paint and wallpaper, hang pictures on the walls, and maybe even finally feel a sense of belonging.

She was determined to turn her house into a home. As she worked, she hoped that Matthew would one day think of it as his home, too, despite the transient mentality the Marine Corps would always expect of him.

She also promised herself that her home would never possess the impersonal qualities of the dormitories in which she'd spent her childhood and adolescence, nor would it have the museumlike echo of her grandmother's mansion. Unlike those places, she decided, her home would house her dreams.

She missed Matthew, longed for him, ached for him, and it saddened her to think of all the simple pleasures he was missing. He should be here, she realized, sharing in the joys and aggravations of turning a collection of boards and nails into a real home.

Still, in her loneliest moments, she reminded herself that she at least had hope for the future no matter how dismal her emotions might become. Many women had only caskets and their memories. Marshaling her hope, Eden used it to advance her sobriety during the long hours, weeks, and eventually months that it took to remodel the small beach house.

It was only at night, when she was alone in the still-unfurnished cottage, surrounded by paint cans and drop cloths and enveloped in her sleeping bag, that she didn't even try to ignore the acutely painful sense of isolation she felt. Being alone had become her reality. It would not go away, and she suspected that it would not end easily or painlessly. Inside herself, she had already begun to accept the fact that she would be alone for a long time, perhaps years, maybe even forever. That thought, that reality, chilled her to the bone.

Eden began testing her decorating skills early in May, effectively utilizing walls she had painted a crisp white and forest-green carpeting as her creative foundation. After supervising the installation of custom-made shutters on all the windows, she selected two large couches in a richly textured cream-colored fabric for the living room and added throw pillows in a contrasting chocolate. She then covered the walls with French Impressionist prints in dark oak frames and scattered clay pots filled with generously limbed ferns throughout the vaulted-ceilinged cottage.

She decided on an oversized brass bed and tall teak bureaus in the master bedroom, and an antique rolltop desk, left to her by her grandmother, graced the spare bedroom/study. A daybed and several bookcases completed the converted room, which also had an added benefit. It contained mementos of Matthew, only recently released from storage by the Marine

Corps. His books, letters written to him by his father prior to the senior Benedict's death in Korea, clothing, and photos taken during various stages of his Marine Corps career, as well as pictures from his childhood. Determined that the room would never become a shrine, she planned to use it as a guest room whenever Tracey had time to visit.

Eden indulged herself with a collection of shining brass pots and pans in the kitchen. Sliding-glass doors on the opposite side of the spacious room led out to a modest fenced patio and garden in addition to offering an unrestricted view of the beachfront and the Pacific. She often began her day seated at the butcher-block table positioned in front of the encompassing view.

It wasn't long before Eden realized that she possessed far too many empty hours. She began having moments of crisis, times when she thought only of Drew and Matthew, mornings when getting out of bed seemed an impossible task, nights when sleep refused to come. She already knew the risks inherent in too much isolation, too much inner thought, too much time spent dwelling on the emotional turmoil that could, if she allowed it, easily consume her. She soon realized that the time had come, once again, to fight back.

"Be honest," Eden challenged herself one morning as she studied her reflection in the mirror above the bureau. "You're just like this house. All dressed up and no place to go. You need people, a life, a *real* life, not this make-believe you've created for yourself." She sighed, and her gaze dropped to a photograph of Matthew. Taken during their courtship, it effectively reminded her of everything that was missing from her life. Suddenly she wanted to scream aloud at the injustice of his captivity.

"Damn it! I'll go crazy if I don't find something to do with myself. I've got to get busy and stay that way." But how? And by doing what? she wondered.

Forcing herself from the bedroom and Matthew's picture, she wandered into the living room. A mug of cooling tea sat on the coffee table, the *San Diego Union* morning edition beside it. Eden dropped to the cushions of the couch and began to scan the headlines, determined to ignore the frustration and bitterness eating at her, as well as the not-so-subtle desire slowing growing inside her for a drink.

She reached the final section of the paper, and an ad reminded her of what Jack Morrison had suggested during their first meeting.

> Volunteers needed. Balboa Naval Hospital—San Diego. Seeking military dependents and civilian personnel, eighteen years of age or older for Red Cross volunteer program. Contact Kitty Hooper, Patient Services. 555-7201.

Jack's observation came back to her. "The medical staff's really hustling down there, and the Red Cross is always looking for volunteers to help the guys in the wards."

Eden reached for the phone. Her thoughts strayed inadvertently to the stack of letters she'd written to Matthew since his capture as she dialed the number listed in the paper. A single page, typed or in longhand, was permitted each week before it was routed through the State Department and then on to the International Red Cross in Switzerland, which would deliver it to Hanoi.

She wondered now, as she wondered each time she wrote to her husband, if he actually received her letters, then quickly told herself that such thoughts were unproductive. She had no control over anything that concerned Matthew, and she wouldn't as long as he was in the hands of the North Vietnamese. Realistically, all she could do was continue to hope and to pray. Frustrated with the direction of her thoughts, Eden reminded herself that the Red Cross was trying to help her. Perhaps, she thought as the phone rang, I can return the favor.

"Patient Services."

Eden tightened her hold on the telephone receiver, determination suddenly growing inside her. "Yes, I'm calling about your ad for volunteers."

"The one we placed in the *Union*?"

"That's right."

"Wonderful! You're my first caller. This is Kitty Hooper. We're expanding our volunteer program here at the hospital. Would you be interested in interviewing for a position with us?"

"I'm interested in hearing about the program. My days and evenings are free."

"If you'll tell me your name, we'll schedule your appointment for tomorrow, then."

"My name is Eden Benedict."

"All right, Eden. I'll look for you at ten in the morning. Have the guard at the gate direct you to my office in the quad behind the administrative offices."

"I'll be there, and thank you." She replaced the receiver and remembered Jack's comment about the "pink palace." She smiled and realized that she was looking forward to seeing the place for herself.

Kitty Hooper glanced up from the completed application form on her desk. She studied the young woman seated on the opposite side of the glass partition, intrigued by her apparent aloofness and composure. An astute judge of character, Kitty sensed that Eden Benedict wasn't typical of the wives of the servicemen she was accustomed to dealing with. Most of the women were outgoing and energetic gypsies, citizens of the world by virtue of their husbands' military careers.

Picking up the telephone, she buzzed her assistant. "Please ask Mrs. Benedict to join me, Grace."

Kitty smiled at Eden and waved her into a chair. "Thank you for coming in today. I must say you've aroused my curiosity."

Eden shot her a puzzled look. "About what?"

"Two things, actually. You haven't listed your husband's duty station on your application form. 'Overseas' covers most of the world. And you've obviously begun a career in the publishing industry. There are book publishers in our area who would appreciate and pay for your skills."

Eden shifted awkwardly in her chair, deciding after several moments of thought that honesty was the only route she could travel at this point in her life even if it had the potential of keeping her from working as a volunteer. "I can understand why you'd be curious. It's not a complicated matter, just one I prefer not to advertise."

Kitty settled back in her chair and removed her glasses. A prominent nose and weak chin didn't detract from the warmth of her personality. "I'm a good listener, Eden."

She nodded. "My husband is missing in action. His F-4 went down over North Vietnam. The Marine Corps has suggested that I remain somewhat anonymous until his status is confirmed."

The older woman felt a twinge of pity, but instinct warned her that the sentiment would not be appreciated.

"I also have personal reasons for maintaining my privacy. When Matthew was shot down seventeen months ago, I was pregnant. Our son"—Eden paused, felt the tenuousness of her control, and cleared her throat—"he died shortly after his birth. I'm now a recovering alcoholic with too much free time. All the unfilled hours are becoming a burden. As to my working for a publisher, I'm not comfortable with the enforced solitude the job often requires. That's basically why I'm here today."

"And you think," Kitty supplied after a brief pause, "that by spending yourself on others, you'll improve your own perspective, as well as the quality of your life?"

Eden exhaled slowly and nodded. She'd begun to relax and realized that the reason was the woman seated across the desk. "I'm hoping that will be the natural result of being a volunteer, aside from the obvious, which is to be of assistance to the patients. The officer shot down with my husband managed to escape, but he was seriously wounded in the process. He spent a year here. In fact, he still returns for physical therapy sessions. He made the original suggestion that I look into the Red Cross volunteer program. Your ad jogged my memory."

Kitty silently studied her, digesting the facts and weighing her own instinctive reaction to Eden. Replacing her glasses, she straightened. "As station director of the Red Cross volunteers, I look for individuals capable of compassion and understanding. I suspect you have a great deal to offer in both those departments."

"I'd like to think I do." Not since Tracey had Eden felt such ease in the presence of another woman. "Whether or not I qualify for the program, I'd like to thank you for making me feel so comfortable."

"It's the only way to get to know people. And people, specifically patients, are my number-one priority. Patients in pain, patients who feel isolated and lonely, patients desperately hungry for compassion. I work at meeting their needs, as do the members of my staff. This isn't just a job, Eden. It's the realization of personal goals. Goals I hope you'll want to share with us, but with one condition."

"Name it," she responded immediately, eager to feel useful and be busy again.

"Our AA program. I want you to sit in on a minimum of three meetings a week during the first six months you're with us. You have a lot to learn, and you'll be under a certain amount of pressure. I want you to have an outlet if things start getting to you."

"I won't miss a meeting," Eden promised. "When would you like me to begin work?"

"How about right now? I've got a ward in Building twenty-six screaming for volunteers, that is, if you don't mind playing gopher for the time being. Actual orientation for new volunteers doesn't begin for another ten days, but I never turn down a willing worker." Eden nodded as Kitty picked up the phone and buzzed Grace. "We need a lab coat and a temporary badge for Eden." She paused. "Just print her name on it. We'll get her a permanent one from supply after her paperwork's been processed. Have Cathy Dunlap take her over to twenty-six when she gets back from lunch."

"Ladies, I want to welcome you to the naval hospital's Red Cross Volunteer Program," Kitty began at orientation a week and a half later. Standing at a lectern in a conference room adjacent to her office, she surveyed the ten women seated in metal folding chairs. "You will participate in a special occupational therapy program recently approved by Captain Blake, as well as numerous other duties which we discussed during your initial interviews.

"As some of you already know, the majority of our patients medevacced from Southeast Asia are in the eighteen to twenty-three age group. Our function is to assist in making their recoveries as comfortable and as smooth as possible. We work in concert with the medical personnel who care for them. Compassion is the key word in your work as a volunteer."

Kitty removed her glasses and rubbed the bridge of her nose. "You will note that I have not used the words sympathy or pity. These young men and women are not to be pitied. They don't want it, and they won't stand for it." Replacing her thick-lensed spectacles, she looked around the room and allowed those assembled time to absorb the full import of her comments.

"Is this an ambitious undertaking? Yes! Will it be a difficult task at times? Most assuredly! For each one of you here today, five have been rejected. This is not a glamorous job, and our standards are extremely high. Our younger volunteers have been cautioned against personal relationships with the patients. The more mature of our group have been counseled against expressing their maternal instincts. This advice is based on past errors in judgment made by volunteers who are no longer with us. You *will* be expected to listen attentively when a patient needs to talk no matter how shocking or painful the tale. You'll write letters, empty bedpans, and feed those men and women who cannot feed themselves.

"When a corpsman isn't available, you'll change soiled linens and remake the beds. If, at any time, you feel you are dealing with a patient who is losing control, you will immediately call a qualified staff member who is properly trained to handle a patient's physical or emotional crisis. Under no circumstances are you to play nurse or doctor. You could endanger a patient, as well as yourself." Kitty paused and looked around the room. "Everyone with me so far?"

The women, without exception, nodded soberly. Eden glanced at several of her peers and noted that no one seemed deterred by the commitment being asked of them.

"Good. Now, since you'll be assigned to a specific ward for eight weeks at a time, you'll be expected to keep a daily record of your patient contact. Clipboards and the appropriate forms will be issued to you at the end of our orientation course. I cannot even begin to stress the importance of these forms. The program depends upon your consistency and compassion with the patients, as well as your record-keeping abilities," Kitty warned. "In six months the occupational therapy portion of this program will be reviewed by Captain Blake. He will then decide if we are providing a valuable service to the patients.

"If you have a problem, come to me. If you've taken on too much by volunteering for the occupational therapy aspects of the program, stay after this meeting and you will be reassigned. To quote the navy, 'This job isn't light duty.' It will demand a great deal of you personally and emotionally. Your sole reward will be the satisfaction of a job well done."

Kitty went on to explain certain portions of the therapy-program procedures. She assured each woman that she would be well versed in the techniques prior to assisting the patients. Captain Blake, the naval hospital administrator, spoke briefly, as did the director of nursing, a dour-faced woman who had been on active duty for more than twenty years. She provided them with a cursory description of the nursing staff and left each volunteer with a distinctly uneasy feeling.

The door to the conference room closed, and Kitty smiled ruefully as she surveyed her volunteers. "Captain Bell is not altogether thrilled with this program. She is justifiably concerned that her nurses will spend a lot of time baby-sitting volunteers instead of doing the jobs they're trained for. This is a good time to remind each of you that you aren't nurses. It takes years to acquire those skills. I trust you will all exercise sound judgment and never presume to interfere with the tasks of the nursing personnel."

"If she doesn't approve of us, won't she convey her resistance to the nurses in charge of the wards?" a volunteer asked. Eden noticed that the faces of several of the women in the room displayed similar concern.

"Captain Bell is a stickler for procedure, but she's always fair. The bottom line is very simple, ladies. We'll have to win the skeptics over to our way of thinking, and the only way to accomplish that is to do one hell of a good job." Kitty glanced at her watch and smiled. "Your next challenge is to locate the cafeteria with the maps you were given earlier today. Since the hospital complex occupies approximately seventy-six acres, I would caution those of you unfamiliar with the area to follow Grace Luna, my assistant. She usually goes to lunch about this time."

Eden smothered a grin. She recalled her own confusion during her first day at the naval hospital. Because the buildings weren't numbered in sequence, it was very easy to get lost at the "pink palace." She gathered her purse, notebook, and first-aid manual together and followed the others as they moved toward the door.

"Eden, stay a moment, please," Kitty requested.

She waited as Kitty collected her papers from the top of the lectern. Once they were alone, Kitty told her, "I've spoken to Captain Blake. He's asked me to assure you that your privacy with regard to your husband's status will be respected."

"Thank him for me, won't you?"

"Jim Blake's a reasonable man. I've known him and his wife for several years. Gloria Blake and I went to college together back in Chicago. They were both very empathetic to your situation." She studied Eden for a moment, her serious expression adding to the lines on her face. "There is one thing I want to caution you against, though. You're the only volunteer whose husband is a POW. You're also at a very vulnerable stage in your own life. You're looking for an outlet for a lot of emotion you've been forced to suppress during the last year and a half."

Eden paled. "Have you reconsidered about admitting me to the volunteer program?"

"Of course not! Don't be foolish. I want you in the program. What I'm trying so ineptly to get at is this: You can't risk devoting yourself totally to the patients. The hospital can only be a part of your life. If you make it your entire focus, you'll stop coping with your own personal problems. I don't want you here at the risk of your peace of mind somewhere down the road. It wouldn't be fair to you."

Eden released the breath she'd been holding. "I know what you mean. I made that mistake with my son. I learned a very painful lesson when he died." She knew she would never forget her agony over Drew's death or her struggle for sobriety, but she also knew that she had made a very real commitment to life and living in recent months. "Your caution is justified, Kitty, but please don't worry, because I do understand what you're saying. Sometimes it's easier to ignore the pain by jumping feet first into another situation, but the solution is usually short-lived."

Kitty patted her shoulder. "Good girl. Now go have some lunch."

Orientation lasted two full weeks. Nurses taught the women to change dressings, constantly stressing the importance of gentle handling of surgical wounds. The trainees made and unmade beds until they loathed the sterile white sheeting placed under and over a patient.

The art of emptying a bedpan became less of a joke when two of the volunteers missed and soaked their feet. They practiced chart logging, memorized ten-syllable Latin medical terms, and attended four days of intensive instruction devoted to emergency first aid. The women focused on the basics of occupational therapy during the second week, learning, to their collective surprise, that something as simple as assembling a model airplane could enhance the dexterity of combat-damaged fingers.

Dress codes became an issue when the youngest member of the group, an admiral's nineteen-year-old daughter, arrived at the hospital one morning in a thigh-exposing miniskirt and knee-high white boots, her long hair frizzed and hanging down to her waist. Kitty wryly suggested that she "save that getup for go-go dançing" and handed her a lab coat and a rubber band before she could cause a riot on her ward.

Eden felt both exhausted and exhilarated by the time orientation came to a close. Her days at the hospital would begin the following Monday after morning rounds. Committed to a six-hour shift in a ward each day, she planned to work five days on and two days off. She also insisted that in the future she be considered for weekend duty, a time she knew the majority of the volunteers would want to spend with their families.

After a light meal and a long walk on the beach, Eden still couldn't sleep despite the late hour. On impulse, she dialed the number of Tracey's New York hotel.

"Hullo?" a sleepy voice mumbled after several rings.

"Hi, Trace."

"Eden? What's wrong?"

"Not a thing. I just couldn't sleep."

"I wasn't having any trouble sleeping. Lord! It's two A.M. here, and I have to be up at dawn."

"But tomorrow's Saturday."

"Tell that to the agency's cola king. The man is driving me up a wall. He will not make up his mind on the presentations we've been working up for him. And now David's convinced the man's hot for my body."

"Are you alone?"

"Of course I'm alone. I don't like cola. You know that," she huffed.

"Where's David?"

"Washington, where else? He had to stay because of a reception at the White House."

"You're not going?"

"Tomorrow, after I finish with my cola king. Why all the questions?"

Eden laughed. "It always takes you at least five minutes to wake up. Sixty questions usually does the trick."

Tracey yawned loudly. "Well, I'm awake now. You know, don't you, that if you were here right now, I'd have your fanny for that crack."

"No pun intended?"

"God," she groaned. "Are you sober?"

"Of course. Stone-cold sober, as a matter of fact. Aren't I allowed to call my best friend and say a friendly hello once in a while?"

"You're in an awfully mellow mood for the middle of the night. And yes, you're allowed to call . . . despite the obnoxious hour."

"Think of it as early," Eden suggested with a smile. "And in response to your observation—yes, I am in a good mood."

"What's going on? When we talked a few weeks ago, you were still heavily into interior decoration."

"I just finished my Red Cross orientation at the naval hospital. I'm worn out, but I'm excited, too."

"Eden, we were candy stripers for a month in high school. Aren't there any decent publishers in San Diego?"

She laughed. "Being a Red Cross volunteer is definitely not the same as candy striping. I won't just be pushing a book cart up and down the halls this time."

Tracey sighed. "So tell me about the hospital."

"It's great."

"If you like hospitals."

"Not everyone on this planet passes out at the sight of a Band-Aid, Sinclair."

"I wasn't that bad!"

"Close, very close," Eden insisted. "I start working with the patients next week."

"Oh, that's nice," she commented, her tone lukewarm. "I was going to call you tomorrow before I left for Washington."

"And tell me what?"

"Big news," she teased.

"Did David finally break down and propose?"

"How did you guess?"

"The man's crazy about you. He has been since he first set eyes on you. Despite my alcoholic haze last fall, it was obvious to me that it was just a matter of time before David popped the question."

"He wasn't going to, not at first," Tracey admitted. "I kind of pressed the issue."

"How and why?" Eden asked, somewhat puzzled.

"He's ten years older than I am, and that bothered him a lot. He'll probably get orders to Vietnam again, and that didn't help at all. So I accused him of having the willies about marriage because he was afraid of committing himself. I also told him that if he didn't love me enough to take a chance on us, then I wouldn't be standing around twiddling my thumbs for much longer. I chewed him out one night and suggested he retreat to Washington or wherever macho marines go when they need to smarten up."

She grinned. "How long did it take him to come to his senses?"

"Less than forty-eight hours, thank God. It's a good thing he didn't take any longer, Eden. I was down to my last long fingernail."

"That's our Tracey. A woman with the heart of an Amazon and the tact of an earth mover."

"As George Patton was fond of saying, 'I don't go into battle expecting to lose.' "

"Since when do you quote generals?"

"David might be one someday," she replied airily. "I've been studying all about them."

"When's the big day?"

"That's the best part. David got his orders yesterday. That's one of the reasons why I was going to call you in the morning . . . This morning," she amended. "We're going to be stationed at Camp Pendleton."

Eden grinned. "That's right up the freeway from me."

"I know. We're going to have our wedding at the base chapel. Dress blues and an arch of swords. The entire Marine Corps tradition. How would you like a temporary roommate as of August fifteenth? I'm selling the Malibu house, putting everything in storage temporarily, and giving my boss two months to replace me. David doesn't report till the end of September, but I thought I'd get an early start on the festivities if I can stay with you."

"Trace, you don't even have to ask. The guest room is waiting for you. But why give up your career? Can't you and David live smack between L.A. and the base? It wouldn't be a bad commute for either one of you."

"As much as I'd like to, it's just not possible. My boss wants me to accept a permanent transfer to the New York office, but David and I don't want to live on opposite ends of the country once we're married. It's been tough enough conducting a courtship this way. I am giving serious thought to starting my own business after we're married and settled. Something small, of course, but it would mean I could stay in advertising. I'm not sure yet. Time will tell." After several moments of silence, Tracey finally asked, "What's wrong? Do you think I'm making a mistake?"

"Oh, no. Not at all." Eden mentally chastised herself for dwelling on her own concerns in the face of Tracey's happy news. She knew she was being selfish when she let her thoughts stray to Matthew, but in this instance she just couldn't help herself. She wanted to be happy, too, and she wanted a chance to plan a future with the man *she* loved. "I was just wondering if David's heard anything new lately?"

Tracey sighed. "I'm afraid not. Not as of last night, anyway."

"What about my letters? Does he know yet if any of them have gotten through to Matthew?"

"He says the Marine Corps and the State Department are doing everything they can. The negotiators are trying to get a guarantee from the North Vietnamese that they're abiding by the Geneva Convention. The International Red Cross is trying to get a list of the prisoners as well as provide the men with the mail that's being routed to them from State. Even the foreign press has been approached now that Hanoi is allowing them to see a few of the POWs. Everyone in Casualty Assistance is at the finger-crossing stage, but, Eden, what I've just told you isn't news. You know how touchy the situation is, especially since Matt hasn't been officially listed as a POW."

"Damn it!" she exclaimed in utter frustration. "Why not? He's alive, Trace. I'm certain of it."

"I believe you."

Eden laughed, the sound jagged, frayed. "What an insane way to live!" She took a steadying breath. "Are any of the wives getting mail from the men?"

"A few, according to David. He's planning on flying out to see you next week. He was going to call you and tell you Sunday night. But back to the letters. I don't know their names, but apparently some of the women receive an occasional letter through regular mail. Don't ask me why. Nobody at Headquarters Marine Corps or State has been able to figure it out."

Eden rubbed her temples. "I'll just keep writing, then."

"You don't really have any other choice, do you?"

"Choice? What's that? I haven't even included the word in my vocabulary since Matthew was shot down. Maybe that's why this situation hurts so much. We don't have *any* choices to make. We're pawns, totally at the mercy of people we'll never even know." She swallowed the sob caught in her throat. "I miss him so much. Sometimes I wake up at night expecting to find him next to me. We only shared a bed for a few months, and I actually find myself reaching for him in the middle of the night. But all I ever wind up with is a fistful of sheets."

"I think we'd better change the subject before this conversation gets too maudlin. What do you say?" Tracey asked with a note of forced cheerfulness in her voice.

"Oh, Trace, I'm sorry. I didn't mean to put a pall on your good news."

"You couldn't. I still haven't scraped myself off the ceiling," she admitted with a giggle.

"I really am happy for you and David. You'll have a good marriage, I know you will."

"I think so, too," Tracey agreed happily before changing the subject. "Satisfy my curiosity, will you? What made you decide to do volunteer work in a military hospital? I know Jack Morrison gave you the original idea, but I'm still surprised. It's the last place I'd expect to find you, especially now. I really thought you'd go back to graduate school once you got the house under control."

"It was either that or start building sand castles in the backyard," she confessed. "I've changed so much I don't even recognize myself anymore. But one thing is certain, I need to feel useful, have a sense of purpose about my life. You never know, maybe I'll even be able to do some good. I know I already feel better about myself and I haven't actually begun working with the patients yet."

"What are they like?"

"Young," she answered quietly. "Very, very young, but their eyes are old. They've seen so much death and destruction, and yet most of them are only nineteen or twenty years old. That was the real shock, Trace, even though I read the daily news accounts of the war. I've always equated war with men, not young guys a year or two out of high school."

Tracey hesitated briefly before asking, "They don't remind you of Matt?"

"Of course they do, but in a positive way. It's hard to explain. Once you get out here, I'll take you down to the hospital and show you around. When you meet a few of the patients and some of the Red Cross volunteers, I think you'll understand what I'm talking about."

"The real world, or at least a part of it," Tracey mused aloud.

"It's about damn time, isn't it? You know, I sometimes think we grew up in a test tube labeled 'socially acceptable.' " She laughed ruefully. "I can't begin to tell you how relieved I am to discover there's more for us than duplicate copies of Barclay Acres and Sinclair Manor."

Tracey laughed. "Strange, isn't it? We thought we were so independent and mature, but it took Matt and David to give us a real taste of life and living."

"And loving," Eden amended softly.

"Amen to that."

After they ended their conversation, Eden reflected on the new Tracey. With David's love and understanding, her friend's life was no longer tainted by the loneliness of a miserable childhood. She was with the man she loved, and they would have a good life together. Eden was happy for her, but she still couldn't deny or dismiss the envy she also felt.

She sank back against the pillows on her bed, thinking that while Matthew's absence now forced her to seek a new identity for herself, his entry into her life a few years earlier had encouraged her to walk away from the protective environment her grandmother had created for her after the death of her parents. She recalled her initial fear and how overwhelmed she'd felt by the enormity of what he was asking of her, but her love for him had negated all other considerations. She'd slipped into the world of wife and lover with surprising ease. The seeming effortlessness of loving had astounded and delighted her, then and now.

Tears filled her eyes, tears of regret and sadness for all the love building inside her that had no outlet. She was tired of passing sleepless nights alone in a bed she should have been sharing with Matthew, and she was even more tired of hugging herself for warmth and reassurance when the isolation and loneliness she felt became so intense that she couldn't quell the sobs born deep in her soul. But, most of all, she was tired of fearing for her husband's safety, his very survival, on a minute-by-minute basis.

Wiping the tears from her face, Eden sternly reminded herself that working at the naval hospital represented not only another in a series of dramatic life changes but also a new sense of focus and direction that had already begun to improve the quality of her world. She would have to learn to live with the helplessness she felt where Matthew was concerned. She had no other choice.

Take satisfaction in the fact that you're growing as a person, she counseled herself. The rest will come when the time is right. Still, she couldn't help but wonder if, alone and frightened, she had the patience and ability to wait, especially since she knew firsthand how easy it would be to fall from the emotional tightrope she'd been forced to walk since Matthew's designation as an MIA statistic.

She fell asleep a few hours later, no closer to the answers she'd been seeking for so many months, lulled by the persistent waves lapping at the shoreline beyond her bedroom window, and listening to Grace Slick and the Jefferson Airplane ask, "Don't you *want* somebody to love? Don't you *need* somebody to love?"

CHAPTER

15

Summer 1969—Hanoi, North Vietnam

Texture.

He skimmed his callused fingertips along a warm velvet length. He realized that he'd forgotten the texture of her, forgotten the feel of supple flesh and the fragrance of scrubbed, healthy skin.

He felt the subtle transformation when coarse grains of sand turned to cool satin beneath his body. Trade winds undulated in the hibiscus-scented air. The moon glowed like a beacon in the midnight sky, defining her shape, enhancing her uninhibited beauty. She pressed herself closer to him, leaning into his hands so that he could cup her breasts.

He strained for contact, his mouth finding her jutting nipples as he grasped the now writhing form whose abundant hair veiled their motions.

Feminine hips surged against his, inviting, welcoming, encompassing.

Two became one as their bodies merged. He felt his senses heighten, expand, then threaten to detonate.

She gasped at the sensation overcoming her, and he increased their pace. He felt her stiffen, and he watched, mesmerized, as she tilted her head back, her throat arched and vulnerable. Bared, gritted teeth muffled her cry of release. He gratefully bore her weight when she collapsed atop him. Shudders racking him, his life force exploded within her.

Sprawled across him, her heart pounded like a triphammer.

He heard her whisper, "A small death so that we can live again."

He tightened his hold on her and rolled their still-joined flesh to one side. Smoothing back the auburn drape that cloaked their upper bodies, he pressed his lips to her damp forehead.

"I love you, paleface."

Her silence made him draw back. He saw her sad smile. Unseen hands drew her from his embrace. His arms no longer filled, he reached out, only to be plagued by a lassitude he did not understand. An invisible weight pressed down on him, holding him in place, but it could not contain his seeking hands as he tried to reach for her.

"Don't leave me. I need you. Eden?"

"Be safe, my love."

He struggled upright, fighting the force that pressed against him, his eyes frantic as he tried to pierce the dense mist enveloping her retreating nakedness. Defeat made him slump back into the sand, now coarse and unforgiving as it scored his skin.

The scrape of his knuckles against the cement wall of his cell awakened him. Matt groaned in frustration. He heard the raggedness of his own breathing and felt the wetness soaking his lower body. Triumph and despair bled together in his veins, sadness reverberating in his mind like the unending echo of a discordant horn.

How long, he wondered, have I gone without the knowledge that I am a man? After months of isolation, months of boredom, and months fearing for my life and my sanity, I now know that I can make love to my wife.

He laughed, the sound wealthy with anger and bitterness. There are no solutions, he reminded himself. There is only survival. And days and nights marked by loneliness and any diversion I can think up that will keep me from shrieking myself into the arms of madness.

He shuddered at the thought and fell back against the thin bedroll covering the cement slab he called a bed. He stared unseeing into the blackness that entombed him, his great dark eyes glistening with tears.

CHAPTER 16

August–October 1969—San Diego, California

"Passengers from American Airlines Flight Sixty-one are now arriving at Gate Five, Concourse B."

Eden stood and stretched, relieved that Tracey's flight was on time. As the last of the passengers straggled from the umbilicallike corridor linking the jet to the terminal, she spotted Tracey. The vivacious blonde balanced an armload of carry-on luggage while she chatted with a fellow traveler, an attractive man who appeared to be in his mid-thirties.

Eden smiled, forgot her fatigue, and raised a hand in greeting. She laughed aloud when Tracey shoved her bags into the arms of the man walking beside her and made her way through the milling crowd.

Clasping Eden's hands, Tracey studied her with a smile. "You look wonderful."

"So do you. Being engaged must agree with you."

She lifted her left hand and displayed a two-karat diamond. "Isn't it fantastic?"

Eden's expression softened. "It's beautiful, but then David is a very lucky man." They grinned at one another and embraced. "Now, are you going to tell me what's going on? Why did you change your plans at the last minute? I thought you were supposed to fly into L.A., get your car, and then drive down to my place."

Tracey rolled her eyes heavenward. "A friend was using my car while I finished my work in New York this week. She managed to total it three days ago. Fortunately, she walked away from the accident without a scratch. My last day of work was yesterday, the house is sold, and everything's in storage till David and I are married." She shrugged. "It seemed kind of silly not to fly directly here, especially since I can buy a new car in San Diego."

"I can't fault your reasoning," she agreed before glancing at the man standing nearby. Eden tensed slightly when she saw the almost intimate smile on his face as he watched her. She quickly masked her reaction to him and told herself that she was imagining things, although she couldn't quite ignore the fact that he didn't seem the least bit annoyed that Tracey had parked her luggage in his arms. "But I do feel sorry for your friend. He's beginning to resemble a Himalayan Sherpa."

"Don't worry about Jim. He's tough." Tracey turned and motioned him forward. "Eden, meet Jim Clayton, an old friend of David's from Washington. He's going to be working in San Diego for the next year or so."

She smiled, briefly met his eyes, and then reached to relieve him of Tracey's cosmetic case. "Welcome to California."

Somehow he managed to make certain that their hands touched before he released his hold on the piece of luggage. "I've heard a lot about you, Eden. It's nice to finally be able to put a face to your name."

She felt the appraising quality of his gaze, and a bright neon caution sign flashed in her mind. Men had openly inspected her in the past, but it had been a long time since anyone had been so obvious, so male on the make. This man made her feel particularly uneasy, and she instinctively resented him and the unwelcome emotion he provoked. Experiencing an almost urgent need to flee his probing eyes, she focused on Tracey and didn't bother to conceal her irritation. "Let's get the rest of your bags."

Startled by the sharpness of Eden's voice, Tracey looked up from the shoulder strap she was adjusting. "I told Jim we could drop him at his hotel after we got all the luggage together. You don't mind, do you?"

She shook her head, turned, and started down the concourse, determined to ignore Tracey's friend.

"Eden?"

She stopped, told herself to calm down, and turned to face them. "Sorry, Trace, I've had a long day. I must be more tired than I thought," she finished tightly.

"You worked at the hospital today?"

Eden nodded. "In orthopedics."

"Tell me about it," Tracey invited as she moved forward to walk beside her. They conversed quietly as they made their way through the airport.

Jim Clayton followed at a discreet distance. He didn't take his gaze from Eden's willowy figure, nor did he speak to her again.

Eden appreciated his verbal restraint but not the feeling that he was touching her with his eyes. Just the idea of such intimacy unnerved her, and she quickened her pace, but down deep inside herself she couldn't deny that she suddenly felt alive and desirable instead of like a facsimile of the woman she'd once been.

Although she had no desire to explore the reasons for her intense reaction to Tracey and David's Nordic-looking friend, her mind refused to abandon them. Not since Matthew had she been so conscious of herself as a woman—a woman capable of attracting and holding the attention of a man. She felt guilty and uncertain and reminded herself of how disloyal she was being to even consider being flattered that a man other than her husband could make her feel so acutely aware of her own femininity and sexuality.

Later that night, Eden and Tracey settled in for a lengthy session of verbal catch-up. Although they spoke frequently on the telephone, they hadn't seen one another since Tracey's trip to New York in March.

Seated at the butcher-block table in the beach-house kitchen, the two sipped mugs of hot tea and snacked on crackers and cheese while they talked. Eden didn't even blink when

Tracey asked the one question she'd been expecting since Jim's exit from her car.

"Why were you so rude to Jim at the airport? He's really a terrific guy."

"Was I rude?"

"You know you were."

She shrugged, the gesture deceptively casual, given the emotions still seething inside her. "Chalk it up to lousy chemistry. I just didn't like him, that's all. I guess he's not my type."

"He may not be your type, but I didn't realize you'd given up making friends."

"I don't want him for a friend," she answered bluntly.

"Eden! You haven't even given the guy a chance. You'd like him if you let yourself get to know him. He's got a great sense of humor, he's intelligent, he has a good education, and he reads like a fiend. You two actually have a lot in common."

She looked away, her facial expression closed. "Sorry, Trace, no sale."

Her eyes widened with sudden understanding. "He appeals to you, and you feel guilty, don't you? My God, Eden, he may be attractive, but I'm not suggesting you sleep with him. I just thought you could get to know one another casually before the wedding. It'll make things easier all the way around."

"I didn't like his attitude."

"He was very pleasant until you snarled at him. Besides, he's going to be in the wedding party."

"Wonderful!" Trying to control a temper she'd only recently discovered in herself, Eden stood and walked to the stove. Without turning to look at Tracey, she repeated, "I don't like the man. He makes me uncomfortable. And don't start reading things into what I'm saying, because there's nothing Freudian about my reaction to him."

Tracey followed her across the kitchen. Leaning against the counter edge, she watched Eden fill their mugs with freshly steeped tea. "Could you at least be polite to him? If not for my sake, then for David?"

She glanced up, the confusion she felt hidden behind her composed features. "If it means that much to you."

"It does." Tracey returned to her chair, followed by Eden. "Jim's wife divorced him while he was overseas a few years ago. I think he does some kind of classified work for the government. David told me he's spent the last couple of years in and out of Southeast Asia, but whenever the guys talk about his job, they get really secretive if I'm in the room. I'm dying of curiosity."

Eden sighed softly and reminded herself of what a mule Tracey could be when she got her teeth into a particular subject. The personality trait was probably very helpful in the advertising career she'd chosen for herself, but it had a tendency to drive her friends up a wall when she didn't exercise a little control.

"Trace, he probably saw and did things that are best forgotten. You know as well as I do that the reports coming out of Vietnam are censored, in spite of what the press and the military would like us to believe." Eden fingered the rim of her cup before saying, "What Jim Clayton does or does not do in Vietnam, or anyplace else, doesn't directly affect either one of us. He can keep his secrets. I'm not interested, and you shouldn't be, either."

"He's not like most of David's Marine Corps friends," Tracey persisted. "I don't know what to make of him a lot of the time, but I know I feel sorry for him. He seems lonely, but if I try to draw him out, he clams up on me."

Eden laughed and shook her head. "David's going to love being married to the world's number-one collector of strays. Look, Jim Clayton's probably with the CIA. If that's the case, then no one will ever get beyond the facade he's erected."

Tracey absently nodded, her attention momentarily on the cheese she was spreading on a cracker.

Eden's thoughts wandered, as they often did when any mention was made of the war in Vietnam. She reflected on the altered relationships and strained reunions she'd witnessed in her three months at the naval hospital. Men with weary eyes and bodies trembling with fatigue and injury greeted youthful wives who hadn't the slightest clue of what their twenty- and twenty-one-year-old husbands had confronted in a jungle war.

She'd already seen too many marriages disintegrate in a matter of weeks when the novelty of being a wifely martyr wore off and the cold, hard reality of amputated arms and legs, blindness, or some other malady would not permit a return to the past. The young women panicked and bolted, while the patients lowered their expectations and learned that survival was a lonely business.

She realized, too, that by accepting the responsibility of waiting for Matthew, she had also learned the loneliness of survival.

Eden shivered and wondered what it would be like when Matthew returned. What unspeakable horrors will he have experienced? How wide will the gulf be between us? She also wondered if the realities would destroy the euphoria of reunion. If they ever had a reunion, she grudgingly amended.

Closing her eyes against the direction of her thoughts, she inhaled sharply against the emptiness throbbing inside her. Jim Clayton reminded her of her vulnerability as a woman, and despite the fact that she knew she was being unreasonable, she loathed him for that unwelcome gift.

"We're different now, aren't we?" Tracey asked in a small voice.

Eden opened her eyes, the emerald pools filled with resignation. "Don't you mean less innocent?"

Tracey nodded reluctantly. "How are you really doing?"

She exhaled softly before responding. "I go from day to day. Some are better than others. The hospital, the guys in the wards—they keep me sane. I probably need them more than they need me." She looked away. "Do you think Matthew will still want me if he ever comes home, Trace? I know I'm not the person he fell in love with. I've changed so much. There's no softness left in me. Sometimes I feel like I've simply become a collection of hard edges, ready to defend myself against one more disappointment or one more siege of reality. A man in my ward asked me the other day why I never smile. I didn't know how to answer him," she whispered bleakly.

"I'm not like the other POW wives. They're becoming visible and vocal about the men. It's all I can do to stay sober and on track. What's wrong with me? Why can't I be stronger, tougher?"

"Nothing's wrong with you, so don't be so damned hard on yourself. None of those women buried their baby a year ago. You're doing the best you can, probably better than most."

"I want to believe you're right, but I don't know anymore."

"I feel guilty," Tracey admitted.

"What on earth for?"

"I have so much to look forward to. While a part of me wants to share everything that's happening in my life with you, another part of me is afraid that all I'm doing is reminding you of what you don't have. Kind of like rubbing salt into an open wound."

Eden straightened, brushed the tears from her cheeks, and managed a wide, if watery, smile. "Don't you dare feel guilty. I'll be all right. I've made it through the last couple of years, and I'll cope with this mess for as long as I have to. Besides, don't you know it's a rule that brides are supposed to be happy all the time? And you've earned all the beautiful bridal memories you're about to have. No more talk about sad things. Let's concentrate on getting you ready to walk down the aisle." She stuck out her hand and grasped Tracey's. "Deal?"

She grinned. "Deal."

Eden reached for a pad of paper and a pencil from a kitchen drawer behind her chair. "First, your wedding invitations."

"Mailed yesterday before I left New York. Two hundred of them."

"Good, that's the biggest headache of all. I've already contacted the base chapel and the officers' club at Camp Pendleton and made your reservations for you. You have an appointment to see the chaplain next week. The club'll cater the food for the reception. And I've got a bakery in La Jolla lined up for the wedding cake, so all you really have to do is pick out your gown and your flowers."

"Sounds easy."

"Don't kid yourself. Weddings are notorious for getting

screwed up at the last minute." Eden smiled. "We'll have to keep our fingers crossed and stay very organized."

"That's your job. My first priority is a tan. It's August, and I'm winter white from working year round."

Eden glanced at her watch and grimaced. With luck she'd manage five hours of sleep before her alarm sounded. "Why don't we finish this list tomorrow? I've got to be at the hospital early." She stood, walked to the sink, and rinsed their mugs.

"I'm beat, too. The time change has made me feel like my head's stuffed with cotton." Tracey followed her down the hallway. "Oh, while I'm thinking about it, don't worry about cooking while I'm here. I'll take kitchen duty for the time being."

Eden smiled and gave her a quick hug. "Sounds good to me. And Trace, I promise you this will be the best wedding ever."

Labor Day weekend unfolded in sharp contrast to the events of the preceding year. Drew's death and Eden's siege of alcoholism following his burial went unmentioned.

Eden and Tracey basked in the tropical sunshine bathing the southern California coastline, as did thousands of others who were equally determined to usher the summer out on a festive note. Eden regretted her weekend away from the hospital only once. Jim Clayton's unexpected arrival during the last afternoon of the holiday jarred her from the relaxed and lighthearted atmosphere at the beach.

Ignoring the tension between Eden and Jim, Tracey eagerly accepted his invitation to dinner that evening at Anthony's Harborside. Tracey's enthusiasm kept Eden from objecting, but it didn't diminish her frustration with herself for allowing a stranger to cause emotional havoc inside her. Several days passed before she was able to rid herself of the memory of his inviting smile and forget her instinctive reaction to his blatant sensuality.

September passed in a blur of prewedding activities. Tracey selected a fitted floor-length gown of organza and French lace. A crown of seed pearls with a veil and train of matching lace, organza-covered heels, and silk lingerie completed her bridal ensemble. Eden's gown, a powder-blue creation also of organza, was a more subtle reflection of the elegance and style of Tracey's traditional wedding dress.

Tracey decided on red tea roses for her bridal bouquet. Her choice was in keeping with the scarlet trouser stripe of the dress-blue winter uniforms the men in the wedding party would wear, as was the single long-stem red rose Eden would carry as her matron of honor. By the time David checked into Camp Pendleton the first week of October, all the arrangements were complete.

It rained the morning of the wedding. After reassuring the bride that the sudden cloudburst was part of the nuptial traditions, Eden employed a combination of maiden-aunt determination and threats to life and limb before she succeeded in coercing a suddenly panicked Tracey into the limo hired to take them to the base chapel.

As she stood beside her best friend at the altar, Eden felt the strength of the military presence that frequently required extreme sacrifices of the brides it so traditionally welcomed. She knew from personal experience that the Camp Pendleton chapel wasn't simply a setting for shared pledges and promises of the future. Its unadorned decor, typical of most military chapels because of their multidenominational use, and the profusion of red-and-white roses in baskets atop the altar and along the center aisle effectively enhanced and emphasized the delicate balance that existed between devotion to duty and marital commitment.

Eden also realized that the Marine Corps could and would take precedence over Tracey and David's marriage in the years ahead, just as it already had in her marriage to Matthew. It was a reality she had learned to live with. She silently prayed that Tracey would be willing to understand and adjust to the uncertainties of being a military wife.

Eden knew from personal experience that war, even an undeclared one like the one in Vietnam, tended to minimize all other commitments, and she seriously doubted that anyone could actually prepare herself for sacrifice and loneliness. She had not been prepared in those silent moments just before dawn when she had realized that something devastating had happened to Matthew. Fate had somehow managed to sweep him from her mental grasp, and no one seemed able or willing to retrieve him, then or now. He had become a victim not simply of war but of political maneuvering.

She sighed softly, refocused on Tracey and David, and knew in her heart that there was really no one left to blame for Matthew's misfortune, not even God.

As she listened to Tracey speak, her voice faint and trembling as she repeated her vows, Eden remembered a simpler but equally poignant ceremony. She remembered the resonant sound of Matthew's voice as he pledged his love and loyalty until death could part them. She remembered the startling intensity of his large dark eyes as he watched her. She remembered the feel of his hands clasping hers and the nervousness that made her fingers shake as she accepted the sculpted gold band he'd chosen for her as a symbol of their marriage. She remembered her awe not only at the fact that he wanted her so completely but that he was willing to say so in front of God and to the world. She remembered how freeing and how limitless their love had felt that day.

And she remembered the barely restrained passion of his kiss, their first kiss as husband and wife, after the priest had said, "What God has joined together, let no man put asunder."

Eden watched Tracey, her slender fingers covered by David's sturdier ones, lower the blade of her husband's ceremonial sword into the multitiered wedding cake. The flash unit of the photographer's camera momentarily blinded her, and she closed her eyes. When she opened them, Jim Clayton stood in front of her. She inhaled sharply, but she held her ground.

Without understanding why, Eden accepted one of the two champagne goblets he held. She frowned, her eyes traveling between the pale liquid and the smile on his face, and then she trembled. When the chilled wine sloshed over the rim of the stemmed crystal and wet her fingers, she handed it to a passing waiter.

"I don't drink, Mr. Clayton." She looked away, her expression cold, dismissive. My mother used to look like this when she was annoyed, Eden realized. The thought was less than comforting.

"The lady doesn't drink, the lady doesn't smile, and the lady rarely speaks . . . to me," he observed, curiosity and speculation in his tone. "What does the lady do?"

A part of her, she realized in quiet desperation, was eager to play his game and indulge in banter rife with sexual innuendo. She wanted to walk into his arms and feel the power of his male body while they danced with all the other couples celebrating the wedding of two good friends. She wanted to relax. She wanted to stop being on guard all the time. And she was so hungry for the tenderness she'd glimpsed in his eyes when he wasn't playing the wolf that she ached.

Another part of her, the rational part, the good girl, the married woman, the sensible part of herself, the part of her that comprehended the insanity of such behavior, was outraged, even horrified. In her mind Eden knew she wasn't a whore or a tramp, although there were those who would accuse her of that kind of behavior if they somehow managed to guess her turbulent thoughts. She was just a woman alone, a woman who had made commitments, a woman who felt very nearly plowed under by the weight of those commitments, even though she was determined to honor them even as she skirted the periphery of her best friend's happiness.

Jim frowned when he saw the array of emotions in her face and eyes. He lifted his free hand, intending to offer some kind of reassurance, but he paused when he saw her flinch at the prospect of being touched.

"I'm busy. What is it that you want?" she asked, sudden fatigue making her sound prim and formal.

He smiled, but the pleasantness of his expression didn't reach his eyes. "I want a great deal. Most people do."

Eden balled her fists into lumps of frustration to keep herself from striking the look of seductive male self-assurance from his face. "What does what you want have to do with me?"

Jim sipped his champagne, casually shifting his gaze from

her tensely set shoulders and white-knuckled fists to the anger blazing in her eyes. "You've been avoiding me. Why?"

"I'm busy," she repeated. "This is Tracey and David's day."

"They'll be leaving for their honeymoon in less than an hour. What's your excuse going to be then?"

"I don't need excuses not to see you, Mr. Clayton. Our lives aren't even remotely connected. The only thing we have in common is friendship with the Markhams, and that's hardly cause for a relationship between us."

"Jim."

She peered at him questioningly, almost as though he'd spoken in a foreign language. "What?"

"Call me Jim." He paused and let his eyes drift across her pale face. "I think I know what you're capable of, Eden, and all the formality you insist on won't change the facts. We're attracted to one another. I've wanted you from the first minute I saw you at the airport. And I believe that you want me, regardless of your denials. Why can't you accept the inevitable?"

"*Mr. Clayton*, inevitability is for animals, not men and women who've made commitments. So why don't you take your ego and all the other male trappings you're so eager to display and offer them to someone else? I'm not interested."

The sound of the band playing a wedding waltz registered in Eden's mind, as did the narrow-eyed determination of Jim Clayton's face.

"No one's ever hated me on sight before. It rouses my curiosity. It also intrigues me." He stepped nearer, effectively reducing the space that separated them to inches. "*You* intrigue me, Eden Benedict."

"Women say no all the time, Mr. Clayton. A man just has to be smart enough to listen to the words."

He smiled and lifted his champagne goblet in a mock toast. "Very few women in my experience have been quite as brutal as you, especially when I haven't really asked for anything yet."

Tears welled in her eyes, scalding tears of pain and fear. "Damn you! Go play your games with someone else and leave me the hell alone."

He reached out and caught her wrist as she turned away. "Why, Eden? Just tell me why?"

"My life is full. There's no room for someone like you in it." All too aware of what an incredible liar she had suddenly become, she began to shake.

He stepped closer and felt the vibrations of her trembling body. "Lady, you're hurting inside, and it's obvious as hell."

"I don't want you anywhere near me," she hissed. "Is that clear enough for you?"

"You're lying to me, Eden. What's even worse is that you're lying to yourself. Only fools do that."

She stared at her wrist and wondered if she would have to pry his fingers, one by one, from her body. "The lady does not like to be handled, Mr. Clayton," she seethed as she wrenched herself free.

She stepped past him, unaware of the shock on his face and the sudden alarm in Tracey's eyes as she watched Eden stride across the room.

"What's with you and Jim?" Tracey demanded as they converged on the ladies' lounge.

"Nothing."

Standing behind Tracey, Eden raised shaking hands to the buttons at the back of her wedding gown. She tried to ignore the red marks on her wrist as she willed her fingers to unfasten the tiny fabric-covered buttons.

Tracey finally slid her arms from the organza and lace that had covered her from throat to toes. "What happened?"

"Nothing worth talking about." She managed a smile as Tracey turned around. "We've got to get you changed in a hurry or you'll miss your plane. David would never forgive me if your honeymoon was delayed."

"If Jim corners you before David and I leave, simply tell him you aren't interested and be done with it."

"I already have."

Tracey grinned as she fussed with her hair and makeup. "He looked as though you'd just punched him in the mouth."

Eden shrugged, trying to appear unconcerned. "His ego is probably a little dented, but I suspect it will regenerate by the end of the day."

"If what you said to Tommy Harker in tenth grade is any indication of your ego-deflation technique, then Jim'll probably be in traction for a month, but he deserved it if he wouldn't take no for an answer. He's known about you and Matt since I first met him."

She handed Tracey her overnight bag and purse after zipping up the back of her short dress. "Subject closed, old friend. Concentrate on your new husband and enjoy your two weeks in Acapulco. I'll see you when you get home."

She nodded and hugged Eden. "Wish me luck?"

"Luck and love always, Trace."

Major and Mrs. David Markham departed the Camp Pendleton Officers' Club under a shower of rice, their faces radiant as they waved from the rear window of their rented limo.

Eden loaded Tracey's clothes, her guest book, and assorted wedding gifts into the trunk of her car. She left the base without another confrontation with Jim Clayton. That her phone rang far into the night and again the following day served to strengthen her resolve that she would ignore his persistent behavior.

She knew her body craved the release a man like Jim could provide, but the turmoil in her heart and mind at the thought of betraying her vows helped her ignore the ringing telephone. She realized, though, that she couldn't behave like an ostrich forever, but facing Jim meant facing her own vulnerability as a woman alone. And she wasn't ready to do that yet.

"Eden, would you join me in my office?" Kitty requested.

Closing the file she'd been working on, she walked into Kitty's office and sank into a metal frame chair typical of the worn furnishings in each of the Red Cross volunteer offices. "Problems?" Eden asked.

"Not as far as the quality of your work is concerned, but I have noticed that you've been staying past the end of your shift in recent weeks. I get the impression you're avoiding going home at night."

She shifted uncomfortably when she saw the extent of Kitty's concern. "You don't miss a beat, do you?"

"I can't afford to."

"I haven't been drinking, if that's what you think. I've just had a lot of free time on my hands since Tracey's wedding," she hedged. "Plus I'm trying to learn as much about Grace's work as your assistant as I can before she leaves next month. The job comes with a lot of responsibility, not just a change in status and a paycheck."

"Are you upset about having to cut your hours on your ward?"

"No, not really. Splitting a forty-hour week between the ward and the Red Cross offices shouldn't be a problem. In fact, I think it'll be a mutually beneficial situation where I'm concerned once I get my routine established."

Kitty frowned and removed her glasses. "I'd like to take your explanation at face value, but I suspect that there is more to this surge of dedication than meets the eye. I respect your privacy, Eden, but if you need to talk . . ."

Eden dug her fingers into the arms of the chair in which she sat and sighed, the action serving as an effective pinprick in a balloon of resistance. Slumping down, she rubbed her temples with her fingertips.

"Do I need to remind you that I was on your ward yesterday when Dr. Richards very casually put his arm around you and you blew up at him like an overheated volcano? Under normal circumstances you'd have accepted his behavior as the gesture of friendship it was meant to be. Even the patients were tiptoeing around you after that incident."

"I know I overreacted, and I'll talk to Mark—apologize to him."

Kitty frowned. "That's not the point, and you know it. Mark Richards isn't in the habit of molesting the women who work in this hospital. An apology is between the two of you, but whatever caused that little explosion, not to mention all the long hours you've been putting in lately, does concern me."

Eden paled. She knew that in the three weeks since Tracey's wedding she'd been in a state of emotional panic. Everything and everyone seemed to remind her of how isolated she was, of how utterly sexless her life had become. Sleeping at night had become an impossibility, her physical distress at an all-time high. Even easing the tension herself didn't solve the problem, since her sexual frustration often reemerged within hours of her efforts at release.

"Eden?"

"I met a man," she began quietly. "He's a friend of Tracey and David's."

"The newlyweds?"

She nodded, her eyes fixed on her hands. "Except for a couple of parties before the wedding, I've managed to avoid him. I feel like I've been angry since the minute I met him. I hate him. He made a pass at me at the wedding reception. I—it was awful, and yet it wasn't. I was secretly glad that he found me attractive. He made me feel like a woman again, a real woman, not some piece of plastic sitting on a shelf and collecting dust." She paused, swallowed against the ache throbbing in her throat, and looked up. "Are you sure you want to hear all this? I already feel like an idiot, and talking about it just seems to make it all sound worse." Tears filled her eyes. "Damn it to hell!" Eden yanked a tissue from the box on Kitty's desk and wiped her cheeks.

"Get it all out," suggested the older woman. "Then we can sort through it together once we know what you're dealing with."

"He knows I'm married, but he's still interested in me. I know I'm married, and I don't even like him very much, but I think I want him. God, this isn't making a dime's worth of sense."

"Eden, you're human. You have needs. Why does it surprise you that you've met a man who reminds you of some of the more basic biological facts of life? You're emotionally and sexually isolated. You have been for two years. Why is it so tough to accept that you're a vulnerable human being just like the rest of us?" Kitty questioned. "The facts are simple. You want what a man can give you physically and emotionally. Wanting to make love simply means that you need the same warmth and affection everyone else needs. Have you ever heard of hormones and logic enjoying a harmonious relationship?"

"But I'm furious with him for reminding me of what I don't have, and I hate myself for being so damned weak. Wanting or needing someone other than Matthew is wrong. I took vows. I love my husband more than anyone or anything in this world, but I get so lonely some of the time."

"For God's sake, Eden, you aren't dead!" Kitty exclaimed. "You're a healthy young woman who's condemning herself for having normal desires. Can't you hear how unreasonable that is?"

"Yes, but . . ."

"But what?" Kitty demanded as she leaned forward and rested her elbows on her desk. "No one in this world is perfect, Eden, not even you, no matter how hard you try to be. We all do the best we can with the situations we're faced with. I'm not suggesting that you run out and sleep with the first man you trip over, nor am I suggesting that you have an affair with this particular man . . ."

"Jim . . ." she supplied. "His name is Jim."

Kitty laughed softly. "I haven't met too many ogres named Jim. Have you?"

Eden colored. "He really isn't all that bad," she admitted.

"Look, we don't need to talk about the ramifications of getting involved with another man while Matthew is missing in action. You're bright enough to know what they are, but please try to remember one thing. . . . This is more a human issue than a moral one. You're a giving, loving woman, a woman with passion and laughter and love that needs to be shared. Those qualities aid you in your work with the patients, but like any asset or skill that's being used, it must be refurbished and revitalized periodically. You can't just give, Eden. You've got to be on the receiving end once in a while."

She nodded and blew her nose with a fresh tissue before admitting, "I've felt so guilty and so alone lately. And I know I've probably built this situation with Jim into more of a crisis than it needs to be. He isn't a bad person, not really. He's attractive, intelligent, and very self-confident. At first those qualities just made me more furious with him, but then I realized I was jealous of him. Jealous of his freedom and jealous of the ease with which he makes friends. And when he tried to get close to me, I panicked."

Kitty's expression, softened by her affection for Eden, revealed the compassion her words expressed. "Your loyalty to your husband is admirable, but how many guarantees do you have? You've told me yourself that you live in fear of Matthew being declared dead. You also know that if he's a prisoner of war and not an MIA any longer, then there's no predicting how long he'll be held by the North Vietnamese. While I'm not suggesting that you have an affair, I do think you should consider tearing down some of the walls you've built around yourself and your emotions, especially where men are concerned. If for no other reason than opening yourself up to the possibility of friendship with them."

"Matthew's the only man I've ever been with, Kitty. My memories are perfect, and I don't want to risk destroying what little I've got left of him."

"Aren't you forgetting something that's as important as your memories?"

"I don't understand."

"You started a new life here in San Diego. You've begun what I believe will be a career with the Red Cross, and you're sober. I grant you that your foundation's a little shaky at times, but you've accomplished a lot more than you give yourself credit for, Eden, and that frustrates me no end. You possess inner strength and courage, and you never seem to realize just how much," she admonished kindly.

"I've only done what I had to do, and not at all well some of the time."

"That's where you're wrong, and I'll go to the mat on this with you. Most people, when they're faced with a crisis, run for cover. You didn't. You opted to get on with your life at a time when it would have been easier to drown yourself in booze. You won't ever get any medals for what you've done, but you'll always have the personal satisfaction of knowing you had the will and the strength of character to fight back."

Eden smiled, startled that Kitty would think her brave. She

hadn't felt that way about herself at all. She had just assumed that she was getting by, one step, one hour, and one day at a time.

"I honestly don't know what I'd do in your place," Kitty continued. "I am certain, however, that whatever choices you make and however you get through this separation from your husband, the only person you owe an explanation is yourself. No one else, other than God, has the right to make moral judgments about how you conduct your personal life."

"I don't know what to say."

"Don't say anything. Just start believing in yourself. I warned you a long time ago that I wouldn't let you bury yourself in hospital work. You need friends and a personal life. Now, get yourself home," she ordered gruffly. "I want to lock up for the night. The hours you've been keeping lately have played havoc with my social life. I've got a date with Captain Price tonight, and at my age I need some time to make myself presentable for dinner at the Admiral Kidd Club."

Eden stood and circled around Kitty's desk. She leaned down and hugged the older woman. "Thanks for being here for me. There have been several times during the past few weeks that I've wanted to come to you, but I was afraid to talk about my feelings for Jim. I see now that I was wrong to try and deal with it alone."

Kitty waved her hand in dismissal as Eden walked to the doorway. "You're worth the effort. Now get going or I'll call the Shore Patrol. And be nice to yourself, young lady. You've earned the right."

She nodded and smiled. "Have a good time tonight."

Eden slept peacefully for the first time in several weeks that night. After showering and dressing the next morning, she stopped ignoring the phone when it rang. Jim Clayton called three days later. Despite an initial awkwardness they both seemed to feel, they chatted calmly for nearly an hour. Neither mentioned the Markhams' wedding reception or what had occurred between them.

Aware that she would be off duty for the next two days, Eden invited him to stop by if he happened to be in the area.

She knew she was ready to see him, talk to him, and establish the ground rules that would be required if they were going to be friends.

She also realized that Kitty was right. She couldn't continue to hide from men who made her aware of herself as a woman. It wasn't rational or sensible. She had to stop running from her feelings and her needs. She realized, too, that if she didn't face Jim Clayton once and for all, she wouldn't be able to deal honestly and frankly with the emotions he aroused in her.

When her doorbell rang shortly before noon the following day, Eden found Jim on her doorstep. No longer panicked by his attention, she invited him in.

"I'm having lunch. Would you like to join me?"

Clearly surprised by her cordial greeting and unruffled manner, he followed her into the kitchen and watched while she made a second sandwich and poured another cup of coffee.

"You going to keep me in suspense forever?" he finally asked once she joined him at the table.

She smiled, glad not to be the nervous one for a change. "That wouldn't be fair, would it?"

"I guess that depends on the rules of the game."

"There are rules in any friendship, Jim. Do you want to hear mine, or would you rather pass altogether since I come with restrictions?"

Adding cream to his coffee, he considered her question for a moment before answering. "I'd like to know *you.* If that means I have to abide by your ground rules, then I'll give it a shot."

"I'm surprised."

"Why?"

"There are plenty of available women around. This is California, after all. The land of body beautiful and free love."

He smiled. "They don't intrigue me."

Sensing that the wolf in him had reemerged, she shifted uncomfortably. "There's that word again."

He shrugged, lowered eyes still filled with a frankly sexual gleam, and reached for his sandwich. "It's the truth."

"You don't mind if I'm surprised."

"This seems the day for it," he mused aloud, his tone vague and noncommittal.

Eden sobered. "I won't sleep with you."

He arched a dark blond brow, the look on his face confident and very male. "That sounds like a challenge."

"It's not intended as one. It's just the truth. I'd hate myself after, and that would be a lousy end result for an effort at friendship, wouldn't it?"

He nodded, his expression suddenly less certain as he ate his sandwich and drank his coffee. They said little after that. There didn't seem to be a need. Companionship suited Eden, though she felt the rusty disuse a woman often feels after being shut up alone for so long and then is suddenly thrust into a social situation with a man.

Later, after he had left and she had washed their lunch dishes, Eden reflected on his surprise and what also appeared to be his relief that she hadn't rebuffed him once again.

CHAPTER

17

December 1969—Hanoi, North Vietnam

Matt fingered the grooves etched into the wall above his bed like a blind man. Counting each narrow indentation was his first ritual of the day; one of several repetitive but sanity-ensuring actions in the darkness of his cell.

Scraping the narrow end of his spoon against the resistant cement, he whispered, "Two hundred and nine." A flicker of satisfaction flashed through him as he brushed away the loosened grains of mortar.

His calendar updated, he moved off the cement platform. He tucked his rice bowl, a soiled change of clothing, and his spoon into his frayed bedding and rolled it into a snug cylinder.

Dropping to his knees, he began morning physical training. Another ritual. As he did the push-ups that had helped him restore the use of his injured right arm, he recalled the rigors of OCS at Quantico, Virginia, and a burly gunnery sergeant who had systematically harassed, bullied, and eventually trained the officer candidates in his platoon. Matt mentally saluted the Marine Corps NCO for the discipline he'd learned prior to his commissioning as a second lieutenant. Had it not been for those murderous ten weeks, weeks that now seemed like child's play, he knew he couldn't have survived the last seven months of isolation.

The jangle of keys in the corridor outside his cell interrupted his exercise and alerted him to the presence of prison guards. Matt limped back to his cement bunk, quietly seating himself despite the chains dragging between his ankles and wrists.

His manacles were a constant, a twenty-four-hour-a-day weight his body grudgingly accepted in spite of the rawness and swelling caused by the dig of unforgiving metal. He stiffened, his body tightening into itself when he heard a key being inserted into the lock of his cell door.

It's not time for food. What now? he wondered.

The memory of his first two months at Hoa Lo deepened the lines of tension around his mouth. He warily watched two guards step into the semidarkness of his cell. With the aid of a flashlight, one pantomimed that he was to gather up his bedroll, while the other waved his rifle in the direction of the cell door.

Matt shuffled down a dimly lighted corridor in front of the two guards and ground his teeth against the frustration of being prodded along like an animal. He found little comfort in the realization that deprivation of spirit was an effective means of subjugation, one artfully employed by the North Vietnamese.

Not even in ten lifetimes, he promised himself, will these sons of bitches keep me from surviving.

Matt again sat in the foul-smelling Room 18, the violent room. He recalled the endless days and nights of torture he'd endured in the oblong-shaped room, and he felt a trembling kind of fatigue invade his body at the prospect of a repeat of those agonizing sessions.

Several hours passed before a North Vietnamese officer entered the room. Matt watched him place a large cardboard box on the table between them. He remained still, kept his spine rigid, and fixed his gaze on a hole gouged into the wall at the far end of the room. Past experience had taught him not to make eye contact with a senior officer unless instructed to do so. Even then it was a calculated risk.

In halting English and a smattering of French, the man inquired, "You are not curious why you have been brought here?"

Matt shrugged. He didn't draw his eyes from the wall.

"Perhaps you will appreciate the leniency being shown you

by the citizens of the Democratic Republic once you have seen the contents of this container."

What's this bastard up to? he wondered. Matt looked at the guards standing on either side of the man before lifting his eyes to the face of his new adversary.

"We are not a cruel people, Captain Benedict. Many of your fellow prisoners have already learned that we can be very generous under certain circumstances."

At what price? Matt wondered. At what goddamned price?

The major lifted the lid of the box and overturned the contents. "Because it is Christmas in your homeland, you will be permitted one letter. As you can see, there are many here, but other than the one you yourself select, the remainder will be held for you. Should you wish to receive additional letters, you will be given the opportunity to express your gratitude to the people struggling for freedom in my country."

More propaganda bullshit!

Matt blocked out the sound of the major's voice until it faded to a hum. He stared at the top of the table. Curious, he leaned as far forward as his bonds would permit. Placing his left hand on the table, he waited a moment to see if the guards would attempt to restrain him. He froze when he recognized the scrawled handwriting on one of the envelopes. He felt his heart constrict. Clenching and unclenching his right fist, he eyed the man standing on the other side of the table. Caution strained the muscles in his now trembling body.

The major repeated, "One letter."

Matt eased his fingers across the scarred surface of the table, ignoring the chain between his wrists as it grated against the wood. She hasn't forgotten me, a voice inside him screamed. All these letters! He struggled to contain the rage echoing in his skull. Two fucking years and these bastards give me one letter! Sweet Jesus, why? Why? Sweat beaded across his brow as he gripped a single letter in his left hand.

"You may read privately for five minutes only. I will then return to discuss your war crimes against the people of the Democratic Republic. At that time you will be given an opportunity to rectify the wrongs you have committed against my country. I strongly urge you to reconsider your past silence on this subject."

The door to the room remained open. The two guards stood at attention in the hallway. Matt ignored them.

He saw that the envelope had already been opened, but he dismissed the invasion of his privacy as unimportant. His fingers shook as he removed and unfolded a single piece of stationery. He couldn't stop his eyes from rushing down the page, nor could he stop the tears that blurred line after line of Eden's distinctive handwriting. Taking a deep breath, Matt forced himself to start at the top of the page.

June 19, 1968

My darling,

Andrew is fourteen days old today. He looks like you, Matthew, with his beautiful dark eyes and his golden skin. Each time I hold our Drew, I feel as though I have you both in my arms. Tracey was with me during my labor and delivery, despite a linebacker-sized nurse who made the mistake of resisting our very stubborn friend.

I miss you, my heart, and I love you. Had you been permanently taken from me, I know I would have felt the loss. In spite of my uncertainty about your status and the passage of time, I know in my soul that you're alive and that you will return to your paleface when you are able. Never forget my abiding love and belief in you. It nurtures me as I hope it will nurture you.

Be safe, my love,

Eden

Matt exhaled shakily and scrubbed at the tears streaming down his face. He was certain that Eden had written this letter. She'd given him clues of authenticity, as well as information she knew he would be hungry for. A son. Andrew. Dear God, thank you for my family. And thank you for giving me a woman who believes in my survival and whose love has such strength. My firstborn is a son, he thought over and over as he reread Eden's letter. Great-grandfather, I have a son!

Footsteps announced the return of the major. He carried a notebook and a pencil, which he placed on the table between them. Matt watched him sit down at the opposite side of the table, but his thoughts remained on Eden's letter. He struggled against wondering about the other messages of love and encouragement contained in the envelopes still scattered in front of him. He tried to tell himself that it was enough that he had been given one. The lie tasted sour.

"We will now concern ourselves with the details of your final mission," announced the major.

Matt quietly folded Eden's letter and slipped it into the waistband of his trousers. Why, after two years, he wondered, would the circumstances of my shootdown be of interest to the North Vietnamese?

"My predecessor failed to extract accurate data from you, Captain Benedict. You will now write in this notebook the exact details of your mission and bailout."

"Benedict, Matthew Alexander. Captain, United States Marine Corps—"

"Do you wish additional letters from wife?" demanded the major.

"Benedict, Matthew Alexander," he repeated, slowly and deliberately. "Captain, United States Marine Corps."

The major pursed his lips, the movement adding emphasis to his already puffy features. Matt watched him withdraw a cigarette from a pack in his shirt pocket and accept a match from one of the guards.

"You will write a confession of your war crimes against the Democratic Republic," he ordered again.

His eyes darted back and forth between Eden's letters and the match. "I am not a criminal."

A short burst of Vietnamese followed, and the two guards moved in on their prisoner.

Matt froze when the major flicked his thumbnail across the tip of the match with the speed of a striking viper. He cried out in disbelief, "Noooo!" as the flame landed in the center of the envelopes.

He lunged forward, trying to smother the smoke and flames with his hands. The guards responded with their rifles, landing blows against his chest and shoulders. The chair to which he was strapped overturned, and he toppled over, slamming his head sharply on the concrete floor. But he was beyond pain. The smell of burning paper, as Eden's letters slowly evaporated to ash, was all that reached him.

He awakened several hours later, chest pain and the scorched flesh of his fingertips reminders of what had happened earlier in the day. Opening his eyes, he focused on the ceiling of his cell. Several minutes passed before he realized that he wasn't confined in the darkness that had characterized the preceding 209 days.

"Starting to feel better?"

Matt carefully sat up. He hugged his ribs and stared at the American stretched out atop a cement platform that ran the length of the opposite wall.

The emaciated man, who was probably in his late thirties, although he appeared much older, mustered a weak grin. "Welcome to my humble abode, such as it is. Name's Bill Porter. Last time I checked . . . Major, U.S. Air Force. My friends call me Scratch."

Matt opened his mouth to answer but found his vocal cords locked against speech. He swallowed several times before managing, "Matt Benedict. Captain, Marine Corps."

"You've got the look of a guy who's been in isolation."

He nodded. "Nearly seven months." He gingerly massaged his ribs as he looked around the small cell.

"What'd they use on you? Rifle butts or boots?"

"Rifles. I freaked when they burned a box of letters from my wife. Guess the assholes figured I hadn't earned more than one."

Bill Porter rubbed the gray stubble on his chin before commenting, "You're lucky you got one. I've been here nineteen months and zip." He tapped the dirty plaster cast that extended from his upper thigh to his ankle. "A couple of the guards used steel-toed flight boots on me when I was first brought in. My leg still hasn't healed properly. You know you're in deep shit when they use your own gear on you."

"Parachute cord," Matt volunteered grimly.

"You've been through hell, haven't you?"

"Not for a while and probably no more than any of the other prisoners. The first couple of months here were the worst, if you don't count the thirteen months I spent out in the boonies at a place called Long Moc."

"Why don't you settle in?" Bill suggested. "Get used to the idea of having someone else around. The guards won't be back until dusk when they bring our chow."

"There weren't any lights where I was before."

Bill nodded sympathetically. Darkness could do one of two things: terrorize a man or give him a false sense of security. "You'll be all right in a day or so."

Flexing his right hand, Matt stood and paced off the ten-by-six cell. He moved with the same noiseless skill he had acquired in solitary. "Ever run across a guy by the name of Chet Holt?" he asked as he noticed the barred window at the top of the wall above his cement bunk and added it to his mental inventory.

"Here?"

"Yeah."

"Don't recognize the name, but that doesn't mean he isn't around. Tell you what, we'll get a message out later on tonight or tomorrow and see if anyone knows him. Were you brought in together?"

"What do you mean 'get a message out'?" Matt demanded suspiciously.

"Relax, we've got our own com network here, so you can stop looking at me like I'm some kind of damned collaborator. I wouldn't have a busted-up leg if I'd given these guys the information they wanted."

"How many?"

"How many what?"

"Are a lot of our guys here?"

Bill pulled himself up from his reclining position and propped his bad leg on his folded bedroll. "I've personally seen at least twenty-three other Americans in the compound in the last year and a half. There are probably more, though. There's also a place the Viets call the Citadel on the northeast edge of Hanoi. Our guys call it the Plantation 'cause there's lots of farms in the area. And I've heard about a prison called Dogpatch up near the Chinese border."

Matt rubbed his neck as he sat down. "Chet Holt's a medium-sized guy, starting to bald . . . a marine lieutenant."

"A good friend?"

"An eternal optimist with a sense of humor. We were at Long Moc together."

"There aren't many marines here. Mostly air force and navy guys, and a few army noncoms. He shouldn't be too hard to track down if he's still here," Bill mused aloud. "He could be over in Little Vegas or Camp Unity. Those are two of the other sections of the prison."

Pulling up his shirt, Matt removed Eden's letter from the waistband of his baggy trousers. He turned it over in his hand several times before unfolding it and rereading the contents. He couldn't help but wonder if the Vietnamese major would send a guard for it.

"Your wife's letter?" Bill asked.

Matt heard the wistfulness in his voice. "Yeah. They'll probably be back for it when they realize they forgot to take it away from me."

"Memorize it. That way they're only taking a piece of paper from you, not the words or what they mean."

"Christmas," Matt muttered in disgust. "Those bastards made a big deal about it. Said I had to demonstrate my appreciation if I wanted more than one. I'd like to demonstrate my fucking appreciation, all right. I'd love to stand their asses in front of a firing squad."

"Sounds like the Rabbit is at it again. He's the CO's interpreter, and he definitely subscribes to the philosophy 'When you have them by the balls, their hearts and minds will follow.' "

Matt almost smiled. "You sure you aren't a marine?"

Bill chuckled. "My younger brother is. Ginny—she's my wife—says I'm a natural gutter mouth. When my brother and I get together, she sends the kids to visit her mother. She's a tough cookie about some things, but I wouldn't trade that woman away for a high-yield gold mine."

Still clasping his letter, Matt offered, "Eden was pregnant when I punched out. We—" He cleared his throat. "I just found out I have a son."

Bill nodded gravely. "My oldest is a boy. I know how that makes a man feel."

"She wrote this letter when he was two weeks old, so he must've been born the first week of June in '68."

"Right about the time I was shot down. It was a rough month back home. Bob Kennedy was assassinated a few days before I was captured. Half the country was in mourning. It sure brought back a lot of memories about his older brother Jack."

"Christ!"

"And from what I've heard, the antiwar movement's really grown. The last guy in here said Richard Nixon is president now and our people are negotiating with the North Vietnamese in Paris. My information's about a month or so old."

"Doesn't sound like I've missed a whole lot." Other than my life, Eden, and our son, he amended silently, and clenched his right fist.

"When exactly did you go down?"

"The end of January '68. My RIO and I were separated." Matt paused, shocked that he hadn't even thought about Jack Morrison in recent months. "He might be here, too, or at one of the other prisons you mentioned."

"F-4s?"

Matt nodded.

"Me, too. The guy in my backseat didn't make it. Damn chute malfunctioned on him."

Matt grimaced and remembered how close he'd come to going down with his plane. Without Jack's cool head and skill, he knew he could have easily been just another KIA statistic.

"How long you been on active duty?"

Matt looked up sharply, but when he saw the calm expression on Bill Porter's face, he realized that the man was simply making conversation, not conducting an interrogation. "Since the Naval Academy."

"Career?"

"Yeah. My old man was regular army."

"Apache or Cherokee?"

He smiled at the fact that Bill had slipped into a shorthand style of speech typical of most aviators.

"Half Cherokee. My father was Italian. After he died in Korea and I finished high school, Mom went back to the tribe. She said tradition would serve her better than trying to adapt to an environment that had always felt foreign to her."

"Sounds like a lady who knows what she wants. Your wife's probably keeping an eye on her for you, though."

He shook his head, and regret filled him. "They've never met. Eden and I only had a few months together and then my R and R. There wasn't time for family. Things were happening too fast then."

"Regrets?"

"A few," Matt admitted. "I may have put her in a situation she won't be able to deal with indefinitely, although if Eden's letter is any indication of how she's handling things, she's trying to hang in there."

"Your son'll keep her busy. Ginny always said the little ones ran her ragged worse than the teenagers she used to teach."

Matt nodded. "Eden's very much her own person. A bit reserved where strangers are concerned, but given her background, it's not surprising." He paused briefly and studied Bill before adding, "I sometimes wonder if what she wanted when we were married is what she'll want when and if we ever get out of this pisshole."

"I worry about that, too, in spite of the fact that me and Ginny have been together for nearly twenty years and have five kids. She's intelligent, a real knockout, and she's put up with a lot of crap being an air force wife all these years. Hell, I know she's been tempted more than a few times to tell me to take a long hike off a short pier. But you gotta decide for yourself whether or not your wife'll be waiting for you when, not if, we're released. That's one fear none of us needs to haul around inside. The Viets give us plenty to worry about as it is."

"You're probably—"

The rattle of keys outside the cell door interrupted Matt. Bill's comment, "That'll be our chow," helped relieve the tension that tightened his insides and narrowed his eyes.

After a meal of rice and boiled chunks of pumpkin, the two men waited until the overhead cell light was extinguished before they resumed their conversation.

"I like the mornings for myself," Bill explained. "How about you?"

"Memory work and PT," Matt clarified, thinking of the exercise session the guards had interrupted earlier in the day. "I try to remember books I've read, complicated math equations, that kind of thing."

"I'm working on the plans for a house I want to build someday. And I write a letter in my head to Ginny every morning. I'll write 'em all down when I get home and give 'em to her." He grinned. "She'll call it porn, but that's how my mind works these days."

Matt smiled in the semidarkness, more relaxed than he had been in months. "Thanks for talking me down when I came around this afternoon, Scratch. It helped a lot."

"No sweat. How about we schedule a couple hours every afternoon, and then again in the evening after lights out, for talking? Having a privacy rule will keep us from getting on each other's nerves."

He exhaled and closed his eyes. "Sounds good to me."

"I'll be tapping a code on the wall after midnight, so don't let it rattle you. It's basically the Morse without the letter *K*. We'll try and establish whether or not Chet Holt is here or if he was moved while you were in isolation."

"Whatever you say, Major."

Scratch laughed. "Can it, Captain. My kids aren't even that respectful."

Matt shared in the responsibility of the tap code within a few days of becoming Bill Porter's cellmate. He found Chet Holt and ascertained his approximate location in the Hoa Lo compound. No one had ever heard of Jack Morrison, and Matt wondered if he had been executed after their captivity or if he was still being held in some remote jungle location like Long Moc.

Matt also learned that a viable chain of command existed among the prisoners. For the first time in two years he allowed himself to really feel the unity and strength of his fellow prisoners.

CHAPTER 18

January–June 1970—San Diego, California

Eden stood on the balcony of Tracey and David's beachfront home. Absorbing the rhythm of the lapping Pacific, she half listened to the sound of the waves merging with the conversation and laughter spilling from the interior of the house. When she heard the screen door of the balcony slide open, she turned and leaned against the railing. Even in the darkness she recognized the man walking toward her.

"Hi, Jim."

"Tracey said I'd find you out here." He handed her a chilled glass. "Orange juice and ice, no booze."

"Thanks. I thought we ran out a little while ago."

"Still don't drink the hard stuff?"

She shook her head.

"I have a hard time picturing you as a lush in spite of what I've heard about that part of your life."

Eden laughed, the sound warm and spontaneous. One of the things she'd come to appreciate about Jim as she'd gotten to know him was that he called a spade a spade, or, as in her case, a lush a lush. "You didn't know me then. Take my word for it, I had to stop drinking."

He raised his wineglass in a toast. "Happy New Year."

"Same to you." She took a sip of her juice. "How've you been?"

"Busy."

"I don't suppose I should ask with what or where?"

He shrugged and turned his face into the breeze. The wind ruffled his pale hair and tugged at his shirt collar. As Eden studied his expression, she wasn't surprised by the neutrality of it. She knew Jim never talked about his work. She watched him lean forward and rest his elbows on the wood railing. Suddenly, she remembered Tracey's wedding, and champagne and anger. She also remembered the tentative start to what she now considered a casual friendship.

"You're thinking about the wedding reception, aren't you?"

"Champagne and anger," she answered, verbalizing her thoughts.

"My champagne, your anger," he clarified, his memories as clear as hers.

"But we buried the hatchet when you visited me that first time," she reminded him.

He nodded and abruptly changed the subject, another habit of his that still jarred her despite several phone conversations during the last few months. "You look good, kind of mellowed out."

"I had some personal things to sort through."

"Did you?"

"Not everything, but I'm working on it."

He glanced at her, his expression guarded, his body visibly tensed. "Your husband's still missing, isn't he?"

"Yes."

"Is friendship really possible between us, Eden?"

"I hope so, but that's up to you, not me."

"Your game, your rules, babe."

"Don't be flip," she said softly. "That's not a side of you I like."

He ignored her last remark. "You know, the about-face you did last fall when I stopped by your house kind of blew me away." He shook his head. "I felt like I'd witnessed a very personal internal kind of war at the Markhams' wedding reception, and I guess now I still don't know quite what to expect out of you."

"You make me sound pretty unstable."

Still focused on his own agenda, he admitted, "I spoke to

David a little while ago. He told me to keep my hands to myself—in blunter terms, of course."

She studied the contents of her glass, embarrassed by the overprotective behavior she seemed to inspire. "David sometimes acts as though he got two for the price of one when he married Trace. He's also become a bit more dedicated in his big-brother role than is necessary any longer. I'll speak to him if you'd like, but I think he realized that I hated you when I first met you."

"A blind man could've figured that out." His voice held a trace of harshness.

"Don't, Jim. You don't understand what it's like to live in limbo, and I'm certain you've never had the kind of doubts I was having about myself when I met you." In a softer tone of voice, she confessed, "You frightened me."

His hands settled on her shoulders. "Don't try and turn me into a priest, Eden. I don't want to be your private confessional."

She wrenched free and stepped back. "You don't seem to realize that in a few short weeks you managed to bring down all the walls I'd spent months building around myself. I wanted you, and I felt vulnerable and angry because of feelings I suddenly had and couldn't control or ignore. But, because of you, I faced what I was doing to myself, and I saw how wrong it was." She lowered her voice and told him honestly, "You *were* and *are* a mixed blessing. Now do you understand?"

"Why say all this now?"

"Oh, hell, I don't know. Call it my resolution for 1970. This is the year I stop candy coating my emotions and accept myself for who and what I am."

"You still haven't answered my question. Why tell me the truth now?"

"Because I like you. Because I don't want you to think I'm a fool simply because I panicked when I realized I was attracted to you. Because you guessed how I felt in spite of the smoke screen I tried to put up. Maybe even because, in the end, you didn't take advantage of me." She shrugged and suggested, "Pick one."

"Eden, I still want you. That hasn't changed."

She stared up at him. When he eased her into his arms, she didn't pull away. Instead, she stood passively in his embrace. His expression revealed nothing other than his desire. Waves broke against the pilings that supported the beach-house balcony.

"Jim, you don't know me, not really," she said softly.

"I know enough to realize that there's more to you than an MIA husband. I know about your baby and what that did to you." He grasped her chin and forced her to face him when she tried to look away. "When I watch you, I see a beautiful woman holding herself apart from the world. I hear laughter concealed behind restraint. I see a smile that can be lighthearted or sensual. You remind me of fine crystal, a piece so fragile that a single discordant note could shatter you. And yet I also sense ingrained strength and determination. I've already confessed to being intrigued, Eden, but I'm wary, too. I find myself caring just enough to stay at arm's length for the time being."

"I love my husband."

"You love your memories," he said harshly.

"You're wrong," she insisted. "I love the man."

He exhaled slowly. "All right."

"That won't change, Jim, not ever."

"I believe you," he grudgingly admitted.

"You must, for both our sakes."

"Even if I don't want to?"

"Oh, Jim, don't you see? It's the chase you enjoy so much, not the end result. Women don't normally say no to you. I did, and that's the only reason you're still interested in me."

"You're wrong."

She smiled at the stubbornness in him. He was like Matthew in that respect. "I don't think so."

"What now?" he finally asked.

Eden released a soft gust of air. "I don't know. I keep remembering a story about children who play with fire and how they're certain to get burned."

"We aren't children."

"No, we aren't, are we?"

"You don't seem to be having a problem with me now."

"This is different, and you know it. There must be fifty people inside. Besides, I won't put Tracey and David in the middle."

"Worried about what they'll think or say?" he demanded. "Be honest with yourself, why don't you?"

"I'm trying to, damn it!" She left his arms, moved to the balcony railing, and stared out at the darkness enveloping the California coastline.

Jim shoved careless fingers through his hair. "Look, forget I said that. I don't want to cause you any more trouble than you already have."

She turned and faced him, hugging herself against the cold night breeze. "Then we know where we stand?"

"For now, Eden. For now. More than that I won't even try to promise."

She nodded as he collected his wineglass and crossed the balcony, self-confidence evident in his long-legged stride and the set of his broad shoulders. Looking back before he opened the screen door, he reminded her, "Nothing lasts forever, babe. Not even good intentions."

Eden gripped the metal post at the end of Howie Turner's bed and watched Corpsman Barnes complete his dressing changes. When she couldn't bear the sight before her any longer, she let her eyes drift to the window above the hospital-bed headboard, but the dreary mid-February weather only served to enhance the grim scene being played out in front of her.

Howie's wounds were multiple and serious. Both his legs were cast from toes to crotch, bandages temporarily swathed his eyes, and two deep unsuturable wounds cratered his right arm. Bone, tendons, and ragged flesh in his upper-arm injury had already been tripped with Dakin's solution and hydrogen peroxide to forestall further infection and promote healing.

Eden concentrated on the clock ticking in her head when she saw the corpsman douse the area with Betadine and swiftly encircle it with sterile gauze. Seventeen minutes had elapsed. Howie Turner was bathed in sweat.

When she heard the sodden thud of blood-soaked bandages land in the waste container attached to the corpsman's dressing cart, Eden quelled her instinctive repugnance to the sound and reached for the rubber ball and newspaper atop her own supply cart.

Corpsman Barnes peeled off his surgical gloves. "You're all set for now, Turner."

"Thanks, Doc," whispered the nineteen-year-old marine as he scrubbed the sweat from his face and chest with the towel gripped in his left hand. "Later, man."

Eden stepped forward, nodded to the corpsman, and exchanged places with him.

She sat in a chair at the side of Howie's bed and studied the youthful combat veteran. A shock of red hair, a crew cut gone wild, stood at attention above the gauze covering his eyes. His fair complexion reminded her of rice paper. She knew from previous therapy sessions that at least an hour would pass before the color returned to his face.

Tremors of pain still shook his lanky body, but like many of the men on the ward, he never expressed the agony he experienced with each dressing change. Stoicism and pride characterized most of the patients. Eden had learned to accept and respect their attitudes, although she still felt a sense of despair for what they'd each experienced.

"That you, Eden?"

She smiled. "Right again, Howie."

"It's your perfume. This place smells worse than hell. I always know when you're around."

She slipped the red ball into his right hand, silently agreeing with his evaluation of the stink that permeated the ward. It was an unwieldy blend of antiseptics, drying blood, rubbing alcohol, pus, and body waste thriving in a greenhouse environment. The men often compared the smell to the aftermath of a jungle battle.

Eden gently closed Howie's narrow fingers around the brightly colored ball resting in his palm. "Have you heard from your folks this week?"

He grinned, his show of teeth like blinding neon. "Yes, ma'am. Pa's got himself four new sows, and with winter gettin' so bad, he and Ma'll be comin' out for a visit soon."

She smiled at his enthusiasm as she unfolded the newspaper. "That's wonderful. I'm looking forward to meeting them. I've got the Indianapolis paper with me today, and you know our deal, Howie. I'll read if you'll exercise."

"Yes, ma'am."

She watched him flex his fingers and then tighten them around the ball. He chewed on his lower lip as he squeezed the therapy device, painstakingly working the damaged tendons and ligaments in his lower right arm. Satisfied that his motion was the same one she'd taught him several weeks before, she began to read.

"The Pentagon reports that there have been ten thousand servicemen lost in Southeast Asia since President Nixon's inauguration one year ago. This, despite his pledge to end the conflict in Vietnam. . . ." Eden paused. "Howie, are you certain you want me to read this?"

He nodded. "That's the *Indy Star*, the same paper my pa reads every mornin' before he does his chores. No disrespect intended, but the Nam ain't goin' away anytime soon. I might as well know what my buddies are up against, even if I ain't there with 'em."

She sighed. She knew Howie wasn't any different from the majority of the other patients on the ward. They all wanted to know what was happening in the hellhole that had touched their lives with such violent intimacy. Concern for friends, the possibility of future orders, a validation that they were no longer there—whatever their individual reasons, Vietnam wasn't a reality they were willing to ignore.

Eden continued to read. She kept her voice even as she read the latest casualty figures, the now daily accounts of antiwar activists, and what she personally regarded as the meaningless speeches of Washington politicians. She finally relaxed when she reached the sports pages.

". . . and in local basketball, Jimmy Gregson scored the final basket in the Ben Davis High matchup against their cross-town rivals Attucks High. The Ben Davis team suffered the only injury of the game when center Dale Everton sprained his ankle, but reports indicate he will be back in action before the play-offs."

She glanced over at the continuous flexing of Howie's fingers before letting her gaze travel upward to his partially bandaged face. Below the gauze that covered his eyes, his nose protruded like a hawk's beak. His thin lips were slanted in a contented smile despite the sweat dripping from his chin and trickling in thin streams down his neck.

"That's it for today, Howie."

His hand stilled, and Eden reached for the red ball before it could slide from his slack fingers. Using his left elbow, Howie levered himself up from his reclining position.

"Ready for me to check your arm?" she asked. Eden hated this part of therapy. Even though she knew it was a necessary part of her job, she still worried that she might inadvertently add to the pain of injured limbs.

Howie nodded. Droplets of sweat from his upper lip slipped into the grimacing line of his mouth.

Placing one hand under his wrist and the other under his elbow, Eden elevated his right arm. "Tell me if I hurt you, Howie. No heroics, please."

In spite of her admonition, he didn't utter a sound as she continued to raise and lower his arm. When a nerve jumped and then bunched in his jaw, she brought his arm down one last time. "What did I just tell you?"

"No pain, no gain," he croaked.

"This isn't basic training, Corporal Turner." His lopsided smile quelled further comment. Eden helped him ease himself back down onto the bed. "You're impossible, but you did really well today. Dr. Richards will be pleased with the progress you're making."

Howie's grin remained fixed. "Yes, ma'am."

"Are you as tired as I think you are?"

He nodded, and a deep sigh escaped him.

Eden pulled up the sheet tucked between his plaster-encased legs and bunched at his waist. Walking around to the left side of the bed, she placed a rectangular object in his open hand. "Have this after you wake up, Howie. Your sweet tooth's become a legend in the Red Cross offices. All the volunteers are leaving chocolate bars in my locker for you."

He was asleep before she reached the end of his bed, the candy grasped in his slender hand.

Eden pushed her cart down the center aisle of the ward. She periodically stopped to collect pieces of physical therapy equipment and chat with patients. A few of the men still worked on the airplane models she'd doled out earlier, and she didn't disturb their concentration.

After stowing her cart in the utility closet at the end of the ward, she checked the letter schedule she'd made up for the patients unable to handle pen and paper. She saw that three of the men would need assistance before her day ended on the ward.

Eden paused at the nurses' station before leaving the thirty-bed orthopedic ward. Lieutenant Evans, the duty nurse, looked up from the chart she was working on.

"You realize, don't you, that Howie Turner's going to follow you around like a lost puppy once he gets out of those leg casts and his eyes heal?"

She grinned at the leggy redhead. "Howie's special."

Toni Evans nodded. "That he is. Seems unfair that kids like Corporal Turner have to go through such hell."

Eden's smile faded. "At least we can help them get back on their feet."

"You're late going down to the cafeteria, aren't you?"

"That's what my stomach just told me. I thought I'd run over to the PX while I'm out, too. Need anything?"

"How about a commander in his mid-thirties?"

"Haven't seen any of those on the shelves lately," Eden teased. "Besides, you're beating the guys back with a stick as it is. Why add to the confusion at your front door?"

"Guess I haven't found the right one yet."

"Try saying yes to Mark Richards the next time he asks you out. You know you're crazy about the man." Before Toni could protest the obvious, she added, "Why don't we talk later? I've got to run or they'll close the cafeteria before I get down there."

Eden left the ward with a wave and made her way through the mazelike corridors of the rambling hospital. The elevator doors opened just before she reached them. She hesitated when she saw Jim Clayton disengage himself from the crowd of exiting passengers.

"You're a surprise," she greeted as she smoothed her hair back from her face and looked up at him.

"We're about to get trampled." He took her arm and led her away from the flow of traffic entering and exiting the elevator.

"Been out of town again?"

"Washington and Europe."

"Busy man."

"Too busy," he answered with a smile.

Eden felt his eyes travel the length of her body. She didn't look away when he lingered in his study of her face. "You look good. Different somehow, though. Even if I can't quite put my finger on what's changed."

Eden silently recalled the six weeks since they'd last talked. Her life had settled into a comfortable routine again, a condition she didn't take for granted. Making peace with herself about her feelings for Jim Clayton had taken time and energy. She wasn't surprised by his comment. She did feel different about herself, and about him. Tucking her hands into the unbuttoned lab coat she wore, she looked at him questioningly.

"I was wondering if you have time for dinner tonight? Mrs. Hooper mentioned you normally leave the hospital around six."

Chalk one up for Kitty. "I'd like that. Cooking for one person gets pretty dull after a while."

"Bully's South in Mission Valley sound okay?"

"I see someone's told you about my weakness for their roast beef sandwiches. I can meet you around six-thirty; that way I won't have to come back for my car."

"Whatever's easiest for you."

"I appreciate the invitation, Jim. I haven't gotten out since

Trace and David's party, and I've been feeling both hospital *and* housebound lately," she admitted as she glanced at her watch.

"Have I interrupted something?"

"A late lunch before I pass out from hunger. I didn't have time for breakfast this morning."

"Want some company?" he asked as they walked to the elevator.

"No time, I'm afraid. I'll have to pick up something and eat on the run as it is. It's letter day for a couple of the men on the ward."

"Letter day?"

"I write what they dictate to their girlfriends and families." She smiled at him. "I also run errands, help with physical therapy, empty bedpans, change dirty sheets—whatever's necessary. Not exactly a glamorous job, but I like it."

Jim held the door as they stepped out of the elevator. "I hate to admit this, but you're one surprise after another. What do you do in your spare time?"

"There isn't much of that," she conceded with a laugh. "But being here makes me feel useful. Since I became Kitty's assistant last fall, I've been coordinating the orientation program for new volunteers. The best part about my schedule is that I've managed to split my hours evenly between my ward and the Red Cross admin office. I do what I can to help, and I try to accept the things I can't change. That's all."

He studied her as they walked. "Very philosophical."

"No, just realistic. AA taught me that, although it was a painful lesson. Sometimes I forget, of course, but there's always a rude awakening of some kind to remind me of just how insignificant I really am in the scheme of things."

"You're surprising me again," he warned, looking puzzled.

"Why, Jim? I'm just one woman who is simply doing the best I can while I wait for my husband's status to be confirmed. There are hundreds of wives like me. Just because we've been forced to create new lives for ourselves doesn't make us remarkable or unique. When I accepted that particular bit of wisdom, I finally found some peace."

"It took a while, didn't it?"

She glanced at him and saw compassion in his eyes. She suddenly realized that behind his aggressive personality there existed a great deal of understanding for the confusion she'd experienced.

"It did take me time. More than it should have, perhaps, but I don't intend to apologize to anyone for that. I'm married and yet, in many ways, I'm not. A war has placed me in an awkward position, and the society I live in expects certain behavior from me. On the other hand, I have to balance all those expectations, as well as the ones I impose on myself, with normal everyday needs. That's tough to do some of the time. Add that to the fact that I was very isolated when Matthew was shot down. I know now that I stayed that way for far too long. That type of situation breeds all kinds of problems, and I sampled a lot of them."

"You mean the booze."

"That and several other albatrosses I voluntary hung around my own neck. Losing my son nearly destroyed me. It took me longer than I realized to come to terms with his death. In a way, maybe that was good, though, because I've rediscovered myself and my own strengths."

Eden paused, surprised by her candidness with a man who until recently intimidated her. *Or was it me I was afraid of?* she wondered.

"Do I know you at all?"

She playfully punched him in the shoulder when she saw his smile. "Hey! Be nice. I know I'm not a tough cookie, but I've got choices, and I'm making some for the first time in years. And I'm glad to feel whole again."

"I like the new you, babe. You've stopped acting like a victim."

Eden stopped at the double doors of the cafeteria. "Here's where I say good-bye for now."

"I'll have a table for us by the time you get to Bully's." He placed his hands on her shoulders and appeared pleased when she didn't pull away. "I suspect you can do without sitting in a bar."

She nodded. "Thanks. I like to avoid them whenever possible."

Jim leaned down and dropped a kiss on her cheek. "Welcome back to the world of the living."

Eden took a sip of her coffee and then placed her mug on the table. "Have you seen Tracey and David recently?"

"I ran into David during happy hour at the Pendleton O Club bar a few nights ago."

"Did he tell you they're planning on starting a family right away?"

"I can't say the subject ever came up." Jim dug out his lighter and put a flame to his cigarette. "Does it bother you that they want to have a baby?"

"I'd be a liar if I said it didn't at first, but I know now that I reacted selfishly to Tracey's announcement."

"Time changes values," he observed, "as well as the rules of friendship."

She glanced at him. "Bingo! But I'm all right now, though I'll admit to a few shaky days. I love Tracey enough to want her happy. Her life with David's everything she dreamed about as a kid. Love wasn't something we could count on when we were growing up," Eden explained. "But she has it now, and the emptiness is over for her."

"Do you mind if I'm still surprised by you?"

She laughed. "No, not at all. I've been surprising the hell out of myself lately."

They fell silent as the waiter put their check on the table and refilled their coffee mugs. When Jim placed a credit card atop the bill, she asked, "Where are you living now?"

"The Pendleton BOQ. Why?"

"Good." Eden reached for her purse. "I'm on your way home."

Jim gave her a considering look. "Don't keep me in suspense."

"I have an unopened bottle of cognac. Very old and very expensive. The parents of one of my patients gave it to me as a thank-you gift, and I didn't have the heart to refuse them. It seemed a shame to throw it out, so I saved it to give to you."

The twenty-minute drive up the coast to Del Mar passed in a blur of headlights and random thoughts, none of which altered Eden's certainty of how her evening with Jim would end. Her mind had known all along, she realized, what her body would ultimately demand. Emotions somewhat aloof, she felt neither guilt nor regret as she collected her purse and got out of her car.

Standing under the light flooding the front steps of her home, Eden inserted her house key into the lock. Jim's silence allowed her to feel the solidness of his presence as he stood behind her. Pushing open the door, she inhaled shallowly.

"Come in," she invited as she reached for the wall switch. Light flooded the room and brought soft earth tones to life. She walked into the center of the room, but before she could turn around, Jim spoke.

"I still want you, Eden."

"I know," she answered softly.

He shoved his hands into his trouser pockets and didn't move. "It's your ball game, babe. Give me the cognac and send me packing or lock the front door."

She hesitated briefly, then turned, retraced her steps, and slid the dead bolt into place. The sound reached into her mind and registered like detonating dynamite before she lifted her eyes to Jim's speculative expression.

"You *want* me to stay?"

She saw his desire in the sudden harshness that defined his facial features and knew it was time for the truth. "I *need* you to stay."

He moved to within centimeters of her body. She stilled under the certainty of his hands as he reached around her and began to loosen the weave of her braid. Exhaling unevenly, he threaded his fingers through the auburn mass.

"Honesty to the bitter end, is that it?" he finally asked.

"Would you rather I lied and told you I love you?"

"Yes, damn you!"

She whispered, "You know I can't. I never will."

She felt his hands knot into fists, but she didn't flinch beneath the pain.

"Is this where you tell me you won't make any promises you can't keep?" he demanded harshly. "One day, one night, at a time?"

She looked up at him and ached for them both. Nothing was easy anymore. Touching his cheek with her fingertips, she asked, "Why are you doing this?"

"Why do I want you so much?" he countered as he unclenched his fists and released her.

Without taking her eyes from his face, Eden lifted the hem of her sweater and drew it from her body. Her breasts swung free, and Jim captured them with his hands. He leaned down and licked hot circles around her nipples. She moaned, and the sound splintered the quiet of the room. In that instant Eden knew she would never forget the feel of Drew suckling at her breast.

Jim straightened and removed his own sweater. "After we make love, I won't want to lose you."

"This isn't about winning or losing," she told him quietly. "It's about needing and surviving. And it's about not being alone any longer." She searched his face for understanding, hoping that it could and would surpass his unrealistic expectations. "I'm so tired of being by myself."

His eyes didn't cease their quest for the truth. His questions continued. "Why didn't you let this happen six months ago? We both knew then it was inevitable."

"Nothing's inevitable, nothing," she insisted, recalling verbatim his words at Tracey and David's wedding reception.

He just looked at her, disbelief and challenge in his eyes.

"We're people, Jim, people with obligations and responsibilities. Nothing can change those basic facts no matter what we say or do."

"Why did you make me wait?" he pressed again.

"I just wasn't ready."

"And you are now?"

She thought for a moment about his last question. She had grappled with right and wrong and all the gray area in between for weeks and months, and she always came up with the same answer. She needed him. He wasn't Matthew, so she knew she wasn't deluding herself. Nor was he a replacement until Matthew came home, because she wasn't that cruel. She simply needed him. Now. In this moment and at this time in her life. Finally, she nodded.

He swore in frustration and gathered her into his arms. "You've lost your innocence, babe."

She stared up at him. Faces drifted through her mind, and tears filled her eyes. Drew, Matthew, young men like Howie. She blinked and put her arms around him, pressing herself into the heat and strength of his male body. She asked softly, "Haven't we all lost something of ourselves?"

Jim muttered, "Another casualty," and lowered their bodies to the carpet.

Eden felt as though time, as she defined it, simply stopped. She also realized that she had finally found a physical and emotional reprieve from the emptiness of the last two years.

Gravel crunched, and Eden peered out the living-room window. She watched Tracey slam her car door and walk to the front steps of the beach house. The sound of shower water ceased as the doorbell chimed.

You'd think I'd be ready for this after four months.

Eden took a deep breath and stepped away from the window. Warm June air and the familiar salt tang of the Pacific wrapped invisible arms around her as she opened the door and smiled in greeting.

"Since you've forgotten our address and phone number, I thought I'd stop in and see if you're still among the living." Tracey walked into the living room and opened her arms for a quick hug. "Where've you been hiding yourself lately? We've missed you."

"You know me. I get in a rut and tend to stay in it." She watched Tracey extract a small black box from her purse before setting the leather bag on the couch. "Come on into the kitchen. The coffee's just finished perking."

Tracey followed her. "Haven't you been up long?"

Eden stiffened when she heard Jim's off-key whistling in the back of the house.

Tracey frowned. "Who's . . ."

Eden ignored her confusion and reached for two mugs from the cupboard near the stove. "Coffee?"

"I've already eaten, but coffee sounds good. Besides, I can't stay long. I'm on an errand for David. It's kind of a present . . ." Her voice died when Jim walked into the kitchen, his hair still damp from his shower.

"Morning, Tracey. Long time no see."

"I've got plenty of eggs and bacon. You sure you won't stay for brunch?"

"Have you completely lost your mind?"

"Don't, Trace. This doesn't concern you," Eden warned.

Jim glanced at Eden. She answered the question in his eyes by saying, "Your coffee's poured. I put it on the table."

Tracey shoved the box she'd been holding into Eden's hands. "Here. David sends it with his compliments. Next time he can deliver his own damned surprises."

"What is it?"

"Matt was promoted. David got the news yesterday. He thought you'd be pleased if he picked up the new insignia for you at the PX." She paused before saying deliberately, "Your husband is a major in the Marine Corps now. Congratulations, Mrs. Benedict."

"Trace, you're my friend, not my conscience."

"Are you nuts?"

"This is not the time."

"You need your head examined, Eden." She whirled around and glared at Jim. "And you . . . you despicable bastard. How could you do this?"

Eden couldn't stop the bitter laughter that escaped her. "Your outrage is showing."

"You've got a husband, or have you decided to overlook that particular fact of your life?"

"You're leaving now." Eden took her arm and led her from the kitchen.

Tracey pulled free and came to a stop. "Not before you explain what's going on between you and Jim."

"It's fairly obvious, isn't it?"

"How are you going to explain this to Matt?"

"You talk as though he's out of town on an overnight business trip."

"This is wrong, Eden. You know it's wrong."

"That's enough, damn it! What would you suggest I do? Shall I write him a letter, on the off chance he even receives the damn things, and confess my infidelity? Will that make you happy, Tracey? Or, better yet, shall I beat my breast and atone for my sins in the public square?" Shaking with anger, she walked the remaining steps to the front door and jerked it open. "Good-bye, friend. In the future, kindly keep your moral indignation to yourself. You've no idea what it's like to live my life. I sincerely hope you never have to find out."

"I don't believe you're behaving this way," she said as she collected her purse and approached the front door.

"And I do not believe you," Eden grated. "You're the lady who has a husband in her bed every night, not me. You're the lady who's ecstatically happy every hour of every day, not me. As I said before, Trace, you're not my conscience. If you want to remain friends, my personal life is not up for discussion or debate. Is that clear?"

"This is wrong, Eden. What you're doing is wrong. Come home with me so David and I can help you sort through this mess."

"Who declared you the moral arbiter of my life, Tracey? I certainly didn't. In the final analysis, the decisions are mine, as well as the consequences. I'm prepared to live with both. Give David my love and thank him for Matthew's insignia. I appreciate his thoughtfulness."

She closed the front door and resisted the urge to lean against it. Walking back through the house to the kitchen, Eden placed the small black box on the counter and slumped forward. Her fingertips sought and found the battering pulse in her temple.

"You always do that."

She didn't turn around. "What?"

"You always rub your forehead or your temples when you're hurting. It's one of the first things I ever noticed about you."

She heard his chair scrape along the floor as he stood. Crossing the kitchen, he slid his arms around her waist and pulled her back against his sturdy body as she sighed heavily.

"You gonna be all right, babe?"

"Maybe in a hundred years."

Eden turned in his arms and looked up at him. *She knew* he'd fallen in love with her. *He knew* she was still in love with her husband. And, like her, he stood on the edge of an emotional precipice so treacherous that there were no answers, no guarantees.

There is only now, she realized sadly. Only now.

CHAPTER

19

June 1970—Hanoi, North Vietnam

A single muffled thump sounded against the cell wall.

Danger!

Matt tensed. Sitting up, he realized that it was morning, an overcast June day thick with humidity and the stink of unwashed flesh. His own.

He glanced at Bill Porter, his cellmate of the last six and a half months. Both waited for the second thump, the signal that the danger had passed. It never happened. They heard instead the measured cadence of booted feet, the shriek of a rusty hinge as a cell door opened down the corridor, and then the protestations of another prisoner, his voice raised in anger as he was prodded from his bunk by the guards.

"That's the second time since dawn," Bill observed from his reclining position on his cement platform.

Matt nodded without speaking. He watched Bill's fingertips stray to his right leg. His cast had been removed during a recent torture session, the improperly set breaks rebroken and now oozing infection.

Matt remained silent, his senses alert to the sound of voices or footsteps. He sat with his back against the stone wall of the cell, his thoughts periodically wandering to the night cries of men being tortured that he'd heard in the last week. He'd already counted six prisoners who'd been removed from the cell block in the preceding three days. None had returned.

Bill groaned. Matt saw him struggle to sit up. Sliding from

his own bunk, he grasped the chain dragging between his ankles, crossed the narrow room, and placed his free hand on the bony shoulder of his cellmate.

"Let me help," he suggested.

Bill nodded. Sweat beaded his forehead, and pain-filled seconds ticked by before he straightened his spine and exhaled the pent-up air trapped in his lungs.

Matt squatted in front of him and eased aside the fabric of his gray pants. Both men studied the protruding stubs of bone at mid-thigh and mid-shin. Neither commented on the weeping, discolored flesh.

"I need to get up."

Translation: "I need your help to use the bucket."

Matt straightened. He lifted Bill, carrying him as one would a frail child. Four shuffling steps led them to the bucket in the corner of the cell. A bucket reeking of feces.

Neither man relinquished his dignity despite the sound of urine streaming into the wooden container.

Several hours later the door to their cell burst open. Matt placed a protective hand on his bedroll. He watched Bill do the same.

"Llole up!"

Roll up, Matt thought in disgust. Speak English, you son of a bitch!

His gaze returned to Bill's face, and he saw a blink of warning. Matt inhaled deeply and reminded himself to stay calm no matter the provocation.

"Stand!"

The two men moved simultaneously. Both tucked their bedrolls under their arms, and both edged toward the ends of their cement pallets. Matt stood first and extended his hand to Bill.

Bill moaned as he struggled upright, and Matt urged, "Lean into me. Give me your weight."

"Silence!"

He ignored the guard and supported his cellmate's right side. "Ready?"

He waited for Bill to nod. The guards continued to make threatening motions with their unsheathed bayonets.

"Ready," Bill finally managed.

They moved slowly from the narrow cell. Matt glanced at the grime-covered cell walls one last time before stepping into the hallway. Home, he thought. Home for six and a half months had been a mosquito- and rat-infested cubicle no bigger than a walk-in closet. He shook his head and tightened his hold on Bill. Now what? he wondered.

A second guard led them down an unlighted hallway. A third fell in behind them. Matt squinted when they entered a large courtyard. The afternoon sun had finally penetrated the hazy sky. Cooking smells and high-pitched Vietnamese assaulted his ears. To his right he saw what appeared to be Hoa Lo's main gate, the same gate, he decided, that he and Chet had passed through sixteen months earlier.

They were led to a second long corridor. Guards stood at attention in every doorway they passed. Another courtyard, smaller than the first, appeared at the end of the hall. Two men collected litter. Matt started in surprise when one of the prisoners looked up and touched his fingertips to his forehead in an abbreviated salute. He glanced down at Bill, heard his sigh of relief, and realized that they had both had the same fear of more torture sessions.

"We're just being moved," Matt whispered.

"Silence! Prisoner no talk!" screeched one of their guards.

Matt and Bill were ordered to a stop at the entrance to a small building in the center of the courtyard.

"Leave lloles! Time wash!"

He welcomed the flow of tepid water across his shoulders and down his body as he leaned against the wall. Bill stood beside him under a second spigot. Using the wall for support, the crippled man twisted and turned his body under the meager supply of soothing water. Even without soap, Matt was certain that this was the cleanest they'd both been in several months.

The water soon trickled to nothing. A guard tossed them thin gray towels. After reclothing themselves, they were marched to a second building on the perimeter of the courtyard. Matt felt his throat close and his chest expand with emotion when he stepped into a twenty-by-thirty-foot room already occupied by more than a dozen American prisoners of war.

The guard nudged them forward. Matt felt the prodding tip of the bayonet and clenched his right fist. Shoving down his irritation, he kept a secure hold on Bill and crossed the room, all the while hungrily drinking in the sight of other American men. They stopped on the far side of the room, in front of an elongated cement ledge that Matt assumed was a sleeping platform.

"Llole here!" shouted the guard.

Matt and Bill silently placed their bedrolls on the platform and remained standing.

"Sit!"

Matt helped Bill find a comfortable position before joining him. He glared at the guard, absently clenching and unclenching his right fist.

"Next time bow!" spat the North Vietnamese guard.

Matt watched him whirl around and stalk from the large cell, his two minions close on his heels.

"You son of a bitch!"

He exhaled raggedly, relief suddenly draining the energy from his body. Remaining seated, he closed his eyes and took several steadying breaths.

"Semper fi, Warrior. I've been wondering where the hell the gooks had hidden you."

Matt felt the sting of tears and blinked. He stared at Chet Holt, saw the familiar lopsided grin of the short, balding marine lieutenant, and reached out to grasp his extended hand. "Long time no see, buddy. How ya been?"

Chet shrugged, but his smile persisted. "Hangin' in there like everyone else."

Matt studied his Long Moc cellmate. Broken front teeth, a jagged scar across his forehead, and the flesh evaporating from his body still failed to diminish the humor shining from his eyes.

Chet squeezed his hand before releasing it. "You've been working on your arm, haven't you?"

He nodded. "My own version of physical therapy."

Chains scraped the cement floor as two men crossed the

room. Matt surveyed the area. He saw curiosity, compassion, and restraint in the eyes of the men who met his gaze with a welcoming nod or smile. No one would crowd him here, he realized.

He glanced back at Chet. "Who's in charge?"

"A light colonel named Jenkins. He's a B-52 driver." Chet turned and motioned forward the man in question.

Matt stood and squared his shoulders. "Benedict, M. A., Captain, United States Marine Corps, sir." He held his salute, knowing it was an example of proper textbook execution. A random memory reminded him of the hours he'd spent in front of a mirror during OCS perfecting the smooth gesture.

Pride. My survival is a matter of pride. The realization strengthened him, helped him stand taller.

"At ease, Captain." The colonel, a gap-toothed, gray-haired man in his early forties, glanced at Bill Porter and saw his struggle to rise. "Stay where you are, Scratch. It's good to see you again. ComNet said you were around here somewhere."

"Thank you, sir."

"Settle in, gentlemen. Get the lay of the land. Chow's not for another few hours. The S-2, Dave Winkle, will debrief you tomorrow. In the meantime," he said, nodding at Chet, "Lieutenant Holt here'll outline our communications network, chain of command, and the rules our senior people in another cellblock have established for us."

They watched the colonel shuffle back to the far side of the oversized cell. The chain dragging between his ankles was muted by the murmur of voices in the room.

Matt looked at Chet and saw reassurance in his expression. Everything will be explained soon, his eyes said. Relax for a minute. I know how disconcerting this change is. Matt nodded and sat down again.

"He's a good man," Chet commented as he joined the two men on the cement ledge.

"I've known him for years," Bill told them. "We were in fighters together until he was transferred into heavy bombers. He's methodical as hell, but he gets the job done."

Matt scanned the room again. This time he counted fourteen men, all involved in one pursuit or another. Some slept, a few exercised, while others participated in what appeared to be small discussion groups. Chet's voice ended his perusal of his fellow prisoners for the moment.

"Isolation?"

"Yeah. Two hundred and nine days' worth and then a double cell with Scratch for the past six and a half months."

"My stretch was for ninety-seven days." Chet grimaced. "I nearly went out of my skull."

Matt's jaw instinctively tightened, and he narrowed his black eyes. The memory of the fifteen months he'd already spent at Hoa Lo surged up inside him like rising bile. He would never forget, he knew, the inhumanity he'd endured at the hands of the North Vietnamese. His mouth tasted sour, and he swallowed.

Chet seemed to sense his tension. "Still a thinker, I see."

"It's his Cherokee blood," Bill chimed in with a grin. "He'll never be accused of running off at the mouth."

Matt smiled grudgingly. Their good-natured kidding helped take the edge off his preoccupation with the past and the bitterness he felt because of his captivity.

"I checked on your buddy Jack Morrison when I got out of isolation. Nobody here's ever heard of him, but he might be up at Briar Patch or out at the Citadel."

"Thanks, Chet." Matt's focus changed, and he voiced the query now dominating his thoughts. "What are the rules the colonel mentioned?"

"The gooks have been playing head games with several of our guys. Promising them things like extra rations, no more torture sessions, and early releases in exchange for intelligence information. We've even been put on display for visiting U.S. peace groups. Those bastards are getting some great PR at our expense. But the bottom line is this—no early release. We all go home together or not at all."

Matt and Bill nodded. Their expressions indicated that comments weren't necessary in a situation where the enemy endeavored to pit the men against one another.

"The concept of unity over self is the rule here," Chet continued. "No bowing in public, either. And we don't admit, verbally or on paper, to any war crimes if we can avoid it."

"Any idea why we were brought in here and not left where we were?" Matt asked.

"There's a subtle change in prisoner policy going on. We started noticing it in February. The Cat's even been replaced as commandant of the prison."

"Major Bui's gone?" Bill clarified, his body suddenly rigid with tension.

Chet placed a hand on his shoulder. "For several months now. They've eased up on most of us. Fewer guys are being tortured. We occasionally get powdered milk with a meal. Some of the guards are even backing off on reporting minor infractions of prison rules. We're not sure why, but according to the newer prisoners, peace talks are still going on in Paris. Word apparently leaked out last summer about the North Vietnamese torture of American POWs. Our government confirmed it, and the gooks found themselves with an image problem in the free-world press. That's about all I know."

"What about an escape committee?" Matt pressed.

Chet sighed. "Not a good idea. Two men tried recently. They didn't even get as far as the edge of Hanoi. Both were captured and tortured. One man's still missing. The capital city, as well as the rest of the country, is an armed camp. An effective disguise is virtually impossible, so our senior people are discouraging any further attempts."

Bill leaned back against his bedroll and closed his eyes. His fatigue obvious, he observed, "It's grin-and-bear-it time again, fellas."

"That's about the size of it," Chet agreed. He watched Matt ease himself into a comfortable position against the cell wall, his bedroll tucked under the base of his spine like Bill's. "I know it's frustrating and we're all climbing the walls in here, but there's very little any of us can do to get out of this pisshole. The good news is that every time there's a snag in the peace talks, the president actually listens to his military advisers and drops a few bombs."

"I get the feeling we're a political hot potato back home," Matt mused aloud.

"Yeah, you're probably right. Between the politicians, the antiwar pukes, and the North Vietnamese, we'll be lucky if this stinking war doesn't drag on for another ten years. According to one new guy who came in last week, even some of our wives are getting into the fray."

Matt looked genuinely surprised, and Chet explained, "The women are giving press conferences, visiting congressmen, and going on talk shows. The *Navy* and *Air Force Times* are running stories about them. It seems they're worried that we'll be forgotten. The mood at home has gone from bad to worse where Vietnam's concerned. One new POW said it wasn't safe to go off base stateside in anything but civvies. Can ya beat that?"

"Our ladies must want us home pretty bad," Scratch murmured. "I bet Ginny's leading the bandwagon. You make that woman mad and there's no tellin' what she'll do."

"Maybe they're horny, too," Chet said hopefully, a lopsided grin on his face. "I know I sure am."

"Do you ever get any letters?" Matt asked quietly after their laughter died down and Scratch announced his intention of getting some shut-eye.

Chet nodded, his expression suddenly subdued. "Two, so far. One at Christmas and then one a few weeks ago, but the postmarks on them were almost two years old."

Matt touched the waistband of his trousers and pressed his hand against the sheet of paper tucked there. The ink had nearly disappeared from constant handling, but the words blazed in his mind. *Be safe, my love.* He looked up when he felt Chet's hand on his shoulder.

"Get some rack time. The other guys will introduce themselves one at a time. No one pushes too hard around here. We all just try to take things day by day."

"What else?" He watched Chet make his way to a spot halfway down the platform ledge. Tears stung his eyes, and Chet's body blurred. His thoughts drifted to Eden, as they always did when he felt the keen bite of loneliness.

I love you, Matthew. I will always love you.

He grimaced and closed his fist around her letter.

Be safe, my love.

Oh, paleface, I'm not safe. I'm in hell. Will you want what's left of me if I ever get out of here? Do you even want me now? Are you waiting for me, or do you hate me for wasting our lives this way?

CHAPTER 20

July–November 1970—San Diego, California

A hand covered her mouth.

Eden stiffened in shock.

"Come with me now," a voice instructed. "It's time."

She nodded. The hand moved away, and she opened her mouth to scream. No sound emerged.

The hand clutched her arm, pulling her to her feet with frightening ease. She felt skeletal fingers close around her wrist, insistent, sharp, punishing fingers.

"What do you want?" she asked, her heart slamming violently against the wall of her chest.

The hand dragged her forward, and she stumbled. Then it jerked her upright as though she had all the vitality of a rag doll. Shivering convulsively, she realized that the hem of her nightgown was trailing in the dirt. She started to laugh, instantly recognized the hysteria of the sound, and ground her teeth together to silence herself.

The hand released her, and she shrank back. Her eyes hesitantly followed the pointing insistence of its bony fingers. She took a deep breath, and relief flowed through her, but then she frowned, puzzled by the splotches on the white wall.

Curious, she eased forward. She fingered the erratic scarlet pattern, expecting coolness. Instead, she felt wetness and a disturbing warmth. In the space of a heartbeat she realized it was blood. She gasped, panic ricocheting around inside her.

"Nooo!"

The hand covered her mouth, shutting off the sound. It died in a gurgle in her throat.

He took her down another corridor, this one darker, longer.

She stumbled again, struggling to keep up. "Who are you? Where are you taking me?"

"Do not speak."

She closed her eyes. The hand tugged at her, relentless as it propelled her forward.

"This isn't real," she moaned. "This is not real."

The hand held her immobile. When had she stopped walking? She opened her eyes, the action violating the resistance in her mind. "No more. Please, no more."

She fought the hand, the implacability of its grip. It yanked her forward, into an empty room. Her eyes touched the walls, and she exhaled in relief. No blood. Looking around, she froze.

Wood-frame beds, the slats showing, lined the walls. Leg irons were attached to the baseboards, skeletons attached to the leg irons. Their bones clacked as they tossed and turned. A voice cried out, "Don't leave me here to rot!"

She felt their agony and cringed. "No more," she pleaded. "No more."

The hand guided her from the cell. Tears fell from her eyes, blinding her, making her stumble. Something she couldn't define pressed in on her. It took her several moments to realize that it was a cloyingly sweet scent. But the sweetness was rotten, not the fragrance of flowers.

She wrenched herself from the hand. It released her. Its willingness puzzled her, but she didn't linger or question her sudden freedom. She ran, tripped, and then tumbled forward. Her hands sank into oozing mud as she tried to right herself at the edge of what she realized was a trench.

She moaned when she saw the carnage below.

Bodies. Dozens and dozens of bodies. Stripped, emaciated, and left to rot in the heat. The stench of overripe flesh merged with her senses, and she gagged. Hundreds of vacant eyes stared at her until the vultures hovering overhead suddenly swooped down, one by one, and captured the swollen red berries.

"Stop this!" she screamed. "Stop this insanity!"

She whirled around to flee, but the hand stopped her. She suddenly saw the body attached to the hand, the bones now clothed in flesh. She looked up. Emptiness occupied the space that should have been a face.

She shuddered. "Who are you?"

"I am not a dream." He waved his hand across the scar carved into the earth. "We are not a dream. Take us home. Do not abandon us as others have."

Her eyes shifted back to the pile of bodies, and she flinched. In the center of the trench sat a man in a rocking chair. He held a baby. He was surrounded by corpses.

"Noooo! Noooo!"

Eden screamed herself hoarse. Sitting in the center of her bed and swaying back and forth, she eventually collapsed into a sobbing heap. It was well after dawn before she realized that she wasn't alone.

"You've been out of it for hours. What happened?"

"Can't . . . talk," she gasped.

Jim frowned and tugged her into his arms. "You sounded like you were in hell, babe. Is there anything I can do?"

Her teeth chattered in spite of her perspiration-drenched body. "Hold . . . me," she finally managed.

She closed her eyes. His solidness offered only momentary reassurance. The dream wouldn't fade. It kept replaying in her mind, refusing to roll back into her subconscious like most of the nightmares she'd had for the last two and a half years.

"You want to tell me about it?"

"No. Not now, anyway." She twisted in his arms and glanced at the clock on the night table. "We have to get up."

"I can think of something I'd rather do."

Eden looked up and saw his smile.

"Why don't we stay in bed? I can book a later flight."

"No!" Her voice was sharper than she intended, and she exhaled slowly. Go away, Jim. Stop talking and leave.

"That nightmare's really got you shook."

She stiffened when his hand strayed under her nightgown and up her thigh. "I need a shower."

"I want you."

She heard his determination but no longer found it appealing. "This isn't a good time."

Pulling her down onto the bed, he promised, "I'll make it good." He found her center, that place on her body that was like a light switch to her desire, and stroked her with his fingertips.

She tried to jerk herself out of his arms. "Don't! I said no."

Jim released her and held his hands in front of his chest in a placating gesture. "Whatever you want."

"I want a shower," she repeated, her voice low as she slipped from the bed.

"Eden?"

She stopped. Turning, she faced him, unaware that she was absently rubbing her temples.

"I love you, babe. Whatever you need is fine with me."

Her eyes touched the expression on his face and flitted away to safety. Don't be understanding, Jim. I don't want you this way. I preferred your aloofness, your indifference. But we can't go back to simply using each other's bodies, can we? You changed the rules and didn't mention it until it was too late. Eden sighed and looked back at him. "You've changed."

He chuckled, the sound oddly mirthless. "That strikes me as more an accusation than an observation."

She stared at him. "I'm not sure what it is." Eden turned and walked into the bathroom. Stuffing her nightgown in the hamper, she stepped into the shower. Make your mind a blank, she told herself. Don't think about the dream or what it might mean. It'll drive you out of your skull if you don't forget it.

Tears spilled from her eyes as she washed herself. She couldn't forget the sight of all those bodies, nor could she rid herself of the smell still suffocating her senses. She grimaced when she heard the medicine-chest door open and close. The shower curtain moved as she reached over to turn off the water. Jim's tanned body came into view, and Eden unconsciously backed against the wall.

Please don't touch me, she thought as her mind and body

tightened against any further intrusion by this man she had so foolishly invited into her life in a moment of loneliness.

"Need your back scrubbed?"

She flinched at the familiarity of his question. It was part of the early-morning patter they often indulged in.

I'm creating rituals with this man!

"Eden?"

She shook her head and stepped around him. "I'll start the coffee." Risking a glance, she saw his confusion. "Jim, I'm all right. Just have your shower." She heard his reply, the curtain closing, and then the splatter of water as it hit the tile wall.

Eden walked into the kitchen after brushing her hair and slipping into a terry-cloth robe. The bewildered expression on Jim's face wouldn't leave her mind. She swore softly. No confrontations and no expectations today, Mr. Clayton, sir. I haven't got the strength.

"*Don't stop loving me, Eden.*"

"Stop it, Matthew! Just stop it!" she cried. Emptiness swamped her, and she doubled over. Wrapping her arms around her middle, she slid to her knees on the cool kitchen tile. She leaned against the cupboard door beneath the sink and sobbed. She sobbed for the isolation and confusion of her life, she sobbed for the awful ache in her heart that never seemed to give her a moment of peace, and she sobbed because she was tired of not knowing how long she would be without Matthew.

Jim found her in the same position ten minutes later, still weeping helplessly.

"Eden!" He dropped to his knees at her side and placed a hand on her shoulder. "For Christ's sake, talk to me!"

She scrubbed at her cheeks with the heels of her hands. "I didn't make . . . the coffee . . . yet."

"Oh, Jesus. Come on. Let me help you up." He saw her dazed look and guided her to the table on the other side of the kitchen. "I'll get the coffee. Instant okay?"

She nodded, her face a blank canvas, her thoughts buried behind her eyes.

"I hate leaving you like this."

"How long will you be gone?" She didn't abandon the sight

of the rolling ocean swells beyond the edge of the beach as she spoke.

"A week, ten days tops." He paused briefly. "I meant it earlier when I said I could delay my departure."

"No, don't." She continued to stare at the water, not really seeing the brilliant July morning sun reflected by the shimmering Pacific. The piercing whistle of the kettle finally brought her back from the haunted place she kept visiting in her mind.

Sighing, she stood, crossed the room, and poured hot water into the two mugs Jim had placed on the counter. Looking over at him and keenly aware of his sudden tenseness, she said, "We'll talk when you get back."

"It's been a long time."

Eden nodded. "Four and a half months." She watched Tracey nervously fold and unfold the napkin on the table in front of her.

"We're . . ." She covered the napkin with her hand and looked up. "David and I are having an anniversary party next weekend. Just a few people. We'd both like you to come if you haven't made any other plans."

Plans? The word made her smile as she studied her old friend. So much had changed. It was almost a year since Tracey's marriage to David and fourteen months since Jim Clayton had stumbled into her life, and eventually her bed. That was over, thank God. Even if it had ended badly. He'd finally stopped phoning two weeks ago, although their final confrontation was still fresh in her mind.

"What do you mean 'end things'?" he had demanded.

"You heard me. I don't think we should see each other any longer. It's just not a good idea."

"Why? What the hell made you change your mind? I thought everything between us was great." His mouth narrowed to a disgusted line, and he raked cruel fingers through his sand-colored hair. "It was that damned dream, wasn't it?

I knew I shouldn't have left you alone to stew in your memories."

"You don't understand . . ."

"He's dead, Eden. You know it and I know it. Why don't you face facts and get on with your life?"

"I have a life, a life I made for myself," she lashed back. "It was the hardest thing I've ever done, but I did it, and I'm proud of it. And for the record, my husband is missing in action, not dead. The Marine Corps hasn't declared him dead, and neither have I. I'd know if he was gone. I'd know, damn it!"

"Would you?" He grabbed her and shook her as though he could force her into believing what he wanted her to believe.

She pulled herself free and put the bed between them. "This hasn't got anything to do with Matthew. This only concerns us. I've been honest with you from the beginning, Jim. I love my husband. Having an affair with you hasn't changed my feelings."

"Oh, I see it all clearly now. You've been talking to Tracey again, haven't you? And she's finally managed to lay some big morality number on you. Christ, I should've expected this."

"You're wrong," she insisted. "Jim, you care too much about me. The longer we drag this out, the harder it will be for both of us. I've never lied to you about my feelings, and I don't intend to start now. Tracey has nothing to do with my decision. She never did."

"You'll change your mind," he had insisted, a stubborn look on his face. "You know where to reach me when you do."

"I won't change my mind, Jim, and I'm sorry if I've hurt you, because I do care about you. But only as a friend. You've always known that."

"Eden?" Tracey said hesitantly. "Will you come to our party?"

She shook herself from her memories. "Of course I'll come. I wouldn't miss it for the world."

"I'm pregnant," Tracey blurted out.

Eden reached across the table and unraveled the shredded

napkin from Tracey's nervous fingers. "I'm happy for you. You've earned this family of yours."

"David and I talked it over. We'd like you and Matt to be the baby's godparents." She saw the lack of understanding in Eden's face and hastened to explain. "The priest told us a proxy can stand in for Matt."

Surprise briefly widened her eyes. "We'd be honored."

"About last June . . ."

Eden instantly felt her awkwardness. "You don't—"

"But I do. You were right when you said I didn't have any idea what your life was like. I had no business acting as judge and jury. Not about Jim. Not about anything. I hope you'll forgive me."

"It's over, Trace, so forget it. I already have."

She nodded and appeared relieved that they wouldn't have to rehash what had happened between the three of them that day she'd dropped off Matt's insignia. "Thanks."

Eden glanced at her watch and slid her chair back from the table. "I've got to get to the ward. Lunch trays are due soon, and some of the men need help."

Tracey nodded and collected her purse. They left the cafeteria and walked to the front entrance of the building.

"I've really missed you," Tracey said, tears welling in her eyes and slipping down her cheeks. She laughed self-consciously. "I've been crying so much lately that David's about to invest in a life preserver."

Eden gave her a hug after handing her a tissue. "I'll see you next weekend. You take good care of yourself."

Deep in thought, Eden traversed the seemingly endless corridors of the naval hospital. The rift between herself and Tracey had been difficult, but Tracey's willingness to bridge the gap created by the affair Eden had had with Jim Clayton was a welcome gift, one she hadn't anticipated. She knew that they probably couldn't ever resurrect their past friendship. Too much water under the bridge and too many harsh words spoken, but perhaps they could have a newer, better relationship, one they could both handle. Eden hoped so.

As she entered the ward, she saw that the lunch cart was already in front of the nurses' station. Toni Evans, with the help of an orderly, handed trays to ambulatory patients, who then served the bedridden troops first. Those able to help with distribution returned for their own food once the task had been completed.

Toni smiled when she saw Eden. She handed her an uncovered meal tray and asked, "Ready to face our resident bear?"

"I gotcha a backup, Eden," the orderly assured her with a toothy grin as he levered the cart around for easier access to the lower shelves.

"I must have a persecution complex. Sergeant Howard ranks right up there with Attila the Hun when it comes to cooperation." She gave them both a wry look. "I'm really getting tired of wearing his food, so wish me luck."

Eden checked the buttons on her lab coat before walking the length of the ward's center aisle. Laughter, snippets of conversation, and the clink of silverware punctuated the air. Billy Ellingen, the patient in the bed next to Army Sergeant Daniel Howard, grinned up at her between bites of roast beef and Jell-O. Minus a leg and an arm, the ever-smiling nineteen-year-old veteran was either high on drugs or just naturally effervescent. Eden couldn't decide which.

"Lunch is ready, Sergeant Howard." She pressed a button at the end of his bed, waiting as it slowly elevated the upper half of his body to a comfortable position. Making her way to the chair beside his bed, Eden automatically surveyed his cast-encased left arm, his bandaged right arm, and the still-suppurating sores on his chest. Her gaze lingered briefly on the dressing-covered stump that had once been his right hand and wrist.

"The roast beef looks excellent today. Will you try and eat something for me?"

He ignored her and continued to stare at the ceiling, his body rigid with an emotion Eden couldn't quite define. She decided to try again. "I think you'll enjoy the food if you'll give it a chance."

"Get the fuck away from me, lady!"

Here we go again, she thought. Glancing at Billy, Eden suppressed a smile. His grin looked stuck, and his eyes reminded her of inflated blue balloons. She took a deep breath, refocused on the sergeant, and reminded herself: The patients are here to be helped, not murdered in their beds when they annoy a Red Cross volunteer.

Keeping her voice low and even, she suggested, "Don't make this any more difficult than it has to be. We both know you need to eat. If you'd prefer help from a corpsman or an orderly, all you have to do is tell me."

"Lady, I said get lost." He kept his eyes on the ceiling. "I'm not hungry."

"Hey, Shooter, I'll take your chow if you don't want it," Billy offered, his grin wider than ever.

Eden frowned at him until he went back to his own lunch. "How do you expect to regain your strength?"

He grunted and closed his eyes.

"Sergeant, if you don't let me feed you, Dr. Richards will be forced to order intravenous feeding. You can't really want that to happen." She saw the muscles in his jaw bunch and pressed her point. "I know this is hard on you, but if we work together, you'll regain your strength, the cast'll come off—"

"Fuck you!" he bellowed.

Eden jumped. She felt his frustration, his profound sense of helplessness. Reaching for him, her fingertips grazed the hand exposed at the end of the plaster cast. He lurched to the side of the bed, his growl of rage exploding around them. His cast connected with her forehead, the lunch tray overturned in her lap, and she slid to the floor after losing her balance.

Roast beef, mixed vegetables, and Jell-O clumped together and slithered down her legs. The mess landed with a soggy plop on the floor between her ankles. Sergeant Howard was sprawled half in and half out of his bed. Silence blanketed the ward. Eden pulled herself to her feet and straightened her lab coat, finally noticing the crowd of curious patients ringing the end of the bed. Squaring her shoulders, she waited while two corpsmen helped the sergeant back into a comfortable position.

Toni Evans handed her a second tray. "Try again?"

Eden released a gust of air and nodded.

"Give her a chance, Shooter. She's just doin' her job," Billy advised, his smile reappearing.

"All right, everyone," Toni called out. "Back to bed. This isn't a circus sideshow."

The patients dispersed, and Eden returned to the chair beside Daniel Howard's bed. "Let's try again. Roast beef, gravy, mashed—"

"Lady," he growled, his muddy-brown eyes stabbing into her like twin daggers. "I don't know what the fuck your problem is, but get the hell away from me and take that pig slop with you."

"I'm not a collie, Sergeant Howard, so stop calling me 'lady.' My name is Eden or Mrs. Benedict, whichever you're comfortable with."

"I don't give a flying fuck who you are."

Eden's shoulders slumped. His pride's fragile, she reminded herself. Go slowly or you'll blow it. You've handled tougher patients than this guy.

He continued to glare at her, his body shaking with barely restrained rage. "I'm not hungry, and I don't need your pity. Now let me be."

"Pity?" The word slammed around inside her brain. "Pity? Damn it to hell! I've had just about enough out of you, mister. Now sit up and cooperate. I'm not in the mood for any more crap from you."

"Get fucked!"

Eden felt her control snap completely. She dumped his lunch tray on the nightstand near the head of the bed. Jell-O bounced and jiggled. The milk overturned, the plastic glass clattering to the floor. The collection of sounds drew the attention of the entire ward. Again.

"Shut your mouth, Sergeant Howard, and listen very carefully, because I'm only going to say this once. I don't give a good goddamn who you happen to be pissed off at. For all I know, you hate the entire world. Well, good for you. You're so damned busy brooding over your own losses that you haven't even bothered to take a good look around you. I suggest you do so and damned soon. Then maybe, just maybe, you'll see that you can still walk and you can still function as a man. A lot of the patients on this ward will never know either luxury again." She turned, seized his lunch tray, and announced, "If I have to get a funnel and siphon this food down your throat, you can damn well bet I'll do just that. Now, Sergeant Howard, it is time for your lunch."

Eden watched him slowly turn and peer up at her. His enigmatic expression offered no clue as to his thoughts, and she found herself struggling against the urge raging inside her brain to strangle him. She nearly dropped his tray when she felt a hand settle on her shoulder. The hushed whispering among the patients reached her at the same moment that she focused on Toni's face.

Eden felt her heart plummet to the soles of her feet. She knew she'd just broken the cardinal rule of patient care when she allowed her own emotions to interfere with her work.

"Come with me, Eden." Toni motioned to the corpsman standing behind her. "Take care of the sergeant."

She followed Toni to the office adjacent to the nurses' station, her footsteps leaden when she felt the eyes of the men in the ward charting her progress.

"You okay?"

"I feel like a fool, but I'm all right. I've probably set him back at least six months."

"You only did what everyone else on the ward's wanted to do since he arrived." She smiled. "Cheer up. It's not the end of the world."

"Do you want me reassigned?"

"Of course not! Eden, that was bound to happen. If not with you, then with someone else on the staff. He goaded you into overreacting. He knows it, I know it, and so does everyone else within shouting distance of this building. I would, however, suggest that you give yourself a day or two to cool off before you try and feed him lunch again."

"I shouldn't have lost my temper. I know better."

Toni shrugged and sipped the coffee she'd just poured for herself. "I suspect you shocked the hell out of him. I know you surprised me. It's kind of nice to see a little fire beneath all that reserve of yours. Relax, will you? You haven't done anything wrong."

"But I hate losing control."

"It's called life, Eden. Look, we all have problems with

certain personalities. It goes with the territory when you work in a hospital. Finishing-school manners aside, you can't expect harmony when you're dealing with sick people. It doesn't work that way." Toni paused and tapped her nails against the ceramic mug she held. "You're spoiled, you know. Those guys out there get one look at your beautiful face and all that gorgeous hair and they think they've died and gone to Florence Nightingale heaven. They'd all stand on their heads if you told them to. Daniel Howard, on the other hand, is too tied up with his own pain right now to even notice Eden Benedict the woman."

She flushed, surprised by Toni's comments. She no longer thought of herself in terms of whether or not she was attractive or appealing to the opposite sex. Jim hadn't even reminded her of her appearance, just of her loneliness and her need for the physical aspects of a relationship with a man.

"Why don't you stop by Mark Richards's office after your shift's over today? He's got Sergeant Howard's file. It might give you some insight into the man, not just the patient. He's had a hell of a lousy life, and he's understandably enraged about the loss of his hand."

Eden nodded. "That's a good idea. Tell me something, would you? Why do the men call him 'Shooter'?"

"He was a sniper in Vietnam. Decorated several times, from what I understand."

"You're right; I'll talk to Mark about him. I need all the help I can get with this guy."

Toni smiled. "So you're willing to keep trying with the illustrious Sergeant Howard?"

"I'm not sure why, but I know I can't give up on him."

Eden found Mark Richards in his office after the end of her shift.

"I heard what happened," he teased with a broad smile.

She flushed. "You and everybody else, it seems. I may never live it down."

Mark chuckled. "We love you, Benedict, flawed personality and all, so don't kick yourself for being human. It's not worth the bruises you'll end up giving yourself." He leaned back in his chair and continued puffing on his pipe as she took a seat opposite his desk. "So tell me, what do you want to know about him?"

"Anything I can use to help him."

"That's a tall order." Mark regarded her thoughtfully before nudging a thick folder across the top of his cluttered desk. "Feel like doing some reading about one of the most decorated snipers to come out of Vietnam?"

"Will it help me get him to eat?" she asked.

"He's a tough case, Eden. Traumatic amputation, temporary prisoner of the Vietcong, wounds left untreated after a fall into a pit of punji sticks."

"Punji sticks?"

"Bamboo rods sharpened to needle point, dipped in human or animal excrement, and placed sharp end up in deep holes or body-sized pits."

She shuddered visibly, unable to ignore the panic and pain the man must have endured. "His hand?" she clarified, wanting to understand the reason why it had been amputated.

Mark nodded. "And his chest, arms, and legs."

"My God!"

"Be careful, Eden. You're liable to get more than flying food if he even suspects that you feel sorry for him. He's a proud man. The fact that he crawled twenty miles through enemy-held territory after escaping the VC proves he's also very courageous. That's the part of him we're trying to tap into right now. So far, though, no luck. We can fix his body . . ."

". . . if he'll eat," she inserted.

". . . but his head's in the care of the shrinks upstairs. I'd send him up to the psych ward in a flash if I didn't believe he's better off in the ward with us." Mark inhaled on his pipe and then exhaled the aromatic tobacco. "His folder's a real eye-opener. Who knows, maybe you can even talk him into physical therapy once his cast comes off. I haven't made much headway, and I dislike making rehab a direct order when I can avoid it."

Eden nodded, her attention on the inch-thick file now in her lap.

"I don't have to tell you this is 'eyes only' material."

"I understand."

He stood and walked to the door. "I've got to see a couple of patients before I check out. Take your time with the file, but lock it in the security drawer in my desk when you're through reading it."

"I will, Mark. And thanks."

He closed the door to his office, leaving Eden to settle in for a long read. She started at the beginning of the file, her amazement and respect growing as she read about Daniel Howard, child of the streets of Chicago, societal misfit, juvenile-hall graduate, army inductee, and decorated soldier.

While page after typed page added flesh to the person the men in the ward called Shooter, Mark's summary notes provided a character essay of the man. Snatches of the file remained in her head in the weeks that followed.

> . . . abandoned at age eight by unemployed, unmarried mother;
> . . . declared a ward of the state of Illinois after mother's disappearance;
> . . . housed in several foster homes and six juvenile-hall facilities from age nine through seventeen;
> . . . selected military over penitentiary when given choice by judge;
> . . . normal progression through basic training;
> . . . qualified as expert marksman and given advanced weapons training;
> . . . two twelve-month tours of duty in Republic of South Vietnam;
> . . . performance evaluations repeatedly stress attitude problem with authority figures;
> . . . charged with insubordination by junior-grade officer—special circumstances cited by CO, charges dropped;
> . . . scores above average in a variety of intelligence tests;
> . . . recipient of DSC, three Purple Hearts, Silver and Bronze stars, as well as other commendations for performance while in combat;
> . . . makes no overt effort to advance through the ranks;

. . . assigned naval hospital, San Diego, at request of army;
. . . age: twenty-four.

Eden smiled as she walked through the ward, her thoughts on the patients and their frantic preparations for the long Thanksgiving weekend. They had reminded her of little kids the day before summer vacation. Armed with detailed medical instructions, nearly two-thirds of the men were on four-day passes, many enjoying their first leave since being wounded in Vietnam. The few who remained on the ward either slept or read. Toni Evans and Mark Richards were in the hospital cafeteria enjoying a relaxed lunch. The duty corpsman was busy restocking the supply closet.

Eden paused at the end of Daniel Howard's bed, and the smile left her face. A month had passed since their explosive confrontation—a month during which they'd managed to establish an uneasy truce. Frowning, Eden recalled the information she'd acquired from some of the patients about the job of a sniper. What she'd been told still had the power to turn her stomach.

So graphic had been the descriptions, she could almost feel the tension of days and nights dodging enemy patrols, hour upon hour of hiding in rice paddies while leeches feasted on exposed flesh, the discomfort of C rats turning to lumps of stone in the stomach when fatigue and fear lowered mental defenses, guts cringing in reaction to the sounds coming out of the jungle at night, and the self-imposed isolation of being a highly skilled killer.

She sighed, profoundly saddened that Daniel Howard had experienced all that pain and more. Stepping quietly to the end of his bed, she studied his sleeping form. Her eyes flew to his face when he gasped. She saw his body tremble and knew it wasn't from the cold, not in the greenhouse environment of the ward.

She frantically looked around the ward and then back at him, her fingers hovering above his exposed foot as she made another sweeping survey of him with her eyes. Sweat covered his face and chest. His trembling grew more pronounced with each passing second.

"Sergeant?" She kept her voice low, unthreatening. Experience had already taught her not to approach a combat veteran suddenly or without warning. Even asleep their reactions could be lethal.

"Daniel?"

Eden watched him stiffen, the tension in his body palpable. Wariness emanated from his still body. "Sergeant Howard, you are having a nightmare." Grasping his ankle, Eden tried to shake it, but he jerked his foot free. Then she heard him whimper, and the sound reached into her soul.

"Goddamned son of a bitch! Can't . . . see . . . him!"

"Sergeant! Wake up!"

His body spasmed. He twisted, throwing himself from side to side on the narrow bed.

I've seen this happen before, Eden realized as she rounded the end of the bed. He'll end up on the floor and do God only knows how much damage to himself.

"Corpsman!"

Daniel screamed, "Incoming!" and made a slow-motion dive for the side of the bed.

Eden bolted forward, her caution forgotten as she flung herself across his chest. She grappled with his heavy cast and the blood-soaked stump of his right arm as he fought her.

"Corpsman!" she called out again. Her braid loosened and fell across her face as she struggled with him. He bucked against her weight, still trying to dive for the floor.

Eden felt it the moment they began to tumble out of the bed. A flash of weightlessness and then the jarring sensation of hard tile as it registered waves of pain up and down her spine. Dan's body weight drove the air from her lungs as he fell atop her. Trapped, Eden groaned when his cast hit the side of her face.

The glancing blow momentarily stunned her. Dan angled his arm against her throat and pressed down. Choking and twisting, Eden struggled, her fists flailing at his shoulders and back as she fought for air.

Sanity finally pierced her panic, and she stilled. She began to hum, a lullaby she'd often sung to her infant son, the sound ragged yet soothing. Relief filled her when his movement became less violent.

"What in hell . . ." a voice began.

"Stay back!" Eden ordered, her eyes on Daniel Howard's face. "Find Dr. Richards."

Although his eyes were closed, Eden saw the tears seeping from beneath his dark blond lashes. She bit her lip to keep from crying, too, and gently rubbed his back in wide circular strokes.

"My hand," he moaned as he wept. "My hand."

She tasted salt as his tears fell on her face, smelled sweat soured by agonizing fear, and finally managed to whisper, "I'm going to sit up now, Sergeant."

He rolled off of her and onto his side. Eden dragged herself up and leaned against the wall. With strength she didn't even know she possessed, she helped him sit beside her on the floor and urged him closer with the simple statement "I want to hold you for a little while."

He leaned into her, his eyes still closed, and allowed her to wrap her arms around him. She felt the sobs that shook him and tightened her hold. Tears streamed down her cheeks, but she ignored them as he grieved. Eden knew that a part of Daniel Howard had died. She understood death. She also knew that because he had just begun to mourn his own loss, he would need someone willing to share it with him.

Footsteps rushing down the center aisle drew Eden's attention. She'd lost track of time, she realized, when she noticed Toni and Mark. She took a ragged breath before she tried to speak.

"The sergeant and I were talking. Mark, would you help him back to bed and take a look at his arm? We took a fall." Her throat closed, and she couldn't say anything more.

Mark and the corpsman got Dan back into bed while Toni helped Eden to her feet.

"He talked to me, Toni. He only said a few words, but he really talked." Her voice shook as she spoke.

Toni shook her head. "Let's get you down to X ray and see if you're going to survive this little triumph of yours. We also need to do something about the black eye you're about to have." Putting her arm around Eden's waist, she helped her back to the nurses' station.

"Did you land on your back?" Toni questioned as she stuffed ice cubes into a plastic bag.

Eden nodded, her fingertips gingerly probing the already puffy skin beneath her right eye while her thoughts lingered on Daniel Howard's breakthrough expression of loss for his amputated hand.

"You're going to have a heck of a shiner." She handed Eden the ice pack. "Hold this over your eye. Maybe we can keep it from swelling up too badly."

Mark stepped into the tiny cubicle. Pulling Sergeant Howard's file from a rolling caddy near the door, he made a few notes and then ran a practiced medical eye over Eden. "As far as I can tell, he's okay. We're going to pop his cast and take a closer look at his left arm after the corpsman gets the amputation site cleaned up, resutured, and wrapped. What the hell happened?"

Eden paled and lowered herself into a chair. The incident returned to her mind with all the subtlety of an avalanche. "Nightmare. I couldn't wake him. He screamed, 'Incoming,' and tried to dive for cover. I saw it happen once before in the burn unit upstairs. I didn't think, Mark. I simply threw myself across his chest and tried to keep him in bed, but we both hit the floor, anyway."

"He landed on top of you?"

"Yes." She half laughed. "He's heavy."

"I don't doubt it. He's a big man. If it's any consolation, you probably saved him from another set of breaks in his arm." His gaze wandered from her face to the awkward way she sat in the chair. "You okay?"

"I'm fine, in spite of how I must look." At Toni's snort of disbelief, she admitted, "Well, maybe a little sore in spots."

"What about your head? You know the symptoms of a concussion."

"I didn't hit my head, Mark. I just got bashed in the face." She readjusted the ice pack and asked, "Can I see him later? After you're finished with him?"

Mark frowned at her request. "Not today, Eden. I want you to check out early, go home, and get into a hot tub. X rays are up to you, but your back's going to stiffen up from the fall you took. Besides, Dan'll be here when you come back to work in a few days. Who knows, maybe he'll even apologize to you."

She shook her head. "Not his style. But if he doesn't ignore me or growl at me anymore, then I'll know I've finally made a dent in that chip on his shoulder."

Two days of tub soaks and liniment for her back, plus aspirin for the headaches her black eye had caused, and she returned to the ward. Mark issued strict orders that she not lift anything heavier than a magazine. Although everyone on the ward knew what had happened, no one mentioned it to Eden as she distributed therapy devices her first day back to work. Following lunch and dressing changes, she pushed a wheelchair to the side of Dan Howard's bed.

"Hi! How about some sun?" she asked, trying to hide her nervousness behind a wide smile. "We can sit out in the courtyard behind the ward for a while if you'd like."

He nodded, a ghost of an answering smile on his face as he carefully moved out of bed.

"Hang on to your IV pole and I'll steer."

Once outside, Eden locked the brake on the wheelchair after glancing up at the sky and positioning Dan so that he faced the sun. She sat on a stone bench a few feet away.

"Take off your glasses."

She fingered the sunglass frames for a moment before sliding them off her nose. Dan frowned as he peered at her face and saw for the first time the discoloration beneath her eye.

"I've never hit a woman before."

"That makes us even. I've never been hit in the face before, unless you count the field-hockey puck I almost ate when I was twelve." She grinned. "The dentist had to rewire my braces after the doctor finished stitching up the inside of my mouth."

He looked away. "Sun's nice."

"It is, isn't it?"

Dan closed his eyes and settled back in his chair. Eden took the opportunity to study him more closely. His crew cut was flecked a premature gray, his face angular, his features even. The width of his shoulders suggested that he probably had an impressive physique under healthier conditions. She returned her gaze to his face and noticed that he was observing her with equal intensity.

"How come you work here?" he asked. "Someone like you—young, pretty—must have better things to do with your time."

She shrugged. "It's simple. This is where I want to be."

"Nothing's that simple."

She accepted his skepticism with a nod. "It is simple." And complicated, she thought to herself. "I needed a good way to spend my time. I needed to feel useful. . . ."

His expression hardened, and his eyes narrowed. "Don't say it. . . . You needed to be needed."

"In a way," Eden agreed. "My son died a little more than two years ago. When I stopped wanting to die, too, I realized that it was up to me to make something of my life."

"What do you want from me?"

She smiled. "There's a price on everything."

"You said it, not me."

"Friendship."

He peered at her, his expression unreadable. "Why?" he demanded suspiciously.

"Why not?" she asked back, as determined to defuse his tension and anger as he was determined to remain skeptical about her motives.

"We're as different as two people can be. Hell, we probably don't have anything in common except for this hospital."

"We have a lot in common, Sergeant Howard."

"Yeah? How do you figure that?"

"A part of you has died." Eden saw him flinch, but she ignored his reaction. "Death is final. Your hand isn't coming back. No more than my son is going to return to me. I think I understand some of what you may be feeling. The whole situation comes down to a choice. You can space out on drugs, like some of the guys do, or you can learn to live with what's happened to you and go on. It's totally your choice, isn't it?"

"What would someone like you know about spacing out?"

"I did it with booze after I buried my baby. I stopped caring, but most of all I stopped fighting back. Someone helped me learn that I didn't necessarily have to accept the injustice of Drew's death but that I could find a way to live with it."

"I don't want your pity," he insisted.

Eden's expression gentled. She'd had plenty of time in recent months to consider the real meaning of friendship. "Friendship isn't pity, Sergeant. It's compassion, warmth, caring, and understanding. It's not judging what a person does, whether it's right or wrong. It's not making rules for that person or setting them up for failure out of some misguided effort to get them to adhere to your own standards of behavior. It's simply offering a hand or an ear or even a shoulder when it's needed or wanted. That's all."

She saw conflicting emotions in his brown eyes. Unwilling to force the issue further, Eden remained quiet until he indicated his desire to return to the ward. Watching him as he climbed into bed, she stepped forward and pulled up the sheet bunched at the bottom of the mattress.

"Eden?"

She lifted her eyes to his face, thinking: Please, God, let him unbend just a little. He needs someone right now, someone who'll cheer for him and weep with him. His momentary hesitation nearly destroyed her hope that she'd finally reached him.

"My friends call me Dan."

She nodded and smiled. "I'll see you tomorrow, Dan."

She started to turn away but paused when he took her hand and briefly squeezed her fingers. Lingering beside his bed even after he released her hand and closed his eyes, she made certain he was sleeping peacefully before she left his side and continued with her duties on the ward.

CHAPTER

21

February 1971—Hanoi, North Vietnam

"You bow when told. You read prepared statement." The interpreter glared at Matt. "Remember! Severe punishment if disobey wish of commandant."

You self-important bastard, Matt answered with his eyes. He then glanced at the guard who had brought him from the communal cell, watching as the enlisted man opened the door to the area at Hoa Lo designated as a "press room." Matt listened intently to the low murmur of voices. He caught snatches of French, as well as what he thought might be Chinese.

The interpreter shook his fist one last time. "Not forget! You prisoner!" He impatiently turned away and spat one last order at the guard before leading the way into the room.

The guard waved his weapon threateningly and pointed to the press room.

Matt peered down at him, his expression scathing. He grudgingly followed the interpreter at a slower pace, his leg irons hampering his steps.

Flashbulbs winked, and bright lights glared in his face. Raising manacled wrists, Matt shielded his eyes. He didn't see the curious faces observing him as the guard prodded him down the center aisle of the room and onto a small stage.

The guard motioned Matt to the only chair on the platform. Once seated, with a cocked rifle aimed at his head, he slowly surveyed the room. Camera equipment, Occidental and Oriental men and women, clean walls, open windows, a table with food and a coffee urn atop it, registered in his mind.

Matt thought about the squalid prison conditions, the tasteless rations, and the rags the POWs were forced to wear. Grimacing, he stared at the floor, frustration raging inside him. He clenched his fists, brought himself under control, and refocused on the faces peering up at him, but their curiosity only served to fuel his anger at being paraded in front of them like a circus freak.

The interpreter spoke for fifteen minutes. Matt listened to the spattering of the words, a sound not unlike a hard rain beating on a tin roof. Vietnamese, French, Russian, and Chinese echoed inside his head as questions were asked. He detached himself from the crowd of onlookers and let himself drift with his memories, something he did more and more now as he began his thirty-seventh month of captivity.

Matt's expression softened as he recalled the words Eden had written. *I know in my soul that you're alive . . . Never forget my abiding love and belief in you.*

A sudden stillness in the press room jerked Matt back to the present. He watched the interpreter through narrowed eyes as the man turned from the podium and approached him. Matt tensed when the man spoke.

"You will read statement now. First bow to commandant's guests. Then read. Punishment swift and severe if prisoner not follow wish of commandant," he warned again.

Matt glanced dismissively at the sheet of typed words the interpreter held. He shook his head.

The man frowned and thrust the paper into his hand. "Do as told!"

The guard moved forward, nudging Matt to his feet with his weapon. Standing at the podium, his face set in stern lines, Matt lifted his eyes and studied the wall at the far end of the room. Raising his hand, he slowly closed his fist around the prepared statement. The sound of crumpling paper crackled in the microphone. Flashbulbs blinked. Voices exploded in surprise.

"Benedict," he bit out. "Matthew Alexander. Captain, United States Marine Corps. Service Number: two-two-nine—" He gasped when a rifle butt slammed into his back. Digging his fingernails into the wood of the podium, he forced himself to remain on his feet. ". . . eight-one-zero . . ."

The interpreter shrilled at the guard. Two additional guards burst into the press room. The reporters strained forward with their cameras. Hands emerged from nowhere and dragged Matt from the podium.

He waited in the silence of Room 18. His nostrils told him that it hadn't changed. If possible, the stink of death was even more pronounced now than it had been during his last experience in the rectangular-shaped room.

Matt closed his eyes against the darkness and exhaled slowly, silently reminding himself of the decision he had made long ago. Just the thought of reading a propaganda statement for the North Vietnamese violated every value he held dear. Whatever the cost, he knew he was prepared to live with the consequences of his actions. He started when the door to the room crashed open. Raising his head, Matt opened his eyes and looked into the face of an old adversary.

Major Han stomped past him and slapped his gloves on the table in the center of the room. He smirked at Matt and loosened the holster strapped to his chest. Matt watched him remove an American-made, snub-nosed .38 and place it on the table.

"We meet again," he sneered in French. "I knew I would one day be rewarded for tolerating your resistance to my authority."

Matt stared at him, his body rigid with disbelief and his mind overwhelmed by memories of Long Moc. Hunger. The oven that had baked his brains. The rats that had scarred his body. The suspended coffin-shaped hell he'd survived. Sergeant Jackson's murder. Hal Caulfield's painful death.

Matt blinked and refocused. Major Han failed to disappear.

Two guards entered the room. One placed a box on the table and then joined his comrade beside the closed door.

Major Han smiled and lifted the lid of the cardboard container. He dumped the contents next to his unholstered weapon.

Matt jerked against his bonds when he saw the handwriting on the scattered envelopes. Eden! His eyes darted back to the major's face, and he froze. He watched Major Han extract a lighter from his shirt pocket and hold the flame under one of the letters.

Not again. Dear God, not again!

"My government has received a telegram regarding your wife . . . from the International Red Cross." He reached for another of Eden's letters and again held the flame under the envelope until only a small scrap of paper remained. Carelessly flicking it to the floor, he continued to repeat the process over and over until the table was a mess of ash and bits of paper.

Matt shook with rage. "You fucking bastard!"

"It is better not to read the letters of one who is dead." He moved the flame to within centimeters of the final letter, and the edge began to curl from the heat.

"Dead?" Matt whispered.

"Your wife is dead. Robbed, raped, and then beaten to death."

Like a serpent's tongue, the blue-red flame licked at the envelope.

"Liar! She's not dead!" Matt challenged, jerking at the parachute cord that held him nearly immobile in his chair.

"She is dead." Major Han took what looked like a telegram from his shirt pocket and unfolded it.

Matt saw the International Red Cross logo and slumped down in his chair. "No," he groaned. "Eden's not dead. I won't believe she's dead. I won't believe it."

Major Han strode around the table and approached his prisoner. Standing behind Matt, he issued an order to the guards. One stepped forward and fastened a swatch of cloth over Matt's eyes. The other remained on the opposite side of the table, his rifle cocked and aimed.

The spinning of the .38's cylinder eventually reached Matt, and he tensed at the sound.

"We are going to play a game. I trust you will enjoy the risk involved. After all, you repeatedly risked my wrath at Long Moc."

Major Han shrugged indifferently when he received no response to his challenge. He emptied five cartridges from the gun. Matt heard them each ping, one by one, as they hit the cement floor and rolled away. He knew the sixth bullet would remain in the .38. The spin of the cylinder sounded again and Matt clenched his fists. His body trembled, and perspiration dotted his face.

Click.

Spin.

Click.

Spin.

Click.

On and on it went. The air moved each time Major Han raised his weapon to Matt's temple. The guards chuckled each time their prisoner flinched and then sagged in his chair. Matt began to smell fear in his own sweat and knew he was losing control.

Spin.

Click.

"Great-grandfather, help me!"

Spin.

Click.

He felt a hand settle on his shoulder, the same hand that had guided him in the hotbox at Long Moc.

"Great-grandfather, my wife . . ." He couldn't make himself say the words.

Spin.

Click.

"You are not alone, my son. I will not abandon you. I have been with you, watching over you, since the beginning. Your grief is my grief."

Spin.

Click.

Darkness arrived. Tension billowed in waves behind his blindfold. Matt felt himself succumbing to exhaustion. Death flirted with his consciousness. And still . . .

Spin.

Click.

Spin.

Click.

Clinging to his memories, he blacked out as dawn crept into the sky over the Hoa Lo compound.

Matt briefly regained consciousness on the cement platform in the communal cell. Bill Porter slept beside him, his face drawn and his body shaking with fever. Chet knelt at his side and passed a damp cloth across his forehead each time the air force major moaned in his sleep.

Chet glanced at Matt and saw that his eyes were open. "We've requested medical care. Bill's sure to die from the infection in his leg if the Viets don't get him to a hospital."

Matt stared at the ceiling. He didn't hear Chet's voice, nor was he aware of Bill Porter's condition. Chet left him to his silence, uncertain about what to do for him and privately wondering how much longer any of them could withstand the emotional and physical abuse that had become the norm of captivity.

Guards finally arrived with a stretcher around noon. They loaded Bill's emaciated body onto it and carried him out with no explanation of his destination. Many of the POWs knew they might never see Bill Porter again. Too many severely injured American prisoners had already disappeared under the guise of medical care.

Matt slept most of the day and into the night. Chet awakened the next morning and found him seated on his bedroll, the chamois band knotted around his neck since Long Moc now fastened across his forehead. He sat cross-legged, his large hands resting on his thighs, his eyes open and unblinking.

Chet didn't recognize the words he quietly singsonged as he swayed back and forth. Leaning toward him, he asked, "What gives, buddy?"

Matt didn't flinch or break rhythm. The mournful entreaty continued, the words foreign to Chet. He placed a hand on Matt's shoulder, worry creasing his face as he studied his friend.

After several attempts at communication, Chet left the cement platform and shuffled across the width of the cell. He stopped in front of Tom Jenkins. "Something serious has happened to Matt. He won't talk to me, and he's chanting some kind of Indian thing."

"Word is he blew a press conference sky-high. He was over in Room Eighteen all night."

Chet frowned. "He doesn't look as though they roughed him up too bad except for a cut on his face and rope burns on his arms. They must've been screwing with his head."

"Keep an eye on him," Tom suggested. "He'll come back down to ground zero when he's ready."

Chet sighed audibly. "He reminds me of some of the battle-fatigued grunts I used to see at Da Nang. I wonder what those bastards did to him."

"We won't know for sure till he comes around. Watch out for him and let me know when he wants to talk."

"Yes, sir."

Chet shuffled back to his six-by-four segment of the cell, understanding that it was now his turn to offer protection.

The months drifted by, and 1971 unfolded with little change in prison conditions. Chet painstakingly ensured the survival of his fellow marine. He led Matt by the arm whenever the guards marched the POWs into the center compound for exercise. He fed him when the mute man was unable or unwilling to feed himself. He stood beside him in the showers once a week and bathed him as he had his own child when she was an infant. And he talked unceasingly, sharing bits of information and words of encouragement despite Matt's lack of response.

Matt, shielded behind an invisible curtain of agony, spent the weeks and months remembering Eden. Every moment he spent in the interior of his mind became an opportunity to examine each second they had shared.

The navy chaplain opened his prayer book and glanced at the marine officer standing in front of him. "Are we ready to proceed, Captain?"

Matt turned to Eden. He studied his bride through emotion-filled eyes. She wore a white linen dress with a strand of pearls at her throat. Her hair flowed to her waist, a thin band of seed pearls draped across her forehead and fastened at the back of her head. He waited for her to look up from the roses she held, and when she did, he saw love and commitment shining from the depths of her emerald eyes.

They joined hands and he said, "We're ready, sir."

"Dearly beloved, we are gathered here in the presence of God to join this man and this woman in the holy sacrament of matrimony. Marriage is the union of two individuals; their personalities, their spirits, their strengths and weaknesses, and their love for one another . . ."

". . . I admonish you here in the presence of God to remember that you cannot know the indescribable blessings of love until you have been privileged to suffer and endure for one another . . ."

". . . I declare that Matthew and Eden are now husband and wife, according to the holy ordinance of God, Holy Mother Church, and the laws of the state of California. In the name of the Father, and of the Son, and of the Holy Ghost."

> May the Lord bless you and keep you;
> May the Lord make His face shine upon
> you and be gracious unto you;
> May the Lord lift up His countenance
> upon you and give you peace;
> Both now and in life everlasting.
> Amen.

The chaplain smiled at them and closed his book. "You may kiss your bride, Captain Benedict."

Eden moved into his arms. Touching his cheek with her fingertips in a gentle caress, she whispered, "I love you, Matthew. I will always love you."

"Are you sorry we went out tonight?"

Matt shook his head. "It just reminded me how temporary this R and R really is."

"We're all stealing a little bit of time away from Vietnam."

Matt tugged her out of her chair and into his lap. "Maybe it's a good thing to be reminded of reality every once in a while. I've managed to forget everything for a couple of days. I'm probably luckier than a lot of guys."

"Seeing so many men in uniform has made me realize that there are things you must need to talk about, Matthew. I just don't know how to help you get them out."

"It's enough that you're willing to listen."

"But it's not," Eden disagreed. "I want to share as much as possible with you before you go back there."

He hesitated at first in spite of the concern he saw in her eyes. "Did you feel their desperation? All those couples in the restaurant, I mean."

"They aren't so different from us. We're aware of the clock ticking on our time together even if we can't or won't admit it to one another." She leaned forward and pressed her lips to his temple. "Are you ever afraid when you fly?"

He smiled. "Only when someone's shooting at me."

"That's not what I meant and you know it."

"I'm serious," he protested. "There isn't time for fear. Eden, think about it. There are only three things that could hurt me or kill me. Ground or air fire, a poorly maintenanced plane, or my own carelessness."

"You're good at what you do, aren't you?"

"I'd better be. Uncle Sam spent a million bucks training me."

"Then you'll be all right. Even though you're lacking sadly in the humility department, I suspect you're a superb pilot." She chuckled softly. "Your letters are starting to read like airline brochures on Southeast Asia."

"I'll switch to sexual fantasies in the next batch if you'd like," he teased.

Eden groaned. "The censors already love you enough! Why do you think I brought most of your letters with me? I want to know what's hidden under all that black ink."

Later that night, on a stretch of deserted beach near their hotel, they stopped to look at the star-studded sky. Matt looped his arms across her midriff as she leaned back against his chest.

"There's a falling star. Let's make a wish." When he didn't say anything, Eden angled her head and peered up at him. "No wishes?"

"Just one."

"Tell me."

"I want you to love me forever, no matter what happens."

She turned in his arms and studied him in the diminishing light. Sensing his seriousness, she tugged his mouth down to her lips and whispered, "I will love you forever . . . beyond forever, Matthew."

He closed his eyes and traced her lips with the tip of his tongue. The answering sweetness of her breath made him tremble, and he felt the certainty of her love reach into him. Trailing one hand down the length of her spine, he pressed her closer, aligning their bodies so that she could feel the extent of his arousal. He tangled the fingers of his other hand in the auburn silk of her unbound hair.

Eden abandoned caution. What did it matter if they made love on the beach? The darkness would protect them. Matthew's need was greater than any concern for propriety.

They dropped to their knees in the sand. Bubbling surf and breaking waves harmonized at the water's edge. Eden unbuttoned his shirt and ran her fingers across the width of his chest. He unwrapped the sarong she'd styled for herself with native Hawaiian fabric.

His breath tore at his lungs when he saw the fullness of her breasts, the hardness of her nipples in the moonlight. He raised shaking hands and cupped them, absently noting the line of pale skin left by her bikini. The sight reminded him that what was protected from the eyes of strangers was his alone to cherish.

"Mine. You're mine," he insisted, the words wrenched from deep within him.

Matt didn't flinch when her fingernails scored the skin of his shoulders. Leaning forward, he teased her nipples with his tongue and heard her pleasure in the moan that escaped her, felt her hunger when she pressed herself more fully into his mouth.

Her hands fluttered down his chest to his straining sex, anxious fingers yanking at the zipper that separated them. He helped her tug the barrier from his body. Poised atop her, her sarong now spread under them as darkness invaded the deserted beach, Matt cupped her face in his hands.

"I need you now, paleface."

"Inside me," she whispered. "I want you inside of me . . . always, Matthew, always."

He took her with swift hunger, plunged into her as she wrapped her legs around his waist and held tightly to him as though he'd become her lifeline. He basked in the wet heat of her as he sank into her flesh, marveled at her wordless cries of love, and felt her quivering body as it thrummed and strained beneath him. He made it last as long as he could, waiting until she reached her climax before he allowed himself his own.

He continued to hold her, remained imbedded within her, ever mindful of parting and ever fearful that their link to one another could somehow be broken. Lifting his head, he gently kissed her brow.

Eden sensed the sadness in him and whispered, "What, love?"

"How can I say good-bye to you tomorrow?"

She hugged him tightly. "We won't ever say good-bye. The words don't exist for us, because we have the future. Nothing can separate us, Matthew," she promised. "Nothing, my love. Not even death."

CHAPTER

22

June 1971—San Diego, California

"How are you holding up?"

Eden lifted her eyes from the sleeping infant cradled in her arms. Regret and loss tugged at her insides as she held Katherine, but she mentally shook herself free of the destructive emotions. The process had been a painful one, but she knew now that she'd recovered from Drew's death.

She smiled at Tracey. "I'm fine."

"I was afraid Katherine's christening would bring back a lot of painful memories for you."

"It's time for you to stop punishing yourself for wanting to be happy, Trace. Drew will always be a part of me because he was my son and I loved him, but my memories of him aren't all sad, you know."

Tracey leaned forward and adjusted the blanket that covered her tiny daughter. "When Matt comes home, the two of you will make another baby."

Eden heard her certainty and was surprised by her assumption. "Who knows what we'll want? I haven't forgotten what I went through when Drew died, and having another baby isn't even a decision I'm willing to consider at the moment. Besides, who can possibly predict what Matthew will want after being gone so long?"

"His dreams won't change. He told us both how much children meant to him."

"Trace, it isn't just his decision. His needs and wants are important, of course, but what I need and want are just as valid. Too many wives come away from the wards asking themselves the same questions. What's wrong with my husband? How can he have changed so much? Why doesn't he still want the things we dreamed about and planned on before he went overseas? I'm not about to kid myself after what I've seen and heard. I also realize that I may not even know the man who comes home to me." Unwilling to continue the direction of their conversation, Eden handed the still-sleeping baby to her mother and stood. "You must be exhausted. I'm going to take off and let you two ladies get some much-needed rest."

"Will we see you again soon?"

"Of course. Why wouldn't you?"

Tracey shrugged.

Eden collected her purse. "How's your incision healing?"

She laughed before saying, "My stomach looks like someone superimposed railroad tracks across it. Bikinis are definitely not a part of my future."

Eden leaned down and traced Katherine's cheek with her fingertip. "I think this young lady was worth it."

"I won't argue with you about that. I'd have walked through hell in bare feet to get this little angel. Having a C-section guaranteed her survival."

"I'll tell David you're going to have a nap with the baby," she offered as she walked to the door.

"How are your plans coming along for the bar-be-cue?"

Eden smiled in spite of the slight edge she heard in Tracey's voice. Jim had been right, she thought as she turned to face her. Time *does* change the rules of friendship. We've grown apart. We're struggling even now to come up with nonthreatening topics of conversation. Is it me? she wondered. Am I so jealous of Tracey that I can't bear to witness her happiness? Or is Tracey the one who's unwilling to accept the person I've become? Or are we both to blame? She sighed, uncertain of the answers.

"Eden?"

"We're all set for the big event. The guys in the wards are really excited about getting out to the beach, Special Services has offered us a bus if one of the corpsmen will drive, and the nurses are pitching in with the food."

"David told me you ran the Red Cross office while Kitty was away on vacation. Did you miss working in your ward?"

Eden groaned laughingly. Shuffling papers was definitely not her forte. "Those were six of the longest weeks of my life. It's not that I mind the administrative details, but I prefer working with the patients. Dan Howard—I think I told you about him . . ."

Tracey blanched. "The guy who beat you up?"

Eden managed to contain her temper in spite of how much she resented Tracey's implication. "That's Daniel, only he didn't beat me up, and you know it. Anyway, he's doing wonderfully. The prosthetic replacement for his hand fits, and he's learned how to use it. He's even helping some of the other amputees adjust to the idea of prosthetics. Dan has more raw courage than any patient I've ever worked with."

She grimaced distastefully. "I'd forgotten about his injury."

Eden suddenly remembered Tracey's aversion to the reality of damaged bodies and shattered spirits. Her one visit to a ward had ended with her throwing up in a bucket in a utility closet. Now she refused to visit Eden anywhere near the naval hospital facility.

"Dan will be at the party, Trace," she told her firmly. "He's my friend as well as a patient, so please try not to let his physical condition upset you if you and David decide to drop by."

"I'm not certain we'll be able to make it," she hedged, her eyes on Katherine as she fussed with the folds of her daughter's receiving blanket. "I'll have to let you know."

"It's up to you." Eden eased the door open. "Take care and have a good nap. I'm call you soon."

Toni Evans stepped into the kitchen and smiled at Eden. "I sure hope we've got more potato salad. Those guys eat like locusts who've been on short rations for the last six months."

Eden laughed as she turned from the sink and wiped her hands on a dish towel. "Check the fridge," she suggested as she sprinkled seasoning over the burger patties she'd just made. "I think you'll find two more of potato salad in there and the cold macaroni Kitty brought. Do you know if Dan's ready for more hamburgers and hot dogs?"

"He said he'd be in soon for another platter. I suspect he wants a cold beer and a break. He's been on his feet for at least four hours now."

"Should we ask one of the other men to cover the grill?"

"I wouldn't. Dan's enjoying himself, and Mark said he'd keep an eye on him."

The sound of laughter and happy voices drifted in from the patio and beachfront. Eden glanced out the window above the sink while Toni inspected the supplies in the refrigerator. Some of the men sat in the sun, drinking beer or lemonade and playing cards. Others, those confined to the patio because of their wheelchairs, played Ping-Pong, balanced paper plates filled with food, or chatted with the medical personnel recruited for the outing. She also saw the lifeguard from the Del Mar beach patrol who'd volunteered to ensure the safety of those patients who wanted to test their water skills.

"Where's my woman?" bellowed a masculine voice.

Eden grinned. Toni flushed and slammed the fridge door. "Get engaged to the man and he thinks I've signed on as his shadow."

Mark strolled into the kitchen, his bathing suit and hair dripping wet, his pipe trailing wisps of tobacco smoke.

"Please tell me you didn't go swimming while you were sucking on that pipe," Toni begged, laughter in her eyes but a peeved look pinching the area around her nose and mouth.

"But of course, my darling Red. I am never without my trusty pipe." He winked at Eden before circling around Toni and tugging her and the bowl she held back against his chest. "Would you have me any other way?"

"Affirmative, Dr. Richards. Sane would be nice. It's a condition I heartily recommend before I introduce you to my parents."

Mark ignored her comments and worked his hands up under the front of her T-shirt.

Toni sidestepped him, turned, and shoved the full salad bowl into his arms. "Make yourself useful, Doctor. Your patients are hungry."

Carrying an empty cake plate, Kitty entered the room as the newly engaged couple laughingly departed. "Those kids can really pack it in."

Eden gestured to the butcher-block table covered with cakes and pies. "Help yourself. We're well stocked."

Kitty gave her a quick once-over. "You look relaxed and happy."

Eden playfully twirled around, posing against the stove in a baggy gray T-shirt that read U.S. NAVAL ACADEMY and barely reached her thighs. With no makeup, bare feet, and her hair in a long, fat braid, she felt eighteen, not twenty-eight. "The latest in beach attire for the well-dressed woman," she quipped.

"I'm proud of you."

"I certainly didn't do all this by myself."

"I'm talking about you, not a beach party."

"One day at a time, Kitty, and my life works."

"I'm still proud of you. Proud enough, in fact, to nominate you as the next Red Cross director at the hospital when I retire next year." Kitty sliced a German chocolate layer cake as she spoke. "Before you say no, you'll be free to reorganize the office, set aside ward time for yourself, and select your own assistant. I won't need an answer from you until December, so you have plenty of time to think about it."

Astounded because other volunteers had been on staff longer and because a few had even voiced their desire to take over once Kitty retired, she finally managed, "I don't know what to say."

"Then don't say anything," Kitty suggested as she walked to the sink and rinsed icing from her fingers. She noticed a trio of college-age young women who'd paused to chat with some of the patients. Everyone was smiling and laughing. One of the girls carried a Frisbee. One of the men held a volleyball in his remaining hand. "This is a good environment for the men. They need to know that they'll fit back into the world once they leave the hospital." Pausing, she turned to look at Eden. "They all treat you like a younger sister even though most of them are only two or three years your junior, but I suppose you've noticed that already."

Eden ducked her face and concentrated on the onion she was slicing. "I've noticed."

"They sense your love for them and your commitment to them. In short, they trust you. And they know about Matthew, don't they?"

Her hands stilled. She placed the knife on the cutting board before she faced Kitty. "Yes. I felt like a cheat, and I wanted them to know we're even. I get as much from them, probably more, than what I give to them. Using them and my work as a crutch seemed wrong. They're my family, and I don't ever have to hide from them."

"Vietnam's made us a family. And no matter how many people criticize the military's role there, they can't take our loyalty to one another away from us." Kitty gave her a hug before she picked up the cake plate and walked to the patio door. "You have an instinctive feel for their vulnerability, Eden. That's why you're the most qualified person to replace me."

Dan filled the doorway once Kitty stepped outside. Eden gave him a damp smile.

"The natives are getting restless." He tilted a beer can and swallowed half the contents as he approached her. "You okay?"

"Of course."

He put his arm around her and tugged her into a brotherly hug. "Truth?"

"Cross my heart." She picked up a slice of onion and waved it at him. "These things make my eyes leak."

She was relieved when he simply nodded, crossed the kitchen, and dropped into a chair beside the pastry-laden table. Kitty's announcement was enough of a surprise without having to explain it to anyone before she had a chance to weigh the pros and cons of becoming the next Red Cross station director. While she was honored that Kitty thought so highly of her ability, she was also aware of the responsibility of the position.

The doorbell chimed. Dan asked, "Want me to get that?"

"Please. I'll finish stocking this tray for you." She grinned when he drained the last of the beer from the can, crumpled it in his fist, and slam-dunked it into the trash can on his way to the front of the house.

"Remind me to tell you about the honey I met on the beach," Dan called out over his shoulder. "She's a physical therapist at UCSD Medical Center."

Still smiling, Eden added hot dogs to the two dozen raw burgers already on the platter. Dan's pride and self-esteem had replaced his rage and frustration. She felt a sense of personal pride at having participated in his transformation from an embittered professional killer to a man capable of compassion and leadership.

When she heard, "She's in the kitchen, Major," Eden rinsed and dried her hands. David, in uniform, and Tracey, clutching a howling Katherine, walked into the kitchen. Dan stood behind them, his expression sober.

Eden read caution and something more in his eyes. The smile left her lips. Matthew, she sighed inwardly. David's miserable, and Tracey does not want to be here. She crossed the kitchen with measured steps, willing herself to act naturally and drawing from within herself the strength to remain calm. No matter what the news is, she told herself, I can and will handle it. I have a life now. A life I'm proud of. A life I can live alone if the need arises, even if it's the last thing I want to do.

She took Katherine from Tracey and hugged the crying infant. Warm flesh and baby smells soothed her. Eden remembered Drew, not painfully but as a comforting reminder that, however briefly, she had once known peace and happiness. That knowledge allowed her to hold on to the idea that she might know such feelings again one day.

Consciously ignoring Tracey's obvious distress and David's strained expression, she chastised, "You two are upsetting my godchild with your grim looks."

Dan responded to her stress and quietly approached her. "So this is the famous Katherine Markham I've been hearing so much about." He peered into the baby's face, muddy-brown eyes meeting cobalt blue. Katherine quieted and looked up at him. She grasped his extended finger and blew tiny bubbles from her pursed lips as she studied him.

David shifted uncomfortably. "We need to talk to you . . . privately if possible, Eden. It's about Matt."

She nodded and looked at Dan, noting the encouragement reflected in his eyes as she handed Katherine to him. And although she had a momentary urge to walk into his arms and hide behind the security of his friendship, she knew such behavior would be an act of cowardice on her part.

"Why don't I show off your daughter to the troops outside?" Dan noticed Tracey's concern and added, "There's no need to worry. There are at least three nurses, two doctors, and four corpsmen out on the patio if she needs a diaper change."

Tracey ignored him and moved forward. Eden frowned and shot a sharp look at David, silently willing him to deal with his wife.

He responded by taking Tracey's hand and gently tugging her back to his side. "Thank you, Sergeant. I'm certain my daughter will be in good hands."

Dan nodded. "Ma'am. Major." He left the kitchen, Katherine peering wide-eyed over his shoulder and the platter of raw hot dogs and burgers forgotten.

David and Tracey followed Eden into the living room. She sat down opposite them, her fingers knotted in her lap and her thoughts in turmoil over Matthew.

David opened his briefcase while Tracey perched nervously on the edge of the couch beside him. Eden resisted the tension emanating from them as she took a steadying breath, but David's uncharacteristic display of uneasiness still grated on her nerves.

"You've had some word about Matthew?" she prompted, trying not to sound impatient.

"I've got a photo of him. We aren't certain when it was taken. Intelligence is still trying to get an approximate date.

The picture appeared in an Eastern-bloc newspaper. The Pentagon managed to convince the wire services to hold it back one day so that you could see it first. Headquarters Marine Corps sent a copy to me by courier this morning."

Eden leaned forward, extended a shaking hand, and then nearly screamed in frustration when David hesitated.

"It's a rough-looking shot. Don't forget Matt's been a prisoner for a long time."

"David, stop trying to protect me. I'm not a child. I see the damaged bodies of American men every day at the hospital." She drew in a ragged breath. "If Matthew's been photographed, then he's alive. That's all that matters now."

"I just wanted to prepare you."

"He's my husband. I don't care how he looks. I just care that he's alive."

David gave her the news clipping. Eden closed her fingers around it and exhaled slowly, her heart beating an erratic tattoo against her breasts. She trembled and her eyes widened when she focused on Matthew's raised arm and clenched fist. The stubborn look on his face reached inside her body and clawed at her heart.

Dear God, thank you. I've waited three and a half years for proof that he's really alive.

Tears filled her eyes, and she blinked them away. The gauntness of his face made her insides ache, and the dark circles ringing his eyes brought a moan surging up from deep inside her. She found herself clinging to his obvious anger, reason translating it to the certainty that he intended to survive, that he was fighting back in spite of everything!

"*I love you, paleface.*"

"Matthew," she whispered, unable to take her eyes from the dark bands around his wrists and the chain hanging between them. She couldn't even begin to fathom why he was chained like an animal, nor could she suppress the fury she felt that anyone would intentionally try to rob such a proud man of his dignity.

Kitty walked into the room. She smiled encouragingly when Eden looked up at her.

"He's alive, Kitty," she whispered. "He's really alive."

"You've always believed he was."

She smiled with satisfaction. "He's furious. He's absolutely furious!"

"Then he'll make it, won't he?"

Eden nodded vigorously. "Yes, he will. Anger's a good weapon. We've seen it make the difference between life and death on the wards." Glancing at David, she clarified, "You have no idea when this was taken?"

"The best guess anyone's come up with so far is the last six to twelve months."

"What can we do to help you?" Tracey asked.

Eden looked at her, puzzled by her question. "Help?"

"We thought you'd want to come and stay with us for a few days. This picture's quite a shock, Eden. You shouldn't be alone right now."

Instinct and pride made her reject the sympathetic tone of Tracey's voice. "I'm not alone. And I'm really all right, just a little stunned, that's all."

"But—"

"I know you mean well," she said firmly, "but this isn't the time for tea and sympathy." Why won't you understand? I've changed. I'm not the frightened rabbit Matthew married four and a half years ago.

Kitty saw the plea for privacy in Eden's eyes. "I don't think anyone will object if you'd like some time alone right now."

Eden nodded, Kitty's intervention making her almost limp with relief. "Would you make my excuses to the guys? I'll talk to them tomorrow at the hospital."

"Whatever you want," Kitty assured her. "We'll just keep feeding them and doling out suntan oil until they feel like calling it a day."

"We can stay with you tonight," Tracey offered as she stood. "I'll just go home and get Katherine's things."

"No, Trace, that's not necessary. It would be silly to disturb the baby's schedule." To Kitty, she added, "Would you ask Dan to stay? I can drive him back to Balboa later if he doesn't want to use the guest room tonight." Eden left the couch, her thoughts on the solitude she would find in her bedroom.

"We'll keep trying to find out when the photo was taken," David offered.

"Thanks, David. There's plenty of food left. Please stay and eat with the others." Eden didn't bother to wait for his reply. She slowly walked down the hall, still clutching the news clipping. Sudden fatigue claimed her as she closed the bedroom door and lowered herself to her bed. She shut her eyes and immediately drifted into a dreamless, restful sleep unlike anything she'd experienced since Matthew's captivity in January 1968.

In the living room, Kitty faced David and Tracey. "She needs to work through this on her own."

"Why does she insist on shutting me out?" Tracey exclaimed.

"Eden's waited a long time for her husband's status to change."

"But why is she shutting us out when we could help her?" Tracey asked again. "I don't understand the distance she seems determined to put between us. We were always so close, but in the last year or so—"

"She must," Kitty insisted gently. "She knows she's capable of dealing with her life and her problems herself. It's taken her a long time to understand what she can and cannot handle. She also knows how to ask for help when she wants and needs it, so don't judge her too harshly."

"We haven't had time for lunch," David interrupted as he slid his arm around Tracey's shoulders.

Kitty smiled. "Better late than never. Eden wasn't kidding when she said we've got plenty of food left. Come on out to the patio. We'll fix you up with an excellent lunch and see how many young men your daughter's already charmed."

Eden glanced out the bedroom window before she walked into the bathroom. Night blanketed the beach, the soft lapping of the waves and an occasional flicker of light from a boat offshore the only evidence that she even lived at the edge of the Pacific. Standing under a hot shower, she lingered until the water ran cold. After slipping into a long kimono-style robe, she made her way to the living room. Dan, who was stretched out on the floor with a pillow under his head, waited for her.

"When did everyone leave?" she asked.

"Around five."

"It's nearly midnight. You must be tired."

"Nope. I crashed in here for a while." He pulled himself into a seated position on the carpet. "Kitty filled me in. How ya feelin'?"

"Relieved. Terrified. Numb. Mostly numb, I guess. I've waited so long for confirmation that Matthew's alive. Now that I know, I'm not sure what the next step is."

"Does there have to be a next step?"

"You tell me," Eden countered as she tossed a few pillows against the side of the couch and settled herself on the floor across from Dan.

"Why not keep doing what you've been doing? Knowing your husband's alive doesn't mean he'll be home tomorrow." He lifted his beer can and gave her a silent salute. "It's your life and your decision, lady."

"Why are you being such a hardass?"

"Wake up, Eden. A picture in a newspaper doesn't change anything. Charlie's still fucking him over. Until he gets back to the world, his life isn't worth shit."

She paled and knew that Dan was right. Any news about Matthew was a mixed blessing. He was still gone, and she was still without her husband. Eden sighed and shook her head, her expression rueful. "Thanks for scraping me off the ceiling. I tend to get anxious for this mess to come to an end, but I always seem to wind up clutching at straws."

"Flimsy things those straws." He drained the remainder of the beer from the can he held. "Your friends decided to hang out for a while."

"And?"

"Mrs. Markham's one uptight broad. Kitty took care of her . . . after Tom Coulter decided to dazzle her with a handshake."

Eden laughed in spite of herself. Tom had lost both his arms in a mine explosion in the Mekong Delta. He now delighted in flustering people with his prosthetic arms and pincerlike hands.

Dan grinned. "She was kind of upset, wouldn't have anything to eat even though everybody kept offering to fix her a plate."

"Tracey doesn't cope well with—" Eden hesitated, searching for the right phrase —"physical imperfections."

Dan frowned at her attempt at delicacy. It wasn't like her to dance around any subject. "Must be hard for her," he speculated. "I got the impression you two were pretty close at one time. She talked about you some, but the person she described didn't sound much like anybody I know."

"We were close, extremely close, but now it's as though our friendship happened to two other people. Tracey spent a lot of time propping me up, probably more than she should have. Things happened fast when Matthew was first shot down. His MIA status, Drew's birth, then his death a few months later, my drinking, getting sober, the move back to California. She went through a lot with me, and I owe her." Eden smiled somewhat sadly. "What can I say? We've changed, gone in different directions with our lives. I'm genuinely uncomfortable around her now. I don't know, maybe I'm jealous of her. I'm not really sure. I just know we can't go back to who and what we were."

Dan nodded, got up from the floor, and wandered toward the kitchen. "Want a soft drink?"

"Please."

He returned with two cans, one of cola and the other a beer for himself. He placed both on the coffee table before lowering himself to the floor. "What do you want to know about Charlie and how he treats his prisoners?"

Eden hesitated. She knew that Dan hadn't been willing to unearth his memories of his own Vietnam experience with anyone but the shrinks until now. She realized that he was about to demonstrate his regard for their friendship with this offer to retrace an agonizing route from his past. "Whatever you want to tell me," she finally answered. "I do wonder what Matthew thinks about when he's alone."

Dan leaned back against the cushions on his side of the

room and studied the ceiling. "I thought about being in control of my own life again, about making my own decisions, about eating and sleeping when I wanted to. I spent a lot of hours planning my escape. And I thought a hell of a lot about being clean and getting laid." He laughed harshly and glanced at her. "You deal with the basics. That's all you can really handle."

Eden fingered the folded news clipping she'd tucked into the pocket of her robe. "Matthew looks like he's been abused, maybe even . . . beaten."

"Spit it out, Eden. You think he's been tortured. Right?"

She nodded. "I've felt the most excruciating pain in my sleep. Sometimes I wake up and my arms ache. So do my wrists and ankles."

"Sounds like you've got a pretty good fix on the physical part. He'll have a lot of scars, bad ones if Charlie's still doing his old number, which I'm sure he is. Manacles and leg irons are always a size too small. They're called squeeze cuffs. The metal digs into your flesh. I spent half my time bleeding and the other half picking off the leeches. Those bastards have a million ways to push a guy to the edge." He clenched his teeth and sucked in enough air to fill his lungs. Eden felt chill bumps rise on her skin as the sound whistled through the room. "Sometimes you just want to give up and die."

"What kept you going?"

"Anger. Vengeance. Hope." He shrugged. "Pick one."

"You were still so angry when you got to the ward," she recalled. "Even the corpsmen cut you a lot of slack."

Dan chuckled. "You didn't."

"I couldn't. I think I was fighting for both of us, even though I didn't know it at the time. I had to follow my instincts with you. You didn't give me any other choice."

He stared at the stump that had once been his right hand. "They took a piece of me. That's not something a man ever forgives or forgets." Glancing over at her, he asked, "Do you still love him?"

His question held all the subtlety of a thrown gauntlet. "I love the man I knew. My memories are warm and comforting." She pulled the news clipping from her pocket, unfolded it, and studied the person she thought of as her husband. "I don't know this man. I sense his rage, and I feel his isolation. I want him home, but I'm frightened, too. I'm sure I'm going to face a stranger, not the man I fell in love with and married. I don't even know how I'm going to tell him about our son. And once he knows, I'm not sure he'll even want me."

"Why wouldn't he want you?"

"He's very proud. I worry he'll think I waited for him out of some misguided sense of loyalty."

"Have you?"

"Of course not. I love Matthew."

"Then you know where you stand. Just make sure he understands how you feel. You've reached a lot of guys in the wards, Eden, and I know 'cause I'm at the top of the list. It takes time, patience, and some good old-fashioned ass kicking to break through the walls, but it works. You've already proven it to yourself and guys like me, and you'll have to prove it to your husband when he comes home." He gave her a considering look. "No one reacts to captivity the same way. It depends on the man and how he stayed alive as well as how much of his self-respect he manages to hang on to."

Eden stared at the news photo. She smoothed the creases folding it had caused, but nothing could remove the starkness of Matthew's emaciated body or the anger captured in his raised fist. She longed to rescue them both from the nightmare they both lived day after day. The harshest reality was accepting that she couldn't.

"Do you know where the picture was taken?" Dan asked.

Eden nodded but didn't look up. "Hanoi."

"There's a prison there called Hoa Lo. It's an old French fortress that has guard towers and thick walls topped with barbed wire and broken bottles. Some of our guys are being held there. Has Major Markham or anyone else from the Marine Corps told you about it?"

"No, nothing at all."

"Shit."

"Tell me, Dan. I have a right to the information even if David won't tell me because he's trying to protect me."

"I don't know a lot, just that it's been verified that the

American POWs are regularly tortured. Medical care's almost nonexistent, the chow's pitiful, the men are left to rot when they aren't being beaten." He shook his head in frustration. "It's a fucking hellhole, Eden. There's just no other way of describing it."

"Why hasn't our government—"

"Done what?" he demanded. "Charlie isn't honoring the Geneva Convention. Says they didn't sign it and won't abide by it. At least that's what I was told when I was captured, but I was luckier than most. I was still in the south when a VC patrol nailed my ass."

"How long?"

"Long enough to watch the Cong turn a couple of tough combat soldiers into mealymouthed babies after weeks of torture." He drained his beer can and stood. "I can still hear them crying for their mothers."

"Dan, don't say anymore if it's too painful for you. I've heard enough."

He ignored her. "Treat your husband the same way you treat the guys on the ward. No matter how much distance he tries to put between you—and he'll do it, so pay attention—don't give up on him. The shrinks'll help him as much as they can, but he'll need you more than anyone else. Don't let him push you away or shut you out, Eden. He'll die inside if you let him get away with that kind of crap." He roughly wiped at the tears glistening on his cheeks. "Love him. That's what will really heal him. I know, 'cause that's how you healed me."

PART THREE

KISSINGER SAYS TALKS HAVE NOT REACHED
"JUST AND FAIR" AGREEMENT; BLAMES HANOI

Front-page headline,
The New York Times,
Sunday, December 17, 1972
Vol. CXXII . . . No. 41,966

CHAPTER

23

December 1972–Hanoi, North Vietnam

Chet led Matt out into the courtyard in the northeast corner of Hoa Lo. The two men walked in silence, past an area known among the American prisoners as the Golden Nugget cells. At the end of the dirt path between the bathhouse in the center of the courtyard and the Riviera cellblock, they veered to the left.

Looking up at his friend, Chet grimaced in frustration. Nothing he'd said or done in the preceding twenty-two months had jarred Matt from the silent world he now occupied. The only time anyone ever heard his voice was when he chanted to himself in Cherokee, but even those moments were few and far between.

They passed a guard who lounged against a cellblock wall. With his rifle propped against his hip and a cigarette dangling from his fingers, he displayed the growing casual indifference obvious in many of the Vietnamese who worked in the prison.

Chet knew that the recent spate of night bombing in and around Hanoi had affected everyone. He also realized that the Viets sensed what the American prisoners sensed. Washington seemed determined to bomb the North Vietnamese back to the negotiating table they had recently abandoned in Paris. And if the newer POWs could be believed, a cease-fire and freedom were close at hand.

Vietnamization, a term Chet often puzzled over, although

he'd heard it several times from the more recent arrivals, was supposedly going on in the southern provinces. American troops were pulling out, leaving behind spent lives and blood-soaked soil.

Matt stumbled, cutting short Chet's wandering thoughts. As was his ritual, he led Matt to a spigot on the exterior wall of the bathhouse. He filled his cupped hands with tepid water, raised them, and waited for Matt to lean down. Chet smiled like a pleased parent when his charge drew the water into his mouth. He then filled his joined palms a second time and soothed his own thirst. The image of a cold brew, the glass beaded with moisture and foam trailing riverlike down its side at a crowded happy-hour bar, filled his mind. He promised himself he would know that simple pleasure once again.

Matt tugged his arm free of Chet's hold and raised his hands. He retied the chamois band at his forehead, tucking thick black shoulder-length hair under the soiled strip of cloth. The task completed, he glanced down at Chet, his dark eyes momentarily focused on the man at his side. Hope sparked inside Chet when he saw the flash of clarity in Matt's eyes, but it waned almost immediately when the shuttered look returned.

As they continued their quiet walk, Chet marveled over the fact that the guards still kept their distance from Matt, whose steady gaze and stoic expression were right out of an American history book. He doubted if any of the Viets knew about or understood Matt's Cherokee heritage, but they did seem to comprehend the fact that he possessed some kind of spiritual protection that they didn't want to risk challenging. Hence, Matt Benedict had the distinction of being the only POW without a shaved head, as well as being the only prisoner spared the continual indoctrination attempts of the North Vietnamese.

They approached the Mint cellblock. Chet automatically scanned the guard tower located above and behind the oddly angled building as they walked. "I got a letter from my wife yesterday. It was a year old, but it sure as hell was good to receive it. The baby's in kindergarten now; at least she was when Kathy wrote the letter. It's hard to believe Maggie's almost six. Last time I saw that kid she was screaming her lungs out while I tried to wrap a clean diaper around her fanny." He shook his head and smiled at the memory.

"I talked to a new man this morning. He bailed out of a B-52 the other night after dumping his load on the other side of Hanoi. Our guys are pounding the hell out of the north right now. B-52s at night, F-111s and A-6s during the day, and F-4s for escort and chaff corridors. There are only six or eight thousand Americans left in-country down south. President Nixon's turning the war back over to the Vietnamese. I guess he figures the little fuckers can blow themselves to hell without our help any longer." Chet tightened his hold on Matt's arm and brought him to a stop. Looking up, he said, "There's a chance we might get out of here soon, Warrior. I just hope to hell a part of you understands what I'm trying to tell you."

A siren suddenly shrieked.

A guard approached them, and Chet muttered, "Smiley's got the duty today."

The man waved his weapon. "Inside. You inside . . . now!"

Chet smiled in satisfaction, not only at the warning klaxon but at the scowl on the Viet's face. Nodding to the guard, he led Matt back to their communal cell. "The bastard's afraid we'll notice his precious city stinks of smoke and death."

Sirens screamed throughout the evening and into the night. Heavy bombers released their ordnance from thirty thousand feet and exited the target area. Explosions rocked the city while SAM missiles streaked into the sky in search of metal and air crews.

Unable to sleep, Chet pulled himself up from his mat and leaned against the cell wall. He closed his eyes, smiled, and savored the destructive force of wave after wave of B-52 bombers, his senses filled with the firepower being unleashed against the North Vietnamese and the mortar dust sifting through the air in the cell.

"Come on, you sweet mothers," he quietly cheered. "Make those loads really count for something."

A few feet from Chet, Matt stared into the darkness. He heard whispered conversations despite repeated admonitions from the guards that the prisoners quiet down. Unconsciously clenching and unclenching his right fist, he belatedly realized that he was in the Las Vegas section of Hoa Lo. He also remembered the press conference, the impact of rifle butts against his ribs, and the rage he'd felt at being displayed like a sideshow freak in front of the press.

A door clicked shut on the far side of the cell, and the sharp sound reminded him of Major Han. He knew that none of what he now remembered had been a dream. Not the destruction of Eden's letters and not the announcement of her death. He felt his guts heave at the thought of never seeing her again.

Raising a shaking hand, he smoothed his fingertips over the strip of chamois wrapped around his head and thought, Great-grandfather, thank you for sharing my grief and for standing at my side in my time of need. I would not have survived had it not been for your courage.

A bomb impacted less than a mile from Hoa Lo, and the voices of the men nearby rose. A guard screamed his displeasure and then slammed the cell door in disgust. Matt remained quiet, slowly reorienting himself to his surroundings as windows opened in his mind and allowed him to fully understand where he was, who he was.

Chet chuckled softly, his delight with the bombing evident. Matt turned his head and studied the marine who'd been his ally since Long Moc. He finally asked, "How long have they been making their runs?"

Chet stared at him. The question, though succinct, came from a voice rusty from disuse. He silently wondered if someone had pulled on an unoiled hinge and he'd mistaken the strange sound for words.

"How long?" Matt asked again.

Chet collected his wits and leaned forward in the darkness. He peered into Matt's face and saw the flash of white teeth. Tears filled his eyes, and he grasped his cellmate by the shoulders. "Jesus H. Christ! I was afraid you'd checked out for good. Now that you're back, are you stayin'?"

Matt nodded. "What the hell's going on?" An explosion punctuated his question.

Chet grinned. "Good old U.S. of A. firepower, that's what! B-52s, F-111s, A-6s and God only knows what else every day and night for the last week except for a thirty-six-hour break over Christmas."

Flashes of white jumped across the sky, casting slivers of light through the louver-covered windows at the top of the cell walls. The two men watched the laserlike slashes as they talked.

"Half of Hanoi must be on fire."

"We're ever hopeful," Chet answered, his curiosity unspoken but etched into his voice.

"Go ahead and ask."

"You've been tits up for nearly two years. What brought you back?"

"I'm not sure. Eden's dead. I think something inside me snapped when I was told."

"But how do you know she's dead? And who told you?"

Raw pain surged up inside him. He opened and closed his right fist and tried to control his rage before he spoke. "Major Han."

"Han? He's here at the Hilton?"

"He was. We spent some time together after I screwed up one of the commandant's press conferences. We even played a little roulette after he gave me the news about Eden."

"Christ! You didn't believe him, did you?"

"I did then, but I'm not so sure now."

"No wonder you checked out." Chet forced air through his teeth in a tuneless whistle. "You hungry? I saved some rice from dinner."

Matt smiled. "Why would I be any more hungry than you are? You've been feeding me."

"You know what happened?"

"Just the basics. It was like watching a slow-motion movie in my head, even though I couldn't connect with anything that was going on around me." He shrugged and studied the nearly bald marine. "I do know you've been taking care of me."

Chet grinned. "Nobody else'd come near you. You should see yourself."

Matt cocked his head questioningly.

"You're a regular throwback to your ancestors. Even the guards stay clear of you. They park your ass in a vacant cell whenever we're inspected. Hell, your hair's longer than my wife's," Chet said with a grunt of humor.

Matt touched the hair that now reached his shoulders. Thank you again, Great-grandfather. You have reminded me of my heritage. It is a reminder I will never forget. Frowning, Matt asked, "What's the date?"

"December twenty-eighth"— Chet hesitated briefly—"1972."

Matt slowly exhaled, finally understanding that he'd lost nearly two years. He shot Chet a crooked grin. "Did I have a good Christmas?"

"Hell of a good Christmas! Turkey, dressing, candied yams, the works. You even got a pair of wool socks and a muffler for our next ski trip."

"I'm glad some things never change."

"What do you mean?"

"Your sick sense of humor."

"Hey! You're talking about the guy who's been holding your hand for the last two years."

Matt's reply was muted by another explosion and a subsequent siren that warned of a new wave of bombers. When the noise finally abated, he murmured, "Thanks, Chet. I owe you."

The smaller man shook his head, his gesture of denial vehement and obvious even in the darkness. "After Long Moc, I'd say we're even."

Matt glanced around. "Where's Scratch?"

"Rumor control says he's somewhere in Hanoi, probably in a Viet hospital if he's still alive. He lost his leg. Gangrene set in. They hauled him out of here the day after you checked into the twilight zone. It took us almost six months to find out where he'd been taken." He paused for a moment before asking the question that had hovered in his mind for nearly two years. "What happened at that press conference?"

Matt shrugged. "I freaked. Instead of reading a prepared statement, I gave the foreign press my name, rank, and service number. That pissed off the honcho running the show. The rest is history."

"As far as I know, nobody else has seen Han."

"Forget it, Chet. It's water under the bridge now."

"You spent the first couple of months chanting some Indian thing. Nonstop, no less. One guy almost stuffed his shirt down your throat to shut you up. You haven't done much of that in the last year or so, though. Just every once in a while. Any idea what you were saying?"

Matt shook his head. "I don't speak my mother's language."

"Believe me, you do. It sounded like a funeral dirge to most of us, but we couldn't get a fix on the words."

"It's over, Chet."

"You don't believe what Han told you about Eden, do you?" he persisted.

Matt passed a hand across his face before admitting, "I don't know what to believe."

"There were letters in a box for you, but the guard wouldn't give them to you 'cause you wouldn't get off the sleeping platform. I tried to talk him into giving them to me, but it was a no-can-do situation."

"Thanks for trying," Matt said in a low voice.

"No sweat."

Matt scanned the room as another streak of light split the sky and flashed across the rectangular cell. He counted more than two and a half dozen reclining men. "I don't remember there being this many people in here."

"New-guy village has been busy," Chet answered. "They're running out of places to stash the new POWs." He laughed. "It's a double-edged sword for the Viets. Every time they put a new man in the cell, we get updates on what's happening at home and in Paris. It's driving them crazy."

Another explosion rocked the compound. Matt and Chet fell silent as the bombing intensified. Night passed and dawn crept into the sky as they calculated the ordnance tonnage that fell in and around Hanoi and speculated on the effectiveness of the sorties that had been launched against North Vietnam.

Chet threaded his way through the clusters of men milling around in the courtyard. He saw the object of his search doing push-ups on the hard-packed earth next to the Thunderbird cellblock. He hurried forward, his elation impossible to conceal.

Matt grunted, "Two hundred and fifty," and sank to the ground. Taking a deep breath, he rolled onto his back, peered up at Chet, and then got to his feet. He brushed the dirt from his hands and knees while he studied the smaller man. "You look like one of those vibrator beds in a cheap motel. What gives?"

"I just got the latest skinny from Jenkins. The Viets are back at the negotiating table."

"So?"

"The bombing—it worked. Our chow's improving. We're getting medical treatment. The guards are killing us with their version of kindness." He grinned, the alteration of his features exposing his missing front teeth. "Hell, they're even fixin' us up so we don't look like a shit detail when they ship us home."

Matt nodded thoughtfully. "You might be right."

The smile disappeared from Chet's face. "I'd better be goddamn right. I can't take much more of this craphole." He began to shake with an emotion other than anticipation.

Matt felt a twinge of regret. Everyone had their own reality, their own way of coping with captivity. Some believed they would soon be free. Others were more cautious, adopting a wait-and-see attitude. He included himself in the latter category.

Taking Chet by the arm, he led him to a quiet corner in the compound courtyard. He leaned against a wall and slid down to his haunches. When Chet remained stiff-legged and tight-lipped above him, he patted the ground. "Join me for a pow-wow, Lieutenant."

Chet reluctantly squatted beside him. Several moments passed before he looked at Matt.

"How can I help?"

Chet shook his head and eased back against the wall. Closing his eyes, he rubbed his forehead, his fingers idly lingering on the puckered flesh of the scar above his eyebrow. He finally brought his emotions under control and whispered, "Sorry."

"For what?"

"For acting like a dumb-assed kid who doesn't know the score."

Matt's expression softened. He loved this man, but he couldn't help but wonder if such emotion would have been possible if they hadn't shared five years of hell. "We all want to go home."

"I overreacted."

"You reacted to what might eventually be good news. Period. End of statement." Matt touched his shoulder in a gesture of comfort. "How long did you think you could hold out as Mr. Sunshine?"

"I think I just ran out of gas," Chet admitted ruefully.

"Try to maintain. That's all any of us can do right now."

Chet didn't try to stop the tears that filled his eyes and then slowly slid down his face. "I want to wake up in bed next to my wife. I want to smell her skin and touch her body the way I used to. I want to hug my kid when she comes home from school. And I want a cold beer at the end of a long day." His voice cracked, but he forced himself to continue. "I'm sick to death of being brave. I don't feel brave. I just feel filthy and hungry and mad. I know we're accountable for how we act in here, but I just don't give a damn anymore. I think I'd sell my soul for one hour with Kathy. How fucked up is that?"

"I feel the same way," Matt admitted. "I ache from needing Eden, and I want my life back the way it was. Part of me almost believes she's still alive in spite of what Han said. I just keep wondering if I'll ever see her or my son again."

Chet scrubbed the tears from his face. "You always seem so together, so confident of your ability to take it one day at a time. Hell! Even your disappearing act was first-class all the way. Sometimes I wish I could check out with such ease."

Matt studied his shaking hands. "I feel like my guts are in chunks and scattered all over this godforsaken country. And I'm afraid of what I'll find when and if we ever get home."

"You don't show it."

He took Chet's arm, his fingers digging into the smaller man's frail limb. "You've fed me, washed me, and held on to me when I've cried myself to sleep, so don't bullshit me now. We're all scared," he insisted, his eyes roving a courtyard filled with emaciated and physically and emotionally abused men. "We're not the same people. None of us knows what to expect from day to day. Living with that kind of fear has changed us all . . . forever."

They both got to their feet. Chet suggested, "Let's make a pact . . . one we'll really keep."

Matt looked at him and knew what he was thinking. He nodded.

"We'll help each other if the going gets rough once we get home. We'll both promise to pick up the phone or grab a cross-country hop if either one of us needs to talk or just get drunk."

Matt smiled. "I'll hold you to it."

Chet extended his hand. Matt accepted his gesture of loyalty, and they solemnly shook on their promise to one another. The rattling chains attached to their manacles served to enhance the gravity of their vow.

CHAPTER

24

January 1973–San Diego, California

Eden stood, stretched, and crossed the living room to turn off the television set, her thoughts on a restful night of sleep. She hesitated when she heard, "Please stand by for a news bulletin of great importance. The White House has requested air time for a special announcement. We now take you to our correspondent in Washington."

"This is Carol Blount reporting to you from the White House. President Nixon has requested air time this evening to announce the results of the government's efforts to bring an end to the war in Vietnam. White House sources close to the president indicate that peace in that region of the world is close at hand. We now switch live to the Oval Office for President Nixon's statement."

Sinking to her knees in front of the television screen, Eden held her breath and silently prayed.

"Good evening," President Nixon began. "I have asked for this radio and television time tonight for the purpose of announcing that we, today, have concluded an agreement to end the war and bring peace with honor in Vietnam and Southeast Asia."

Eden slowly exhaled, stunned by the news. "Matthew?" she whispered. Tears filled her eyes, but she blinked them back and leaned forward, her body tense and all her senses alert to the president.

". . . and the cease-fire will take effect . . ."

She finally heard the relentless pounding on her front door

and pulled herself up from the floor. Without taking her eyes from the dour-looking man who dominated the television screen, she made her way to the door and yanked it open.

"It's already started?" David asked as he stepped into the living room.

Eden nodded and resumed her kneeling position in front of the television. David lowered himself to the edge of the couch.

". . . within sixty days from this Saturday, all Americans held prisoner of war throughout Indochina will be released."

The air left her body in a disbelieving gust. Covering her face, Eden struggled for control. When she found it, she looked up at David.

"I've been trying to reach you all afternoon. My office received advance word about the announcement. I'm sorry I wasn't here to prepare you for the news."

"I had a late meeting at the hospital, and then I stopped for dinner on my way home. The phone was ringing when I got in a little while ago, but I didn't catch it in time. The only reason the TV's even on is because I decided to have a cup of tea before I got ready for bed."

"You okay?" David asked.

Eden nodded despite the stunned look in her eyes. "I'm sorry. It's just that none of this seems real."

"We'll have a complete list of the men by Saturday if everything goes according to schedule. The North Vietnamese have agreed to give us the names of all the men they're holding. Can you hang on until then?"

"I'm an expert at hanging on."

"Would you like me to stay for a while?"

"No, that's all right. You go ahead home. I need some time to . . . to absorb all this." She waved her hand, the gesture as disoriented as she felt inside. "Really, David. Go on home. I'll be fine."

He nodded and stood. "Call me if you need me. It doesn't matter what time. If I'm not at the house, Trace'll know how you can reach me." He crossed to where she sat, reached down, helped her up, and gathered her into his arms. "Don't fight what you're feeling right now. Once the shock wears off, you'll have a lot of questions that you'll want answered. I'm available for anything you need. Okay?"

"I understand."

Releasing her after giving her a reassuring hug, he walked to the door.

"David?"

He turned and looked at her.

"The waiting—it's really almost over, isn't it?"

"He'll be home soon, Eden, so just hold that thought for the time being." He smiled and left her to the privacy she wanted and needed.

She returned her attention to the television as David pulled the front door closed. Turning up the sound, she listened to several newsmen dissect each word the president had uttered. Annoyance filtered through her at their endless interpretations of each phrase. And although she forced herself to pay attention, Eden couldn't help but wonder why the announcement itself wasn't sufficient for the media. Why did the ceasefire have to be picked apart and examined under a microscope? She didn't give a damn about the political ramifications, and she knew that none of the other POW families did, either, because, like her, they simply wanted their men home.

Ten minutes later the phone rang. Eden picked up the receiver.

"This is Dan. I just heard the news. Need anything?"

"No. I'm fine, really. Go back to whatever you were doing." She heard him grunt and asked, "What were you doing?"

"*Who* would be a better question."

She smiled at the suggestive cockiness in his voice. "Knock yourself out, Dan. I'll see you when you come in for therapy on Thursday."

"You plannin' on stickin' with the guys at the hospital?"

"Dumb question, Daniel."

"Right."

"Night, Dan. And thanks."

Eden severed the connection and left the phone off the hook. She craved time for herself. Time to think. Time to plan. Time to worry before Matthew came home. Time to consider the reality of a stranger walking into the center of what had become a well-ordered life. A stranger she still loved.

She didn't want to ask herself if he would still want her, but the question nagged at her as she turned off lights, slipped out of her clothes, and crawled into bed. It nagged at her all through a sleepless night, as did her memories of the preceding five years.

And she remembered, more than she really wanted to, because her mind had suddenly become a tumult of emotion-filled flashbacks.

She remembered Drew. She remembered the joy of having him and loving him, as well as the agony of losing him and of having to put his tiny body into the earth. She knew she'd buried more than her son that muggy August day. She had buried her innocence and her dreams. But time and sobriety and self-discipline, when she had the strength for it, had saved her. She had continued her life and built something of value, something she could now point to with confidence and pride.

Red Cross station director. Who would have expected her to achieve so much? What would Matthew think? When he left for Vietnam, all she'd wanted was to be his wife and the mother of his children. Now she had a career, professional commitments, people who depended on her. She'd become a decision maker, a leader, a woman who contributed and made a difference in the lives of others. Would one role now have to be sacrificed for the other? Or would he understand that she'd changed and grown, that she needed both?

Matthew. The lack of him in her life had been an agony, too. Hours, days, months, and then years of not knowing if he was even alive. But I survived, she reminded herself as she stared into the darkness, and, hopefully, so has he.

They would face one another awkwardly, she realized, altered forever by what they had individually experienced. Strangers. She wondered if they could start over. Or would one or the other of them opt to back away from the vows they'd taken, like so many of the couples she'd seen at the naval hospital?

Jim. She'd used him, as he'd used her. But he had changed the rules. She would never forget the power struggle their affair had become before he had finally accepted the reality that she couldn't ever love him. Although his anger had stayed with her for months, she knew her guilt had ended when she understood and accepted that frailty was part and parcel of humanity. She'd eventually forgiven him. More important, she had forgiven herself for needing someone other than Matthew.

Eden left her bed at dawn and took a long walk on the Del Mar beach. Warming her hands with a mug of steaming tea, she watched two playful black Labradors race down the beach. Their master jogged behind them, his running shoes leaving a trail of footprints for the waves to assault.

As she made her way around tiny tide pools at the edge of the strip of beach near her house, she considered, too, the singularity of her life, as well as the sense of isolation that had given birth to the definition of the person she had become. She'd learned to be gentle with herself, and she had also learned of her capacity for compassion where the men and women at the hospital were concerned.

Recalling the nothingness she'd transformed into commitment at the naval hospital, Eden knew that a sea of scotch would have claimed her had not the patients on the wards. The temptation to anesthetize her wounds would always be a flaw in her character, a war she knew she would never be able to stop fighting.

Eden crossed the sand-littered patio and entered the beach-house kitchen. After refilling her mug, she walked down the hallway to the spare bedroom. She dragged two heavy trunks from the closet and knelt between them. She lifted the lids and began to reacquaint herself with her husband. Trembling as she removed the tissue paper from the trunk shipped to her from South Vietnam after Matthew's shootdown, she trailed her fingers across the top layer of clothing and then closed her eyes on the sigh that escaped her.

Matthew's extra flight suits, his shaving kit, a razor still coated with dried soap, the plastic-wrapped bundle of letters she'd written to him, the paperbacks he'd thumbed through so many times in his quonset hut at Chu Lai, all reached inside her and clutched at her heart. She slowly looked through the photo album she'd assembled after their Hawaii R and R: the candid shots of her modeling her first bikini and Matthew building a monstrosity in the sand he'd finally labeled a castle. She smiled at the memory, shivering slightly when she thought of the gentleness of his hands on her body. God, how she still wanted and needed him!

Drawing in a steadying breath, Eden lifted his robe from the collection of folded clothing and pressed her face to the fabric. His special smell lingered, the mothballs she'd scattered in the bottom of the trunk five years earlier unable to diminish totally his masculine scent.

She finally gave in to her tears as she knelt on the floor. She hugged his faded terry-cloth robe and sobbed, a great gasping sound that replaced the awful ache that had plagued her all through the night, a sound that told of isolation and fear, emptiness and hope, pain and relief.

The emotion finally spent, Eden discovered within herself the knowledge that she was capable of confronting the future on her terms. She knew she'd survived Matthew's captivity in her own way, as he had survived in his. Neither one of them had the right to judge the other. She also understood that the only thing worthy of examination was how they would spend the months and years ahead. Alone. Or together. Whatever happened, she knew she would be able to deal with it.

Late Saturday afternoon the front chime pealed and Eden ran to the door. Pulling it open, she saw a smiling trio—David, Tracey, and baby Katherine.

"Tell me," she insisted as she tugged them inside.

David grinned from behind two enormous antipasto trays. "Hope you haven't eaten dinner yet, Mrs. Benedict. We bring greetings from the commandant of the Marine Corps, great news about your husband, and a party."

"You're certain?" she whispered. "He's alive?"

"His name's on the list," David assured her. "He'll be in the first group out of Hanoi because of how long he's been a POW."

Eden looked from David to Tracey, finally able to believe what he'd just said when Tracey plopped a conical-shaped paper party hat on her head.

"First in, first out is the policy. The men decided themselves."

Eden saw his pride in their decision in his eyes, felt his emotion, his sense of being a marine. She felt a wall tumble down inside her. These people were her friends. They cared about her, and they'd shared her pain even when she'd been forced to shut them out of her life. Tears filled her eyes. "Thank you both . . . so much."

The front chime sounded again. David smiled and went to answer the door. With Katherine still in her arms, Tracey hugged Eden, saying quietly, "We love you. We always have, even when you couldn't let us into your life."

She nodded, her throat too tight for words.

"Great! You made it before the press."

Eden turned to see Kitty and Dan step into her living room. She smiled through her tears and moved forward into a three-way bear hug, holding on to her hospital connection with all the strength left in her body. "I'm so glad you two are here, but aren't *you* supposed to be in Hawaii?" she asked Kitty before she turned to Dan and scolded, "And you! I've been trying to call you all day."

Kitty brushed the tears from her cheeks and demanded, "Where else would I be on a night as special as this?"

Eden laughed. "With your new husband, of course. Enjoying your honeymoon and your retirement."

Kitty shrugged. "He understands. Besides, I'm flying back to Honolulu tomorrow afternoon."

Eden glanced at Dan, and he promptly threw his hands up in surrender. "Who do you think's been cleaning out the deli section of every major grocery store between here and Camp Pen?"

"The man's a genius with antipasto trays," Tracey supplied, and then laughed when she saw the surprise on Eden's face.

"Okay, people," David interrupted. "I don't know about the rest of you, but I'm hungry. We've got champagne, apple juice for Eden and Katie, and a ton of food. Let's dig in."

"Plates and napkins coming right up," Kitty promised as she headed for the kitchen.

They toasted Matt's safe return far into the night. Katherine gurgled her juice from a plastic cup, Eden sipped hers from a crystal goblet that had been a wedding gift, and the others polished off two magnums of California's finest.

The press arrived at dawn. Dan read a prepared statement as he stood on the front steps of the beachhouse. The media dubbed him Mrs. Benedict's brother. Eden saw no reason to correct their error.

PART FOUR

Operation Homecoming

CHAPTER 25

February 1973—Hanoi, North Vietnam

Matt shifted his stance and looked around the main courtyard of the Hoa Lo compound. Nearly a hundred American POWs waited in the early-morning drizzle. Guards formed a loose perimeter around the men, and the prison's main gate yawned open to reveal a line of buses.

From his position in the two-abreast formation, Matt noticed the curious looks of civilian North Vietnamese who strolled, pedaled bicycles, or prodded mule carts down Hoa Lo Street. He glanced back over his shoulder at Chet, who stood two men behind him. When the smiling marine nodded, Matt gave him a thumbs-up gesture.

As he continued to study the activity in the courtyard, he couldn't help wondering about the suddenness of the North Vietnamese announcement that the Americans would be released. Hot showers and soap, a first in five years, milk, fresh fruit, medical attention, and the new clothing they'd been issued further enhanced the unreal quality of their situation.

Matt felt the tension in the men around him. Like frail tin soldiers, all dressed in dark gray trousers and light gray shirts, they stood poised on a precipice of freedom.

Home. He turned the word over and over in his mind. Bitterness at the way they'd all been forced to exist for so many years still eroded his ability to believe that they were truly going home.

Like a delicacy that one has heard about, discussed, and then anticipated, he wondered if the end result would be too rich, too overwhelming to the senses. After a diet of rice, moldy bread, tasteless vegetables, torture, and isolation, he personally considered the prospect of release both appealing and intimidating.

Home. He relished the very sound of the word. Home meant Eden, her gentleness, her love, and her ability to make him feel like the sole focus of her life. He allowed a small part of his mind to actually believe that she might be alive.

Home also meant seeing his son for the first time. Andrew. He shook his head in frustration. Almost five years old and I've never even seen him. It jarred him to think of walking into the middle of a child's life without warning. He promised himself he would go slowly with such a little boy. Build confidence, share time. Do all the things a father dreams of doing with his son.

I need my wife and my son. I need to get into my uniform and resurrect my career in the corps. I need to be a person again, not an animal bent on survival. But first, he realized, I need to learn how to feel again.

He clenched his right fist, as much in determination as in the need to reassure himself that he'd done everything in his power to repair the damage done to his wrist and hand. Only rarely did the feeling fade from a few of his fingers, and even then he knew how to provoke a renewal of sensation. He could still handle the controls of an F-4. He could still fly. I will fly, he promised himself.

And I'll teach my son to navigate the clouds when he's old enough, he decided with a smile. A long-forgotten poem drifted into his mind. The exact phrasing of the verse was blurred by the emotion churning inside him, but he still recalled the essence of the words. As a pilot, according to the poet, he'd touched the face of God. In the sky and in the isolation of Long Moc and Hoa Lo, Matt knew a higher power, perhaps God, had been with him.

God. As a child he had learned that a warrior never walks alone. He still wasn't certain he believed in a God defined by other men, but he accepted the presence of a supreme being, one who had the ability to create even as man inflicted destruction and one who had the compassion to offer surcease when man again inflicted unbearable pain.

His wandering thoughts turned again to his wife. Eden, please be alive. My memories of you kept me sane even in my darkest moments. When Great-grandfather could not reach me, I knew I could depend on you when I felt myself weakening. He shuddered, closed his eyes, and lifted his face to the weeping sky. I can almost smell your skin, Eden. And I can almost feel the texture of your hair rippling like silk through my fingers. Please be alive, paleface. I need you so much.

He suddenly recalled the comment Chet had made during those stressful days that followed the bombing of Hanoi. "*I'd sell my soul for one hour with Kathy. How fucked up is that?*"

Chet wasn't fucked up, not by any stretch of the imagination. Supremely rational, perhaps. What man among the married POWs hadn't been willing at one time or another to make a deal with the devil if he thought he might be able to share a few moments with his wife?

Matt opened his eyes, squared his shoulders, and held his head high when he heard the voice of one of the senior POWs.

"Attennn . . . shun!"

He counted to three during the brief pause that followed.

"Forward. March!"

He savored the crispness of the words, a simple reminder of sanity and order, a welcome change from the abortive attempts at English by the North Vietnamese.

The Americans filed forward across the courtyard, their footsteps raising tiny puffs of dust as they silently passed through the main gate and boarded the buses lined up in the street. Matt felt, as he was certain the others did, the anxiety that existed like a separate entity all around them. He drew in a deep breath in an effort to control the worry raging inside him and quietly prayed that this was not yet another in a series of cruel hoaxes so skillfully perpetrated by the North Vietnamese.

After taking his seat in the old French bus, he pressed his fingertips to the filthy strip of chamois tied across his forehead. Despite the orders of the guards, he had not relinquished his token, his connection to his heritage. And beneath the waistband of his trousers was Eden's letter, the paper soft from handling and the ink faded by his sweat and the passage of time.

Are we really going home? he wondered over and over again.

The question haunted him, ate at him, even as the buses pulled away from the prison. He couldn't bring himself to cast so much as a cursory glance at the twenty-foot-thick walls of Hoa Lo, nor was he willing to acknowledge the guard towers, the barbed wire, or the broken glass embedded in the tops of the walls. He would take with him the memory of hunger, torture, and isolation. Those memories were sufficient, and he knew they would last him a lifetime.

He shoved away the possibility of another prison, more punishment. He wanted, needed, had to believe that he was on his way to freedom.

Few commented on the ruin that was Hanoi. Their silence reflected a collective and tenuous hold on their sanity as the buses crept along the streets of what remained of the capital city.

Rain pinged against the top of the bus, droplets darting down the windows. Matt absently studied the knife-cutting pattern, the sound of thunder periodically drawing him from his suspended state of mind. A hand settled over his opening-and-closing right fist, startling him. He glanced up to find Chet standing in the aisle.

"Look up ahead. You won't believe your eyes."

Matt did as he urged. Even the guard stationed at the front of the bus seemed fascinated by the condition of the Paul Dormier Bridge.

"Do you suppose anyone will ever know how many of our guys died trying to knock out that particular piece of real estate?"

Matt exhaled heavily. "Guess we'll have to leave it to the historians," he conceded as the driver slowed the bus and carefully navigated the cratered earth and pavement of the French-built bridge.

Chet hunched nearer. "I remember seeing recon shots of this area. We have to cross this bridge to get to Gia Lam Airfield." He grinned. "We're goddamn going home, Warrior."

He nodded, emotion suddenly stinging his eyes. Feeling Chet's hand on his shoulder, he covered it with his own. "Home," he managed, the word a barely recognizable croak.

The guard glanced back at the POWs, heard the eagerness in their voices without understanding the words, and placed his rifle in the stairwell of the bus. Relaxed, he chatted with the driver as the man steered the bus through a throng of civilian and military North Vietnamese and parked at the edge of the tarmac.

"Where the hell's the air force?" growled one man.

"Nobody said we'd be flying home in our own birds," countered his seatmate.

"Look at that ceiling."

"We're socked in. Who in his right mind would fly in this crap?"

"Those 141 guys can fly into anything," disagreed an air force major. "Why, I saw some crazy-assed kid out of Warner-Robins drop right into the middle of a monsoon downpour a duck wouldn't even want to tackle."

"Who said anything about C-141s?" questioned a man in the rear of the bus.

"Come on, rice brain, do you think they'd send choppers for all of us?"

"The rain's stopped," observed a heretofore silent passenger in the front row.

The men quieted. The door to the bus scraped open. The guard exited and then returned a few minutes later. He motioned the men to their feet and pantomimed a "follow me" gesture.

"Now what?" someone muttered. No one answered him.

They stood in formation beside their respective buses. A dark-complected man at the front of the group peered around the nose of the bus and then quickly stepped back to his place in the line. "Our people are here. Pass it along."

The announcement swept the men like a fast-moving brushfire. As a group, they relaxed. Some chatted, while others silently pondered the past as well as the future.

The mist returned. Within minutes rain splattered heads and faces. A North Vietnamese dressed in a Western business suit scurried across the flight line, barked an order at the guards, and motioned the men back into the buses. They remained subdued even when the guards passed out packs of European-made cigarettes and books of matches.

Two hours crept by.

Matt watched the North Vietnamese and Americans, both civilian and military personnel, as they moved in and out of a tent set up at the edge of the Gia Lam flight line. Consciously comparing himself to the robust, well-fed men of his country, he realized that he'd lost more than fifty pounds. As he studied his hands and arms, he also accepted the fact that he looked and felt like most of his peers. Skeletal, exhausted, and older than time.

The ceiling slowly lifted. The rain tapered off, first to a light drizzle and eventually to a whispering mist. Again the guard motioned the men from the bus. He carelessly propped his weapon against his hip and smiled amiably at the Americans. Several of the men lit the cigarettes they'd been given on the bus and listened in amazement to the animated voices of the onlookers crowded against the fence in front of the airfield terminal.

Another sound filled the air. A sound so comforting and familiar that many of the men openly wept. Matt kept his eyes on the far end of the runway. Within seconds an air force C-141 Starlifter came into view, its behemoth body and extensive wingspread a portrait of camouflage-painted beauty.

"Goddamned truck," muttered a fighter pilot. "Never thought I'd be so glad to see one of those hulking babies in all my life."

"We really are going home," whispered another man, his voice filled with awe.

Matt turned and glanced at Chet, who moved forward. They shook hands before embracing one another. Chet whispered, "Semper fi, buddy. Semper fi."

They drew apart, wet faced and shaking.

Matt laughed, the sound ragged. "I sure hope your wife's been warned you're on your way home. I predict you'll need a new bed in less than six months."

Chet grinned, but he quickly sobered. "Eden's alive. I feel it in my gut."

Matt nodded, wanting to believe him even if he wasn't totally sure himself.

The North Vietnamese official in Western clothing returned, his Oxford accent surprising many of the men. "You will form a line in order of your captivity." He paused while they did as he requested. "Follow me. Your names will be called. You will file forward, one at a time, and present yourself to the men at the table in front of the reception tent. You will then be escorted to the aircraft."

He led them past the guards, the assembled crowd at the terminal fence, and several North Vietnamese dignitaries. Matt noticed a few hastily scrawled placards wishing the POWs well. By the time his name was called, he felt as though he had been transported to another time zone.

"Benedict, Matthew Alexander. United States Marine Corps."

He moved forward, his steps measured, his spine ramrod straight as he saluted the senior ranking American officer at the table. After signing a document with shaking fingers, he turned and accepted the handshake of a Marine Corps officer standing nearby.

"Colonel Cal Windley, Major Benedict. I'm your escort home. We'll be heading for Clark Air Force Base in the Philippines for debrief, any immediate medical attention you may require, and all the steak and eggs you can eat."

Matt stared at him, numbness and confusion preventing a reply.

Cal smiled. "You were promoted a few years back. Dave Markham, your wife's liaison officer from Headquarters Marine—"

Matt gripped his arm. "My wife?"

He nodded. "Yes, your wife. Major Markham supplied her with your oak leaves when your promotion came through."

"Eden's alive?" he clarified, his fingers tightening on the man's arm.

The colonel cocked his head and placed a reassuring hand on Matt's shoulder. "Your wife is just fine, and very much alive. According to our records, she has a small house near San Diego, and she's the Red Cross station director at Balboa Naval Hospital. She's lived there for almost four years now."

"I thought—she's not dead?"

"Who told you that?" Cal pressed.

Matt clenched and unclenched his right fist before finding his voice. "Charlie."

"Bastards!" The spit-and-polish Marine Corps officer swiftly brought himself under control. "You'll be able to talk to her shortly after we land at Clark. The air force is putting in a bank of phones at the hospital where you'll be temporarily housed." He paused and studied the man at his side, his expression grim as he continued, "I plan to fill you in on her entire situation once we're P.I. bound."

Matt nodded. Relief surged through him, making him tremble. "Thank you, sir."

"No need to thank me for anything, Major." Cal took his arm and guided him to the waiting C-141. "Why don't we get aboard this MAC flight and get the hell out of this pisshole? There's a second bird due in to pick up another load of our guys as soon as we take off."

Twenty minutes later, Chet found Matt strapped into his seat. He handed him a sweating beer can and buckled himself into the adjoining seat. "The crew got together and bought us a couple of cases of suds before they took off this morning."

Matt savored the feel of cold aluminum in his hand. Lifting his can, he tapped it against Chet's. "To freedom."

"To freedom," Chet echoed before chugging half the contents. Grinning, he offered a second toast. "To our ladies, who probably really believe that if the corps had intended for us to have wives they would have issued them."

Matt grinned. "To our wives." He leaned his head back against the seat top and closed his eyes. "If this is a dream, don't wake me up."

Chet chuckled. "If this is a dream, then everyone on this fucking bird is having the same one."

Shortly after the C-141 was airborne, the pilot announced, "Gentlemen, we are now entering international air space."

The POWs roared their approval, then repeated the deafening sound after listening to a brief message from President Nixon over the plane's PA system.

Medical personnel who accompanied the Operation Homecoming team circulated among the men. Nurses lingered in the aisle, understanding that the men needed time with round-eyed women who reminded them of their wives and sweethearts at home. Several men napped, emotional fatigue taking its toll. Others chatted with the escort officers assigned to each returning POW.

Matt joined Cal Windley in a draped-off area in the forward section of the aircraft after asking about Jack Morrison. The two men sat opposite one another. Cal offered Matt a cigarette and his lighter. Matt sank back against his seat, grateful for the first American-made smoke he'd had in several years.

"Captain Morrison escaped his half of the patrol that nailed you after the shootdown. I had a chance to speak with him at Headquarters Marine Corps last year. His leg was badly damaged during a firefight before he was picked up by friendlies, but he's okay now. He's presently attached to VMFA-314 at El Toro."

"Then he's flying F-4s again?"

Cal nodded.

"He always said he'd put in thirty years if the corps'd have him."

"He's a fine officer," Cal agreed.

Matt suddenly sensed that something important had yet to be said. "There's something you're not telling me, Colonel. Is it about Eden?"

"That's right. Look, Matt, there's no easy way to say this, so I'm just going to lay it on the line."

"Spit it out," he responded tersely, convinced now that Eden's feelings for him had changed during their years apart. His thoughts strayed to the possibility that she might have divorced him, but he reminded himself that he still had a son.

"You knew about your wife's pregnancy when you went down?"

"We had a son in June of '68."

Cal looked surprised.

"His name is Andrew," Matt clarified. "Eden calls him Drew."

"Then you received your wife's letters?"

"One. The rest were burned." His voice was flat, his eyes momentarily focused on a sight other than Cal Windley's lined forty-year-old face.

"She wrote you every week via the State Department and the International Red Cross."

He blinked and refocused. "I was only given one letter from Eden."

"Matt . . . your son died when he was two months old. His lungs collapsed. Your wife found him, but she wasn't able to revive him."

"Died? Drew? My son died?"

"I'm sorry, but he's dead."

Matt felt something give way inside his body. He tried to pull into himself, tried to safeguard his emotions the way he had during captivity, but even that skill now eluded him.

"I have a son. I can't even begin to imagine how a man lives with the death of a small child, especially when he's spent four or five years thinking and dreaming about the time when they'd be together."

"I never saw him."

Cal sighed and leaned forward. "Your wife went through hell after she lost him. It took her quite a while to get herself together."

"Why?"

Cal didn't even try to answer Matt's real question. Who understood why infants died? What entity decreed that children, and not old people or soldiers, should be taken from their families? "The doctors call what happened to your son a crib death. When we get to Clark, I'll ask someone from pediatrics to talk to you about it."

Matt just stared at him, his eyes a dark void, his hands hanging slack between his knees.

"There's a chaplain on board. Do you want me to get him for you?"

He shook his head.

"Then I'll leave you alone for a while. Just let one of the stewards know if you need me."

"What's the date?"

"February twelfth."

"Five years and two weeks gone . . . totally wasted." He lowered his face to his hands and wept for all that he had lost.

Cal turned to find Chet on the other side of the drape partition.

"Matt in there? I got him another brew."

"He'd probably like some privacy right now."

Chet frowned. "I thought his wife was okay."

"She is."

"What's wrong, Colonel?"

"I had to give him some tough news."

"Tell me," Chet insisted.

He hesitated briefly before saying, "His son died a few months after his birth."

"Jesus H. Christ! He never even saw the kid."

"You two are pretty close, aren't you?"

Chet unconsciously straightened. "We're like brothers, sir."

Cal nodded and stepped aside. "He'll need you now."

Chet parted the drapes, stepped into the small enclosure, and studied Matt's bowed head. "Colonel Windley told me about Drew." He reached out and placed a comforting hand on Matt's shaking shoulders.

He finally lifted his head, released a strangled rush of air, and said, "I wonder which one of us he would've looked like if he'd lived."

"Eden'll have his baby pictures."

"Why, Chet? Why did it have to happen this way?"

"Why were we shot down? Why did Tom's wife divorce him and marry another man? Why did Bob's mother have a heart attack and die last week? Where's Scratch?" he answered, cataloging the conversations taking place throughout the aircraft. "Life goes on. Unfortunately, so does death."

Chet kept his hand on Matt's shoulder as he grieved for the son he would never know. They eventually spoke of what they had shared, of their memories of their wives, and of their apprehension about the days and weeks ahead.

Shortly after touchdown at Clark in the Philippine Islands, Chappy James, a barrel-chested black air force general, boarded the C-141. He welcomed the men with a short speech. A second man, the base's public information officer, explained that the media planned to broadcast their arrival to all the major news networks in the United States.

CHAPTER 26

February 12, 1973—San Diego, California

"Here's the last of your juice, Sam."

Eden tucked a straw between the man's lips and held it in place while he sucked in the liquid, a major feat since Sam Cavanaugh was missing one side of his face thanks to a grenade explosion.

"News bulletin, Eden!" shouted a patient from the far end of the ward.

She forced herself to keep a steady hand on the plastic cup she held for Sam. Despite her resolve, Eden knew her entire body was trembling.

A phone conversation she'd had with David during her lunch break drifted through her mind. "The media's covering the POW arrival at Clark. With a little luck, Matt'll be on the first plane. Stay near a television if you can manage it."

She waited for Sam to lift the corner of his lip and release the straw. When he did, she blotted his chin with a napkin.

"Husband," he whispered.

"When you're finished, Sam. How about some pudding?"

He shook his head. "Not . . . now. Sherry . . . come . . . soon. Help . . . food," he insisted, despite the discomfort of speaking from a mouth only half filled with teeth.

Eden nodded and placed the cover on his meal tray. "Can I get you anything else?"

He jerked his head from side to side, his good eye flashing impatiently. "Go."

"Come on, Eden. The plane just landed," yelled a corpsman from the solarium that doubled as a TV room.

She smoothed the front of her lab coat with damp hands.

Sam frowned. "Enough! Husband . . . you . . . need . . . see."

"I'll be back in a few minutes."

He captured her wrist and squeezed it. "He . . . nervous . . . too."

Tears burned her eyes. "Thanks, Sam."

She raced down the center aisle, her footsteps slowing once she saw the television screen and the patients grouped around it. They made a space for her in front of the set. Conscious of their eyes on her, Eden didn't mind their curious stares. She'd stopped hiding from them a long time ago. She knew a fleeting sense of pride at the thought.

"I'll find you a chair," offered a patient.

"I'm fine right here." She sank to her knees on the tile floor, her hands clasped tightly together in her lap, her body rigid with anticipation, and her expression uncertain. A hand settled on her shoulder, and she looked up. One of the men had rolled his wheelchair forward. Several others followed suit. She covered the supportive hand with her own, grateful for these men who were willing to share the final moments of waiting with her.

They all silently watched the transport jet roll to a stop near a podium with a half-dozen or more microphones attached to the top of it.

"Protocol! Look at all those heavy hitters," commented another patient as a group of military and civilian dignitaries gathered at the bottom of the stairs to the plane. "Why don't they get on with it and let us see our guys?"

Eden silently echoed their sentiments as she watched the men on the television screen. They disappeared into the aircraft while a news commentator rattled on about the arriving POWs, the crowd of Clark-stationed air force families waiting to welcome the men, and the convergence of the media on the Pacific island.

After a wait that could be measured by the drops of perspiration sliding down her back, Eden saw the dignitaries leave the C-141. A white-haired man in drab gray shirt and pants followed them. The crowd cheered its approval from behind the cameras, and the newsman announced his name. Eden recognized him as the husband of a San Diego woman active in the League of Families of POWs/MIAs.

Eden didn't notice Dan until he dropped to his knees beside her and slipped an arm around her waist for a quick hug. She tore her eyes from the television screen long enough to flash him a look that asked, "Where have you been?"

"Around," he mouthed with a wink.

One by one the men exited the plane. Medical personnel carried a few off on stretchers; others walked unaided despite their obvious physical frailty. Several limped, while a few depended on crutches to support their weight.

Eden held her breath as the newsman slowly ticked their names off his list. Then an unusually tall man ducked his head before stepping through the doorway. He paused at the top of the stairs and squinted against the glare of the bright Pacific sunshine.

Eden moaned and reached out. Tears spilled from her eyes, blurring her vision.

"Marine Corps Major . . . Matthew Alexander Benedict."

"Way to go!" shouted a patient.

"All right!" cried another.

Eden swayed. Dan grabbed her shoulders and steadied her.

"I'm okay," she whispered, not taking her eyes from Matthew as he walked the length of the receiving line, shook hands with the dignitaries, and then stepped into place beside his fellow prisoners. "Oh, my God! He's so skinny, but he looks wonderful." She turned to Dan. "He's alive! He's really alive."

"Worth the wait, wasn't he?" Dan asked after mopping awkwardly at her cheeks with his handkerchief.

She nodded and laughed at the same time, then heard the patients gathered around her chuckling and talking as they shared her joy. Eden got to her feet and slowly circled the solarium, hugging each man, although she was unable to verbalize her appreciation for their support. A part of her sensed, though, that they understood how jumbled her emotions had become as well as her gratitude for their love and compassion.

She turned and saw Toni Evans standing in the doorway, her cheeks wet and her nose red. Eden walked into her arms and hugged her. "I saw him. He walked off that plane all by himself. He's skinny as a rail, but he looks so good!" She laughed self-consciously. "God, I can't stop talking."

Toni dabbed at her face with a tissue and cleared her throat. "Dave Markham just called. Their arrival was actually taped several hours ago. There's a seven- or eight-hour time difference between here and Clark. The men are going to be allowed to call their families after their initial medical workups at the base hospital. He thinks you'll hear Matt's voice either late tonight or early tomorrow morning."

"But he doesn't know my phone number!"

Toni and Dan both laughed at the horrified look on her face. "David said it's all taken care of."

She gave them both a blank look.

Dan grinned at her lack of composure. "How about starting with hello?" he teased. "That usually breaks the ice."

"But there are probably things that I shouldn't say—things that might upset him."

"Didn't we have this conversation about eighteen months ago?" Dan questioned with a frown.

Eden nodded. "You're right. Thanks for reminding me."

"Anytime." He looped his good arm around her shoulders. "I'll walk you down to your car when you're ready to leave."

She glanced at her watch. "Let me check on Sam Cavanaugh. My shift's over, but I want to make sure his wife's here to help him finish his supper."

She discovered Sam and his wife arguing good-naturedly about who was going to finish Sam's dinner. Sherry won and started siphoning pudding into his mouth. As she left the ward, Eden heard Sam moaning about people who ganged up on cripples. She was still smiling when she found Dan waiting for her in the Red Cross office.

Opening her locker, she exchanged her lab coat for a tan corduroy jacket that matched her slacks while Dan looked on, a measuring look in his eyes. Eden hesitated before slowly turning to face him.

"You look like a truck just hit you."

"One just did. My brain feels like scrambled eggs right now."

"You're not talking about Matt, are you?"

"Partly. I'm worried about his mental condition. Five years in a prison under lousy conditions is not going to make our reunion very easy."

"That's not a surprise."

"No, it's not. But, Dan, I've gotten used to not knowing when he'd finally come home, of living in a self-enforced state of limbo. I've prayed for an end to all of it, but down deep I don't honestly think I ever really expected not to have to live this way. And now that things are about to change, I don't quite know what to do."

"What do you want to do?"

She glanced around the room before answering. "Keep working here, keep putting one foot in front of the other where my sobriety's concerned. I—"

"Say it," he urged.

"I want to still be able to love him once he's home. I don't want him to have changed so much that we can't put our lives back together."

"You won't know any of that until you've seen him, talked to him, and spent time with him."

"I know. It's just that—"

"You're scared," he supplied when she paused.

"Totally, completely, irrationally witless with fear. Isn't it ridiculous? Me, scared of my husband. Dumb, really dumb."

He shook his head. "Not dumb at all. That's how he feels, too. Frightened out of his mind because he's been gone so long and hasn't a clue about who and what he's coming home to. That's how I felt even with no one waiting for me."

Eden leaned back against the locker doors and crossed her arms. "So, how do I handle it?"

"What do you think?"

"I think I've got two choices. I can keep my feelings to myself and just take it a day at a time, or I can get my uncertainty out in the open and deal with it. Individually *and* with Matthew."

"It's your ball game, friend, but my instincts tell me you're inclined to confront the problem and handle it rather than sidestep it and have it blow up in your face later."

She nodded. "You're right, I am." Picking up her purse, Eden reached inside and found her car keys. "I can't help thinking about how much I've changed in the last five years, though."

Dan followed her from the Red Cross offices, pausing briefly while she locked the door. "We all have to grow up, Eden. Personally, though, I think we just lose our innocence."

She remembered another man who had made the same observation, but that seemed as though it had happened in another lifetime altogether and to another person. "Matthew used to talk about seeing my promise, the person I'd become as the years passed, but I still think he's going to be surprised. I seriously doubt I'm who he expects to find waiting for him."

"Probably," Dan agreed.

"You're a big help!"

He grinned and took her by the arm. "One day at a time, Eden. You know how to do it."

She nodded, saying little as they left the hospital complex and made their way to the sprawling parking lot across the street.

"Do you want me to follow you home?"

"Not necessary. I'll save the waterworks for later."

Dan took her keys, unlocked her car, and waited for her to get settled before he closed the door. When Eden rolled down the window, he suggested, "Let's celebrate after you've gotten your call and you have a better idea of when you'll actually see him."

"Sounds good."

"One of the guys over in admin mentioned a special ward the brass's setting up for the local POWs. Two wards, really. Six C and D over in Building Twenty-six. The hospital's turning the two bedrooms into small suites so the families can spend time with the men."

"I wondered about the furniture I noticed being hauled in there this afternoon. Do you have any idea how many men they expect?"

"My sources tell me eighteen or twenty guys."

"What about the press? They've been driving me nuts since Nixon's announcement. That's why I had to get that unlisted number."

"Don't remind me. Dave Markham had to track me down when he couldn't get through to you."

She laughed, remembering the temporary confusion she'd set into motion after not getting any sleep three nights in a row.

"One of my other sources mentioned special clearance badges for the men and their families. Dave'll probably have yours for you before Matt lands at Miramar."

"The naval air station?"

"Best place to land a jet transport other than Lindberg Field."

"Who told you that?"

He shrugged. "Logic."

"Don't wander off, okay? You're the only person I know with a pipeline to the powers that be."

"Glad to be of service, friend." He straightened and started to step back from the side of her car.

Eden caught his prosthetic appliance with her outstretched hand. "You've got a terrific bedside manner, Daniel. I'm not scared anymore."

He studied the placement of their hands, one real and warm and alive, the other a man-made substitute. Slowly raising his eyes, eyes filled with the depth of his affection for her, he quietly admitted, "You're the one who taught me the uselessness of fear and anger. I owe you a lot more than a few minutes of conversation."

She tugged him closer. When he bent down, she kissed his cheek. "You don't owe me at all, but please promise not to disappear from my life when Matthew comes home. You're an important person in my world, Dan. You always will be."

He winked, his grin again in place as he straightened. "Get your butt in gear and head on home. I'll see you on the ward after I finish up in therapy tomorrow afternoon."

She nodded and started her car. In the reflection of her rearview mirror, she watched Dan climb into his jeep. As he followed her from the hospital parking lot, his radio blaring

"Let it Be" by the Beatles, she reflected for a moment on how different their relationship might have been had he not been such an instinctively honorable man and had she not been forced to face her own inadequacies well before their first meeting.

Eden sighed softly before whispering to herself, "Thank God I didn't have to try and get through the last two years without your friendship, Daniel Howard."

CHAPTER

27

Clark AFB Infirmary—Philippine Islands

"You can get dressed now, Major." Winding his stethoscope into a tight circle, the doctor stuffed it into the pocket of the lab jacket he wore over his summer-weight uniform shirt.

Matt pulled on a pale cotton robe. He remained seated on the examining table, his long legs hanging over the side.

"You're in surprisingly sound medical condition given the length of your captivity. And although you've lost about forty-five pounds, you have managed to maintain reasonably good muscle tone throughout the majority of your body." The doctor removed his wire-rimmed glasses and massaged the bridge of his nose. "The scars on your back, shoulders, ankles, and wrists speak for themselves. They may fade, but they'll never disappear completely."

"I wasn't expecting them to." Matt absently clenched and unclenched his right fist, his gaze fixed on the activity outside the examining room. He wondered how long it would take him to accept as normal American men and women smiling and talking to one another or the sight of a small child clinging to its mother's hand as it toddled down a sidewalk. He didn't notice the compassionate look on Dr. McKee's face, nor did he realize the hunger in his own eyes.

"You mentioned some concern about muscle damage in your right wrist area," the doctor encouraged, the notes he was making in Matt's file momentarily forgotten.

Matt brought his gaze back to the doctor and nodded. "I think a nerve was damaged. The feeling in my wrist and hand came and went at first. It usually depended on how tight my squeeze cuffs were, but I exercised as much as I could."

"The orthopedic team at the naval hospital in San Diego will do an extensive evaluation once you're stateside, and surgery, if necessary, but you appear to have handled the situation with excellent results." The doctor lifted Matt's arm, noting that a bullet had passed though his wrist, leaving a puncturelike scar on top and a dime-sized outcropping of scar tissue on the inside. "You're worried about getting back into the cockpit again, aren't you?"

"Yes, sir."

"I wouldn't be surprised if you're in the air within six months, assuming, of course, that the shrinks give you the go-ahead and your retraining is successful."

He exhaled slowly, relief etched into his fatigued facial features. "Other than my wife and the baby she was expecting when I went down, flying's all I've thought about for the last five years."

"I know you're probably tired, but I'd like to talk to you about the child you and your wife lost."

Matt glanced at the bulging folder the doctor held. "All I know is what Colonel Windley told me."

Ben McKee watched Matt grit his teeth and swiftly avert his eyes to cover the emotion welling in them. "Although you need dental care, physical therapy, vitamins, three squares a day, and time with your wife, you also need to deal with the death of a son you ultimately expected to find waiting for you. We can talk now, or I can set you up with the Clark shrinks for a couple of sessions before I release you for transport stateside."

Matt looked back at the doctor and saw compassion and concern, but he couldn't feel anything other than the numbness that seemed to entomb his entire being. "I expected a son." Gesturing at his surroundings, he exhaled sharply. "I don't know if I'm dreaming or having a nightmare. Nothing seems real."

The doctor pulled a chair to a position beside the examining table and sat down. "You need time."

"Time! I've just wasted five years of my life."

"Through no fault of your own. Don't forget that. Now, do you think the answer to your problems is to jump on some merry-go-round and throw your emotions even farther out of whack?"

Matt ran his fingers through his newly cropped hair in a gesture of frustration. "Probably not."

"Then try going very slowly. From what I've read about prisoner-of-war situations, I gather a man has to learn to pace himself while in captivity."

Matt nodded. "It's the only way not to go stark raving mad."

"Then you have to handle the next few months with the same kind of caution, don't you? Test yourself. See what appeals to you and what drives you crazy. Figure out the best route back to a world that right now seems very foreign to you."

"When I was in flight school," Matt recalled, "I was strapped into a contraption called a Dilbert Dunker. After a gunnery sergeant gave the signal, the Dunker dropped into a swimming pool like a boulder and turned upside down. I had to release the harness, reorient myself, and reach the surface without help. I panicked at first, but I managed to bring myself under control and pass the underwater-cockpit escape test on the first try." He scrubbed the sweat from his upper lip before going on. "That's how I am right now. Threatened and disoriented. I don't like the feeling."

"If you didn't feel that way, I'd set you up for mandatory psychiatric counseling and delay your return to California," admitted the doctor.

"You've made your point, Doc."

"Good. Now we need to talk about your son's medical condition at the time of his death."

"Yes, sir."

Ben McKee flipped through several file pages, grunting when he found the data he wanted. "What precisely did Colonel Windley tell you?"

"Not much. He mentioned something called crib death."

"Crib death is a new name for an unexplained phenomenon that's been with us since the beginning of time. Infant mortality, at least in my medical experience, usually involves the twenty-eight-day period following birth. Your son was, however, two months old at the time of his death. In crib-death cases, one of two things generally happens. The lungs collapse, causing severe respiratory distress, or the heart simply stops beating. In Andrew's case, his lungs collapsed."

"Was he sick? Did Eden have any kind of warning?"

"None. Your son was healthy, he'd gained the right amount of weight for his age, and he had the added benefit of being breast-fed."

"Then why? None of this makes any sense. It sounds as though Drew had everything going for him, not against him."

He closed Matt's file and admitted, "You're right. I'm afraid no one can really give you a logical explanation of why your son died. What's worse is that this kind of thing is increasing, despite the advances being made in pediatric medicine. All I can say is that the researchers are at work, but I'm afraid they've got a long road ahead of them."

"Does your file say anything about Eden? I mean, I can guess what Drew's death must have done to her. Did she have anyone with her?"

Matt sensed Ben McKee's hesitation when the man resettled his glasses on the bridge of his nose and straightened the name tag on his lab jacket.

"Doc?"

"Dave Markham, your wife's liaison officer from Headquarters Marine Corps, got involved in her case a few months after your son died."

"Eden contacted him?"

"Not exactly. Major Markham apparently guessed she was having a serious problem after a phone conversation he had with her. It turns out she'd been drinking very heavily by the time the major entered the picture. It took some time, but Major Markham and a woman friend of your wife's were able to help her sober up and join AA."

Matt stared at him. "Alcoholics Anonymous?"

He nodded. "She blamed herself when your son died, which is somewhat typical of a new mother who loses a small child."

"But it wasn't her fault. You just said as much."

"She knows that now, but think about the position she was in at the time. You weren't officially listed as a POW until the summer of 1971. When the baby died, just eight months after you were shot down and listed as an MIA, she probably thought she'd lost both of you."

"What happened in June of '71?"

Ben extracted a news clipping from Matt's file, a copy of the same news clipping Eden had been shown some twenty months earlier. He handed it to Matt, saying, "This photo was the first evidence of your POW status. It appeared in an Eastern-bloc-nation's party newspaper."

Matt clutched the news photo and stared at it, feeling once again the rage he'd experienced during that press conference and the emotional agony he'd endured because of Major Han. "That was the day they told me Eden had died." He swallowed convulsively. "I wanted to die, too."

"Then you can imagine how she felt when she lost your son."

He nodded and handed the photocopy back to the doctor. "She's had time to live with what's happened."

"And you haven't," the doctor finished for him. "And you're concerned about opening old wounds."

"Yes. Even though I never saw my son, he was alive and real to me. It's almost as though he died today, not four and a half years ago."

"Let Eden help you. The work she does at the naval hospital has placed her in intimate contact with tragedy and pain. She started as a part-time volunteer with the Red Cross, and now she's the station director of the unit. She's obviously learned how to handle some very difficult situations. I suspect she also understands and empathizes with the grief you're experiencing right now."

Matt slid off the examining table, a thoughtful look on his face. "I hope you're right, Doc. I don't want her to have it any tougher than she's already had it the last five years."

"Don't hide your own pain to protect your wife, Major Benedict. You *cannot* afford to do that. Understood?"

"Yes, sir."

"Good. You're scheduled for extensive debriefing in the morning. For now, though, you can make a phone call home and then grab some chow and some rack time. If you'll come with me, I'll escort you down to the Com Center."

Matt extended his hand. "I appreciate the time you've taken with me," he said after a brief handshake.

Ben smiled, opened the door, and escorted Matt down the long hospital corridor. "You aren't finished with me yet. I'll be the one signing your Clark release papers before you leave here. If there's anything you need, just let me know. The nurses' station on your ward can always reach me." Pausing outside the open door of a room lined with telephone cubicles, he continued, "I'm personally delighted to be a part of the Operation Homecoming team welcoming you home. I wasn't so fortunate where my brother was concerned."

Matt knew he didn't have to say anything. He also realized that everyone had paid a price for Vietnam, not just the prisoners of war.

CHAPTER 28

February 13, 1973—San Diego, California

The phone rang, jarring Eden from a restless sleep. As she fumbled for the receiver, she pulled herself up against the headboard of her bed. "Hello?"

"Eden?"

"Yes?"

"Is that you, Eden?"

"Yes, it's me. Matthew? Where are you?" Stupid question, she groaned silently. You know where he is.

"I'm still at Clark." He paused, then asked, "Can you hear me all right?"

"Oh, yes! Your voice is very clear."

"I'll be arriving in San Diego in a few days. Probably at Miramar."

She smiled through the tears creeping down her cheeks. "I can't wait to see you. Do you know if I can meet you?"

"I'm not sure about the arrangements. You'll have to check with the Marine Corps."

"I saw you on television yesterday afternoon. You looked wonderful. Too skinny, of course, but wonderful. How do you feel?"

"Tired," he answered, his voice noticeably subdued. "Kind of ragged around the edges, too."

She glanced at the clock on her night table. Eight A.M. California time. "It must be late there. Matthew?"

"What?"

"I . . . I've missed you."

"I know about Andrew," he answered.

She sighed, not aware that he heard the sound thousands of miles away. "I wanted to tell you myself, to explain what happened, but I was told not to say anything in my letters. Did you get any of them?"

"Just one. We can talk about him when I get home."

"All right."

"I heard you bought a house."

"Yes, I did. About four years ago. The rental in Massachusetts was full of painful reminders of Drew, and it was too hard on my mental health, so I decided to relocate."

"I'd always hoped . . ." Static suddenly cluttered the connection. ". . . sound so different, more sure of yourself."

"I guess I am different, but I think you'll still know me."

"How big is it?"

"The house?"

"Yeah."

"Not terribly big. More the size of a spacious cottage with two large bedrooms. I think you'll like it. The neighbors are nice, and the ocean's our backyard. I decorated it myself, painted the walls, pasted up wallpaper, that sort of thing." She stopped talking for a moment and took a deep breath. "I'm sorry to keep going on about the house."

"I'm sure it's very nice."

"Matthew, we sound like polite strangers."

"Tell me about your job," he urged, sidestepping her observation.

"You've certainly been getting an earful about me, haven't you?" When he didn't answer, she said, "I'm the station director for the Red Cross facility at the naval hospital. I split my time between admin work and the wards. The patients are terrific guys, mostly combat veterans. I love the people and the job."

"I'll be staying there for a while."

"I know. Dave Markham confirmed the rumors floating around the hospital when I talked to him last night. He's married to Tracey. Had you heard that?"

He chuckled at the news. "So she married a marine, did she?"

Eden relaxed somewhat when she heard his amusement. "They have a daughter. Her name's Katherine, and you're her godfather. Tracey and David had one of their friends stand in as proxy for you at her christening. And your friend, Jack Morrison—"

"Eagle?"

"That's right. He called last night, too. He's been a very supportive friend, Matthew. He asked me to give you his best and to tell you he's going to be TAD at Beaufort for the next few months, but he'll be by to see you as soon as he gets back."

"Did he tell you what happened?"

She heard the sudden intensity in his voice. "Yes, he did. He visited me during a convalescent leave from the hospital while I was staying at Tracey's place in Malibu. In fact, he was the first person to tell me about the Red Cross volunteer program at the hospital."

"It'll be good to see him again."

"What about me?" she asked before she could stop herself.

He inhaled sharply.

"What is it? Don't you want—" to come home to me, she almost asked. The Red Cross worker in her stepped in while she tried to cope with her rattled emotions. "If you're not ready for the trip, just tell the doctors that they're rushing you. They'll understand if you need more time for yourself."

"I know that."

"I'm sorry. This is such an awkward way of communicating with one another for the first time. I'm at as much of a loss as I'm sure you are." When he didn't say anything, she asked, "This whole situation's pretty unnerving, isn't it?"

"Why would you be nervous?" he questioned after several silent seconds.

"Because I don't know if you still love me or want me," she blurted out.

"Eden . . ." he began, sweat beading his forehead as he gripped the receiver and his knuckles turned white from the pressure.

"Don't pay any attention to me right now. I haven't had much sleep with everything that's been happening this week, so I'm probably not making any sense." She reached for a wad of tissues from the box on her night table and wiped her cheeks. "It's all right, Matthew. Really. I know we have plenty of time and that I shouldn't get ahead of myself. It's just that I've missed you so much and I've dreamed about having you home safe and sound. I'm almost afraid to believe this is really you and you're finally out of that awful place."

"I wasn't sure if you'd—" He thought he heard her start to cry and fell silent.

"You weren't sure if I'd what?" she asked once she brought her erratic emotions under control.

"Everything's happening so fast, Eden. I'm not sure of anything right now."

She heard his confusion, and her heart ached for him. "Matthew, whatever happens, we can handle it together. Please try to trust me on that."

"I guess I should get off the phone now. There are a lot of guys still trying to reach their families."

"Two days, Matthew?"

"Yes."

"And you'll call me if you decide to delay your arrival?"

"Of course."

"They're fixing up a special ward for you and the other San Diego area men."

"We'll need it."

"I have your trunks from Chu Lai and all the things you left in storage. And I made a scrapbook for every year that you've been gone."

"Sounds like you've kept busy."

She laughed. "It's the only way to stay sober and sane."

His voice gentled. "I'll be home soon, Eden."

"I've counted days, weeks, months, and years. Now I can start counting the minutes." She silently told herself to stop delaying the inevitable. "Have a safe flight, Matthew. I . . ."

The phone made a whirring sound and then clicked in her ear.

". . . love you," she finished to the empty room.

CHAPTER

29

February 15, 1973—Miramar NAS, San Diego, California

Eden leaned forward and lowered the window of the limo provided by the Marine Corps. David stood a few feet away, periodically speaking into a walkie-talkie.

"Much longer?" she asked.

"A few more minutes. The Miramar tower says they're on final approach."

She exhaled slowly and sank back against her seat. She could hear the low hum of voices from the crowd of well-wishers and media standing behind the waiting line of limousines. Closing her eyes, Eden gingerly rubbed at the pounding in her temples.

She froze when the pitch of the voices abruptly changed and exploded into a loud cheer. Turning in her seat, she saw smiling faces and pointing fingers.

Looking toward the end of the runway, she saw a plane touch down, its mammoth wheels sending up puffs of dust. The aircraft lumbered down the runway, its engines screaming and its enormous body vibrating as the pilot applied his brakes. It finally rolled to a stop less than a hundred feet from the podium set up at the edge of the flight line.

The numbness left her, and fright took its place.

She noticed faces peering from the windows of the plane. Men's faces. Smiling men. Nervous men. Eager men. Men searching the crowd with darting eyes. Men straining to see their wives and loved ones.

The aircraft engines died. A door opened and was lowered to form a short flight of stairs.

Eden leaned forward again, struggling against the urge to leave the car until David's signal that she could greet her husband.

The men filed off the plane. Eden gripped the edge of the seat until she saw Matthew in the doorway. When he ducked his head and descended the stairs, she felt tears burning her eyes. Each former POW shook hands with the small group of assembled dignitaries before the senior member of their number stepped up to the podium and gave a short statement.

Car doors opened. Wives, children, parents, brothers, and sisters surged forward.

David yanked open the limo door and helped Eden from the backseat. He gave her a quick hug and whispered, "Go get your man."

She moved forward, her footsteps hesitant as she watched Matthew scan the converging crowd. She saw his uncertainty and then a flash of recognition in his dark eyes when she broke into a run. Eden forgot about her short skirt riding high up her thighs as she raced toward him. All she wanted or cared about was only a moment away.

She flung herself into his outstretched arms. Lifting her up, he whirled her around, his arms like steel bands around her body, his breath raging harshly into the auburn cascade she hadn't cut since his capture. She clung to him, chanting his name over and over again. Tears rolled down her cheeks and laughter escaped her all at once. She felt the hardness of his chest, the shudders vibrating through his body, as he held her. She embraced him more tightly, unwilling to leave his arms for even an instant.

Without releasing her, Matthew lowered her until her feet touched the pavement. They stared at one another, dazed and disbelieving.

"Welcome home," she whispered.

He nodded, a hundred emotions shining in his eyes as he studied her. Raising a shaking hand, he cupped her face. Her beauty startled him. He'd always thought that he'd remembered every detail of her face while in captivity, but now he realized that his memories had been dimmed by isolation and anguish.

And her body. He felt the change in her. The added fullness of her breasts as they pressed against his chest, the feminine width of her hips, the trimness of her waist, and her long, graceful legs, now revealed by the short skirt she wore. She wasn't coltish any longer. Pregnancy had matured her, fine-tuned her physical assets in a way he wouldn't have ever imagined. Her eyes, though, hadn't changed. They still sparkled like bright emeralds.

"I can't get over it," he managed, still staring down at her.

"What?"

She searched his face, her mind registering the gray laced through his midnight hair, the lines of tension and fatigue grooved into the skin around his eyes and mouth, and the pallor that she would never have expected, given his dark complexion. Oh, Matthew! You need so much love and care. You need the beach, beautiful sunsets, and time to rest. She promised herself that she would give him those things and more as soon as he checked out of the hospital.

"You can't get over what?" she asked again.

"You. You're so beautiful."

She heard his bewilderment in the hoarseness of his voice. "Your body's changed."

She nodded, her expression now cautious. "Since Drew."

"I like you this way."

She moved closer, resting her head on his shoulder and twining her arms around his waist. She felt his breath against her neck as he buried his face in the curve of her shoulder. They stood quietly for several minutes, both finally believing that this reunion wasn't a dream, that miracles were indeed possible more than once in a lifetime.

Eden opened her eyes when she heard the clicking sound of a camera. The photographer seemed intent on recording every intimate detail of their first moments together, giving little thought to their obvious need for privacy. She touched Matthew's face before stepping back. "Why don't we get out of here? I want you all to myself for a while."

"Sounds good." Matt placed his arm around her shoulders,

and they walked to the waiting limo. David met them halfway, his hand extended in greeting.

"Welcome back, Matt. Glad to see you're in one piece."

"You must be Dave Markham."

"That's right. Eden's casualty assistance officer, courtesy of Headquarters Marine Corps."

Matt smiled as they shook hands. "And Tracey's husband."

David grinned. "Right again." He ushered them to the open car door. "We're going to take the scenic route through Balboa Park before we deliver you to the naval hospital. That way, you two'll have about thirty undisturbed minutes before the medical types get their hands on you."

They climbed into the limo, shutting out curious looks and anxious cameramen. David joined the driver in the front seat. The glass partition remained up.

Matt stretched his long legs out in front of him and leaned his head back against the seat top. Closing his eyes, he exhaled slowly and began to relax. Eden took his hand, felt the answering squeeze of his fingers, and smiled.

"I'm not sure what to say first," she told him.

"I know how you feel."

"That was quite a crowd at Miramar."

He opened his eyes and glanced down at her. "The same thing happened this morning for the guys we dropped off at Travis."

"You didn't mind the fanfare, then? The newspeople and the photographers?"

"We all wondered what it would be like when we came home, especially after all the antiwar freaks Charlie had touring the Hilton," he recalled, his voice suddenly tense and bitter.

"It's over, Matthew. You're home now and you're safe." She fought back the tears swelling in her throat. "No one will ever hurt you that way again."

"I'm only just starting to believe that."

"I'm so glad you're back. It's been such a . . ."

". . . nightmare?"

She nodded, relieved when he drew her into his arms and

held her in silence for the remainder of the drive to the hospital.

A marine guard escorted them to the ward in Building 26. He handed Matt the key to his rooms, stepped back, and saluted. Matt responded in kind, saying, "Thanks for the escort, Marine."

"Happy to be of help, sir." The youthful enlisted man flashed him a quick smile. "And, sir?"

"Yes?"

"Welcome home, sir."

He nodded and watched the escort guard, shoulders squared, head erect, uniform and boots a testament to the exacting grooming standards of the corps, stride down the hallway, his mission complete.

He turned to Eden, a sad smile on his face. "I remember being that young and idealistic once, but it was a long time ago."

"You've learned something even more important. Perhaps he will, too, someday."

"What's that?"

"Courage," she answered softly.

Matt shrugged, then walked through the sitting room and into the bedroom. Eden hesitated at the door when she noticed a nurse she knew hurrying toward her. "Check your husband's blood pressure for me, will you? That way I won't have to disturb you two until tomorrow morning."

She accepted the cuff and stethoscope. "I'll leave these at the nurses' station for you later."

"Great! Oh, one more thing, Eden. The hospital kitchen's on call for the men twenty-four hours a day. If the cooks don't have what they want, someone'll go out and find it for them."

"Thanks, Jean." Eden eased the door closed and locked it. Dropping her purse and jacket on the couch, she quietly entered the bedroom and discovered that Matthew had already changed into a pair of blue pajama bottoms. He stood at the window, his attention focused on the quad beneath his second-floor rooms. She covered her mouth with her free hand to keep from crying out when she saw the scars on his back, arms, and shoulders.

Matt sensed her presence and slowly turned to face her. "If they bother you, I'll wear a shirt."

She lowered her hand and shook her head. "What bothers me is that people are capable of such cruelty. I can't even begin to imagine the pain you must have endured."

He gave her a look she didn't understand and returned his attention to the activity beyond the window. Eden joined him, smiling when she saw the bedsheet hanging from a window in the building on the opposite side of the quad, WELCOME HOME, MAJOR BENEDICT unevenly printed across it.

"The fellows in my ward have been busy."

"What do you mean?"

"The sign across the way. That's my ward. I was working the day you landed at Clark. The men watched your arrival with me in the solarium."

When he didn't say anything, she waved the stethoscope and cuff at him. "I need to check your blood pressure. After that, we can order dinner and relax. And no medical exams until tomorrow morning, according to the head nurse. Okay with you?"

He nodded and walked to the bed. Seated on the edge, he watched Eden loop the cuff around his upper arm, adjust the stethoscope, and pump up the pressure gauge. She winked at him when she noticed his curious look.

"One hundred ten over seventy," she told him.

"Is this part of what you do here?"

"Sometimes. Red Cross workers are really ward gophers. We do whatever's needed, and then some. Write letters, feed patients, help with physical therapy, change beds, run errands, referee during food fights, handle lab paperwork. Just the usual stuff." She grinned as she placed the cuff and stethoscope on the nightstand. "They don't let us operate, so the patients are safe."

Matt frowned and clenched his right fist.

Eden reached out and touched the indentation above his wrist. "Tell me about this."

"As my wife or as a member of the hospital staff?"

She brought his scarred hand to her lips and pressed a kiss to the puckered flesh. "As your wife, Matthew. Only as your wife."

He continued to study her, caution and restraint etched into his face and in the rigid way he held his body.

Eden reminded herself to go slowly, not to push him. She also remembered how Dan had hidden behind his pain. "Jack said you were wounded before you bailed out. Enemy ground fire, I believe he called it." She glanced at his wrist, noting the entry and exit scars on either side. "Is this the result?"

Matt nodded and didn't pull away.

Pleased by his reaction, Eden continued talking. "I know this is all confusing to you right now. The press, the hospital, all the people who'll want to know about your captivity. How you decide to handle everyone but me is up to you, but what concerns you concerns me."

He looked faintly amused at the determined sound of her voice. "You sound very certain about that."

"I am. I don't know how you survived being a POW, but I hope you'll be able to tell me about it. I do know how I spent the last five years, and I'd like to share it with you." She read conflicting emotions in his eyes but decided to forge ahead. "We both need to talk, probably as much as we need to listen to each other. And we've both been isolated for a long time, but I don't want that fact to keep us apart now."

"Are you saying you want to stay married?"

Hearing his uncertainty, she felt her heart splinter and wondered how long he'd tortured himself with the same doubt that had plagued her during their years apart. "I love you, Matthew, and I want us to have the opportunity to stay married."

He tightened his hold on her hand, nearly crushing her fingers with the pressure. "You're sure?"

"Very sure, even though I know we've both changed. If we talk, though, I think we'll be all right. And I want us to be all right. I want that more than anything in the world."

He pulled her into his arms and held her, shaken by her honesty and determined to be equally truthful. "I've changed so much. I don't even recognize myself most of the time. I had to learn how to . . ."

". . . protect your emotions?" she filled in when he hesitated over the words.

He nodded. "I feel numb, Eden. Numb to everything and everyone around me."

"That's how I felt after Drew died. Empty and drained."

Easing their bodies apart, he studied her. "Tell me about my son."

"He was very beautiful, and he was everything precious to me, and I loved him for both of us. And then he died, without warning and without reason." Holding back the emotion she felt, Eden continued. "His death paralyzed me, and I know now that nothing and no one will ever cause me that kind of pain again. It simply isn't possible to feel any more helpless than I felt when I realized he'd died in his sleep. At that point in my life, I was convinced that I'd lost both of you."

"The doctors at Clark told me the basics."

She blinked back the tears shimmering in her eyes. "Then you know about my drinking?"

"Yeah."

"I fell apart," she admitted. "Totally and completely caved in. I just couldn't live with what had happened."

"But you're okay now?"

She produced a watery smile. "Other than being a little nervous, I'm fine."

"Still?" He tugged her back against his chest and threaded his fingers through the silkiness of her long hair.

"Just a little. I feel pretty secure when I'm running the Red Cross office or dealing with patients, but I haven't had a husband in a long time. I may need some practice time."

"For what I'm worth, you've got me to practice on," he offered tiredly.

She hugged him, her words as fierce as her hold. "You're worth everything to me, Matthew Benedict. Everything! I love you. I never stopped loving you and praying you'd come home. And even though we were separated by thousands of miles, I always felt connected to you. Two or three days before I was told you'd been shot down, I started having nightmares. I knew you were in terrible pain, and I felt so damned helpless. I hated that feeling."

"You weren't alone with your hate. I spent five years surviving on it. I think I've become an expert at hating. What a fucked way to exist!"

"You're here with me now. That's all I care about. We can be happy again, Matthew, if we want to badly enough and if we're willing to work at it."

"Are you always so optimistic?" he questioned, thinking of Chet for the first time in several hours and wondering how his friend was dealing with his reunion.

Eden laughed. "It's the number-one rule for Red Cross workers. I don't permit sour faces or bad attitudes around the patients."

"That's some job you've got."

Her expression softened. "It's more than a job. I have a career with the Red Cross, one I'm committed to."

"More changes," he murmured as he shifted position and relaxed on the bed.

Eden remained seated beside him. "You're right, but a change that's made me a more complete person." His silence prompted her to speak for him. "You're wondering where you fit in, aren't you?"

"Something like that."

"I made some friends, but they never took your place. I have a career that began as a means of staying sober and holding myself together. And I bought a house that I hoped would eventually be a home I could share with you. Now that I look back on the last five years, I wouldn't change what I've done, because it worked for me."

"Do you think I'm asking you to?"

"No, I don't. But neither do I think you know quite what to make of the way in which I've lived with your captivity. Drew's death forced me to make choices. Choices I didn't want to make without you. But I did. I didn't have any other alternative. That's what I meant earlier about changing. I've changed in ways you don't realize yet." Eden took his hand and laced their fingers together. "I'm very different from the person you married. I've experienced things I didn't ever want to experience. We both have, but I know in my heart that we've learned a lot about ourselves as individuals in the process. I loved you with such innocence in the beginning. Now I think I love you even more, but my feelings are based on events and emotions we weren't able to share."

"I want you. I always have."

She smiled gently. "I hope so, Matthew."

He frowned and freed his hand. Resting his upturned wrist on his forehead, he closed his eyes. Eden pulled a blanket to his waist. "Rest now. We'll talk more after you've had a nap." When he nodded, she eased herself from the bed and walked to the bedroom door.

"Eden?"

She turned at the sound of his voice. "Yes?"

"I'm sorry."

"For what?"

"For all of it. The last five years. For having to face Drew's death alone. Mostly, for having to live through such a mess because of me."

She swiftly returned to his bedside. She didn't speak until he opened his eyes. "Don't ever apologize for something that wasn't your doing. Especially to me. Guilt doesn't have a place in our marriage unless one of us has hurt the other purposely."

"You're serious, aren't you? And you're angry."

"Yes to both, Matthew. Any more questions?"

"I don't remember this side of you."

"You had the good fortune never to see it."

He grinned up at her. "I like it, though."

"Well, good for you."

"Now what's wrong?"

"My legs feel like marshmallows, that's what's wrong. I shouldn't be yelling at you already."

"You were going to wait awhile?"

"No! Yes! Oh, hell!"

"Come here," he urged as he tugged her down beside him on the bed and looped his arm around her. "I thought a lot about what it would be like to see you again."

"I won't believe you if you tell me you fantasized about me losing my temper and yelling at you."

"It is a little out of character for the woman I married," he conceded.

She flushed and then admitted, "I discovered the Irish fishwife in my heritage after I'd been working on the wards for a few months."

"You have every right to be on edge. And you're right, you know, about us needing time to figure out how we fit together. I sure as hell need to know who I've become."

"We'll take all the time we both need, Matthew."

He smiled and closed his eyes. Eden stayed at his side until his breathing deepened and the arm around her shoulders relaxed.

While Matt slept, Eden retrieved her overnight bag and a photo album from her locker in the Red Cross office, checked on the substitute she'd assigned to her regular ward for the day, and chatted with several POW family members gathered in the solarium between Wards C and D in Building 26.

She found an orderly setting up dinner for two in the sitting room when she returned. She greeted the orderly, a man she knew from working the wards, before she let herself into the bedroom.

Eden quietly made her way to the far side of the room when she saw that Matt was no longer in bed. As she'd suspected, he was wrapped in a blanket and asleep on the floor. She knelt near his feet, her expression considering. Deciding to wake him, she touched his ankle. "Matthew?"

He shot straight up into a seated position, his arms instinctively raised in front of him. Disoriented and wary, he studied her for several silent seconds.

She kept her voice even, unwilling to betray her frustration with herself at having startled him into a gesture of self-defense. "How about some supper?"

He lowered his arms and tried to get his bearings. "What did you say?"

"Are you hungry, Matthew?"

He nodded, consciously willing himself to take deep breaths as he sat on the floor.

Eden stood. "Don't be too long. Your steak'll get cold."

He watched her walk from the room, the long-limbed grace of her body another reminder that he was free. When his breathing returned to normal, he got to his feet. Shrugging into a robe that he found draped across the end of his bed, he joined Eden at the small dinette in the sitting room.

Halfway through his steak and eggs, Matt asked, "Do you find a lot of people on the floor around here?"

Eden smiled, lowered her fork to her plate, and recalled the comments made by one of the psychiatrists who'd spoken to the POW families. "If your husband is willing to discuss behavior patterns that could be considered somewhat unusual, then it's possible he won't go through the denial process experienced by many former prisoners of war. But remember, it's best if he initiates any conversation about his actions or what he experienced as a POW."

"What's so funny?"

She shook her head. "I was just thinking about your question."

"Then you don't find a lot of people on the floor?"

"On the contrary. The new arrivals complain about the mattresses, especially if they've been sleeping on the ground for several months. But they don't make the trip from the bed to the floor if their wounds are serious. When they do, though, it only lasts a few days. What no one realizes is that the supply officer orders the firmest mattresses the navy can buy." She noticed the relaxed expression on his face and decided he could handle the truth. "Besides, the Balboa homecoming team briefed the wives yesterday morning. We were told to give you all the time you need to reacclimate yourselves. They also told us that many of you have slept on plank beds or cement slabs during the major portion of your captivity."

Matt chuckled, the sound rueful. "I wonder how many of the men opted for the floor."

"Almost everyone, from what the wives in the solarium were saying."

"Comparing notes?" he asked sharply, returning his eyes to the food on his plate.

Eden ignored his sudden defensiveness. "Not really. I walked in on the tail end of the discussion. I had to stop in at my office for my overnight bag, and I ran by my ward to see how my sub's holding up."

He raised his eyes. "You can stay with me?"

She nodded. "If you want me to."

Matt reached for the orange juice beside his plate. His hand shook as he lifted the glass to his mouth and took a long swallow. After placing the empty glass on the table, he said, "I'd like you to stay."

"Fine. Then I will."

He returned his attention to the food in front of him. Eden accepted his silence for what it was, although she had to remind herself how new everything seemed to him.

After finishing his meal, Matt pushed his chair back from the table. Eden knew what he wanted the instant he began a silent tattoo atop the table with his fingertips. She also realized that after so many years of lowered expectations and outright deprivation she would have to anticipate many of his needs in the weeks and months ahead.

Getting up from the table, she crossed the room, opened her purse, and pulled out a pack of cigarettes and a lighter she'd filled with fluid a few days earlier. Returning to her chair, she slid the two items into the center of the table. "I found this," she said, tapping the top of the silver lighter, "when I was going through your things the other night. I thought you might like to use it again."

Matt closed his hand around the small rectangular shape, his knuckles white as he gripped it. "You said you have all my things from Chu Lai."

"Yes, plus everything you left in storage before you went overseas. David had the Marine Corps release it all to me after I bought the house in Del Mar."

"Everything?"

"Everything," she assured him. "Your dad's letters, family pictures, books, clothes, trophies. It's all at home."

He glanced down at his body. "My clothes won't fit. I look like a scarecrow."

"That won't last long, especially with the food the hospital's planning on feeding you. Besides, I've already had a few pairs of pants taken in for you, and I shopped for some sweaters I thought you might like. I decided you'd want to wait, though, before you have your uniforms altered. For the time being, all you'll need is a spare set of pajamas, a robe, and slippers."

He took a deep drag of his cigarette and leaned back in his chair. "Any idea when they'll let me out of here?"

Eden laughed. "Now you sound like the guys on my ward."

He arched a dark brow. The roguish gesture reminded her of the Matthew she'd fallen in love with, of the Matthew who'd spoken volumes with his eyes and changing facial expressions, of the Matthew who could be funny and serious all at the same time, and of the Matthew she knew she would always cherish in her memories. The Matthew she wondered if she would ever know again.

"You haven't even spent one night here and already you're talking about leaving? I can think of a lot of people who'd be crushed if they could hear you right now."

He shrugged. "It's a nice place to visit . . ."

". . . but you aren't exactly crazy about the beds," she finished for him.

"Something like that," he agreed, his tone of voice suddenly less buoyant.

Eden sobered and reached for their plates. As she piled silverware, dishes, and glasses on the orderly's cart, she paused. "It won't be long. I'll be able to take you home soon."

Matt didn't respond. Instead, he focused on his cigarette, watching as the smoke trailed through the air and sought escape through the partially open window a few feet away.

Eden returned to her place at the table, a photo album in her hands. "The pictures in this album are of Drew. I thought you'd want to see them tonight." She pushed the book across the table, acutely aware of every painful beat of her heart. "I'll tell you anything you want to know about our son. All you have to do is ask me."

He straightened and ground out what remained of his cigarette. The look he gave her as he lifted the album from the table provided few clues about his thoughts and emotions. A protective mask seemed in place, but still she saw his reluctance to open the album as he ran his fingers along the edges of the plastic-coated cover.

Matt gingerly lifted the cover. Air hovered in his lungs but refused to be released when he looked at a photo of Eden in the final stages of her pregnancy. Big with their child, she wore an old Marine Corps T-shirt he'd given her during their courtship. Standing beside Tracey, the two proudly displayed a bassinet and rocking chair wedged into the backseat of a small sports car.

With shaking hands, he flipped the page. Eden, looking limp but radiant, held their minutes-old son.

He lowered the album to the table before looking up. "He doesn't look very happy."

She smiled. "My labor lasted more than twenty-four hours. Neither of us had too much pizzazz left when the picture was taken."

"How much did he weigh when he was born?"

"Six pounds thirteen ounces."

Matt nodded and continued to turn the pages. He studied a picture of Drew as he slept, his legs tucked up under him and his diapered fanny in the air; a naked Drew in the tub with Eden, bubbles wreathing their bodies; Eden sitting in a rocking chair and cradling their week-old son in her arms; Tracey in the same rocker, this time with a mountain of unfolded diapers at her feet; and, finally, Eden looking almost Madonna-like as she breast-fed Drew.

He made a choking sound, and his tears dripped onto the pictures. Eden swiftly circled the table and leaned down. Wrapping her arms around his shoulders, she pressed her cheek to the side of his face and held on to him as he finished looking at the album. Drew in his stroller, surrounded by little girls with their pretend babies.

The final photo was of a small grave and marker.

"Where?"

"Massachusetts," she answered softly. "Near the house I rented. I went back last summer. We can go together when you're ready."

He took her hand and drew her into his lap. Tears continued to slide down his cheeks. "How did you stand it, alone like that? I kept imagining the two of you together, with you raising him and loving him for both of us until I could make it back. My God, Eden, how did you handle it?"

"I didn't. Not at first."

"I felt as though someone had shoved a knife in my gut when I was told."

"I know," she whispered through her tears. "He was such a good baby. You'd have loved holding him and watching him when he was little. He looked so much like you, only his skin was a bit lighter, almost golden." She wiped the tears from her cheeks with her fingertips. "I adored him, Matthew. He was everything to me. And I tried so hard to be a good mother, but then . . ."

"It wasn't your fault."

"I've known that for a long time, but it doesn't lessen the sense of loss I still feel. I expect to always feel that something's missing from my life without Drew."

"I had so many plans for him, things I wanted to teach him, places I wanted to show him when he was old enough to understand about my mother's people on the reservation." Shifting Eden forward, he tugged a folded piece of paper from the waistband of his pajama bottoms. "I received this letter a year and a half after you wrote it. It took that long before I even knew we had a son."

She accepted the tattered paper, unfolded it, and then frowned at the blank piece of what she realized was her old stationery.

"The ink's disappeared, but you wrote me two weeks after Drew's birth. You told me about Tracey being with you in the delivery room, and you described the baby."

"But I wrote you every week for five years except when I was drinking so heavily. This is all they gave you?"

Matt nodded, his expression grim. "About two years ago . . . I was told you'd died."

"Matthew!" she exclaimed, horrified by the mental and emotional agony he'd suffered. "Oh, my darling. You've been living in hell for so long."

He closed his fist around the faded letter hanging from her fingertips, pain, stark and haunting, in his eyes. "I don't remember most of the last two years."

"What happened?" she asked, almost afraid to hear his answer.

"I couldn't take it any longer. The living conditions, the torture, the constant threat of death. When Han told me you were dead, something snapped inside me. A friend took care of me until the December bombings a few months ago." He shrugged and blinked, forcing himself back to the present. "I'm still trying to get it all straight in my mind."

"You've only had a few days. Give yourself time to really feel free."

He tensed. "Everybody keeps telling me that. 'Give it time. Give it time.' I've already wasted so much time," he said bitterly.

"Why would the North Vietnamese tell you I was dead? I don't understand."

"It doesn't matter now."

She stared at him. "Of course it matters. The State Department and the Red Cross kept very close tabs on all the families. Births, deaths, moves—everything we did was carefully documented so there'd be no confusion when you were all released."

He shook his head and abruptly moved her off his lap. "I can't talk about it right now."

Eden didn't press him further when she saw the sweat beaded on his upper lip and forehead. She busied herself with the orderly's cart, rolling it out the sitting-room door and into the hallway. Collecting her overnight bag, she went into the bathroom to shower. She returned to the bedroom in a long silk nightgown and discovered Matthew already in bed, his eyes closed.

She hesitated at the side of the bed. "Would you rather I slept on the couch?"

"Why? Have you changed your mind?" he asked tersely.

"No, but if our sharing the same bed could cause you a problem, I need to know about it now." Relax, she told herself, you're both nervous. In a softer voice, she said, "If our being together is happening too fast, you'll have to tell me."

"Nothing's happening." His voice was flat, empty of emotion.

Her shoulders slumped. "All right, Matthew."

She climbed into bed beside him, felt the rigidity of his body, and didn't attempt to move into his arms. Exhausted from the stress of the day, she soon fell asleep.

A troubled sound alerted Eden to Matt's absence from the bed. Rolling onto her side, she squinted into the darkness, straining to locate him. He mumbled incoherently, giving away his position on the floor. When he finally quieted, she got out of bed and made a pallet of blankets for herself beside him. She awakened at dawn to find him propped on an elbow, watching her.

She smiled sleepily. "Hi."

His amusement obvious, he asked, "How do you like the floor?"

She groaned and rolled toward him. "I don't know how you stand it. I ache everywhere."

"Then why are you down here?"

"I didn't see any reason to sleep alone."

He trailed his fingertips down the side of her face, startled by the softness of her skin. "Why don't you get back into bed and sleep a little longer? It's not even six yet."

"Can't. I have to be on the ward before rounds this morning, and then I've got a staff meeting at ten. You have a busy day ahead of you, too."

"You're working today?"

She nodded. "But I'll be back to have lunch with you." Noticing the strip of fabric hanging around his neck, she ran her fingers across it. "What's this?"

"My token."

"A token of what?" she asked when he rolled onto his back and stared up at the ceiling.

"My heritage. Survival."

Eden pulled herself up and peered down at him. "Isn't this what you used to wear under your helmet to keep the sweat out of your eyes when you were flying?"

Matt met her gaze, his expression equally curious. "How did you know?"

"You wrote me once about wearing a strip of chamois to soak up your perspiration when it got really humid out."

He snorted. "Great topic for a letter."

"Hey!" She playfully shoved his shoulder. "Your letters were wonderful. I've reread every one of them at least five hundred times. They helped keep me going when I felt lonely."

"If you say so."

She grinned. "I say so, *Major* Benedict."

He smiled back at her. "That was a nice surprise."

"David bought your new insignia for me when you were promoted. I have the box in my purse."

"Thoughtful guy."

"Most of the time." Eden chuckled. "He's probably even happier to have you home than I am. I don't think baby-sitting your wife was exactly how he envisioned spending his career in the Marine Corps." Recalling the times when she hadn't been willing to accept David or Tracey's concern and friendship, she admitted, "I made things pretty tough for David, especially after he and Tracey were married. I'm almost ashamed to admit it, but I couldn't stand how happy they were. As a result, I put a lot of distance between us."

"Has your relationship with Tracey changed that much?"

She nodded before tugging her blanket up and around her shoulders. "That's one of the things I was talking about yesterday when I said I'd changed. Trace quite literally propped me up when you were first listed MIA. But once I moved to San Diego, our lives went in completely different directions. She had a hard time accepting my work at the hospital, and she had an even rougher time abandoning her role as my personal easel. Katie's birth helped fill in the gaps for her, though."

"That must've hurt," he offered quietly.

"More than I wanted to admit at the time." She smiled, her pleasure genuine now. "Our godchild's a very special little girl. She's tiny like Trace, but she's got David's low-key temperament."

Matt shifted onto his stomach, lowered his cheek to his folded hands, and kept his eyes on her. Eden took it as a signal that she should continue talking.

"They bought a house on the beach in Encinitas. Trace took one look at Camp Pendleton's housing and called Hawks and Hawkins, the accountants who handle her trust fund. She located a realtor, went house hunting, and put an enormous down payment on the beachhouse while David was in D.C. one week. Escrow took all of ten days. She was moved in before he knew what hit him."

"I don't remember her as subtle, now that I think about it."

"No, she isn't." Eden pulled herself up from the floor, stifled a groan, and unraveled herself from her blanket. Without a word, she began to massage his lower back, her fingers moving in wide circles as she gently kneaded his flesh. Matt sighed heavily and closed his eyes, and she congratulated herself on trusting her instincts.

"You haven't lost your touch."

She smiled, thinking of all the things she'd learned about herself and about life, although most of them couldn't even be cataloged. "I get a lot of practice on the ward. It helps take a patient's mind off the pain after a rough therapy session."

Matt unexpectedly turned over. Surprised by his sudden move, Eden's hands remained suspended in the air above his chest.

"You care a lot about the people here, don't you?"

Sobering, she lowered her hands to her lap. "Yes. They've helped me find myself."

"Gentleness and caring were always a part of you."

She shrugged. "Maybe."

He tugged her down across his chest. "There's no maybe about it."

"The hospital's a two-way street, Matthew. I get as much, probably more, than I give. I need them, and they need me, as well as people like me."

He nodded, his eyes searching her face, his fingertips tracing her collarbone and the slenderness of her shoulders. "*I* need you, Eden. So much," he whispered before taking her chin and guiding her mouth down to his.

He traced the curve of her lips with his tongue, then groaned when she parted them and welcomed him into the heat and moisture of her mouth. Running his hands the length of her spine, he reacquainted himself with the narrowness of her back, waist and the flaring shape of her hips. Then, with trembling fingers, he found the hem of her nightgown and tugged it upward.

Eden lifted her hips and slid onto her side in order to free herself of the confining fabric. She separated their mouths for an instant and yanked her silk gown over her head. Settling back against Matthew, she felt the solidness of his chest and the pounding of his heart against her breasts. She caught her breath when he smoothed his hand across her pelvis, then eased his fingers into her body. She tensed slightly and then arched into his touch, finally believing that the emotional and sexual hunger she'd endured would soon be at an end.

Matt brought himself up on one elbow and eased Eden onto her back, his fingers still gently exploring the give of her body. She felt his gaze and opened her eyes to the desire blazing in his dark eyes. She reached for him, then hesitated when he shook his head. "Not yet, Eden. Let me love you now. I've waited years to touch you this way."

Eden bit her lip, nodded, and lowered her hands. Though still anxious to touch him, she understood his need to set the pace of their loving. She gasped and then moaned when he leaned forward and began to suck on her nipples. She felt the hardness of his sex against her thigh, a sign of life she'd been warned not to expect for a long time. But the doctors had been wrong. Matthew's desire was insistent, inflaming her senses and provoking her need to smooth her fingertips along his body.

"Matthew, I can't *not* touch you." He nodded, and she reached for the tie at the waistband of his pajama bottoms.

He helped her, hurriedly peeling them from his body. Eden felt him shudder when she closed her hand around him, heard the hissing sound of air escape his clenched teeth.

"Matthew, please . . ."

"Soon, love, very soon," he promised. Trailing his fingers across the flatness of her abdomen, he followed each caress with his lips as he traced the pale scars left by her pregnancy. "I wish I'd been with you when you carried our son."

Tears burned her eyes, but she made herself smile. "I was enormous at the end."

He turned and looked at her, his cheek resting on her stomach. "I saw the pictures. You were beautiful. I'm so sorry I missed sharing it all with you."

"You're here now. That's all that matters." She trailed her fingertips down the side of his face. "Hold me?"

Memories of the past crashed in on him as he gathered her into his arms. Happier times. Shared laughter. Their honeymoon. Making love on an empty beach at dusk during their Hawaii R and R. His breathing quickened. Again, he thought of his son inside her body. The image in his mind made him even hungrier for her, and he moved over her, bracing himself on his arms.

His flesh prodded, gentle and demanding all in the same instant. Eden saw the desire and the question in his eyes.

"Oh, yes. Now, please." She reached for him, her hips rising to meet his, her hands cupping his face, her need and her love for him never greater.

She cried out when he entered her, not in pain but with relief. The sound echoed in her head and reverberated in her ears as she savored the sense of completeness she'd craved for so very long, the heat and hardness of him inside her as he reclaimed her as his wife and partner.

Urgency and wildness marked their actions. He groaned, straining to reach the heart of her as they repeatedly surged against one another. Her cry was low at first, starting deep inside her and reaching her throat as the building pressure of her climax finally exploded in and around her. She absorbed his release as her own seemed to seize her and lead her on a quest for completion.

He collapsed atop her, his breathing harsh in her ear, his heartbeat branding her breasts. Arms around her, he rolled them to one side and pulled up a blanket over their still-joined bodies.

When she could speak, Eden opened her eyes and looked up at him. "Now you're really home."

He nodded and pressed her cheek to his shoulder. "I love you. Even when I thought you were dead, I loved you."

The tears she'd held back now refused to remain at bay. They slipped from her eyes, scalding her cheeks before they reached his skin. He tightened his hold on her as her sobs shook her, somehow understanding that she was crying not just for their mutual losses but for the fact that fate was now offering them a second chance at a life together.

"Sorry," she finally whispered a little while later.

"You needed to cry, Eden. You always held your emotions inside you too long. That much hasn't changed."

She laughed, the sound damp. "You remember that about me, do you?"

He tilted her chin up and studied her face. "I remember every minute we had together. And while I know you're five years older, very mature, and incredibly strong, I also know that parts of you will never change."

"What can I say to that?" she teased.

"That you love me," he answered quietly. "Because I need to hear the words as often as you can stand to say them."

Her chin trembled, and her eyes filled with tears again. "I do love you, Matthew. More than anyone or anything on this earth."

"I think that's what kept me alive. Knowing you loved me enough to wait for me."

"Why wouldn't I have waited?"

"Some of the wives didn't."

She heard accusation and more in his voice. "Don't judge them too harshly. Those who survive all this will be the ones who made a conscious decision to get through it any way they could."

"You sound awfully certain about that."

She didn't say anything for a moment because she wasn't at all sure what to say. She knew it wasn't her place to judge the other women. Nor was it her prerogative to condemn. She also realized that the choices she'd made could easily be labeled as betrayal, in spite of the fact that she'd learned that loneliness provokes individual responses. Her experience with Jim had taught her that much. She realized, too, that while she and Matthew couldn't change the last five years, they could determine for themselves how they would spend the future.

"Eden?"

She touched his cheek. "I'm very sure, Matthew, because I made the choice, as you did. Not everyone is able to choose. That doesn't make us better people, but it should allow us to recognize what we've accomplished and take some pride in it, as well as allow us to have compassion for those who couldn't, whatever their reasons."

"You've become very wise, haven't you?"

"No, my love, just realistic."

A knock at the sitting-room door temporarily interrupted their privacy a few minutes later. As Matthew pulled on a robe and left the bedroom, Eden went into the bathroom. She climbed into the shower as soon as the water was hot enough, not at all surprised when her husband soon stepped in behind her.

"I think I still remember how to wash your back," he commented as he took the bar of soap from her, worked it into a lather, and covered her with suds from shoulders to thighs.

She turned and grinned up at him. "Still remember how to do both sides?"

He frowned, but his eyes twinkled playfully. "How's this for starters?" Massaging her breasts with one hand, he explored her hips and thighs with the other.

"Excellent," she murmured, her knees suddenly weak as a result of his intimate stroking. "Remember that morning in Hawaii when we used the hotel's supply of hot water before we went down to breakfast?"

He nodded, his eyes on her breasts as he molded and shaped

them with his hands. "You kept telling me you were hungry, but I couldn't get you out of the shower."

"*You're* the one who woke me up at zero dark-thirty because you were hungry. After, I might add, you made us miss our dinner reservations the night before."

He tapped the end of her nose with his soapy fingers. "Old age is catching up with you, wife. You had the hots for my body. I recall the entire episode very clearly."

She scowled at him, laughter in her eyes as she rinsed the soap from her body. "I can see that I'm going to have to keep a very accurate diary of our life in the future."

"Do that," he suggested as he dropped to his knees in front of her and pressed his cheek to her stomach. Circling her hips with his hands, he held her against his mouth, his tongue stabbing at the tender flesh of her body.

"Matthew?"

"You're moaning, Eden."

"Who was . . . at . . . the door?" she enunciated with some effort.

Matt briefly lifted his head. "Some doctor."

"Which doctor?" she gasped when he returned to his task.

"Hurley."

"The head of medical services? What did you tell him?"

"That I was getting reacquainted with my wife and he'd better come back later. Now, will you kindly shut up?"

"Of course." With that, she clutched his shoulders to keep herself upright and tried to forget that she would be joining Dr. Hurley for a meeting later that morning.

Matthew cooperated with the schedule established for him by the medical team organized to care for the former POWs. Extensive dental care, vitamin therapy, psychiatric evaluations, additional debriefing by Headquarters Marine Corps, minor surgery to fix the nerve damage in his wrist, a balanced diet and all the snacks he wanted, and nights with his wife occupied the next month.

But as the weeks passed, Eden couldn't shake the feeling that Matthew was hiding something from all of them, especially himself. She sensed but couldn't justify the feeling that he was routed on a collision course without an identity. Unable to verbalize the exact nature of what she suspected, she decided to bide her time and keep a close eye on her husband. She also realized that she really had no other choice until Matthew decided to share what was bothering him.

CHAPTER

30

Mid-March 1973—San Diego, California

Eden cast a worried glance at the contents of the trunk before looking up at Matthew. "I hope we've got all your things."

"The ward nurse said she'd pigeonhole anything I might have left behind, so stop worrying." He closed the trunk and handed her the keys. "How's the mattress at your house?"

She saw the laughter in his eyes. "Extra firm. I ordered a new one just to be safe." Holding out the keys, she asked, "Feel like driving?"

"I haven't renewed my license yet."

Eden grinned. "I won't tell if you don't."

He nodded. "Let's give it a shot, then."

He held the door for her as she slid into the passenger side of the front seat. Walking around to the opposite side of the car, he rubbed wet palms on his jeans before opening the door. Matt moved the seat back, climbed in, and inserted the key into the ignition.

Eden reached for his hand when he hesitated over the emergency brake. "How about a couple of turns around the parking lot before you test your wings on the freeway?"

"Value your hide, do you?"

Leaning toward him, she planted a kiss on his cheek. "Something like that."

He gave her a sage look. "Your suggestion has a certain merit."

She laughed. "I'm glad you think so."

Settling back in her seat, Eden watched him start the car and put it into reverse. While she silently congratulated the hospital staff on their decision to release Matthew to outpatient care, she also realized that he was entering a new phase of postcaptivity adjustment, one that was certain to challenge them both in terms of day-to-day living.

She continued to study him. Having gained almost twenty pounds since his return, he looked like a new man. Dressed in Levi's, a cable-knit sweater, and loafers, his appearance now only hinted at how he'd spent the previous five years.

There were reminders, of course, especially when he would clench and unclench his right hand if he was nervous or on edge or when he'd get that faraway look in his dark eyes. She never intruded on those private moments, certain inside herself that Matthew would eventually share the details of his captivity with her. Frequent calls to and from Chet Holt, a man he frequently described as his "brother," seemed to lessen his tension when he felt ill at ease. But Eden couldn't help wondering how long Chet could be his private avenue to solace when his memories plagued him.

Sighing heavily, she refocused on her husband.

He chuckled as he rounded another row of parked cars and brought them to a teeth-jarring stop. "Is my driving that bad?"

Eden smiled. "You're doing great." She placed her hand on his thigh, the gesture unconscious, totally natural, and a throwback to the days of their courtship when they couldn't seem to get enough of touching one another. "I'm just happy you're coming home with me today."

He covered her hand and squeezed her fingers.

After several minutes, as well as frequent and smoother stops and starts, she asked, "It's like riding a bicycle, isn't it?"

He nodded, shifting into second as he drove past the administration building at the front of the hospital complex. "But it'll be a while before I'm ready for the cockpit."

"Does that worry you?"

"It did at first but not now. I'll be fine after retraining at

Yuma." Matt pulled into position behind a line of cars at a red light. "You my RIO this trip?"

"Definitely. Turn left here, then follow the signs for Route 163 into Mission Valley."

Matt stayed in the slow lane on the two-lane road that wound through Balboa Park. As his confidence grew, so did the speed of the car. Eden directed him west toward Mission Bay, then north on I-5. Twenty minutes following their departure from the hospital parking lot, they left the interstate for a slower drive through Del Mar.

"The house is on the beach on the north side of town," she told him, not missing the darting glances he directed at the buildings that lined both sides of the main street.

"You can afford the real estate around here?"

Eden shifted in her seat, aware that she couldn't side-step this particular conversation any longer. "I used some of the money that Grandmother Barclay left me. The house is small compared to the ones around it, and it wasn't priced very high because of the condition it was in when I bought it."

"How much, Eden?" he asked, not taking his eyes from the cars in front of him.

She told him the amount, and he whistled, the sound tuneless and grating.

"I considered apartment living, but I couldn't talk myself into it." I did the best I could in an impossible situation, she reminded herself. "I needed the privacy of my own home. And, as time passed, I realized I'd made the right decision when I bought the cottage."

Matt tightened his hold on the steering wheel. "I still don't understand why you refused to use the allotment checks the Marine Corps sent you each month."

"I've already explained that. I wanted the money there for you when you got home. It's really that simple. Please don't interpret my actions any other way, because they had nothing to do with your ability to provide for me. I made a decision, that's all. In retrospect, perhaps it was the wrong one. If so, I apologize."

"I guess we can invest it."

Eden had a thought and voiced it. "You always talked about getting yourself a Corvette someday. Now you can, and you'll still have plenty of money left over to invest."

"I'd forgotten about that," he admitted.

She smiled. "I didn't. You spent hours dragging me through one car lot after another before we got married. You talked for hours about the cherry-red Corvette you were going to buy yourself when you got home from Vietnam. Oh, take a left at the next corner." She kept her eyes on Matthew as he nodded, signaled, and accelerated during a break in traffic.

Guiding the car down the rutted road that ended in a cul-de-sac, he glanced at the tennis courts that lined one side of the narrow street and then at the unusual examples of California oceanfront architecture opposite them.

"It's the white one-story with the gray flower boxes. You can use the gravel space by the side of the house for parking."

Matt turned off the engine and removed the keys from the ignition as he looked around. "Looks nice. Maybe we can keep it after we're reassigned."

"I'd planned to!" she exclaimed, already nervous about his reaction to the home she'd made for them.

"I see."

She reached out and caught his shoulder before he could reach for the door handle. "No, Matthew, you don't see, not at all. This is the only home I've had since Drew died. It means a lot to me. And now it's ours. I thought that maybe after you retired from the corps we could live here again."

"Maybe, but that's a long way off. Five, ten, fifteen years. Who knows?"

"Then we'll talk about it later, when *we* decide what we're going to do."

He frowned. "If you think we need to."

She nodded. "*We* definitely need to talk about your career and several other things. Perhaps now that you're home we can."

He exhaled slowly, opened the car door, and got out. Eden didn't wait for him to open her door. She let herself out, dug into her purse for her spare house key, and walked to the front door.

"Need your keys?" he asked after opening the trunk.

She shook her head. "Nope. I've got a set. Those are yours now." Turning, she unlocked the front door and stood to one side as he carried two pieces of luggage into the living room.

He paused just inside the front door, taking in the subtle earth tones and comfortable furniture Eden had selected for her home. He noticed his carved aviation wings above the fireplace and his old squadron plaques positioned on either side of the sculpted length of Philippine monkey pod. Emotion surged up inside him, momentarily eliminating his ability to speak.

"Why don't you leave those things in here for the time being? We can unpack after you've had a chance to see the rest of the house."

He nodded and lowered the suitcases to the floor.

"Do you want the ten-cent tour, or would you rather wander around by yourself?"

"The tour sounds pretty good."

Eden took his hand and led him through the dining room, past an oval oak table surrounded by four burgundy-corduroy-covered chairs, and into the kitchen. "The patio's small, but the retaining wall is low enough so that our ocean view isn't blocked." Fingering the pale finish of the butcher-block table in the breakfast nook, she told him, "I usually have my meals in here."

Matt nodded, his eyes straying to the mug tree on the kitchen counter near the stove. He walked toward it, his thoughts on the various squadrons he'd served in during the ten years that had preceded his Vietnam orders. Lifting one of the mugs, he fingered the squadron insignia baked into the finish.

"I've been using them since they were shipped to me. I hope you don't mind."

He studied her, a perplexed look on his face.

"It helped having your things out, Matthew. Using your coffee mugs, wearing your old T-shirts, things like that. It made it all a lot easier to bear when I felt alone."

He slid the mug onto the counter. Despite the play of uncertain emotions on Eden's face, he found he couldn't offer verbal reassurance. Instead, he pulled her into his arms and held her, his grip tight, his eyes squeezed shut as shudders swept the length of his body.

"Matthew?"

Clearing his throat, he raised his face from the top of her head and tried to smile. "Any more to see on this tour?"

Eden fought the questions racing around inside her head and slowly nodded. "Follow me." As she led him back through the dining room, living room, and down a long hallway, she thought again of the promise she'd made to herself that she wouldn't pressure him into conversations he wasn't yet ready to tackle.

She stepped into the first doorway and flipped a light switch. "One bathroom for company."

A faint smile appeared on his face as she grinned up at him. Taking his hand, she led him across the hall to a second doorway and flipped another light switch. "One study that doubles as a guest room."

Standing beside him, she watched him scan the room and noticed that his gaze lingered on one particular wall, which was covered with photographs of their respective pasts. Eden had long ago dubbed it the family gallery. Selecting and framing the pictures had occupied several lonely nights during her first months in San Diego.

"Great-grandfather," he whispered, his eyes snagged on the most dominant photo. His hand shook as he touched the dark oak frame and then skimmed his fingertips across the glass that covered the black-and-white picture of a small black-haired boy seated on the knee of an aging Indian man. Tears burned in his eyes before slipping unheeded down his face.

Eden moved forward, relieved when Matthew drew her into the crook of his arm and held her against his body. Reaching up, she turned his face toward her. "What's wrong?"

"Nothing. Nothing at all."

"Then why the tears?"

He glanced back at the photograph. "He was with me. He helped me stay alive."

"I don't understand. Your great-grandfather's dead."

"He never left me. Not once in five years."

"He's dead, Matthew. He has been for a long time."

He nodded. "I know, but he was with me at Long Moc and at the Hilton. He gave me his strength and his courage so that I could survive."

"You did that for yourself, love. Why aren't you willing to take credit for what you've accomplished? It doesn't make sense."

"It does to me. He reminded me of my heritage, the heritage of my people."

"Stories are one thing, Matthew, but the guts to actually do it—that's something else altogether. You survived because you decided to. A dead man can't keep anyone alive."

"You don't understand."

"You're right, I don't But maybe I would if you'd tell me about it." She glanced at the photo. "I wasn't sure who he was when I found the picture, but I did recognize you from some of the other photos in your album. I framed it because I saw the resemblance to Drew in your face."

"He protected me, Eden. Believe it, because it's the truth."

"If you say so."

He took her hand. "When I can, I'll tell you about it, explain about Great-grandfather."

"All right. Ready to play follow the leader again?" she asked, suddenly uneasy with his references to a dead man.

After one last glance at the picture of himself as a child with his great-grandfather, he followed her to the end of the hallway and paused at the entrance to what was clearly the master bedroom.

Eden stood uncertainly at the end of a large brass bed. "I hope you like it."

He stepped into the room, taking in the oversized bed, the tall teak bureaus lining one wall, the mirror-covered closet doors, and the picture window that provided a view of the ocean. "It reminds me of you."

"If there's anything you'd like to change, all you need to do is tell me."

"Why would I want to change your home?"

She exhaled a rush of air. "Because it's *our* home now; at least I hope it will be."

He watched her raise her fingertips to her forehead and recalled the nervous gesture. "This place is yours, Eden, despite the fact that my things are scattered through it. You told me to give myself time to adjust to being free again. Perhaps we should both give me time," he suggested quietly.

She lowered her hand and nodded. "You're right. I shouldn't be so damned jumpy. I don't know what's the matter with me today. You haven't even spent an hour here and I'm insisting you act as though you've always lived in this house."

Several silent seconds ticked by as they studied one another. Matt finally said, "Why don't I get the rest of my things?"

Eden lingered in the bedroom, needing a few minutes to herself. She realized that in spite of the experience she'd gained at the hospital, she wasn't doing such a great job of dealing with her husband. Torn between her desire to give him the time he needed to reaccustom himself to a life together and her own need for reassurance, she felt frustrated and angry, emotions she knew would yield nothing but chaos between them if they didn't open the lines of communication fairly soon.

A pall seemed to settle over them as the day passed. Matthew kept to himself, unpacking and sorting through books, clothes, and other personal items that Eden had stored for him in the spare-room closet. Conversation during their evening meal consisted of ice cubes clanking in iced-tea glasses and fork tines spearing food. And although they went to bed at the same time, neither spoke. Eden awakened in the middle of the night to find Matthew asleep on the floor, something he hadn't done since his second week at the hospital.

Dan joined Eden at her table in the cafeteria and handed her the cup of coffee she'd asked for. "You look like hell! What gives?"

She shrugged and took a sip of her coffee.

"Matt's been out of the hospital a month now, and every time I see you, you look worse."

"Four weeks, three days, and"— Eden glanced at her watch—"five hours."

"You sound like you're counting down the hours to a death sentence." He paused for a moment, then moved around the table to sit beside her. "If it's too personal to talk about, say the word, but if I can help—"

"Everything's so screwed up!"

"Care to be a little more specific?"

She hunched over her coffee and stared at the black liquid. "You don't have the time for a laundry list on what's wrong with my marriage."

"Give me a try," Dan urged. "Or have you forgotten that I was at your house two weeks ago?"

She looked up. "I wish I could forget. It's a good thing you brought a date to dinner that night. Otherwise, the entire evening would have been a real disaster."

"He thinks we've slept together."

Eden flinched. "Blunt but true. He won't actually come right out and say it, but that's what he thinks."

"There's more to this than jealousy."

"A whole lot more," she agreed. "I dread going home at night."

"Why? Because you might have to tackle the past and be honest with one another?"

"I'm willing, Dan; he's not. And I don't know if he'll ever be ready for the kind of honesty we need between us."

"You're not a quitter. How come you're acting like one now?" he demanded.

"Because I'm afraid, damn it!"

"Of what?"

"Of messing up. Of losing Matthew because I'm not clever enough or smart enough to figure out how to reach him. Of going home to a man who's well on his way to becoming invisible, with his eternal silences and brooding expressions. Of being shut out of his life so completely that I'll never find a way back inside. Of his constant mood swings. Of finding him, night after night, on the patio, regardless of the weather, because he can't stand to be alone in *my* house." She slammed her fist on the table. "Pick one!" she challenged before whispering again, "Pick one."

"You were warned before he landed at Miramar. Didn't you believe what the docs told you?"

"I guess not. I guess I thought Matthew would be different. I kept remembering his strength. How else could he have survived all those years if he hadn't been like the Rock of Gibraltar?"

"Christ, Eden! He's just a man. A man," he repeated insistently. "He had to dig deep inside himself to live through that hell. Don't you think he deserves some time to be vulnerable, time to have doubts about himself and his life?"

"But he keeps shutting me out. He acts like a guest in our home. A home, I might add, he refuses to accept as belonging to both of us." She lifted her cup and took a swallow of her coffee. "I'm so damned tense all the time that I feel like dynamite looking for a place to detonate. I don't know how much longer I can handle the situation."

"Do you love him?"

"God, Daniel, you know I do. Even more now than I did when we were first together."

"Then what are you going to do about it?"

"What can I do? I don't want to push him too far."

"So you'll push yourself instead, is that it?" He made a disgusted sound and shook his head. "Talk to him, Eden. Say everything you've been saving up for the last five years. Forget about the fact that he's hiding things and quit tiptoeing around him because you're afraid he might break. He won't. He'll talk when he's ready, and not before. You were able to understand that simple ethic on the wards. Why not put it into practice now, with Matt?"

"This is different. We're discussing my husband."

"Were the men on the wards less important to you when you were fighting for their survival?"

"Of course not."

"Then what the hell are you waiting for? A referee of some kind to keep the two of you from drawing blood?"

"Are you volunteering?" she shot back with a smile.

"I'm your friend, not a fool."

"Thank God for that."

"Eden, even if he just listens, you've at least begun the process of searching for common ground. It'll be a beginning, and that's what you're looking for, isn't it?"

She nodded and slipped her arms around Dan for a quick hug. "You're the best friend I've ever had." Even better than Tracey, she realized, because you don't let me dodge reality.

"Then listen to your friend," he urged, "and go home."

A short time later Eden parked her car on the street in front of the cottage, the single parking space beside the house already occupied by Matthew's new Corvette, his only purchase in the weeks since his discharge from the hospital. He refused to shop for clothes. He also declined all social invitations, as well as any suggestions from Eden that they go out for an occasional meal.

"No more hiding, Matthew," she decided aloud as she unlocked the front door and walked into the living room. "I cannot and will not live like this any longer."

Depositing her purse and jacket on the couch, Eden walked into the dining room. Her footsteps slowed when she heard Matthew's voice. Eavesdropping was not a habit she admired in anyone, but she decided that his current behavior justified a breach of the good manners ingrained in her.

"You're not listening, Chet. She doesn't need me. All I'm doing is messing up her life. She's young, intelligent, and beautiful, and she deserves better than me. Why should she be saddled with an old man who can't even handle taking her out to dinner once in a while?"

Eden forced herself to remain still, forced herself to listen as he continued speaking.

"It's not that I want to leave her, but I know I have to. I'll be doing her a favor. We're driving each other nuts. She's so careful about everything she says and does. She can't keep on this way. It's killing her. And it's killing me to watch her struggle to do what she thinks is best for me."

He paused, apparently to listen to the voice at the other end of the line.

"No, I won't change my mind. I've got sixty days before I'm scheduled to report to Yuma. If I don't get my head unfucked now, I'll never do it." He laughed shortly, the sound bitter. "Yeah, they did do a number on us, didn't they?"

Eden blinked back the tears welling in her eyes, squared her shoulders as she stood in the dark dining room, and waited for the conclusion of his conversation with Chet.

"I haven't made any decisions past getting my ass back to Oklahoma soil, but if I end up anywhere near Cherry Point, I'll give you a ring. Thanks for trying, buddy."

Eden walked into the kitchen in time to see Matthew replace the receiver of the wall phone. "We need to talk."

He turned and watched her cross the room, flip the gas burner to a high flame, and deposit a water-filled kettle on the stove. "There's not much to say."

"We haven't even started," she told him in a tight voice. Pulling a mug from the tree near the stove, she dropped a tea bag into it and then turned to face him. "When are you leaving? And when were you planning on telling me?"

"I'm sorry you had to hear it that way. I'd planned to tell you."

"When? Five minutes before you walked out on me?"

He crossed his arms and leaned against the wall near the phone. "I'm not walking out on you."

"What would you call it, then?"

"I need some time alone."

She stared at him, bewildered by what he was saying. "You spent five years alone, Matthew, and you've had four and a half weeks of absolute solitude since you left the hospital. Damn it to hell! You're running away. From me. From yourself. From whatever happened to you in North Vietnam. And for only one reason. Because you refuse to talk to me about what happened to you there."

The kettle began a high-pitched scream, startling them

both. Eden turned down the flame, filled her cup, and left it to steep on the counter.

"I'm leaving in the morning."

"You're going to Oklahoma tomorrow?"

He nodded, the expression on his face closed, unrevealing.

"To see your mother? The very same person who refused every effort I made at communication for the entire five years you were gone. Or to see a dead man?"

"To see my mother. As you just said, Great-grandfather is dead."

"And I'm not welcome," she concluded, relieved that he comprehended the difference between the living and the dead.

"Not this time."

"When do I get an invitation back into your life, Matthew? When there's nothing left of you at all?"

He straightened and crossed the room. "I don't know yet."

"Then figure it out," she yelled as she grabbed his arm and forced him to look at her. "How long am I expected to watch you disappear into yourself? There won't be anything left for us if you don't stop this silence of yours."

He looked down at her, his eyes filled with a mix of emotions as he removed her hand from his arm. "I'm leaving in the morning. You can't change my mind. If you can't live with what I have to do, then maybe you'd better see a lawyer."

Her eyes widened in shock at what he was suggesting. "I don't want a divorce. My God, we haven't even had a chance to be married yet." Fury fused with the pain seething inside her at the thought of another separation. "God damn you, Matthew! This is insane. You've got to stop running away."

"I remember everything about you, but I don't remember you swearing quite so much." He gave her a puzzled look and then suggested, "Drink your tea. It's getting cold."

"I don't want the damn tea!" she yelled. "I want you! I want a chance to make a life with you. I want a chance to forget years of watching the world pass me by, of seeing other couples who laughed, enjoyed themselves, fought and made up, and had babies. I watched them until I thought I'd be sick to my stomach if one person told me how happy they were.

"You don't get it, do you? I was in prison, too. We both were. I grant you mine was prettier, the food better, but it was a jail cell nonetheless. Do you think for one minute I haven't suffered? I buried our son, and that nearly destroyed me. And then I held on to my sanity with my fingernails once I sobered up long enough to recognize what was going on around me. After that, I learned how to wait, how to mark the days, one by one, off the calendar without ever knowing the extent of my sentence."

He reached for her, but she fled his hands. Lurching across the kitchen, she grabbed the counter edge in front of the sink for support. Between gasping breaths, she told him, "I've grown to hate Chet Holt. . . . I don't even know the man, and I hate him. . . . You trust him, but you don't trust me . . . and you act as though you're the only one who's suffered through all this." She twisted around to face him, tears streaming down her cheeks and her arms wrapped around her middle. "Well, you're wrong, Matthew. Totally wrong. I just hope you find that out before it's too late for us."

Standing near the doorway that separated the kitchen and the dining room, he held his arms rigidly at his sides and clenched his fists to keep from going to her. "I feel like I'm dying inside, Eden. I can't change what's happening without help, but you aren't the person who can help me." He took a step forward, once again considered the wisdom of touching her, and decided to hold his ground. "I know you don't understand what I feel about my Cherokee heritage, especially since I haven't been able to explain about Great-grandfather in a way that makes sense to you."

"He's dead. He can't help you. I'm alive and I love you. Why doesn't that count for anything?" she asked, confusion and anguish tearing her apart inside.

"It'll mean everything when the time is right. Try to understand. I have to go home. I have to bring harmony back into my life. I can't do that as long as I'm here." He turned and walked to the kitchen door, pausing briefly to look back at her. "I can't even ask you to wait, because I know I haven't the right to do that."

Eden moaned, unaware that the sound tore at his insides with all the subtlety of razor slashes. Raising her fingers, she massaged the pulse battering her temple, thought about what a mess they'd managed to make of everything, and said softly, "I hope you find what you're looking for, Matthew."

CHAPTER

31

April 1973—northeastern Oklahoma

Matt pulled into the entrance of his uncle's farm after leaving the narrow road that wound through the farmland north of Tahlequah. Opening the car door, he unfolded himself from the cockpitlike interior of the dust-covered red Corvette, pocketed his keys, and walked to the barbed-wire fence line that surrounded the property. Gentle hills covered with wheat extended for several miles in any direction he looked.

Memories of childhood and stories he recalled of the land softened his expression. He listened to the grinding of an ancient oil derrick sluggishly coaxing black crude from the earth, his thoughts on those who had survived the Trail of Tears to claim the property still held by his mother's family; those same men and women who had arranged the boundary markers, tilled the soil, planted the first crop of wheat, harvested it, and then loaded their wagons for the trip to market.

Shifting his gaze to the sky, he knew he had come home to sample, once again, the lessons of the past. He wondered if they would somehow aid him in forming a bridge to the future, a future that he hoped would include Eden. Turning away from the fence, he tugged a cigarette from the pack in his pocket and shielded the flame of his lighter with his free hand. Inhaling deeply, he walked back to his car.

Matt thought of his mother as he drove the final five miles to the three-story frame house he had visited as a child. Like those before her who had poured their sweat into the land, she had labored as a girl behind a mule-drawn plow. Her absence from the farm during her years with his father had not blunted her love of the land. She had returned to the cyclic nature of a harvest-yielding soil and had taught her son to value the traditions of his ancestors.

A woman worked methodically in the garden beside the house, her still-slender figure bent over a row of seedlings, a watering can at her elbow. The coronet of gray braids encircling her head brought a lump of emotion to the throat of the man now towering over her.

"Mother?"

Serena Benedict looked up and extended her hand. "I've been expecting you, my son."

He didn't release her after helping her to her feet. "You haven't changed." Gathering her into his arms, he pressed his face against her neck and filled his senses with the smell of lavender, earth, and perspiration as he hugged her. "I've missed you," he managed despite his tears.

When he finally set her free, she reached up to touch his cheek, unable to ignore the lines of hardship etched into his features. "You have suffered much, Matthew. It is good that you have returned to your people."

"Great-grandfather guided me through the difficult times."

She nodded and took his hands in her own. "He has always protected your spirit. Even as a child, you shared a special relationship with him."

"You look wonderful."

She smiled, her dark blue eyes sparkling with life. "Although my brother enjoys reminding me that I have passed sixty winters, I am well."

He hugged her, his embrace lifting her from the ground. "You know you've never looked your age. When I was a child, no one believed you were old enough to be my mother."

"Now you flatter me. And between mother and son, such talk is unnecessary," Serena chided. "Especially since I still bear the marks of having carried you in my body, should anyone doubt the truth."

Matt noticed the fleeting surprise that touched her face when she glanced at his car. "I've come alone," he admitted.

"Why have you not brought your wife?"

"I couldn't."

"She wrote many letters, words of fear and words of encouragement. She didn't understand that I knew you would return to us."

"Why didn't you write her?" he asked, his voice empty of criticism.

"You know of my experience with white women. They have little desire to understand the ways of the Cherokee."

"She's not like most whites. She gives of herself, openly and without restraint."

"Did you tell her of her responsibility to come to me for safekeeping?"

He shook his head. "We didn't have much time together before I went overseas."

"Her place was here with me. Instead, she thought she should care for me."

"It's her nature to look after others."

"There is no need to explain further. She will join you soon?"

"No, I asked her not to."

Serena frowned. "You are very troubled, my son. Your uncle will be home soon. He will talk to you when the time is right. For now," she said, taking his hand and leading him into the house, "you will eat. You're much too thin."

Matt smiled down at her. "I've just gained twenty-five pounds."

"That is still not sufficient for a man of your stature." She motioned him to the table in the center of the kitchen. "Sit down while I prepare your meal and we will talk."

Upstairs, a baby cried. Matt stiffened when he heard the sound. He looked around, his expression curious. Slowly lowering himself into a chair, he let the air suspended in his lungs escape in short bursts. He glanced up at his mother when he felt her hand on his shoulder.

"The child is simply announcing his desire to end his sleep. He is the firstborn of your cousin David. Your Uncle Jesse's second boy."

Matt nodded and leaned back in his chair.

"You think of your son?" Serena pressed.

"You know about Drew, then?"

"Your wife sent me a photograph taken a few days after his birth. She also told me of his death." Her expression softened as she studied him. "You will give her more children, Matthew."

"Maybe," he whispered. "If she waits. If she's willing to understand why I had to come here. If she can forgive me for leaving her behind." He closed his eyes and rubbed at the fatigue in them.

"You're tired."

"I drove straight through."

"That was not wise. I don't understand this side of you. You were always wise as a child. Even as a little boy you considered the results of your actions."

"I'm not the same. Nothing's the same."

"Does it surprise you that the world went on without you?"

He watched her place a bowl of sliced fruit and a pitcher of milk on the table before he answered. "I suppose it shouldn't."

"The future is your concern, Matthew. The past is only a means of learning from our mistakes. Your great-grandfather taught you that when you sat at his knee and accepted the wisdom of his years."

"Perhaps that's why I've come home," he answered. "To relearn the old lessons."

May 1973—San Diego, California

Eden forced herself to continue her full-time schedule at the hospital, although the temptation to sit home near the phone periodically warred with her commitment to the patients. But, in the end, the patients won. She hadn't forgotten their loyalty to her when she'd needed them most, and even though Vietnam had been consigned to the past by Washington, the healing process for many had just begun.

While Matthew's abrupt departure was a painful reality,

Eden promised herself that she would give him time to come to terms with himself, but not so much time that their marriage would be irrevocably destroyed. At dinner with Tracey, David, and Jack Morrison, who had recently returned from temporary duty overseas, she shared her plans.

"Have you heard anything from him yet?" Tracey asked as their waiter poured coffee and served after-dinner drinks to David and Jack.

"Not yet."

"How long's he been gone?" Jack questioned, his expression intent.

"Three weeks."

"But you know where he is," he clarified.

Eden nodded. "I have a post-office box number for his mother's home in eastern Oklahoma."

"What are you going to do?" David finally asked. "Sit tight for a while longer?"

She looked around the table at the concerned friends who had consistently offered her support and understanding. "He's got one more week."

"Then what?"

"I'm going after him."

"Just like that? What about work?"

"My assistant's about to get her baptism by fire. I'm going to take the month of June and try and reach some kind of a compromise with Matthew. I've already cleared it with the chief of staff at the hospital."

Jack took a sip of his cognac and then smiled. "I think you're making the right decision. Whatever made Matt take off in the first place was serious. And from what you've said, he was still pretty disoriented and couldn't seem to get his bearings. He's nobody's fool, Eden. He knew he was in trouble, and he knew where to go for help. And we all know that if he's going to fly again, he's got to have his act together."

She nodded. "That's the conclusion I came to after I calmed down and stopped feeling sorry for myself. I've also been doing some reading about the Cherokee way of life, their culture, their belief that peace is the natural state despite the fact that they are taught to always be prepared for war when they, or those they're allied with, are threatened. And, even though the accounts I read were all historical, I think I caught a glimpse of what Matthew's great-grandfather must have represented to him in captivity."

"You're the single most important person in his life," Jack reminded her. "Even if he feels a bond to the past and even if he's turned on about his heritage, he still needs you in his life."

"I don't know how accurate your conclusion is, but I want to believe you."

Jack slid his brandy snifter onto the table and leaned forward. "The man loves you. He always has and he always will. You were the first person he thought about when we realized we were going to be taken prisoner. And if I know him as well as I think I do, you, his memories of you, and his thoughts about a future with you kept him alive when he was a POW. Don't bail out on him now."

She mustered a smile. "I wasn't planning on it. I just hope he hasn't bailed out on me."

Jack shook his head, provoking amusement from the others at the table with his vehement expression. "Go! He needs you and wants you as much if not more than you need and want him. Don't forget . . . I spent months listening to him itemize every sterling aspect of your character and your feminine charms. He wants you!"

"Leave it to a marine to get things down to basics," Tracey commented with a laugh before hugging her husband and winking at Eden.

"Well, I'm going to Oklahoma, come hell or high water. And if the blasted river rises, then I'll buy a boat. I want my husband back!"

Jack grinned, obviously satisfied with Eden's determination. "Tell the Warrior I've got a few words of wisdom guaranteed to undent his skull if he gives you any crap. I need to fly with a top-notch pilot again."

David laughed, and Tracey raised her coffee mug. "A toast to Eden and Matt. May they soon reside in the same tepee."

Eden groaned. "The Cherokee are much more sophisticated than that, Trace. They tend to prefer well-constructed homes, higher education, free enterprise, and they've historically treated their women with more respect and dignity than any other Indian nation on this continent."

"Guess I've seen too many John Wayne movies."

Eden ruefully shook her head. Feeling relaxed and hopeful, she enjoyed the remainder of her evening with friends she loved and valued.

Eight days later, Eden traveled the same roads Matthew had traversed the month before in a car she rented at the Tulsa airport. Driving southeast around the Gibson Reservoir waters to Fort Gibson and then northeast into Cherokee County, she followed the Illinois River north after receiving instructions from the postmaster at Tahlequah. And, like Matthew, she savored the rolling crop-covered hills and the rich smell of fertile soil.

The open gate to Reese Farm encouraged her entrance. When she first saw the white frame house from atop a rise in the rutted gravel road, she felt a sense of certainty about her decision to follow Matthew, a sense of coming home after an arduous journey. She realized that he must have experienced the same emotional relief she was now feeling, but on an even greater scale.

She noticed the woman standing on the front porch of the house as soon as she got out of the rental car. Tall and slim, Serena Reese Benedict possessed a dignity unique to her tribal origins.

"You are Eden, wife to my son," she said.

Eden nodded, lifted her hand to shade the setting sun from her eyes, and watched Matthew's mother descend the short flight of stairs.

"I'd hoped to find him here with you."

"He is not here."

Eden's shoulders slumped. Serena crossed the driveway, stopping a few feet from her daughter-in-law. "At first I hoped you would not follow him. Selfishness on my part, I think. But now I'm glad you've come."

"I guess I shouldn't have waited so long."

"My son will return."

"I should have come to you at the very beginning. I've only

just begun to discover the traditions of the Cherokee in time of crisis."

Serena reached out, took Eden's hand, and led her to an old wooden swing on the porch. "There are many books about the Cherokee, but it is best to experience the people yourself, to gain understanding with your mind and your heart."

"How is he?"

"He will be well soon. The medicine man has taken him to a private place to cleanse him of the sickness that infects his spirit." She studied Eden in the diminishing light. "My son told me of the purity of your heart. I see now I should not have doubted his words."

"I've been worried about him. After four weeks without even a phone call, I decided to see for myself that he's all right."

Serena smiled. "My son is a very proud man. He was taught as a boy to rely on himself for his survival. While I believe those lessons have aided him greatly, Matthew has failed to understand the necessity of sharing his burdens with his wife. You have decided wisely. You will be here for him when he returns."

"Will he be gone long?"

"Until the time is right and he is at peace with himself." She saw Eden's confusion and added, "It is not my intent to be evasive with you. I only wish to counsel patience. Healing cannot be rushed. My son has suffered much at the hands of others these past five years. There is an emptiness inside him that must be replenished if he is to walk in harmony with this world."

"I want him to feel whole again. I know how important that is for him even if he decides we can't share the future."

The older woman frowned. "Why would he not wish to remain with his wife?"

Eden gave her a helpless look. "I don't know what he wants anymore."

"You should not worry about things that are not likely to happen."

"Did he say anything to you about our life together since his release?"

"Very little," Serena admitted. "When he first arrived, he was more troubled than I have ever seen him. But as he spent time with his uncle and cousins in the fields, he began to relearn the simple lessons of the past. And when his uncle requested the aid of the medicine man, it was only to assist him in regaining total harmony. We teach our young the value of courage and endurance against pain, but those strengths often become weaknesses when the need for them has passed. This is a time of change for my son. His respect for the past will help him, but so will his love for you."

"You have such faith," Eden marveled as she studied her own white-knuckled fingers.

Serena reached out and lifted Eden's chin. "I know my son. You have had very little time in which to know your husband. I also know the values his father and I taught him as a child. His great-grandfather was his teacher, too, although he died when Matthew was still very young. But what they shared surpassed the death of an old man's body."

"He kept telling me that his great-grandfather protected him. I refused to believe him. His explanations sounded so mystical. I was afraid of losing him if he got too caught up in something I didn't understand."

"And did my son offer to explain his feelings and beliefs?"

"Yes, but not until he returned. I was so hurt by his insistence that he had to leave that I struck out at him with anger instead of patience."

"You, too, have been alone. You, too, have suffered with the death of your son. I am afraid Matthew was too occupied with his own troubles to be a thoughtful husband to you."

"That's what I accused him of."

"Child," Serena soothed as she gathered Eden into her arms, "you cannot be all things to my son, nor can he be all things to you. That is the greatest lesson a young wife must learn. To be joined in marriage is not to know all the secrets of your partner. We do well to share dreams and goals with those we love. And it often requires great courage to simply stand side by side and face what the world asks of us. Much more comes with many years and great wisdom. You must be patient with yourself."

Eden couldn't stop the tears that spilled from her eyes. "I love him so much."

"There is no need to weep. My son is not lost to you."

"Thank you," she whispered, easing back from Serena's embrace and wiping the tears from her cheeks.

"Why do you thank me? I am only doing what I should have done long ago."

Eden looked around, finally noticing that the sun had dropped behind the horizon, as well as hearing for the first time the muted sound of voices from the interior of the house. "It's getting late. I must be keeping you from your family."

The older woman smoothed back a lock of hair that had fallen across Eden's cheek. "You would wish to wait with me?"

"If I'm not intruding," she answered, hope in her voice.

"You are most welcome. You are wife to my son, Eden, and therefore daughter to me. My only regret is that my resistance to most whites has kept me from welcoming you into our home before this night. We've lost many years because of my foolishness and injured pride. Years that I hope will remind us both of the necessity of sharing our lives in the future."

"I hope so, too."

"Come inside, then," Serena invited as she stood and drew Eden from the swing. "You will meet the other members of your family and share our evening meal. Then you will sleep in the bed of your husband while you await his return." She led the way to the front screen door but looked back over her shoulder to add, "If you are at all like me, you treasure the comfort offered by your husband's possessions."

Eden laughed in response to the seemingly feminine trait. "I sleep in Matthew's T-shirts because they smell like him. That must sound foolish to you, though."

"Not at all, my daughter. For many years after my husband's death I still cherished the smell and feel of his clothing."

Serena opened the screen door and walked into the living room. Eden followed her more slowly. Matthew's mother sensed her hesitation and gave her a questioning look.

"Being here with you is everything I hoped it would be."

The older woman smiled gently. "And you are all that I hoped my son would find in a wife."

Matt closed his eyes and listened to the melodic chanting of the shaman. Although he didn't understand most of the words, they served to soothe, comfort, cleanse, and heal by turns. Each prayer seemed to bring him nearer to the harmony he sought. Absorbing the scent of fragrant sweet-grass burning in the fire pit nearby, he lost track of time, content to remain seated on the sacred ground and oblivious to the night cold or the heat of the day.

Above him, around him, Matt sensed the spirit of his great-grandfather, a protective force, concerned but not intrusive on the prayers offered by the medicine man seated on the opposite side of the fire.

Sweat drizzled from his naked body, washing from him the pain and loneliness of Long Moc and Hoa Lo, the fear he'd known for Eden's safety, and the immeasurable loss of returning to find his son buried in infancy.

The hard earth on which he sat possessed an oddly welcoming texture, and the trees overhead formed a canopy, as though ready to embrace a star, should one fall from the heavens. The scented air, offered in supplication, filled his nostrils and brought new life into his body.

The shaman continued to chant, the words an age-old medicine against sin and sickness of the flesh. Like a baptismal rite, his spirit was slowly cleansed, and his body separated itself from uncertainty, torment, and grief.

Serena heard Matthew's booted footsteps as he came down the stairs. Lowering the shirt she was mending to her lap, she faced her son when he entered the kitchen. Her eyes as well as her instincts told her that he had returned intact from a difficult journey. She also noted his awareness of his wife's presence at the farm.

"Eden has gone to the pasture to watch the new foal sired by Black Star."

"When did she arrive?"

"The same day that you departed with the medicine man."

"Four days. I'm surprised she waited."

Serena folded her mending and placed it in her sewing basket. "Your words are foolish for a man who has just returned from the wise one. She loves you, Matthew. Do not make her a sacrifice to your pride."

"I don't intend to."

"It took great courage for her to come here. She is your wife, and she is my daughter. You will treat her as such?"

He crossed the room, leaned down, and placed a kiss on his mother's forehead. "Until the last breath I draw."

She smiled, pleased by his pledge. "You will have many years together as well as many sons. Now go to your wife. It is your turn to listen and to understand."

"I know," he answered, although he made no move to leave the house.

"Why do you hesitate?"

"I'm aware of the risks I've taken."

"And the time of secrets has passed," she finished for him.

"Yes."

She rose and stood before her son. "You are like the lion who has fought for what is his and then cannot accept the fierceness of his own nature." Serena shook her head in maternal frustration. "Aren't you the one who told me of Eden's gentleness and loving spirit? And aren't you the one who urged me to open my heart to her because she is deserving of my trust?"

He smiled at his mother's lack of subtlety. "I understand what you're saying."

She patted his shoulder before stepping back. "Good. Now find your wife and treat her as you would a bride."

"The south pasture?" he confirmed, already at the door.

"Yes. Take her to the home place. It has been prepared for you."

Serena lingered in the kitchen doorway, a pleased smile on

her face as she watched her son find his way back to the woman he loved.

Eden sensed his presence even before he touched her, but she didn't take her eyes from the foal scampering about on the other side of the pasture fence when he slid his hand across her shoulders. Sighing softly, she realized, not for the first time, how much depended on the last four days. At the gentle insistence of his fingertips sliding up and down the back of her neck, she turned and looked up at him. "It's beautiful here, Matthew. I can see why the people and the land mean so much to you."

He didn't remove his hand, nor did he say anything as his eyes glided over her face.

"You look more relaxed than I've seen you in a long time."

He smiled. "Peace agrees with me."

"And have you found the kind of peace you were searching for?"

He nodded. "In my own way."

"I'm happy for you, then. Now you can get on with your life."

"You really mean that, don't you?"

"Of course." She turned, felt his hand slip from her shoulder, and rested her upraised arms on the top rung of the fence.

Matt leaned against the fence and lifted his face to the warmth of the morning sun. Several moments passed before he asked, "Why did you follow me?"

"I think I realized that this was our last chance."

"I didn't walk out on you, Eden."

"I believe you now, but I didn't when you first left San Diego." Shifting her gaze away from the activity in the pasture, she looked over at him and found he'd been watching her. "I thought you were running away from me as well as the years you spent in captivity. I realize now that that wasn't the case. I started doing some reading a few days after you left. I couldn't sleep at night because I couldn't stop thinking about what a mess we were making of our lives. So I went to the library and checked out everything I could get my hands on about the Cherokee people and their traditions. I was desperate to understand what was driving you. I'm just sorry I didn't do it sooner."

"You weren't ready," he offered quietly. "And there wasn't enough time for me to explain." He shoved his hands into the pockets of his jeans. "I was too wrapped up in my own needs to take the time to talk to you. For that, I'm deeply sorry."

She heard not only regret but sorrow and admitted, "I don't think I would have listened despite what I said to you that last night. You frightened me with all your talk about your great-grandfather. I couldn't equate a dead man with your image of him as a protector. And I was still nursing my own emotional wounds when you were released, only I didn't realize it at the time. But the more I read, the more I understood why you kept needing the traditions you were taught as a boy."

"I respect the past, Eden. And I had to depend on the lessons of the past as well as my own inner resources to bring me back to the world I left five and a half years ago."

"You learned your lessons so well that they became an instinctive part of you. I learned to understand and accept them after you left San Diego."

"A hard lesson?" he asked, knowing already what her answer would be but understanding that she had to admit it aloud.

She bit her lip before admitting, "A very hard lesson, Matthew, but one I needed to learn. Your mother's helped me a great deal, too. She's a very compassionate woman. I'm just sorry I didn't get to know her sooner."

"She thinks of you as her daughter. That's the highest compliment she can pay you."

Eden blinked back the emotion welling in her eyes. "Serena and I understand one another now that we've had a chance to get acquainted. She's an extremely important part of our lives."

He tugged her against his body and held her with a fierceness that underscored his relief at her words. "I'm glad you're here, paleface. I've missed you, more than you know."

Eden's smile faltered. "You haven't called me that since you came back."

"I didn't have the right." Taking her hand, he urged her away from the fenced pasture. "Come with me. There's something I want to show you."

Twenty minutes later they stood in front of a rough-hewn cabin of logs and dried mud. The porch sagged in the center, the roof had seen better days, and the windows were filled with beveled panes of glass, yellowing lace panels visible from the outside.

"This is the home place, the first house built on Reese land more than a hundred and thirty years ago. No one's lived here for several generations, but the family won't tear it down. After the Trail of Tears, the Cherokee people had few possessions. They lived in the open, cleared the land, and struggled to feed themselves after their removal from Cherokee tribal lands in Georgia. Five winters passed before they built this cabin."

"*Nunna-da-ul-tsun-yi,*" Eden said slowly, the words awkward on her tongue.

Matt glanced down at her, his surprise evident. "You know the legend, then."

"*The trail on which they cried,*" she quoted. "Your Uncle Jesse told me the parts of the story that weren't in the books I read. I couldn't really grasp the emotion behind the history when I first started reading, but Jesse was able to help me feel what happened, how betrayed the tribe felt after doing everything in their power to honor all the treaties they'd signed with the federal government."

"I'm impressed."

"I needed to know all this. It's a part of you."

He led her onto the porch and into the cabin. Eden looked at him in surprise. "You didn't have to duck."

He chuckled as he crossed the room. "The tribe grows 'em tall."

"I thought it was just your family."

"Not by a long shot. We've always been taller than the other tribes. Elongated genes, I guess," he teased with a grin.

Eden looked around the interior of the cabin. Everything looked fresh and clean despite the fact that Matthew had just said that no one lived there any longer.

He saw her puzzled expression and explained, "Mother wanted us to have some time alone. She fixed up the place for us."

"That was thoughtful of her," Eden said as she took a seat at the table near the front window of the small cabin.

Matt joined her, a relaxed look on his face. "I think you have some things you'd like to say to me. I'm ready to listen if you're ready to talk."

"I am. And I want to start with Daniel Howard. He's my friend. Probably the best friend I'll ever have other than you. I've never gone to bed with him, although I might have had the circumstances been different," she admitted honestly. "He's a good man, and it's very important to me that you understand my relationship with him."

"Go on," he urged.

"When I first met him, he'd just lost his hand. He'd also been a prisoner of the VC for several months somewhere in the Mekong Delta region. He was well on his way to shutting out the entire world when he first hit the ward. I tried patience, tact, reason, and compassion. When that didn't work, I lost my temper and screamed my lungs out at him. Something I'd never done before with a patient, but I just couldn't give up on him. It took us a while to find common ground. We eventually did, but not until after he'd given me a black eye and I'd delivered a rather large piece of my mind to him for his listening pleasure. After a while, we declared a truce of sorts, and I offered him my friendship. He accepted my offer and gave me his in return. I cannot bring myself to sacrifice my friendship with him because you don't like him or trust him. It would be the worst kind of betrayal."

"I don't expect you to, nor do I think you've ever slept with him, even though I may have behaved as though I did."

"And," she continued, "I don't expect you to give up your friendship with Chet Holt. Once I recognized my jealousy for what it was, I stopped hating the closeness you share with him. I've also had a chance to think about what the two of you must have experienced together, and I can accept the love you have for him and the confidences that only he can ever understand. But I would like a chance to get to know him and care for him, too."

Matt smiled and reached across the table. Eden brought her hands up from her lap and accepted the comfort and warmth of his fingers.

"You have more you need to say?"

She nodded. "I won't be ready for a while yet to even think about having another baby. We need time alone, just the two of us. Time to strengthen our love and our friendship. I don't regret getting pregnant or having Drew, so please don't misunderstand me. I do want us to have another child, but not right away."

Matt tightened his hold on her. "I'll trust you to tell me when you're ready. There's no need to rush where children are concerned, and I agree that we need time for the two of us."

She sighed, her relief obvious. "There's something else that's important to me, too."

"Your career?"

"Yes. I'm good at what I do, Matthew. Very good. And I love the work. Since you'll be in Yuma for retraining and then assigned to El Toro, I'd like to continue as Red Cross station director. It would mean living in Del Mar or some place near there in order to keep our commuting time fairly even. I'm also willing to sell the house if it would be easier for you. We can always buy another one."

"The house never bothered me, Eden. It was what was inside me that I couldn't handle."

"You don't hate the house? And you don't resent the fact that I bought it with my own money?" she persisted, wanting to get everything out in the open.

"No to both your questions. The hate and resentment I felt had nothing to do with the decisions you made while I was gone."

"You're certain?"

"Very certain." He glanced down at their joined hands, his thoughts on the separate roads they'd traveled to reach this place in their lives. Eden's honesty, her ability to express her desires for the future, and her obvious love prompted him to continue speaking. "All the while I was in captivity, three things kept me alive and sane. You, the baby we'd made, and Great-grandfather. I never once doubted your love for me. What I did doubt was whether or not you'd want what was left of me if I ever got out of that place. Isolation forces a person to take life one minute, sometimes one second, or even one centimeter of space at a time."

"Like sobriety when you first sober up and decide to stay that way."

"Yes!" he exclaimed. "You do understand, don't you? Anyway, I was in isolation for months at a stretch. I literally began to starve to death for contact with people I could trust. For some of the men, that kind of starvation went on too long, and their minds snapped. I came very close to permanently checking out of the real world at one point. If it hadn't been for Chet, I would have."

She nodded, empathy simmering inside her. "Dave Markham kept me from going over the edge after Drew died."

He shook his head, overwhelmingly frustrated with himself for not realizing the extent of the lessons in humility and humanity that she'd also been forced to learn during the last five years. "I should've given you more credit for understanding what I was feeling."

"It's all right, Matthew. We're talking now. This is what counts, not the mistakes we made. They're in the past."

"You probably know from talking with my mother and Uncle Jesse that my great-grandfather was a very important part of my life when I was a kid."

"Serena said you two were closer than two people ever get."

He nodded. "We were. I think we always will be. When I couldn't handle the pain after a torture session or if I became disoriented after days without food or water, Great-grandfather would appear in my mind. I could almost feel his hand on my shoulder, and I thought I heard his voice, reassuring me, comforting me, reminding me of the Cherokee tradition of strength against my enemies. He kept me from going over the edge several times, especially in the early days of captivity. He always seemed to know when I needed him most. You know I'm not a really religious person, and I never gave a lot of thought to my heritage until I was a POW and had to face the kind of deprivation the North Vietnamese inflicted on all of us."

Eden saw intensity and renewed perspective in the depths of Matthew's large black eyes when he looked up from their joined hands. "I'm sorry I resisted what you were trying to tell me before you left San Diego. I was just so unnerved by what you were suggesting about a dead man. I feel foolish now."

"There's no need. I know I wasn't making much sense at the time. The only thing I was really sure of was that I couldn't be a husband to you, much less a person of any value, unless I could let go of the last five years. I needed help, and I knew in my gut that the purification ceremony was my only shot."

He exhaled sharply, released her hands, and slumped back in his chair, his consternation with himself obvious. "I'm no good with words, Eden, so all I can tell you is that I felt dead inside when I came home. I couldn't seem to shake the feeling. And no matter how hard we tried to make a normal life, all we did was screw each other up more. I figured the only way to stop the tension building up inside me and between us was to get away, clear my head, face the past, and decide what kind of a person I'd become. And then hope like hell you'd still want me if I came out of this in one piece."

She leaned forward, her expression earnest and compassionate. "That's one of the reasons I decided to come after you. I sensed you still wanted us to be together in spite of how you felt about yourself when you left. I know I have a lot to learn about being your wife and about being a real partner in a marriage. And I realize now that I can't be everything to you, Matthew. I can only offer you my love and my willingness to stand beside you in the future. We can't change what's happened, but I really believe we can have a good life together if we work hard and we're always honest with each other about how we feel," she finished softly.

"I love you, Eden. I always did, even when I didn't know who or what I'd become."

"Then we can try again?"

He smiled, stood, and walked around to her side of the table. Drawing her to her feet, he took her in his arms and looked down at her, love shining from his dark eyes. "The priest who married us said that unless we suffered and endured for one another, we'd never know the true strength of our love. I think he was right, even though when I heard the words the first time it didn't occur to me that he was charting the course of the first five and a half years of our marriage."

Tears slid down her cheeks as she smiled up at him. "I love you more now than I ever thought it was possible to love another person, Matthew."

"No more than I love you, paleface." Lowering his head, he claimed her mouth. When the lingering kiss ended, he lifted her into his arms and carried her to the quilt-covered bed on the other side of the room. Lowering her to the feather-stuffed mattress, he promised, "The past can't hurt us ever again. It's over, Eden. We've proven the strength of our vows to one another."

She watched him untie the chamois band wrapped across his forehead. When he dropped it on the table beside the bed, she asked, "You don't need your token any longer?"

He sat down beside her, one hand resting against her cheek, the other releasing the buttons of her blouse. "My token was only a symbol of my desire to survive. It guaranteed nothing. What lives between us is the true measure of what we've survived."

EPILOGUE

December 1983—Washington, D.C.

Eden skimmed her fingertips along the shining black granite, stopping now and then to trace the etched name of a fallen veteran before her eyes strayed from the trailing list of faceless dead to her husband. She saw the rigidity of his posture, the way his uniform hugged the rawboned bigness of his body. She also felt the strength of his pride in himself and his peers in every move he made, every step he took.

Still and silent, her breath shallow puffs of steam in the frozen morning air, she watched Matthew slowly make his way the length of this sweeping wall of tribute, this testament to the sacrifices made by tens of thousands of veterans. She realized that this trip was his personal farewell to those with whom he had served.

Both Eden and Matthew realized that Vietnam wasn't really over despite the peace treaty signed almost ten years earlier. It would continue to live in the minds of the hundreds of thousands of men who had served there for as long as their generation walked the earth. And for the families of twenty-four hundred men this powerful symbol of honor would continue to remind them that resolution of their personal anguish over the fate of their loved ones had yet to occur.

She sensed the depth of his pain when he briefly bowed his head in prayer, then stepped back a pace, straightened, and saluted for the eleventh and final time. Matthew hesitated before turning away. Eden glimpsed the tears brimming in his eyes, saw the hard set of his jaw as he struggled with his emotions and traced the name William L. Porter, known among his fellow prisoners at the Hanoi Hilton as Scratch, with his fingertip.

Eden moved forward, her touch gentle as she stroked his arm to remind him that he was not alone. Colonel and Mrs. Benedict embraced before joining hands. They slowly walked away, leaving others to the privacy of their memories, ghosts of the past, and the never-ending silence of the Vietnam Memorial.